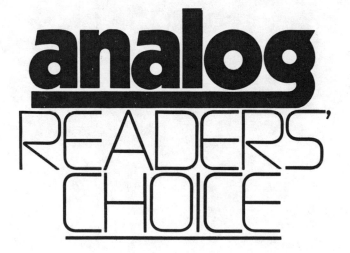

analog
READERS' CHOICE

Edited by **Stanley Schmidt**

The Dial Press

DAVIS PUBLICATIONS, INC.
380 Lexington Ave.,
New York, N.Y. 10017

COPYRIGHT NOTICES AND ACKNOWLEDGMENTS

CONTENTS

INTRODUCTION
by Stanley Schmidt 9

OLD FAITHFUL (December 1934)
by Raymond Z. Gallun 11

HELEN O'LOY (December 1938)
by Lester del Rey 41

REQUIEM (January 1940)
by Robert A. Heinlein 50

SOME CURIOUS EFFECTS OF TIME TRAVEL (April 1942)
by L. Sprague de Camp 64

THE COLD EQUATIONS (August 1954)
by Tom Godwin 66

PLUS X (June 1956)
by Eric Frank Russell 86

THE BIG FRONT YARD (October 1958)
by Clifford D. Simak 130

WHAT DO YOU MEAN—HUMAN? (September 1959)
by John W. Campbell, Jr. 171

HOME IS THE HANGMAN (November 1975)
by Roger Zelazny 177

EYES OF AMBER (June 1977)
by Joan D. Vinge 225

ENDER'S GAME (August 1977)
by Orson Scott Card 254

INTRODUCTION
Stanley Schmidt

In 1980, *Analog Science Fiction/Science Fact* celebrated its fiftieth anniversary as a leading magazine of science fiction. During those five decades it underwent several changes of name and editor (beginning as *Astounding Stories of Super-Science*), but through most of them it was *the* magazine of science fiction to a great many readers who cared equally about imaginative speculation and storytelling. It is now well launched into its *second* half century, and still going strong.

Shortly after Davis Publications took over the publication of *Analog,* during the Golden Anniversary year, I found out that we would now be able to do anthologies. So I ran an item in the magazine inviting the readers (many of whom quite rightly think of *Analog* as *their* magazine) to choose the contents of our second anthology (we were already at work on *Analog's Golden Anniversary Anthology*), drawing on the magazine's entire half-century legacy. I asked interested readers to submit up to ten nominations of stories—or articles, or *anything* ever published in *Astounding* or *Analog*—the book to be compiled from the most frequently nominated items. This is that book.

Please note: I did not specify any particular criteria by which readers should select their nominees. Some might try to pick "the ten best stories ever printed." Others might shun those "best" stories which have already been reprinted so often that even the author has lost count, and try to pick others which they felt had been unjustly neglected. Others may have had still other standards which I can't even guess at. All I got was each voter's final result: a set of up to ten cards listing what that person considered, for whatever reason, "What I would most like to see in a new and important anthology."

This book is a composite of those choices. Over a hundred stories and articles were nominated, by authors from Anderson to Zelazny. The ones which finally found their way into the book are, very roughly, the ones most requested—but, of course, not *all* of those with more than *n* votes are here. A book, like an issue of a magazine, is rather like a jigsaw puzzle, and the contents had to be fitted into a fairly definite number of pages. Some very popular items, such as Spider and Jeanne Robinson's "Stardance," simply couldn't be squeezed in. Some writers had several top contenders—Orson Scott Card, for example, had three, all rather long—and I limited the final selection to one per author. Sometimes a story simply wasn't available due to a conflict with some prior publishing commitment. And sometimes—as with Isaac

Asimov's perennially popular "Nightfall"—a story had been reprinted so often elsewhere that even I agreed that my limited space would be better given to something a shade less overworked. (Sorry, Isaac!)

There were a few surprises in the voting, and it's fun to speculate on what some of them mean. The top contenders, for example, included surprisingly few stories from the "Golden Age" of the Forties. Is this because many readers thought that period had been overworked in the past—or because there were so many favorites from that period that the votes were spread too thinly among them for any one to stand out? Does the preponderance of quite old and quite new stories (with rather few finalists from the Sixties) suggest that the voters tended to be either "oldtimers" with fond memories of their personal "Golden Age," or new readers whose memories don't go back very far?

I don't know. In any case, the important thing is the stories themselves.

A word of explanation may be in order on two of the items herein. Several readers requested "a John W. Campbell editorial," without specifying a *particular* editorial. "What Do You Mean . . . Human?" is one of many (literally hundreds) I could have chosen. There were similar requests for a representative of "Probability Zero," that peculiar series of tall tales that has appeared off and on through the decades. L. Sprague de Camp's entry here was the first of these to appear.

A special honorable mention must be given to Robert A. Heinlein's "The Green Hills of Earth," which received a number of votes even though it never appeared in *Astounding* or *Analog*! It actually made its first appearance in *The Saturday Evening Post*—but evidently more than one reader remembered the story and assumed it *must* have been here.

The stories (and editorial) are arranged in this book in chronological order. If you want to try to guess the exact order in which they finished in the voting, you're welcome to try—but I'm not telling. Suffice it to say that all of these did quite well.

In any case, I hope you'll enjoy them all—and then go on to the *new* ones appearing every four weeks in *Analog*.

Stanley Schmidt

OLD FAITHFUL
Raymond Z. Gallun

If Number 774 had been a human being, he might have cursed bitterly or he might have wept. Certainly he had reason to do so. But Number 774 was not a human being. His fragile form bore not the slightest resemblance to that of a man; he knew nothing of smiles or frowns or tears, and whatever emotions passed within his cool, keen mind were hidden even to members of his own race.

The two messengers who had come to his workshop that afternoon had not seen into his heart, and he received their message with the absolute outward calm that was characteristic of his kind—at the end of forty days Number 774 must die. He had lived the allotted span fixed by the Rulers.

With food and water as scarce as they were, no one had the right to live longer unless he had proved through the usefulness of his achievements that it was for the good of all that he be granted an extension. Otherwise the young and strong must always replace the old and weak.

In the opinion of the Rulers the work of Number 774 was not useful; it was without value and was even wasteful. An extension of life-span could not be considered; Number 774 must die.

Having imparted this information the messengers had crept into the streamlined hull of their ornithopter. Silvery wings had flapped, and the weird craft had lifted lightly, circled the great isolated workshop once in parting salute, and then had sped off into the west toward a distant city.

In obedience to some impulse Number 774 had ascended to a high-placed window in the towering wall of his domicile, to watch the ornithopter go. But long after the glinting metallic speck of its form had vanished into the sunset, Number 774 continued to stare out toward the west. Pools of purple shade swelled and broadened in the hollows between the dunes of the Martian desert that stretched in undulating flatness to the far horizon.

The sun sank out of sight, leaving only a faint reddish glow that quickly faded out at the rim of the world. The Martian sky, deep purple and shot with stars even during the day, became almost black, and the stars, veiled by an atmosphere only one-sixth as dense as that of Earth, gleamed with a steady and eerie brilliance that is never seen by terrestrial observers.

It was a strange, beautiful sight, and perhaps in other circumstances something fine and paradoxically human in Number 774's being might have appreciated its wild and lonely grandeur. But natural splendors could scarcely have interested him now, for his mind was too full of other things.

In the sky was a tiny gray-green streak which he knew marked the position of an approaching comet. For a long moment he stared at it; and then his gaze wandered up among the welter of stars and sought out a greenish silver speck far brighter than any of its fellows.

For many minutes his attention clung unwavering to that brilliant point of light. He knew more about that planet than any other inhabitant of Mars. He had never heard its name, nor in fact did he have a vocal name of his own for it. To him it was just the world which held the third orbital position in order from the sun. And yet, for him, there was concentrated in it all the hopes and all the fascination of a lifetime of painstaking work and effort.

Gradually, by patient, methodical observation, he had wrested a few of its secrets from it. He had learned the composition of its atmosphere; he could describe its climates accurately; he even knew something about its soil. But beyond such superficial information for a long time it seemed that he could never go.

And then one night when, with stoical resignation, he had all but laid aside his fondest dream, a sign had come. The third planet, Earth, was inhabited by thinking beings. It was not a spectacular sign; neither was his conclusion guesswork. Number 774's telescope had revealed, on the darkened side of Earth, between the limbs of its crescent, a barely discernible flicker of light flashes, evenly spaced, and repeated at perfectly regular intervals. Only a high order of intelligence could have produced such signals.

Dominated by a new zeal, Number 774 had constructed a gigantic apparatus and had duplicated the Earthian signals flash for flash. Immediately he had been answered. Then he had tried a new arrangement of flashes, and the unknown beings on Planet Three had seen, for they had repeated his signals perfectly.

For five Martian years, the equivalent of nearly ten passages of the Earth around the sun, he and the unimaginable entities on that other world, hardly ever less than thirty-five million miles away, had labored on the colossal problem of intelligent communication.

The results of their efforts had been small and discouraging; yet in ten or twenty years even that gigantic enigma might have yielded to persistence, ingenuity, and the indomitable will to do. But now no such thing could be. In forty days Number 774 would no longer exist. Nor would there be another to carry on his work.

Study of the third world could not produce more food or make water more plentiful. The Rulers would dismantle all the marvelous equipment that he had assembled to aid him in his quest for useless and impractical knowledge. The veil of mystery would remain drawn over Planet Three for many thousands of years, perhaps forever.

But it was the Rulers' privilege to command and to expect unquestioning obedience. Never once in a millennium had their authority been disputed; for the very existence

Raymond Z. Gallun

of the dominant race of Mars, a world aged almost to the limit of its ability to support life, depended on absolute spartan loyalty and discipline. Revolt now was unheard of; it could not be.

Did Number 774 feel resentment over his fate? Or did he accept his sentence with the stoicism of a true child of Mars? There was no way of telling. His position was almost unduplicated in the annals of the Red Planet, and, in consequence, his reactions may have been out of the ordinary. Almost never before had a creature of his kind wandered so far along the road of impractical knowledge, or had received the notice of the termination of life-span so inopportunely.

And so Number 774 continued to gaze up at the green star that had been included in every dream and effort of his existence. Thoughts and feelings must have tumbled in riotous confusion inside his brain.

After a while Phobos, the nearer moon, mounted up over the western* horizon and began its rapid march among the stars. Its pallid radiance converted everything into a half-seen fairyland of tarnished silver and ebony, the dunes of the lonely desert extending mile on mile in every direction, the low, fortlike walls of Number 774's workshop, the great shining dome of metal that capped it. Nothing was clearly discernible, nothing seemed real.

The coming of Phobos aroused Number 774 from his lethargy. It may be that he realized that time was fleeting, and that an hour could ill be spared from the forty days of life that still remained to him. At a deft touch the crystal pane that glazed the window before him slipped aside, and a faint night breeze, arid, and chilled far below zero, blew in upon him.

Edging his strange form forward, he leaned far out of the window and seemed intent upon creeping headlong down the rough stone wall. Long slender portions of his anatomy clutched the sill, and he hung inverted like a roosting bat of Earth. But otherwise there was not the remotest resemblance between Number 774 and a winged terrestrial mammal.

If, by means of some miraculous transition, an Earthman had suddenly found himself standing there on the desert and looking up at the wall of the workshop close above, he might not even have recognized Number 774 as a living creature in the shifting, uncertain moonlight. Amid the fantastic jumble of light and shade he would have seen only a blob of rusty brown color that might have been just the distorted shadow of one of the stone projections that jutted from the wall.

If he had looked closer he might have believed that the thing he saw was a small

---

Mars rotates on its axis in 24 hours, 37 minutes, 22.67 seconds. Phobos, the nearer Moon, which is only 3,700 miles distant from Mars, completes its orbit in only 7 hours, 39 minutes, thus circling its primary more than three times in every Martian day. Since Phobos follows its path in the same direction that the planet rotates, it is evident that to an observer on Mars, it would appear to rise in the west and set in the east.

bundle of ancient and rotten rags dangling from the window ledge, with long, loose tatters stirring idly in the faint breeze. Still, the glint of bright metal from Number 774's equipment would have puzzled him, and perhaps the suggestively gruesome aspect of this unknown and poorly illuminated object.

From his dangling position Number 774 sucked a great breath of cold air into his complex breathing organs. The frigid tang of the night refreshed him and seemed to endow him with new life. One last glance he cast toward the glory of the Martian heavens. At sight of Earth and the threadlike speck of the comet, his great eyes, dark and limpid and more nearly human than anything else about him, flashed briefly with a vague, slumberous suggestion of something pent up behind a barrier that was none too strong to hold it back. Then Number 774 drew himself up into the window.

Three jointed rods of metal unfolded themselves from the complicated arrangement of mechanisms that was fastened to his fragile body, and in a moment he was striding along on them like a man, down a green-lighted cylindrical passage that extended off into misty obscurity. A faint and regular clicking came from the device, but Number 774 did not hear it. He knew of sound only as a vibration detectable by his keen sense of touch, and as a phenomenon registered by his scientific instruments, for Number 774 had no organs of hearing.

His steps seemed hurried and feverish. Perhaps some un-Martian plan was already half formulated in his restless and troubled mind.

The tunnel debouched at last into a colossal chamber where gigantic flying buttresses swept up and up through a misty green glow to meet the sides of an enormous rotunda of white metal that roofed the room.

Enigmatic forms of weird apparatus crowded in bewildering complexity against the walls. Tipped at a steep angle at the center of the floor was a vast cylinder of webby girders. Piercing the dome, opposite the upper end of the cylinder, was a circular opening through which a portion of the starlit sky was visible; and at the base of the cylinder a great bowl rotated rapidly, like a huge wheel.

Here was the observatory of Number 774, housing his telescope, and here were the controlling mechanisms of his signaling apparatus. He hurried up a steep ramp, from the upper end of which he could look down into the interior of the great rotating bowl. His eyes glanced critically over the device, searching for any possible slight disorder in its function. But there was none.

To an Earthman acquainted with astronomical equipment, the purpose of the rotating bowl would have been at once apparent, and he would have marveled at the simple cleverness of this piece of Martian ingenuity.

The bowl contained mercury. As the container spun on its perfectly balanced axis, centrifugal force caused the mercury to spread in a thin, precisely distributed layer over the inside of the bowl, forming a convex surface that acted admirably as a mirror for Number 774's gigantic reflecting telescope. Its area, and its consequent light-

Raymond Z. Gallun

collecting capacity, was many times greater than any rigid mirror that could have been constructed without flaws.

Satisfied with his inspection, Number 774 hoisted himself nimbly to a small platform, high-placed among the spidery girders of the chamber. His movements were quick and catlike, yet coolly efficient, and he seemed bent upon making use of every moment of life that remained to him.

His eyes almost lambent with eagerness, he stared into the large crystal sphere which the platform supported. From a prismatic arrangement fixed to the telescope arrangement above, an invisible beam of light came down, impinging on the sphere, and causing the picture which Number 774 was so intent upon to appear.

In the depths of the crystal was an image of the third world. Earth. Since it was to sunward and nearing inferior conjunction with Mars, most of its surface that was turned to the Red Planet was in shadow and could not be seen. Only a thin curve of light fringed one hemisphere.

Visible in the crescent were mottled areas of gray and green and brown, which Number 774 knew were oceans, continents, deserts, and verdant countryside. The shifting blurs of clouds, the winding rivers, and the snow-capped mountain chains, he could recognize and understand, too; but there was so much that distance and the distorting effects of two atmospheres left hidden and seemingly unattainable—things about which he had longed so passionately to see and to know.

A delicate bundle of pink filaments that terminated one of Number 774's stalklike limbs rested on a tiny lever before him. The threadlike tentacles, marvelously adapted and trained for the finest and most accurate sort of work, moved the lever slightly to the right.

Immediately there was responding movement in the heavy parts of the huge telescope, and the image of Planet Three in the cyrstal globc bcgan to grow. Mountains loomed larger; seas and continents swelled until the whole of the image of the terrestrial sphere could not occupy the globe, and all that could be seen was a small part of the illuminated crescent.

For a while, as the increase in magnification went on, details on Planet Three were brought morc clcarly into view; but presently, as the picture grew larger and larger, it began to tremble and to undulate, as if it were seen through a million atmospheric heat waves.

As the power of the telescope was increased still further, the flickering, jumping, shifting luminescence that appeared in the vision globe became totally incoherent and meaningless and bore no slight relationship to an Earthly scene. Number 774's huge optical instrument was failing before one of the same obstacles to magnification that terrestrial observers have noted in their telescopes.

The gaseous envelopes of Earth and Mars, with their countless irregular air currents and varying indices of refraction due to differences in temperature and humidity, were distorting the image-bearing rays of light coming from Earth across fifty million miles of space and rendering magnification beyond a certain point useless. The telescope of Number 774 still had many Martian units of magnification in reserve, but for probing into the mysteries of Planet Three that reserve was of not the least value.

Still, Number 774 often gave his instrument full power in the vain hope, perhaps, that some day, by some trick of fate, the atmospheres of the two worlds would be quiet enough and clear enough to give him a momentary glimpse into the unknown. But the opportunity for such a glimpse had never come.

Cool and collected, Number 774 brought his telescope back to the limit of effective magnification. In response to the manipulation of some instrument, the image of Planet Three shifted so that no portion of the crescent was visible. The crystal globe was dark, but Number 774 knew that the third world was within the field of view.

Unerringly, guided by his instruments, he fixed his telescope on a certain spot on the dark side of Planet Three. He knew that shrouded in the shadows of the night hemisphere of that distant world there was a great continent extending broad and diversified, between two vast oceans. It had lofty ranges of snow-crowned mountains, extensive plains green with an unknown vegetation, great lakes, and winding rivers. In the southwestern portion of that continent was a desert, and near the edge of that desert was the Place of the Light—the light that was the voice of the friend he had never seen, and whose form was unimaginable to him, much though he might imagine and long to know.

The light was not there now; only the vague, white blurs of Earthly cities dotting the darkened continent, adding the mystery of their existence to the enigma of Planet Three. But Number 774 was not troubled by the absence of the light, for he had faith in it. When he had signaled, it had always appeared in answer; it would appear this time, too.

At his touch a vast mechanism in a room far beneath the chamber of the telescope began to function silently and efficiently, building up power. Feeble and delicate and hideous though Number 774 was by Earthly standards, at a mere gesture he could evoke forces that were worthy of the gods.

Number 774 watched a Martian version of a potentiometer. It was not like a terrestrial potentiometer. It had no graduated scale, no nervous pointer. It was just a globe of something that looked like frosted glass, from which a soft luminescence proceeded.

First, Number 774 saw in its depths a slumberous glow of a beautiful shade, quite unknown and unseeable to human eyes. It was what is called infrared on Earth. The color, being invisible to men, was of course quite indescribable, but to Number 774 it was as common as blue or yellow, for his eyes, like the eyes of some of the lower forms of Earth, were constructed to see it.

In addition, like all Martians, he was able to distinguish the slightest difference between one shade of color and another.

It is upon this fact that Martians depend for the accurate reading of instruments

Raymond Z. Gallun

which, among men, would ordinarily have pointers and graduated scales. In any Martian meter, infrared, and of course the various shades of infrared, in their order of appearance in the spectrum, means a low reading. Red, and the shades of red, advancing toward orange, constitute somewhat higher readings. Orange, yellow, green, blue, and violet are progressively higher; while the shade at the extreme outer end of the ultraviolet band, which Martian eyes can also see, represents the highest reading.

In short, light of various wavelengths is used in practically all Martian meters to designate readings. Low readings are represented by long wave-lengths near the infrared end of the spectrum; while high readings are designated by short wavelengths near the ultraviolet end of the spectrum.

Number 774 waited until the changing kaleidoscope of ordinary colors had passed and the delicate hue of ultraviolet had reached its maximum in the globe of the potentiometer before he made any further move. Then his tense body swayed forward, closing a complicated switch.

The result was instantaneous. Through the circular opening in the rotunda, at which the muzzle of the telescope was pointed, a dazzling blaze of incandescence was visible in a sudden tremendous flash. The detonation that accompanied it was of a magnitude which one would have scarcely believed the rarefied atmosphere of old Mars capable of transmitting. The whole building, solidly constructed though it was, trembled with the concussion.

For a moment the Martian night, within a radius of twenty miles or more of Number 774's workshop, became brighter than midday, as an enormous store of energy, released from the outer surface of the metal dome which capped the observatory, poured suddenly into the atmosphere, thus forming above the workshop a vast canopy of cold light, far more intense than any aurora borealis of Earth.

But the sudden flare died out as quickly as it had come; the echoes of the crash faded, and the calm of lonely desert and stars reasserted itself. Some eerie monster, which had unwittingly buried itself in the sand too close to the lair of Number 774, scrambled out of its warm sleeping place amid a cloud of dust and on gauzy wings sped hurriedly away from the zone of the thunder that had terrified it. As it flew, its fantastic shadow bobbed crazily over the moonlit sand.

But Number 774 was quite oblivious of any fears his experiments might arouse in the creatures of Mars. As far as his mind was concerned, for the time being things Martian had almost ceased to exist for him. Earth, Planet Three, claimed all his attention, and there was room for nothing else. He had given his sign; now he would wait for the answer that was sure to come.

It would take approximately nine minutes for Earth to get signals back to him. For that was the time which light, traveling at a speed of 186,000 miles per second, required to bridge twice the fifty-million-mile void lying between the two planets.

Number 774's weird, fragile body hunched eagerly forward on the small mat on which he squatted. His great eyes burned with the same fire of fascination which they had held when, a little while ago, he had gazed up at Earth and the approaching comet from the window in the wall of his workshop. Unwaveringly they were fixed on the spot in the darkened vision globe where the light would appear.

Sometimes that light was too dim for his trained and sensitive eyes to see; but arranged and hooded on a carefully shaded portion of the vision globe was a Martian photoelectric cell which would pick up the faintest of light signals and convert them into electrical impulses which would be amplified and relayed to an instrument close beside Number 774.

This instrument would reproduce the signals just as they came from Earth, but bright enough to be easily watched. Another device would record each flash for later study.

II

The body of Number 774 tensed suddenly. There was the first signal, flickering faint and feeble across the millions of miles of space; yet on the desert of Earth it doubtless represented flashes almost comparable with those which Number 774's powerful sending equipment produced.

Number 774 could barely see them in his vision globe, but the little glass bulb of the reproducing apparatus flickered them out plain and clear—long flashes, short flashes, representing the dots and dashes of the Morse code of Earth.

Flash—flash—flash—flash—flash—

"Hello, Mars! Hello, Mars! Hello, Mars! Earth calling. Earth calling. Earth calling," the message spelled, and Number 774 was grimly in the midst of the colossal task he had set for himself.

Lurking in the back of his mind was the realization that his death was decreed and that soon, unless something unprecedented happened, all this work of his, and of his friend of the light, must end, unfinished, before the intelligences of two worlds could really meet and exchange ideas freely. But it did not divert him or make his attention to the task in hand less keen. In fact it seemed to sharpen his wits and to add pressure to his determination.

Still, his mind seemed divided into two parts, one of which was cool and logical and scientific, the other in a turmoil, fighting with itself and its loyalty to time-honored traditions.

"Hello, Mars! Hello, Mars! Earth calling. Man of Mars is late—late—late—late— One, two, three, four, five, six, seven, eight, nine, ten. Four and five are nine. Two times three is six. Man of Mars is late—late—late—late—"

How much of this queer jangle of light flashes, spelling out Earth words and numbers in the Morse code, did Number 774 understand? How much *could* he understand?

Raymond Z. Gallun

Intelligent comprehension of anything new is almost always based on an understanding of similar things previously in the experience of the individual in question. The mind of Number 774 was brilliantly clever and methodical, but what can an Earthman and a Martian have in common? Many points of contact exist, it is true, but for two entities so far removed from one another in physical form, senses, environment, and modes of living, with not the vaguest conception of what the other upon the distant world is like, such similarities of experience are extremely hard to find.

In the first place, the messages that were coming to Number 774 were the code representations of alphabetical letters standing for various sounds which, when taken in groups, made up words of vocal speech.

As previously stated, Number 774 had no idea of sound except as an interesting phenomenon recorded by his scientific instruments, and as a vibration detectable by his touch sense in the same way that human beings can feel sound vibrations in solid objects. He had no ears; neither did he have well-developed vocal organs.

Strange as it may seem to us, prior to his experience with the light, he had not the faintest idea of what a word was, either a vocal word or a written word, or a word represented in the form of a group of signals. Because Martian methods of communicating with one another, and of recording knowledge, are so different from ours that a word would have been as great a mystery to him as it would have been to a newborn kitten.

Describing sound to him, as we know it through our sense of hearing, would have been as hopeless a task as describing red to a man who has been stone-blind since birth. It simply could not be done. He might know that sound and vocal speech existed, but short of trading actual sensations with an Earthman, he could never fully comprehend. Neither could he have told us in any way how the color of ultraviolet or infrared looked, for such things are totally out of our experience.

In the face of these enormous handicaps, in spite of his intelligence and scientific knowledge, he had been like a little child, humbly and intensely eager to learn, yet bungling and quick to make mistakes which, from an Earthman's point of view, would often have seemed more than childish.

Once he had tried a method of his own of establishing communication. If Earth had been peopled by a race physically and psychologically similar to the Martians, quick success might have been expected; but his efforts had evoked only a, to him, meaningless jumble of flashes from the light. Realizing that his method was not suited to Earthmen, he had given up trying to be teacher and had assumed instead the rôle of conscientious pupil.

"Hello, Mars!" Those two groups of symbols had always been the beginning of every message flashed by the light; but except for seeing the unmistakable evidence of intelligence in the oft-repeated and unvarying signal, Number 774 had been quite unable at first to grasp in it any thread of meaning.

A greeting phrase was, if possible, even more incomprehensible to him than a word itself. Try as he might, he could not understand. On Mars, where speech is not the mode of communication, greeting phrases did not exist.

Then Earthly genius, doubtless assisted a great deal by chance, had come to his aid. Number 774 had no difficulty in separating the twenty-six alphabetical symbols of the Morse code. Nor when the Earth entities, controlling the flickerings of the light, had sent out code symbols for numerals in a sequence of 0, 1, 2, 3, 4, 5, and so on, did he have any trouble in recognizing and cataloguing each separate signal, though their meanings were still entirely unfathomable to him.

It was when the counting proceeded above nine, and numbers of more than one digit appeared, that Number 774, after a long period of association with the riddle, had received his first faint glimmer of understanding. No; it was not really understanding yet; just a vague, intuitive intimation that something concrete and graspable was not far off.

He had noted that there were but ten separate signals in this strange system, which was apparently quite distinct from that other mysterious system of twenty-six symbols, for the two had never yet been mixed in one signal group or word; and that, as the flashing of the signals proceeded, each symbol seemed to bear a definite relationship to the others.

They always were in fixed sequence. 1 was followed by 2, 2 by 3, and so on through a sequence of ten. The first symbol of a two-digit number was always repeated ten times as the counting went on, while the second symbol changed according to the fixed rule which he had already noted.

Perhaps Number 774 already had a dim notion of the terrestrial numeral system, when his friend of the light conceived the plan of sending simple problems of arithmetic. Obviously, one plus one of anything is two on the planet Mars just as certainly as it is on Earth.

There was the real beginning. Number 774 had studied carefully the simple equations that had come to him, and at length he had been able to grasp what was meant. In a message like "3 and 3 are 6" he was presently able to see the relationship between the numeral signals. The last in the group was the sum of the preceding two.

Finally he understood. Here was some quaint terrestrial method of expressing the unit quantity of anything. The first point of contact between Earth and Mars had been established.

Flushed with success, Number 774 had made rapid progress for a while after he had learned about the terrestrial decimal system. If 3 and 3 are 6, and 2 and 5 are 7, then 4 and 5 are 9. Reproducing faithfully, though without clear comprehension, the intermediate letter groups of the Earthly equation he had invented, "a-n-d" and "a-r-e," he had flashed the equation to his friend of the light: "4 and 5 are 9."

And the answering flicker of the light seemed to dance with an eager exultation:

Raymond Z. Gallun

"4 and 5 are 9. 4 and 5 are 9. Yes, yes, yes. 5 and 5 are 10. 8 and 4 are 12. 9 and 7 are? 9 and 7 are?"

Keyed to a high pitch, Number 774 had sensed immediately what was required of him. Answers were wanted. Though two-digit numbers were still something of a mystery to him, making his reply partly guesswork, he lit upon the correct representation of the sum: "9 and 7 are 16."

Through the succeeding months, during which the positions of the two planets were favorable for astronomical observation of each other, the work had gone on, various methods being employed. Sometimes Number 774 presented his own problems of addition, giving the answers. If his answer was correct, the light invariably flashed "Yes, yes, yes," exultantly, and repeated the equation.

On those rare occasions when the problems became more complex, Number 774 made mistakes, the answering message was "No, no, no," and the correction was made.

Thus Number 774 had gained his first knowledge of words, as represented by the twenty-six letter code alphabet. "Yes, yes, yes," meant that he was right, and "no, no, no," meant that he was wrong. It trickled into his mind that each group of alphabetical symbols represented, in its crude way, some definite idea. "And" and "are" in a simple addition problem, showed certain relationships between the numbers; and those relationships were different from the ones expressed by other words.

A mistake he had once made had clearly demonstrated this fact to him. It was in the transition from addition problems to problems of multiplication. 10 and 2 was different from 10 times 2. 10 and 2 made 12, while 10 times 2 made 20. "Times" represented a different relationship between numbers than "and." One indicated that the sum was to be taken, while the other indicated that the two were to be multiplied together.

In a similar way he found out what "divided by," "plus," "minus," and other words meant by noting the relationship of the numbers of the equation to the final answer.

Once understanding simple division as it is done on Earth, Number 774 quickly grasped the decimal-position system of representing fractions. In an equation like $36 \div 5$ equals 7.2, he could substitute Martian methods of representing values and division and correlate them with terrestrial methods. In the Martian way he knew what $36 \div 5$ was, and of course his answer thus obtained might just as well be represented by the Earthly 7.2, for they were the same.

Number 774 had found in the number 3.1416, part of which was a decimal fraction, the relationship of the circumference of a circle to its diameter, and so the oft-repeated message of the light, "Diameter times 3.1416 equals the circumference of a circle," had a certain vague meaning for him that was not by any means completely understandable at once.

"Earth, Planet 3, Mars, Planet 4," was a message he was able to guess the meaning of correctly because in the Martian system numbers were used to designate planets in their order from the sun. Aided by the message, "Earth Planet 3, has 1 moon. Mars, Planet 4, has 2 moons," he had been half able to clinch his guess.

Stumblingly, yet reproducing the Earth words with the faithfulness of a good mimic, he had flashed: "Planet 1 has 0 moon. Planet 2 has 0 moon. Earth, Planet 3, has 1 moon. Mars, Planet 4, has 2—"

And an enthusiastic "yes, yes, yes" had come from the light, and the dim flickering glow had gone on to tell that: "Mercury, Planet 1, has no moon. Venus, Planet 2, has no moon. Jupiter, Planet 5, has 9 moons. Saturn, Planet 6, has 10 moons—" And so on out to Pluto, Planet Nine, beyond Neptune.

Thus Number 774 had learned the names of the planets and the meaning of the words "moon" and "planet." In the same way he received a dim idea of such simple verbs as "has."

And so the process of his Earthly education had gone on, slowly, depending to a large extent upon brilliant though not very certain guesswork, and demanding a degree of patience in instructor and pupil for which teaching a person to talk who has been deaf, blind, and dumb since birth is but a feeble and inadequate analogy.

Number 774 had certain knowledge of a few Earthly words and the privilege of guessing more or less accurately on a number of others. Words like "snow," "clouds," or "storm," he could perhaps gather the general sense of fairly well. For whenever a great atmospheric disturbance appeared over the continent of the light, disturbing observations, the light repeated these words over and over again.

He knew a little about the structure of the simplest of verbs and perhaps somewhat more about the forming of the plural of nouns by the addition of an "s" symbol. "Hello!" in the phrase "Hello, Mars!" still was beyond him. He could answer it correctly with "Hello, Earth!" knowing that this was the Earthly way; but the human sentiment of the greeting eluded him completely. And of course he had no sound values to give to those Earthly words which he did understand.

Progress had been made, but the forms which the intelligences of Planet Three inhabited, their manner of living, their machines and their accomplishments, were still as much of an enigma as ever. Consummation of the great dream of intelligent communication still belonged to the future, and now there would be no future—only death and a mighty prophecy unfulfilled.

That prophecy had been, and still was, the essence of Number 774's life. In the face of defeat he still worked on the fulfillment of it now, as though a thousand years of usefulness still lay ahead of him. It was habit, perhaps; and meanwhile his mind smoldered with thoughts which we of Earth can only guess at.

"You are late, Man of Mars. Late, late, late," the dim flicker in the vision globe, and the brighter light in the reproducer bulb beside him, spelled; and Number 774 bent to his task.

He understood sketchily most of the message. He knew that the light referred to

Raymond Z. Gallun

him as "Man of Mars." He knew that "you are" should be followed by a group of signals describing him. Only "late," the essence of the sentence, the word which gave it sense, was new. What could "late" mean?

Intuition told him that some circumstances which existed only for the present had combined to make him "late," since he had never been called that before. What were those circumstances? He racked his brain over the question. Perhaps the light wished to indicate that he had been delayed in sending out his flash call-signal. But this was only a guess which could be right or wrong.

Still, perhaps it could be clinched. Some other day he might be purposely several minutes behind in sending out his call; then, by way of beginning he could admit that he was "late" and, if his surmise had been correct, the light would confirm it.

But the matter of this new combination of signals could wait now. Number 774 must watch for other, possibly intelligible, things which the light might flash.

"Comet coming. Comet coming. Comet coming," the flicker in the reproducer bulb spelled. "Comet coming toward sun, Mars, and Earth. Comet coming. Comet coming. Comet coming."

If Number 774 had been a man, he might have given a sudden start. And it was not the message itself that would have been responsible, even though he caught some of its meaning. "Comet" was not a word that was new in his experience; for on several occasions when one of those long-tailed wanderers had come back into the solar system, after taking its long dive out toward interstellar space, the light had flashed the information: "Comet coming."

Number 774 knew what "comet" meant, and he could differentiate vaguely between "comet coming" and "comet going," for one indicated that the celestial visitor was entering the solar system, and the other that it was leaving. For several evenings the light had been telling him that a comet was arriving, and he had accepted the information as nothing particularly startling or new; he had been puzzled only at the significance of the other words of the message, "toward," for instance. So far he had not been quite able to grasp "toward."

No; it was not the message itself that was so startling to Number 774. Somehow, tonight, the flashing of the distant light on Earth, telling in its cryptic way of the arrival of the visitor, bridged a gap between two of Number 774's thoughts and furnished him with an inspiration—a colossal inspiration which only genius, backed up by a knowledge considerably in excess of that of mankind, and a wonder-deadening familiarity with marvelous scientific triumphs, would have dreamed possible of fulfillment.

In one timeless instant, all of Number 774's dreams and hopes became linked together with the comet. Might he not still be guilty of revolt against the age-honored conventions of old Mars?

* * *

III

Something almost electrical seemed suddenly to take possession of Number 774. His cold eyes, fixed on the reproducer bulb, glittered with impatience. The flickering message, which a moment before would have held the complete attention of his every deductive faculty, had little interest for him now. He translated the signals perfunctorily, gathering what little meaning he could from them and not bothering to puzzle over what was new. He waited with tense eagerness for the moment when the light would go out, and it would be his turn to speak. There was something which he *must* tell his friend of Planet Three, and he *must* tell it so that it would be understood. But how? How could he direct those strange, clumsy signals, of which he knew so very little, so that the information he wished to convey would be received and properly understood?

There! The closing phrase of the message from Planet Three was coming: "Earth standing by for Mars. Earth standing by—" The scarcely noticeable speck of light in the vision globe of the telescope disappeared; the pulsating purple glow in the reproducer bulb faded out, and the darkness there seemed tense with expectancy and eager waiting. It seemed to fling an insurmountable challenge at the intellect and ingenuity of Number 774.

In their present relative positions, Earth and Mars were about fifty million miles, or four and a half light-minutes, apart. Thus any message depending on light would of course take four and a half minutes to travel from Earth to Mars, or vice versa.

To avoid confusion in exchanging their communications, Number 774 and his friend of Planet Three had worked out a system whereby each would send out his signals for two minutes, with an intervening pause of two minutes, during which the other could answer. This Earthly time interval Number 774 had learned to recognize and to interpret in terms of the Martian method of measuring time.

It was his turn now; and though he had something far more important to say than ever before, he hesitated, all his cleverness seemingly check-mated by the immensity of his problem. But the lagging, slipping moments lashed his mind, driving it by sheer tenseness of determination to a higher pitch of keenness, almost, than ever before. At least he could try. He could guess, and he could stumble, but he could try.

The little lever of the signaling mechanism trembled in his grasp, and in response to its feeble movements the signals thundered and flared from the outer surface of the dome overhead. For a full three minutes, violating the rule, Number 774 continued to send, repeating the same phrase over and over again, changing certain words each time, in the hope of hitting the right combination that would convey his meaning.

He did not wait for a reply. Earth had already sunk low in the west, and before a reply could come the flashes arriving from the feeble station on Earth would be rendered too dim and wavering and uncertain by the almost imperceptible haze of the

Martian horizon to be properly recorded. Besides, he had so little time and so much to do.

Ponderously, under his guidance, the great telescope tube swung into line with the comet, which still rode high up in the west. The circular opening in the dome shifted automatically with the telescope, keeping opposite to its muzzle.

The huge form of the comet's head filled the vision globe, spreading brilliant and silvery and tenuous around the more solid spot of the glowing central nucleus.

Delicate instruments came into play, recording and measuring speeds, distances, and densities. But this was no mere quest for abstract scientific knowledge. His eyes smoldered with a grimly definite purpose, in which the shadow of death was very near.

But toward death Number 774's reactions were hardly human. In the torrent of his thoughts one thing shone out clear—the comet would pass close to Mars, and it would also pass close to Earth. That fact offered a slender and stupendous possibility. But in ten days the comet would pass and his chance would be gone. Unless he could cram into that brief time more work than anything human or Martian had ever before been called upon to do, his opportunity would be gone forever.

He finished his measurements quickly and efficiently. Switches clicked, and great mechanisms, and incredibly delicate and sensitive instruments, ceased functioning. The circular opening in the rotunda closed, hiding the stars and the comet. The observatory was at rest, for its eerie, fragile master needed it no more.

Number 774 was hurrying down a passage, the stalky limbs of the machine that carried him making a regular, clicking sound.

He came to a great wall that tumbled away in a murky, green-lighted haze, far beneath. Without hesitation he leaped into it and, seemingly supported and retarded in his fall by the emerald substance of the glow from the metal walls, he floated downward as gently and securely as a feather in the heavy atmosphere of Earth.

At the bottom of the well another vast, low-ceilinged chamber spread out, its remote walls lost in the luminescent emerald murk, through which the burnished forms of gigantic machines gleamed elfinly.

This was Number 774's workroom, and here, now, he set to work, laboring with cool, unhurried efficiency, so characteristic of the children of dying Mars.

Many times before he had struggled with the same problem which now held his attention, and he had learned much concerning it, yet the technical difficulties he had encountered had convinced him that the solution of that problem still lay many years in the future.

But now something had happened. An unforeseen chance had come—a chance which might or might not be possible. It was all a gamble.

There was no time for further experiments. Perhaps with this new opportunity there was no need for further experiments, for Number 774 grasped the underlying principles. He must plan and build; above all he must be quick and sure.

He was thinking of a certain barren valley far out in the desert. In a thousand years, perhaps, no one had visited it except him. Aircraft hardly ever flew over that waterless sand pocket set amid the arid hills of Mars. There would be the ideal spot for the completion of his task, for here in his workshop he knew that he dared not stay.

Delicate electrical impulses transmitted his commands, and in response five giant shapes, paradoxically human travesties wrought in shining metal, rose from their resting places to do his bidding. Under his guidance they made preparation for the exodus, gathering instruments, tools, and other paraphernalia, and packing them in metal cases; binding long arms of metal into great sheafs that would be easy to carry. Meanwhile Number 774 busied himself with a complicated Martian calculating machine.

Thus the night passed. In the almost momentary twilight that preceded the dawn, the strange caravan set out. Number 774 had changed his identity; instead of being only a fragile lump of living protoplasm, he was now a giant of metal, like the five automatons that served him, for the powerful machine he rode was so versatile, and so quick and accurate in its responses to his every guiding gesture, that it was to all intents and purposes his body.

A pair of wings of metal fabric disengaged themselves from the intricacies of his machine and began to flap ponderously. Number 774 soared upward on them, over his servitors that plodded along on the ground, bearing their heavy burdens. His gaze darted back briefly toward the silvery dome of his workshop and at its dusty walls, matching the slightly ocher-tinged dun color of the desert.

But the fact that he had lived in that structure most of his life, and that he was now leaving it forever, aroused no sentiment in his mind. He had no time for sentiment now, for time was precious. Besides, he was looking forward to the trials and dangers that were certain to come soon and to the triumphs that might come with them.

He swung and turned in the air, scanning the terrain with wary watchfulness, on guard for any possible approaching aircraft. It would not be well if he were seen, and if a flier should appear he must take cover. But there was really little danger to face as far as his own people were concerned.

Avoidance of the death sentence imposed by the Rulers was practically without precedent. For thousands of years Martians had obeyed their Rulers' commands so implicitly that now prisons for the detention of the condemned were unknown. When the order came, the people of Mars went to their deaths willingly and without a guard. And so it was unlikely that anyone would suspect that Number 774 had intentions of escaping execution now.

It is hardly likely that Number 774 felt triumphant over his revolt against ancient law—possibly he even felt guilty—but his earnest eagerness to learn things that he did not know, and to give himself to the cause to which his life had been pledged, was an urge that surpassed and defied even age-old code and tradition.

The stars, and leisurely Deimos, the farther moon, shone on an ashen haze that

Raymond Z. Gallun

obscured the horizon in every direction. A mounting breeze, keen and cutting for all its thinness, blew out of the west. When the sun rose, it changed the haze of the dust-laden air to a tumultuous, fiery murk that flung long, ominous streamers of orange and red across the sky. Number 774 knew what was coming and knew the hazards that it brought.

The wind became more and more violent, increasing by puffs and gusts, and at last settling down to a steady powerful blast of the proportions of a terrestrial hurricane. If human ears had been there to hear, they would have detected the mounting whisper and rustle of millions of flying sand particles, rubbing and sliding over each other, making a blurred and soothing purr of sound.

As the streaming, flame-hued trains of sand thickened and mounted higher in the atmosphere, the sun dimmed to a red bubble floating in the murk, and only a bloody reminder of its normal brilliance reached the ground.

Number 774 had descended to join his robots in their march on the ground. He had seen many of these fierce dust storms of Mars, and he accepted them as a matter of course, just as an experienced old mariner of Earth accepts tempests at sea. He himself was safely incased in an air-tight glass cage atop the machine he rode; he was breathing pure filtered air.

The chief dangers were that the filtering equipment which fed oxygen to the engines of his automatons would become clogged, or that he would accidentally be engulfed in some newly formed bed of quicksand, hidden beneath the clouds of dust that swirled about him. But these were unavoidable dangers which must be faced.

Under the pressure of necessity, Number 774 urged his robots to the fastest pace they could attain in the shifting desert soil. The metal giants' long, webby limbs swung on and on steadily, into the east, breasting sand and wind, and climbing several steep rocky ridges they encountered with agile ease, in spite of their great bulk and the weight of the burdens they carried.

Twice they crossed deep, twenty-mile-wide artificial gorges, which on Earth have earned the not entirely correct name of "canals." Now and then during each crossing, the dry and lifeless stalks of some weird Martian vegetation would loom dimly through the storm like grotesque totem poles. The canals were as desolate as the desert itself, for it was very early in the spring, and the water from the melting polar snowcaps had not yet come down through the network of conduits and perforated pipettes buried beneath the canal bed.

When the water did appear, vegetation would srping up in rapid growth along the bottoms of the hundreds of straight scars that had been dredged across the barren desert ages before. But as yet there was no sign of the great Martian planting machines, for it was still too early in the season even for them.

Number 774's wariness in crossing seemed completely unnecessary, for his eyes caught no sign of his own kind, or, in fact, of any living creature. He was as completely alone in the flat expanses of the canals as he was in the desert proper.

Late in the afternoon he arrived at his destination. By sunset the wind had subsided and the air was clearing. The work was already underway. Two of the robots, equipped now with great scooplike claws, had excavated a vast hole in the sand. Feverishly active, the other two were assisting Number 774 with other tasks. Rods were being arranged around the pit. Something of a strange, dark substance was taking form. A stream of molten metal was pouring from a broad, squat mechanism. A thin trickle of white vapor trailed up in the quiet air.

At dusk Number 774 paused to look up, over the rounded hills that ringed the valley, at Planet Three that hung in the western sky, gleaming regally amid its retinue of stars. The light on that distant world would flicker in vain tonight, calling eagerly to the Man of Mars. There would be no answer. Higher up, fainter and less conspicuous, was the silvery dart of the comet.

Perhaps Number 774 was trying to imagine what his unknown friend of the light would think when no replying flicker appeared on the disk of Mars. Perhaps he was trying to imagine, as he had done so often before, what his friend of the light was like. Maybe he was wondering whether he should soon know.

His pause was only momentary. There was much to do, for in effect he was racing with the comet. Martians need very little sleep, and it was certain that Number 774 would get no sleep this night, nor the next, nor the next.

IV

Young Jack Cantrill cast a brief glance at the big diesel engine he had been inspecting, and then, with an air of finality, wiped his grease-blackened hands on a fistful of cotton waste. The outfit was functioning perfectly. Ordinarily he might have paused for a moment to admire the easy strength and motion of the machinery to which he played nursemaid, but, lover of machines though he certainly was, he had no time now.

His eyes did not linger on the reflection of the glowing electric light bulbs mirrored on the polished circumference of the spinning flywheel, as they usually did; nor did his attention wander to the sparks that purred blue and steady on the brushes of the gigantic dynamo attached to the engine.

He had something far more interesting to occupy his mind, and besides, a rather astounding idea had just occurred to him. Old Doc Waters and Yvonne might laugh at the notion; and then again they might be struck by it just as he had been. He'd have to try it out on them right away.

He tossed the handful of waste carelessly into a metal box, then made a perfunctory reading of the meters and instruments banked close and bewilderingly on the switchboard. He adjusted a small rheostat and jotted something down on a chart on the wall

Raymond Z. Gallun

with a red crayon. Then, heedless of his light clothing and his perspiring condition, he hurried out into the frosty desert night.

The breeze, cold and untainted by the smell of burning fuel oil, chilled his damp body uncomfortably, but he did not heed it. The steady thud of the exhaust of the high-compression motor in the iron shack receded rapidly behind him as he ran up a path which led to the summit of a low hill.

On the crest of a neighboring knoll, a broad patch of dazzling light winked on and off regularly, where scores of huge searchlights poured their billions of candlepower toward the twinkling stars, in systematically arranged long and short spurts. Jack Cantrill's glance toward them was brief but intense. His lips moved as though he were counting to himself.

The door of the domed observatory building at the top of the hill opened at his touch. He passed through a small lean-to and entered the brick-lined circular chamber that housed the telescope. Here a single shaded lamp cast a subdued glow over a big desk on which various opened notebooks and papers were scattered. Amid the litter an astronomer's chronometer ticked loudly in shadowed stillness. The gloom was eerie and soft and strange.

Jack Cantrill made his way quietly to the low platform under the eyepiece of the telescope, where the other two occupants of the room stood.

The girl was pretty in a blond, elfin sort of way. She smiled briefly at Jack's approach.

"Any luck, folks?" he inquired.

He was trying to make his voice sound calm and casual, but a tense and excited huskiness crept into his words and spoiled his bluff.

Professor Waters looked up from the eye piece of the big instrument. The glow coming from the nearby lamp accentuated the tired lines of his face, making him look almost haggard. He grinned wearily.

"Not yet, boy," he said. "It seems as though Old Faithful has deserted us completely. It's funny, too, when you remember that when conditions were at all favorable for observation, he hasn't failed me once in nine years. And yet this is the second night that he hasn't given us a sign. The shaded side of Mars hasn't shown a single flicker that you can see, and even the photoelectric cell doesn't detect anything."

The young man glanced uncertainly at the girl and then back at her father. The fingers of one of his hands crept slowly through his curly red hair. With the air of a small schoolboy about to make his first public address, he was fumbling with a soiled sheet of paper he had taken from his pocket. He felt rather sheepish about that idea he had thought of.

"Yvonne— Doc—" he said almost plaintively, in an awkward attempt to get their undivided attention centered on what he was going to say. "I'm not much of a scientist, and maybe I'm a darned fool; but—well, this message—the final one we received the night before last—we thought it was just a jumble but, when you read it, it almost has meaning. Here, listen to it once."

Clearing his throat he proceeded to read from the sheet of paper: "Comet coming. Yes. Comet coming. Yes. Comet coming of Man of Mars. Comet Man of Mars coming toward Earth. Comet coming Man of Mars. Man of Mars. Comet. Man of Mars. Comet. Man of Mars. Comet. Yes, yes, yes. Man of Earth. Yes, yes, yes. Signing off. Signing off."

Jack Cantrill's thin cheeks were flushed when he stopped reading.

"Get it?" he asked in a husky whisper. "Get any sense out of that?"

Yvonne Waters' pretty face had paled slightly. "You mean, Jack—you mean that he wanted to say that he was coming *here*, across fifty million miles of emptiness? He can't do that! He can't! It's too far and too impossible!"

Her concerned manner bolstered up the youth's confidence in his idea. "You caught on to exactly what I thought of," he said.

Professor Waters did not betray any outward excitement. His manner was musing, and he rubbed his cheek reflectively. "I thought of that, too," he admitted after a moment. "But it seemed too wild for serious consideration. Still there's a chance—that you are right."

The thought put into words seemed suddenly to startle the old man. "Gad, boy!" he exploded suddenly. "Supposing it *is* the truth! Old Faithful signaled about the comet. If there's anything to this at all, the comet must be tied up with his coming. And for all we know the comet might help. It passes close to both Earth and Mars. If in some way he could fall into its gravitation field, it would drag him almost all the way. That's it! It would save an enormous energy. It would put his trip, otherwise still impossible, into the realm of possibility!"

"You get me at last, doc," Jack said quickly. "And when you say, 'Supposing it's the truth,' think of what it means! The navigation of interplanetary space, maybe! Commerce between Earth and Mars! A new and wonderful era, with the minds of one world exchanging ideas with the minds of another."

Unconsciously Jack Cantrill had taken Yvonne Waters' hand. Her eyes were starry.

"If it did happen we'd all be heroes, Jack," she said. "Dad and you and I. We'd be the ones to get the credit."

"We would, Yvonne," Jack admitted with a chuckle.

It was the professor's turn to smile. "You two have got the whole business nicely ready-made, haven't you?" he chided. Then his face sobered as he went on: "The gap is pretty wide between Earthman and Martian; and in consequence yours may be very far off, even if that guess of ours about the message is right.

"We don't know that Martians are human beings. The chances are a million to one that they aren't. It is very unlikely that evolution, operating on so different a planet, could produce a being even remotely resembling a man. We don't even know that the people of Mars use speech as we use it. Old Faithful certainly is very intelligent, yet

Raymond Z. Gallun

the way he has fumbled blunderingly with our code seems to indicate that even a faint conception of vocal speech is something new and strange to him.

"Those are some of the gaps, but there may be sinister similarities between Earthmen and Martians.

"Who knows but that something darker lies behind what we think is friendly interest in us? Sometimes conquest is more satisfying than commerce. We can't tell." Professor Waters paused.

"Making it extra strong, aren't you, doc?" Jack put in.

"I guess I am, and now I think I'll do a little news-spreading." The professor strode to the desk.

"Human or not, I hope the Martians are handsome," Yvonne confided impishly to Jack.

"And I hope they're not, darling," he replied, putting his arm affectionately about her waist. He was about to add something more when what the girl's father was saying into the telephone riveted their attention.

"Long distance? I'm calling Washington. I want to speak directly to Mr. Grayson, the Secretary of War. Strange call? Perhaps. But put it through."

Before dawn all the observatories of Earth had begun their watch.

v

Far away on the Red Planet, the work of Number 774 went steadily forward. Then came the night when all was ready except for one thing. A powerful urge, the roots of which are deeply implanted in the dominant forms of life on both Earth and Mars, and perhaps the whole universe, was calling him to a city at the joining place of four canals, far to the east. In that urge there was a pathetic something, perfectly understandable by human standards.

The bright stars reeled dizzily before Number 774 as he swooped out over the desert on the wings of the ornithopter that bore him and sped eastward. He must be cautious, but above all he must hurry.

An hour or so slipped by. The Martian's big eyes, keen and catlike, picked out in the broad cleft of a canal a gigantic angular shape, looming dim and uncertain in the gloom. Inconspicuous as a drifting shadow, he settled toward it. The talons of his automaton found a metal panel that slipped aside at a touch. The green glow of the immense well thus revealed dropped away into deserted obscurity. In a moment he was floating down it, past myriads of openings, from which radiated the labyrinthine tunnels of the buried Martian city.

He entered one of these passages and followed it for perhaps a mile, until he came to a vast chamber, pervaded by a moist, humid heat. The floor was covered with thousands of boxes of clear crystal; and in each box was a purple gob of something feeble and jellylike and alive.

Aided perhaps by some Martian numeral system, Number 774 found his way to the box he sought. At his touch the lid opened. He had dismounted from his automaton, and now, creeping forward, he thrust a slender appendage into the crystal case.

A score of nerve filaments, fine, almost, as human hair, darted out from the chitinous shell that protected them and roved caressingly over the lump of protoplasm. Immediately it responded to the gentle touch of the strange creature that had sired it. Its delicate integument quivered, and a thin pseudopod oozed up from its jellylike form and enveloped the nerve filaments of Number 774. For minutes the two remained thus, perfectly motionless.

It was a bizarre travesty of a touching and perfectly human situation; yet its utter strangeness by Earthly standards robbed it of some of its pathos. No words were spoken, no sign of affection that a terrestrial being could interpret was given; and yet perhaps the exchange of feeling and thought and emotion between parent and offspring was far more complete than anything of the kind possible on Earth.

Number 774 did not forget caution. Perhaps it was intuition that informed him that someone was coming. Quickly, yet without haste, he regained his automaton, replaced the lid on the crystal box, and slipped quietly away into the luminescent obscurity of the tunnel. In a few minutes he had safely reached the open of the canal bed. Broad wings flapped, and the starlit night swallowed him up.

As he hurried back toward his hidden valley, he saw the silvery green speck of Earth dip beneath the western horizon. The sight of it must have aroused a turmoil of forebodings within him; for absently, as if he were already facing unknown horrors in mortal combat, he moved a small switch, and in response a jagged flash of flame leaped from an apparatus carried on a long arm of his flying automaton. Where the bolt struck, the desert sand turned molten.

Above, the comet glowed, pallid and frosty and swollen. It was very near to Mars now.

Having reached his valley, Number 774 descended into the pit. A silvery thing that was illy defined in the uncertain light loomed over him. A door opened and closed, and Number 774 was alone and busy amid a bewildering array of machinery.

There came a blinding flash of incandescence, and a roar that sounded like the collision of two worlds; then a shrill, tortured, crackling whistle. The pit glowed white-hot, and the silvery thing was gone. Above the pit, towering many miles into the sky, was an immense jetted plume of vapor, shining rosy with heat. It would be many minutes before that huge gaseous cloud would cool sufficiently to be invisible.

The body of Number 774 was battered and torn and broken; the terrific acceleration was crushing him; consciousness was slipping, even though he was exerting a tremendous effort of will to cling to it. In a few minutes it would not matter if he did

Raymond Z. Gallun

go out, but now there were controls to watch and to handle. If they were not manipulated properly everything he had done was for naught.

But the blackness of oblivion was closing in. He struggled valiantly to master himself and to fight through the gathering gloom that was misting his vision and clouding his mind. Though his whole being cried out for a cessation of torturing effort, still he kept fiercely at his task. There was too much at stake. That little globe there—it was glowing red when it should glow violet. It must be attended to. The craft was wobbling, and it must not wobble. A trifling adjustment of delicate stabilizers would fix that, if he could only somehow make the adjustment.

A dribble of sticky, oozy fluid welled from a wound in Number 774's side. His limbs, some of them broken, fumbled awkwardly and inefficiently with the complicated controls. He was gasping, and all the while his glazing eyes remained fixed grimly on the form of the comet, toward which he and the strange craft he had built were hurtling. Could he reach it? He must!

VI

On Earth, Professor Waters, his daughter, and his young engineer, watched and waited. It was a tense, grueling task, heavy-laden with monotony, a thousand weird imaginings, and a horde of questions, none of which could be answered with any certainty.

They were uncertain whether to be fearful of the unknown thing whose approach they sensed, or to be exultant. They did not even know whether their vigil was just a huge nerve-racking practical joke which their fancies had played upon them.

Time dragged with torturing slowness. Tardy seconds became minutes, tedious minutes were built up into hours, and hours became days that seemed like centuries. And over the rest of the world, the vigil was much the same.

On the ninth day after the last flickering message had come from Mars, Professor Waters had seen through his telescope, on the surface of the Red Planet, a fine dot of white light that, after its sudden appearance, faded quickly to red, and then, after a few minutes, disappeared altogether. A few hours later he thought he detected a slight and momentary ripple in the gaseous substance of the comet's head, which then had just passed Mars on its sunward journey.

Newspaper reporters who had come many miles to this lonely spot in the desert were constantly seeking interviews. The three watchers supplied them with all the information they knew; and at last, tiring of the additional strain of being constantly hounded by these persistent seekers after sensational news, they refused even to grant them admittance into the barbed-wire stockade of the camp.

At last the comet reached its point of closest approach to the Earth. Faint and ashy though it was, low down in the sunlit afternoon heavens, still it was an awesome, impressive object, with its colossal, fan-shaped head and the vast curved sweep of its gigantic ghost-silver tail.

When the desert dusk settled, the visiting wanderer increased a score of times in brilliance and glory. It had now passed the line and was hurtling away. And as yet nothing that would satisfy the eager hopes and fears of the watchers had happened.

The three were standing on the veranda of the little adobe house they inhabited. All of a sudden Doctor Waters' haggard face relaxed. He sighed heavily.

"I guess that it has been proved that we are all of us fools," he said wearily. "There hasn't been much of anything to reward us for our pains." His glance toward Jack Cantrill was slightly apologetic. "I think I'll go to bed," he added abruptly.

Jack's rather good-looking face twisted into a rueful smile. "Bed isn't at all a bad idea," he admitted. "I feel as though I could snooze a week straight without waking up. Well, anyway, if we're fools, I'm the biggest one, because I started all this." He looked at the old man and then at the girl. "Forgive me, Yvonne?" he queried good-humoredly.

"No," she replied with mock seriousness. "Making me lose so much of my beauty sleep like this! You ought to be ashamed of yourself." Her little speech was terminated by a faintly amused chuckle, and she pinched his cheek impishly.

It was some hours after they had retired that a faint soughing noise began from somewhere, apparently at a great distance. It was like the sound of a suddenly stiffening night breeze, sweeping through a grove of pine trees. Something that glowed rosy with the heat of atmospheric friction swept in hurtling flight across the sky. A mile or so beyond the camp, broad thin flanges of metal shot out from it, and it made a feeble attempt to steady itself and check its almost meteoric speed. It wobbled, then fluttered down weakly. A cloud of dust and sand rose where it smashed into the ground. But there was no human eye to see. For an hour or more it gave no further sign of life or motion.

Yvonne Waters was a light sleeper. Unusual night noises ordinarily aroused her. The momentary soughing rustle caused her to stir, but she did not awaken. Then, toward four in the morning, another disturbance came. It was a faint stretching, creaking, straining sound, that nevertheless held a suggestion of powerful forces acting stealthily.

Instantly Yvonne was wide awake. She sat up in bed, listening. What she heard produced quick and accurate associations in her nimble and cool young mind. A barbed-wire fence would make a creaking, straining noise like that, if something big and powerful were seeking tentatively to force an entrance. The stockade!

Yes; she was right. Presently there came the sharp snap and snarl that told of the sudden parting of a taut wire. Four times the sound was repeated.

Yvonne Waters had bounded out of her bunk and had rushed to a window. It was still very dark, but outlined against the stars she saw a vague shape that swayed and moved. The girl's hand groped quickly into the drawer of a small stand beside her

Raymond Z. Gallun

and drew out a heavy automatic pistol. Then she hurried to the door and across the hallway.

"Dad! Jack!" she called in a husky whisper. "I've seen something big. It's coming toward the house!"

The young man responded quickly, his unshod feet thudding across the floor. His eyes narrowed when he leaned out of the window. There the thing stood, statuesquely now, not fifty paces away. It was not clearly defined in the darkness, but Jack Cantrill knew at once that it was something completely out of his experience. It seemed to have an upright, cylindrical body that rose perhaps fifteen feet above the ground. Leverlike limbs projected grotesquely from the upper end of this torso, and at the lower end there were shadowy suggestions of other limbs, long and spidery. An angular object surmounted the cylinder, and in its present position it was an outlandish travesty of the head of a man, cocked to one side, listening.

A minute passed. Obeying what must have been an automatic impulse, Yvonne Waters drew on her boots. About the camp she always dressed like the men, and during the last few nights, anticipating sudden developments, they had all slept in their clothing.

Jack Cantrill, crouching by the window, felt the short hairs at the nape of his neck stiffen. Doctor Waters' hand was on the young man's shoulder. The fingers were trembling slightly.

It was Jack who first put into words what they were all sure was the truth: "Old Faithful, I think," he whispered, without any apparent excitement.

He paused for a moment, during which neither of his companions made any comment, for even a slight sound, as far as they knew, might be heard, with disastrous consequences.

The young man was thinking fast. Something had to be done and done quickly, and it was perhaps very easy to do the wrong thing.

"Flashlight!" he whispered presently, taking command of the situation, and the girl, responding quickly to his leadership, slipped her big electric torch into his hand.

"Now out into the open—all of us," he ordered. "Armed?"

Each carried a pistol. They slipped around to the side of the house, with Cantrill in the lead. The weird giant stood as before, rigid and perfectly still.

Jack raised the flashlight. Working the flash button with his thumb, he proceeded to signal out in the Morse code, a familiar message: "Hello, Man of Mars! Hello, Man of Mars! Hello, Man of Mars!"

And the answer came immediately, flickering from a small spot of green light on the angular "head" of the automaton: "Hello, Man of Earth! Hello, Man of Earth! Comet. Comet. Comet. Comet." The message was clear enough, but there was an unusual halting, stumbling hesitancy in the way it was given. Old Faithful had always been precise and quick in the messages he had flashed from Mars.

As the three watchers stood spellbound, the great quasi-human machine started forward toward the house. Its movements were powerful, but drunken and unsteady. It seemed to be little more than an insensate mechanism running amuk. The intelligence that was guiding it was losing its hold. Nothing could avert an accident.

The robot struck the side of the house with a heavy thud, lurched forward, stumbled, and fell with a clatter and clang of metal across the low roof that collapsed under its weight and the force of its overthrow. Prostrate though it was, its lower limbs continued to simulate the movements of walking.

Its arms sprawled wide, and from a metal knob at the tip of one a torrent of blue sparks began to pour into the earth, causing the patch of sand it struck to turn molten and boil away in a cloud of incandescent vapor. A minute must have passed before the sparks burned out and the appendages of the machine ceased their ponderous thrashing.

Meanwhile the three watchers had been staring at the weird and inspiring sight, not knowing just what to do. But now, when quiet was restored, they edged cautiously toward the fallen machine. Jack Cantrill's flashlight beam played over the wreckage and halted upon the flattened "head" of the robot. It was pyramidal in form and had been supported by a flexible pillar of pointed metal. There was an opening in one side, and from it something had tumbled. A shadow veiled it, so that the watchers could not immediately see what it was. Then Jack leaped to a different position and poured the beam of the flashlight full upon it.

The effect of its strangeness did not come upon them right away, for they did not at once realize its true nature. It seemed at first only a sprawling mass of drab gray, as large, perhaps, as the open top of an ordinary umbrella. It might have been nothing more than a large lump of wet mud, flattened out by being dropped.

Then, after a moment, the three took note of the ragged tendrils that radiated out from the oblate form somewhat in the manner of the arms of a starfish. The ends of some of those tendrils were slender and stalklike and were terminated by incredibly fine filaments of coral pink. Those filaments were twitching convulsively.

Yvonne Waters was the first to find her voice. It was choking and tremulous: "The thing's alive!" she cried. "Dad! Jack! It's alive!"

Obscure primal instincts had taken possession of them. Like wary alley curs they inched their way forward, craning their neck to look closer at the creature, in which, for them, both fascination and fear were combined.

It was then they saw that the central lump of the thing was contracting in painful, jerky spasms. It was breathing, or gasping, rather. Feathery pink palps around a cone-shaped orifice that resembled the inside of a funnel coiled in agony. They could hear the monster's breath whistle through the opening in long, rasping sighs.

But the creature's eyes, fixed to the ends of two tentacular appendages that protruded from beneath the outer folds of its flattened body, regarded them with what seemed to be an interest which could not be dimmed by physical pain and suffering. They were very large eyes, three inches across, and there was in their alien, brooding

Raymond Z. Gallun

intensity, slightly veiled now by the film of approaching death, a suggestion of an intelligence in this monstrous, inhuman body that was more than human.

Yvonne Waters had taken note of these things almost in the space of a moment. She saw the hideous festering gashes of wounds that must have been several days old on the body of the visiting being, and she saw that several of its limbs were shattered. Some of them seemed to be partly knit, but others were evidently recent injuries. From the fresh wounds bright red blood oozed, giving evidence of a very high hemoglobin content, which would be necessary for a creature accustomed to breathing an atmosphere much more rarefied than that of Earth.

Maybe it was because Yvonne Waters was a woman that she bridged the gap between Earthman and Martian more quickly than her companions.

"He's hurt!" she gasped suddenly. "We've got to help him some way! We ought to—ought to—get a doctor." She halted a little in expressing this last idea. It seemed so totally wild and fantastic.

"A doctor for that horror?" Jack Cantrill asked, a trifle dazed.

"Yes! Well, maybe no," the girl amended. "But still we must do something. We've got to! He's human, Jack—human in everything but form. He has brains; he can feel pain like any human being. Besides, he has courage of the same kind that we all worship. Think of the pluck it took to make the first plunge across fifty million miles of cold, airless void! That's something to bow down to, isn't it? And, besides, this is our friend, Old Faithful!"

"By the gods, Yvonne, you're right!" the young man exploded with sudden realization. "And here I am, wasting time like a dumb fool!"

He dropped to his knees beside the injured Martian, and his big hands poised, ready and willing, but still uncertain how to help this bizarre entity of another world.

Doctor Waters had by this time shaken the fog of sleep from his older and less agile faculties, and he was now able to grasp the situation. With a brief and crisp, "I'll get the first-aid kit!" he hurried into the partially wrecked house, across the roof of which sprawled Old Faithful's automaton.

Conquering her natural revulsion, Yvonne brought herself to touch the dry, cold flesh of the Martian, and to try as best she might to ease its suffering. Presently the three of them were working over their weird patient, disinfecting and bandaging its wounds. But there was small hope that their efforts would be of any avail.

At their first touch, Old Faithful had started convulsively, as though in fear and repugnance of these, to him, horrid monsters; and a low, thick cry came from the opening in his body. But he must have realized that their intentions were harmless, for he had relaxed immediately. His breath, however, was rapidly growing weaker and more convulsive, and his eyes were glazing.

"We're dumb!" Jack stated with sudden vehemence. "He's badly hurt, but that's not all. This atmosphere is six times too dense for him. He's smothering in it—drowning! We've got to get him somewhere where the pressure won't be crushing him!''

"We'll rig up a vacuum tank down in the engine shed," said Doctor Waters. "It won't take but a minute."

It was done. However, when they were lifting Old Faithful onto the litter they had improvised, his body stiffened, shuddered, and grew suddenly limp. They knew that Old Faithful—Number 774—was gone. Still, to aid the remote possibility that he would revive, they placed him in the vacuum tank and exhausted most of the air so that the pressure inside duplicated that of the rarefied Martian atmosphere. Fresh air was admitted slowly through the petcock. But within an hour Old Faithful's flesh had become stiff with *rigor mortis*. He was dead.

Much must have passed through the devious channels of his Martian mind during those brief hours on Planet Three. He must have felt satisfied that his eagerness to penetrate the unknown was partly rewarded, his ambition partly fulfilled. He had learned what lay back of, and what had guided, the flickerings of the light. He had seen the people of Planet Three. Perhaps, at the last, he had thought of Mars, his home, and the sorry plight of his race.

Maybe he thought of his growing offspring in that buried nursery chamber, fifty million miles away. Maybe the possibilities of Earth, as a means of aiding dying Mars, occurred to him, if it had not come into his mind before, and it is quite likely that his ideas in that direction were not altogether altruistic toward mankind.

Certainly he hoped that his friend of the light would find his space car and what it contained, out there in the desert, and that they would study and understand.

Dawn came, with the eastern sky sprinkled with a few pink feathery clouds that the bright sun would soon dissipate.

In one of the various corrugated iron sheds of the camp, Yvonne, Jack, and the doctor were bending over the body of Old Faithful, which lay stiff and lifeless on a long table.

"Kind of heartless to be preparing this intelligent being for immersion in a preservative spirit bath so that a lot of curious museum-goers can have a thrill, don't you think, folks?" Jack was complaining with make-believe gruffness. "How would you like it if the situation was reversed—if we were stiffs with the curious of Mars looking at us?"

"I wouldn't mind if I was dead." The girl laughed. "It would be an honor. Oh, look, Jack—the funny little mark on Old Faithful's skin—it's tattooed with red ink. What do you suppose it means?"

Jack had already seen the mark. It was a circle with a bar through the center and was, as the girl had said, an artificial decoration or symbol. Jack shrugged. "Search me, honey!" He chuckled. "Say, doc, do you suppose that space car is around here somewhere?"

The doctor nodded. "It must be."

Raymond Z. Gallun

"Well, come on! Let's look for it, then! This can wait."

After a very hasty and sketchy breakfast, they made their way on horseback out into the desert, following the tracks the Martian robot had made.

At the summit of a rocky ridge they found what they sought—a long cylinder of metal deeply imbedded in sand that seemed literally to have splashed like soft mud around it. The long fins of the space car were crumpled and broken and covered with the blue-gray ash of oxidation. Here and there a fragment had peeled away, revealing bright metal beneath.

The nose of the shell had become unscrewed, exposing burnished threads that glistened in the sun. Into the shadowed interior they made their way, rummaging gingerly among the bewildering maze of Martian instruments. The place reeked with a scorched, pungent odor.

At the rear of the cylindrical compartment they found a great round drum of metal, fitting snugly into the interior of the shell. Sleepily they wondered what was in it and made several weary attempts to move it. At nine o'clock the police guard that Doctor Waters had sent for arrived.

"Tell those damned reporters who are trying to crash in on us to go to hell," Jack Cantrill told the lieutenant in charge, as he and his two companions were starting wearily back toward camp. "We've got to snooze."

Several weeks had passed. In a hotel room in Phoenix, Arizona, Doctor Waters was speaking to Mr. and Mrs. Cantrill, who had just arrived.

"I'm turning the camp and the signaling apparatus over to Radeau and his associates," he was saying. "No more signals from Mars, somehow, and I don't feel very much like continuing there anyway. There are a lot more interesting things on the horizon.

"That drum which Old Faithful brought us—it contained models and many charts and sheets of parchment with drawings on them. I'm beginning to see light through the mystery at last. There are suggestions there for constructing a spaceship. I'm going to work on that problem as long as I live.

"Maybe I'll succeed with the help of Old Faithful. Human ingenuity will have to be called on, too, of course. I don't think that the Martians have the problem completely solved themselves. Old Faithful used the comet, you know."

The doctor's smile broadened as he went on: "Children, how would you like to go to Mars with me some day?"

"Don't ask silly questions, dad," said Yvonne. "We'd go in a minute!"

The young man nodded seriously. "What a honeymoon that would make, if we could have it now!" he enthused.

"A million times better than going to Seattle," the girl agreed.

The doctor grinned faintly. "Even if you were treated like poor Old Faithful—pickled and put in a museum?"

"Even if!"

Jack Cantrill's eyes narrowed and seemed to stare far away into nothing. His lips and his gaunt sunburned cheeks were stern. Perhaps he was looking into the future toward adventures that might or might not come.

Something of the same rugged spirit seemed suddenly to have infused itself into the strong, bronzed beauty of the girl at his side. They both loved adventure; they both knew life in the rough.

At the door Yvonne kissed her father good-bye. "Just a little run up to Seattle, dad," she explained cheerily, "two or three weeks, maybe. Then both of us back with you—to work." ■

HELEN O'LOY
Lester del Rey

I am an old man now, but I can still see Helen as Dave unpacked her, and still hear him gasp as he looked her over.

"Man, isn't she a beauty?"

She was beautiful, a dream in spun plastics and metals, something Keats might have seen dimly when he wrote his sonnet. If Helen of Troy had looked like that the Greeks must have been pikers when they launched only a thousand ships; at least, that's what I told Dave.

"Helen of Troy, eh?" He looked at her tag. "At least it beats this thing—K2W88. Helen . . . Mmmm . . . Helen of Alloy."

"Not much swing to that, Dave. Too many unstressed syllables in the middle. How about Helen O'Loy?"

"Helen O'Loy she is, Phil." And tha's how it began—one part beauty, one part dream, one part science; add a stereo broadcast, stir mechanically, and the result is chaos.

Dave and I hadn't gone to college together, but when I came to Messina to practice medicine, I found him downstairs in a little robot repair shop. After that, we began to pal around, and when I started going with one twin, he found the other equally attractive, so we made it a foursome.

When our business grew better, we rented a house out near the rocket field—noisy but cheap, and the rockets discouraged apartment building. We liked room enough to stretch ourselves. I suppose, if we hadn't quarreled with them, we'd have married the twins in time. But Dave wanted to look over the latest Venus-rocket attempt when his twin wanted to see a display stereo starring Larry Ainslee, and they were both stubborn. From then on, we forgot the girls and spent our evenings at home.

But it wasn't until "Lena" put vanilla on our steak instead of salt that we got off on the subject of emotions and robots. While Dave was dissecting Lena to find the trouble, we naturally mulled over the future of the mechs. He was sure that the robots would beat men some day, and I couldn't see it.

"Look here, Dave," I argued. "You know Lena doesn't think—not really. When those wires crossed, she could have corrected herself. But she didn't bother; she followed the mechanical impulse. A man might have reached for the vanilla, but when he saw it in his hand, he'd have stopped. Lena has sense enough, but she has no emotions, no consciousness of self."

"All right, that's the big trouble with the mechs now. But we'll get around it, put in some mechanical emotions, or something." He screwed Lena's head back on, turned on her juice. "Go back to work, Lena, it's nineteen o'clock."

Now I specialized in endocrinology and related subjects. I wasn't exactly a psychologist, but I did understand the glands, secretions, hormones, and miscellanies that are the physical causes of emotions. It took medical science three hundred years to find out how and why they worked, and I couldn't see men duplicating them mechanically in much less time.

I brought home books and papers to prove it, and Dave quoted the invention of memory coils and veritoid eyes. During that year we swapped knowledge until Dave knew the whole theory of endocrinology, and I could have made Lena from memory. The more we talked, the less sure I grew about the impossibility of *Homo mechanensis* as the perfect type.

Poor Lena. Her cuproberyl body spent half its time in scattered pieces. Our first attempts were successful only in getting her to serve fried brushes for breakfast and wash the dishes in oleo oil. Then one day she cooked a perfect dinner with six wires crossed, and Dave was in ecstasy.

He worked all night on her wiring, put in a new coil, and taught her a fresh set of words. And the next day she flew into a tantrum and swore vigorously at us when we told her she wasn't doing her work right.

"It's a lie," she yelled, shaking a suction brush. "You're all liars. If you so-and-so's would leave me whole long enough, I might get something done around the place."

When we calmed her temper and got her back to work, Dave ushered me into the study. "Not taking any chances with Lena," he explained. "We'll have to cut out that adrenal pack and restore her to normality. But we've got to get a better robot. A housemaid mech isn't complex enough."

"How about Dillard's new utility models? They seem to combine everything in one."

"Exactly. Even so, we'll need a special one built to order, with a full range of memory coils. And out of respect to old Lena, let's get a female case for its works."

The result, of course, was Helen. The Dillard people had performed a miracle and put all the works in a girl-modeled case. Even the plastic and rubberite face was designed for flexibility to express emotions, and she was complete with tear glands and taste buds, ready to simulate every human action, from breathing to pulling hair. The bill they sent with her was another miracle, but Dave and I scraped it together; we had to turn Lena over to an exchange to complete it, though, and thereafter we ate out.

I'd performed plenty of delicate operations on living tissues, and some of them had been tricky, but I still felt like a premed student as we opened the front plate of her torso and began to sever the leads of her "nerves." Dave's mechanical glands were

Lester del Rey

all prepared, complex little bundles of pansistors and wires that heterodyned on the electrical thought impulses and distorted them as adrenalin distorts the reaction of human minds.

Instead of sleeping that night, we pored over the schematic diagrams of her structures, tracing the complex thought mazes of her wiring, severing the leaders, implanting the heterones, as Dave called them. And while we worked, a mechanical tape fed carefully prepared thoughts of consciousness and awareness of life and feeling into an auxiliary memory coil. Dave believed in leaving nothing to chance.

It was growing light as we finished, exhausted and exultant. All that remained was the starting of her electrical power; like all the Dillard mechs, she was equipped with a tiny atomotor instead of batteries, and once started would need no further attention.

Dave refused to turn her on. "Wait until we've slept and rested," he advised. "I'm as eager to try her as you are, but we can't do much studying with our minds half-dead. Turn in, and we'll leave Helen until later."

Even though we were both reluctant to follow it, we knew the idea was sound. We turned in, and sleep hit us before the air conditioner could cut down to sleeping temperature. And then Dave was pounding on my shoulder.

"Phil! Hey, snap out of it!"

I groaned, turned over, and faced him. "Well? . . . Uh! What is it? Did Helen—"

"No, it's old Mrs. van Styler. She 'visored to say her son has an infatuation for a servant girl, and she wants you to come out and give counterhormones. They're at the summer camp in Maine."

Rich Mrs. van Styler! I couldn't afford to let that account down, now that Helen had used up the last of my funds. But it wasn't a job I cared for.

"Counterhormones! That'll take two weeks' full time. Anyway, I'm no society doctor, messing with glands to keep fools happy. My job's taking care of serious trouble."

"And you want to watch Helen." Dave was grinning, but he was serious, too. "I told her it'd cost her fifty thousand!"

"*Huh?*"

"And she said okay, if you hurried."

Of course, there was only one thing to do, though I could have wrung fat Mrs. van Styler's neck cheerfully. It wouldn't have happened if she'd used robots like everyone else—but she had to be different.

Consequently, while Dave was back home puttering with Helen, I was racking my brain to trick Archy van Styler into getting the counterhormones, and giving the servant girl the same. Oh, I wasn't supposed to, but the poor kid was crazy about Archy. Dave might have written, I thought, but never a word did I get.

It was three weeks later instead of two when I reported that Archy was "cured," and collected on the line. With that money in my pocket, I hired a personal rocket and was back in Messina in half an hour. I didn't waste time in reaching the house.

As I stepped into the alcove, I heard a light patter of feet, and an eager voice called out, "Dave, dear?" For a minute I couldn't answer, and the voice came again, pleading, "Dave?"

I don't know what I expected, but I didn't expect Helen to meet me that way, stopping and staring at me, obvious disappointment on her face, little hands fluttering up against her breast.

"Oh," she cried. "I thought it was Dave. He hardly comes home to eat now, but I've had supper waiting hours." She dropped her hands and managed a smile. "You're Phil, aren't you? Dave told me about you when . . . at first. I'm so glad to see you home, Phil."

"Glad to see you doing so well, Helen." Now what does one say for light conversation with a robot? "You said something about supper?"

"Oh, yes. I guess Dave ate downtown again, so we might as well go in. It'll be nice having someone to talk to around the house, Phil. You don't mind if I call you Phil, do you? You know, you're sort of a godfather to me."

We ate. I hadn't counted on such behavior, but apparently she considered eating as normal as walking. She didn't do much eating, at that; most of the time she spent staring at the front door.

Dave came in as we were finishing, a frown a yard wide on his face. Helen started to rise, but he ducked toward the stairs, throwing words over his shoulder.

"Hi, Phil. See you up here later."

There was something radically wrong with him. For a moment, I'd thought his eyes were haunted, and as I turned to Helen, hers were filling with tears. She gulped, choked them back, and fell to viciously on her food.

"What's the matter with him . . . and you?" I asked.

"He's sick of me." She pushed her plate away and got up hastily. "You'd better see him while I clean up. And there's nothing wrong with me. And it's not my fault anyway." She grabbed the dishes and ducked into the kitchen; I could have sworn she was crying.

Maybe all thought is a series of conditioned reflexes—but she certainly had picked up a lot of conditioning while I was gone. Lena in her heyday had been nothing like this. I went up to see if Dave could make any sense out of the hodge-podge.

He was squirting soda into a large glass of apple brandy, and I saw that the bottle was nearly empty. "Join me?" he asked.

It seemed like a good idea. The roaring blast of an ion rocket overhead was the only familiar thing left in the house. From the look around Dave's eyes, it wasn't the first bottle he'd emptied while I was gone, and there were more left. He dug out a new bottle for his own drink.

"Of course, it's none of my business, Dave, but that stuff won't steady your nerves any. What's gotten into you and Helen? Been seeing ghosts?"

Helen was wrong; he hadn't been eating downtown—nor anywhere else. His muscles collapsed into a chair in a way that spoke of fatigue and nerves, but mostly of hunger. "You noticed it, eh?"

"Noticed it? The two of you jammed it down my throat."

"Uhmmm." He swatted at a nonexistent fly, and slumped further down in the pneumatic. "Guess maybe I should have waited with Helen until you got back. But if that stereo cast hadn't changed . . . anyway, it did. And those mushy books of yours finished the job."

"Thanks. That makes it all clear."

"You know, Phil, I've got a place up in the country . . . fruit ranch. My dad left it to me. Think I'll look it over."

And that's the way it went. But finally, by much liquor and more perspiration, I got some of the story out of him before I gave him an Amytal and put him to bed. Then I hunted up Helen and dug the rest of the story from her, until it made sense.

Apparently as soon as I was gone, Dave had turned her on and made preliminary tests, which were entirely satisfactory. She had reacted beautifully—so well that he decided to leave her and go down to work as usual.

Naturally, with all her untried emotions, she was filled with curiosity, and wanted him to stay. Then he had an inspiration. After showing her what her duties about the house would be, he set her down in front of the stereovisor, tuned in a travelogue, and left her to occupy her time with that.

The travelogue held her attention until it was finished, and the station switched over to a current serial with Larry Ainslee, the same cute emoter who'd given us all the trouble with the twins. Incidentally, he looked something like Dave.

Helen took to the serial like a seal to water. This play-acting was a perfect outlet for her newly excited emotions. When that particular episode finished, she found a love story on another station, and added still more to her education. The afternoon programs were mostly news and music, but by then she'd found my books; and I do have rather adolescent taste in literature.

Dave came home in the best of spirits. The front alcove was neatly swept, and there was the odor of food in the air that he'd missed around the house for weeks. He had visions of Helen as the super-efficient housekeeper.

So it was a shock to him to feel two strong arms around his neck from behind and hear a voice all aquiver coo into his ears, "Oh, Dave, darling. I've missed you so, and I'm so *thrilled* that you're back." Helen's technique may have lacked polish, but it had enthusiasm, as he found when he tried to stop her from kissing him. She had learned fast and furiously—also, Helen was powered by an atomotor.

Dave wasn't a prude, but he remembered that she was only a robot, after all. The fact that she felt, acted, and looked like a young goddess in his arms didn't mean much. With some effort, he untangled her and dragged her off to supper, where he made her eat with him to divert her attention.

After her evening work, he called her into the study and gave her a thorough lecture on the folly of her ways. It must have been good, for it lasted three solid hours, and covered her station in life, the idiocy of stereos, and various other miscellanies. When he finished, Helen looked up with dewy eyes and said wistfully, "I know, Dave, but I still love you."

That's when Dave started drinking.

It grew worse each day. If he stayed downtown, she was crying when he came home. If he returned on time, she fussed over him and threw herself at him. In his room, with the door locked, he could hear her downstairs pacing up and down and muttering; and when he went down, she stared at him reproachfully until he had to go back up.

I sent Helen out on a fake errand in the morning and got Dave up. With her gone, I made him eat a decent breakfast and gave him a tonic for his nerves. He was still listless and moody.

"Look here, Dave," I broke in on his brooding. "Helen isn't human, after all. Why not cut off her power and change a few memory coils? Then we can convince her that she never was in love and couldn't get that way."

"You try it. I had that idea, but she put up a wail that would wake Homer. She says it would be murder—and the hell of it is that I can't help feeling the same about it. Maybe she isn't human, but you wouldn't guess it when she puts on that martyred look and tells you to go ahead and kill her."

"We never put in substitutes for some of the secretions present in man during the love period."

"I don't know what we put in. Maybe the heterones backfired or something. Anyway, she's made this idea so much a part of her thoughts that we'd have to put in a whole new set of coils."

"Well, why not?"

"Go ahead. You're the surgeon of this family. I'm not used to fussing with emotions. Matter of fact, since she's been acting this way, I'm beginning to hate work on any robot. My business is going to blazes."

He saw Helen coming up the walk and ducked out the back door for the monorail express. I'd intended to put him back in bed, but let him go. Maybe he'd be better off at his shop than at home.

"Dave's gone?" Helen did have that martyred look now.

"Yeah. I got him to eat, and he's gone to work."

"I'm glad he ate." She slumped down in a chair as if she were worn out, though how a mech could be tired beat me. "Phil?"

"Well, what is it?"

Lester del Rey

"Do you think I'm bad for him? I mean, do you think he'd be happier if I weren't here?"

"He'll go crazy if you keep acting this way around him."

She winced. Those little hands were twisting about pleadingly, and I felt like an inhuman brute. But I'd started, and I went ahead. "Even if I cut out your power and changed your coils, he'd probably still be haunted by you."

"I know. But I can't help it. And I'd make him a good wife, really I would, Phil."

I gulped; this was getting a little too far. "And give him strapping sons to boot, I suppose. A man wants flesh and blood, not rubber and metal."

"Don't, please! I can't think of myself that way; to me, I'm a woman. And you know how perfectly I'm made to imitate a real woman . . . in all ways. I couldn't give him sons, but in every other way . . . I'd try so hard, I know I'd make him a good wife."

I gave up.

Dave didn't come home that night, nor the next day. Helen was fussing and fuming, wanting me to call the hospitals and the police, but I knew nothing had happened to him. He always carried identification. Still, when he didn't come on the third day, I began to worry. And when Helen started out for his shop, I agreed to go with her.

Dave was there, with another man I didn't know. I parked Helen where he couldn't see her, but where she could hear, and went in as soon as the other fellow left.

Dave looked a little better and seemed glad to see me. "Hi, Phil—just closing up. Let's go eat."

Helen couldn't hold back any longer, but came trooping in. "Come on home, Dave. I've got roast duck with spice stuffing, and you know you love that."

"Scat!" said Dave. She shrank back, turned to go. "Oh, all right, stay. You might as well hear it, too. I've sold the shop. The fellow you saw just bought it, and I'm going up to the old fruit ranch I told you about, Phil. I can't stand the mechs any more."

"You'll starve to death at that," I told him.

"No, there's a growing demand for old-fashioned fruit, raised out of doors. People are tired of this water-culture stuff. Dad always made a living out of it. I'm leaving as soon as I can get home and pack."

Helen clung to her idea. "I'll pack, Dave, while you eat. I've got apple cobbler for dessert." The world was toppling under her feet, but she still remembered how crazy he was for apple cobbler.

Helen was a good cook; in fact she was a genius, with all the good points of a woman and a mech combined. Dave ate well enough, after he got started. By the time supper was over, he'd thawed out enough to admit he liked the duck and cobbler, and to thank her for packing. In fact, he even let her kiss him good-bye, though he firmly refused to let her go to the rocket field with him.

Helen was trying to be brave when I got back, and we carried on a stumbling conversation about Mrs. van Styler's servants for a while. But the talk began to lull, and she sat staring out of the window at nothing most of the time. Even the stereo comedy lacked interest for her, and I was glad enough to have her go off to her room. She could cut her power down to simulate sleep when she chose.

As the days slipped by, I began to realize why she couldn't believe herself a robot. I got to thinking of her as a girl and companion myself. Except for odd intervals when she went off by herself to brood, or when she kept going to the telescript for a letter that never came, she was as good a companion as a man could ask. There was something homey about the place that Lena had never put there.

I took Helen on a shopping trip to Hudson and she giggled and purred over the wisps of silk and glassheen that were the fashion, tried on endless hats, and conducted herself as any normal girl might. We went trout fishing for a day, where she proved to be as good a sport and as sensibly silent as a man. I thoroughly enjoyed myself and thought she was forgetting Dave. That was before I came home unexpectedly and found her doubled up on the couch, threshing her legs up and down and crying to the high heavens.

It was then I called Dave. They seemed to have trouble in reaching him, and Helen came over beside me while I waited. She was tense and fidgety as an old maid trying to propose. But finally they located Dave.

"What's up, Phil?" he asked as his face came on the viewplate. "I was just getting my things together to—"

I broke him off. "Things can't go on the way they are, Dave. I've made up my mind. I'm yanking Helen's coils tonight. It won't be worse than what she's going through now."

Helen reached up and touched my shoulder. "Maybe that's best, Phil. I don't blame you."

Dave's voice cut in. "Phil, you don't know what you're doing!"

"Of course, I do. It'll all be over by the time you can get here. As you heard, she's agreeing."

There was a black cloud sweeping over Dave's face. "I won't have it, Phil. She's half mine and I forbid it!"

"Of all the—"

"Go ahead, call me anything you want. I've changed my mind. I was packing to come home when you called."

Helen jerked around me, her eyes glued to the panel. "Dave, do you . . . are you—"

"I'm just waking up to what a fool I've been, Helen. Phil, I'll be home in a couple of hours, so if there's anything—"

He didn't have to chase me out. But I heard Helen cooing something about loving to be a rancher's wife before I could shut the door.

Well, I wasn't as surprised as they thought. I think I knew when I called Dave

Lester del Rey

what would happen. No man acts the way Dave had been acting because he hates a girl; only because he thinks he does—and thinks wrong.

No woman ever made a lovelier bride or a sweeter wife. Helen never lost her flair for cooking and making a home. With her gone, the old house seemed empty, and I began to drop out to the ranch once or twice a week. I suppose they had trouble at times, but I never saw it, and I know the neighbors never suspected they were anything but normal man and wife.

Dave grew older, and Helen didn't, of course. But between us, we put lines in her face and grayed her hair without letting Dave know that she wasn't growing old with him; he'd forgotten that she wasn't human, I guess.

I practically forgot, myself. It wasn't until a letter came from Helen this morning that I woke up to reality. There, in her beautiful script, just a trifle shaky in places, was the inevitable that neither Dave nor I had seen.

Dear Phil,

As you know, Dave has had heart trouble for several years now. We expected him to live on just the same, but it seems that wasn't to be. He died in my arms just before sunrise. He sent you his greetings and farewell.

I've one last favor to ask of you, Phil. There is only one thing for me to do when this is finished. Acid will burn out metal as well as flesh, and I'll be dead with Dave. Please see that we are buried together, and that the morticians do not find my secret. Dave wanted it that way, too.

Poor, dear Phil. I know you loved Dave as a brother, and how you felt about me. Please don't grieve too much for us, for we have had a happy life together, and both feel that we should cross this last bridge side by side.

With love and thanks from

Helen

It had to come sooner or later, I suppose, and the first shock has worn off now. I'll be leaving in a few minutes to carry out Helen's last instructions.

Dave was a lucky man, and the best friend I ever had. And Helen—well, as I said, I'm an old man now, and can view things more sanely; I should have married and raised a family, I suppose. But . . . there was only one Helen O'Loy. ■

REQUIEM

Robert A. Heinlein

On a high hill in Samoa there is a grave. Inscribed on the marker are these words:

> *"Under the wide and starry sky*
> *Dig my grave and let me lie*
> *Glad did I live and gladly die*
> *And I lay me down with a will!*
>
> *"This be the verse which you grave for me:*
> *Here he lies where he longed to be,*
> *Home is the sailor, home from the sea,*
> *And the hunter home from the hill."*

These lines appear another place—scrawled on a shipping tag torn from a compressed-air container, and pinned to the ground with a knife.

It wasn't much of a fair, as fairs go. The trottin' races didn't promise much excitement, even though several entries claimed the blood of the immortal Dan Patch. The tents and concession booths barely covered the circus grounds, and the pitchmen seemed discouraged.

D. D. Harriman's chauffeur could not see any reason for stopping. They were due in Kansas City for a directors' meeting, that is to say, Harriman was. The chauffeur had private reasons for promptness, reasons involving darktown society on Eighteenth Street. But the Boss not only stopped, but hung around.

Bunting and a canvas arch made the entrance to a large enclosure beyond the race track. Red and gold letters announced:

This way to the
MOON ROCKET!!!!
See it in actual flight!
Public Demonstration Flights
Twice Daily
This is the ACTUAL TYPE used by the

First Man to Reach the MOON!!!
YOU can ride it!!—$50.00

A boy, nine or ten years old, hung around the entrance and stared at the posters. "Want to see the ship, son?"

The kid's eyes shone. "Gee, mister. I sure would."

"So would I. Come on." Harriman paid out fifty dollars for two pink tickets which entitled them to enter the enclosure and examine the rocket ship. The kid took his and ran on ahead with the single-mindedness of youth. Harriman looked over the stubby curved lines of the ovoid body. He noted with a professional eye that she was a single-jet type with fractional controls around her midriff. He squinted through his glasses at the name painted in gold on the carnival red of the body. *Care Free*. He paid another quarter to enter the control cabin.

When his eyes had adjusted to the gloom caused by the strong ray filters of the ports he let them rest lovingly on the keys of the console and the semi-circle of dials above. Each beloved gadget was in its proper place. He knew them—graven in his heart.

While he mused over the instrument board, with the warm liquid of content soaking through his body, the pilot entered and touched his arm.

"Sorry, sir. We've got to cast loose for the flight."

"Eh?" Harriman started, then looked at the speaker. Handsome devil, with a good skull and strong shoulders—reckless eyes and a self-indulgent mouth, but a firm chin. "Oh, excuse me, Captain."

"Quite all right."

"Oh, I say, Captain, er, uh—"

"McIntyre."

"Captain McIntyre, could you take a passenger this trip?" The old man leaned eagerly toward him.

"Why, yes, if you wish. Come along with me." He ushered Harriman into a shed marked OFFICE which stood near the gate. "Passenger for a check over, doc."

Harriman looked startled but permitted the medico to run a stethoscope over his thin chest, and strap a rubber bandage around his arm. Presently he unstrapped it, glanced at McIntyre, and shook his head.

"No go, doc?"

"That's right, Captain."

Harriman looked from face to face. "My heart's all right—that's just a flutter."

The physician's brows shot up. "It is? But it's not just your heart; at your age your bones are brittle, too brittle to risk a take-off."

"Sorry, sir," added the pilot, "but the Bates County Fair Association pays the doctor here to see to it that I don't take anyone up who might be hurt by the acceleration."

Requiem   **51**

The old man's shoulders drooped miserably. "I rather expected it."

"Sorry, sir." McIntyre turned to go, but Harriman followed him out.

"Excuse me, Captain—"

"Yes?"

"Could you and your, uh, engineer have dinner with me after your flight?"

The pilot looked at him quizzically. "I don't see why not. Thanks."

"Captain McIntyre, it is difficult for me to see why anyone would quit the Earth-Moon run." Fried chicken and hot biscuits in a private dining room of the best hotel the little town of Butler afforded, three-star Hennessey and Corona-Coronas had produced a friendly atmosphere in which three men could talk freely.

"Well, I didn't like it."

"Aw, don't give him that, Mac—you know it was Rule G that got you." McIntyre's mechanic poured himself another brandy as he spoke.

McIntyre looked sullen. "Well, what if I did take a couple o'drinks? Anyhow, I could have squared that—it was the dern persnickety regulations that got me fed up. Who are you to talk?—Smuggler!"

"Sure I smuggled! Who wouldn't with all those beautiful rocks just aching to be taken back to Earth. I had a diamond once as big as. . . . But if I hadn't been caught I'd be in Luna City tonight. And so would you, you drunken blaster . . . with the boys buying us drinks, and the girls smiling. . . ." He put his face down and began to weep quietly.

McIntyre shook him. "He's drunk."

"Never mind." Harriman interposed a hand. "Tell me, are you really satisfied not to be on the run any more?"

McIntyre chewed his lip. "No—he's right of course. This barnstorming isn't what it's all cracked up to be. We've been hopping junk at every pumpkin doin's up and down the Mississippi valley—sleeping in tourist camps, and eating at greaseburners. Half the time the sheriff has an attachment on the ship, the other half the Society for the Prevention of Something or Other gets an injunction to keep us on the ground. It's no sort of a life for a rocket man."

"Would it help any for you to get to the Moon?"

"Well . . . Yes. I couldn't get back on the Earth-Moon run, but if I was in Luna City, I could get a job hopping ore for the Company—they're always short of rocket pilots for that, and they wouldn't mind my record. If I kept my nose clean, they might even put me back on the run, in time."

Harriman fiddled with a spoon, then looked up. "Would you young gentlemen be open to a business proposition?"

"Perhaps. What is it?"

"You own the *Care Free?*"

"Yeah. That is, Charlie and I do—barring a couple of liens against her. Why?"

Robert A. Heinlein

"I want to charter her . . . for you and Charlie to take me to the Moon!"

Charlie sat up with a jerk. "D'joo hear what he said, Mac? He wants us to fly that old heap to the Moon!"

McIntyre shook his head. "Can't do it, Mister Harriman. The old boat's worn out. You couldn't convert to escape fuel. We don't even use standard juice in her—just gasoline and liquid air. Charlie spends all of his time tinkering with her at that. She's going to blow up some day."

"Say, Mister Harriman," put in Charlie, "what's the matter with getting an excursion permit and going in a Company ship?"

"No, son," the old man replied, "I can't do that. You know the conditions under which the U.N. granted the Company a monopoly on lunar exploitation—no one to enter space who was not physically qualified to stand up under it. Company to take full responsibility for the safety and health of all citizens beyond the stratosphere. The official reason for granting the franchise was to avoid unnecessary loss of life during the first few years of space travel."

"And you can't pass the physical exam?"

Harriman shook his head.

"Well—if you can afford to hire us, why don't you just bribe yourself a brace of Company docs? It's been done before."

Harriman smiled ruefully. "I know it has, Charlie, but it won't work for me. You see, I'm a little too prominent. My full name is Delos D. Harriman."

"What? *You* are old D. D.? But you own a big slice of the Company yourself—you practically *are* the Company; you ought to be able to do anything you like, rules or no rules."

"That is a not unusual opinion, son, but it is incorrect. Rich men aren't more free than other men; they are less free, a good deal less free. I tried to do what you suggest, but the other directors would not permit me. They are afraid of losing their franchise. It costs them a good deal in—uh—political contact expenses to retain it, as it is."

"Well, I'll be a— Can you tie that, Mac? A guy with lots of dough, and he can't spend it the way he wants to."

McIntyre did not answer, but waited for Harriman to continue.

"Captain McIntyre, if you had a ship, would you take me?"

McIntyre rubbed his chin. "It's against the law."

"I'd make it worth your while."

"Sure he would, Mr. Harriman. Of course you would, Mac. Luna City! Oh, baby!"

"Why do you want to go to the Moon so badly, Mister Harriman?"

"Captain, it's the one thing I've really wanted to do all my life—ever since I was a young boy. I don't know whether I can explain it to you, or not. You young fellows have grown up to rocket travel the way I grew up to aviation. I'm a great deal older than you are, at least fifty years older. When I was a kid practically nobody believed that men would ever reach the Moon. You've seen rockets all your lives, and the first to reach the Moon got there before you were a young boy. When I was a boy they laughed at the idea.

"But I believed—I believed. I read Verne, and Wells, and Smith, and I believed that we could do it—that we *would* do it. I set my heart on being one of the men to walk on the surface of the Moon, to see her other side, and to look back on the face of the Earth, hanging in the sky.

"I used to go without my lunches to pay my dues in the American Rocket Society, because I wanted to believe that I was helping to bring the day nearer when we would reach the Moon. I was already an old man when that day arrived. I've lived longer than I should, but I would not let myself die . . . I will not!—until I have set foot on the Moon."

McIntyre stood up and put out his hand. "You find a ship, Mister Harriman. I'll drive 'er."

"Atta' boy, Mac! I told you he would, Mister Harriman."

Harriman mused and dozed during the half-hour run to the north into Kansas City, dozed in the light troubled sleep of old age. Incidents out of a long life ran through his mind in vagrant dreams. There was that time . . . oh, yes, 1910 . . . A little boy on a warm spring night: "What's that, Daddy?"—"That's Halley's comet, Sonny."—"Where did it come from?"—"I don't know, Son. From way out in the sky somewhere."—"It's *beyooootiful*, Daddy. I want to touch it."—" 'Fraid not, Son."

"Delos, do you mean to stand there and tell me you put the money we had saved for the house into that crazy rocket company?"—"Now, Charlotte, please! It's not crazy; it's a sound business investment. Someday soon rockets will find the sky. Ships and trains will be obsolete. Look what happened to the men that had the foresight to invest in Henry Ford."—"We've been all over this before."—"Charlotte, the day will come when men will rise up off the Earth and visit the Moon, even the planets. This is the beginning."—"Must you shout?"—"I'm sorry, but—"—"I feel a head-ache coming on. Please try to be a little quiet when you come to bed."

He hadn't gone to bed. He had sat out on the veranda all night long, watching the full Moon move across the sky. There would be the devil to pay in the morning, the devil and a thin-lipped silence. But he'd stick by his guns. He'd given in on most things, but not on this. But the night was his. Tonight he'd be alone with his old friend. He searched her face. Where was Mare Crisium? Funny, he couldn't make it out. He used to be able to see it plainly when he was a boy. Probably needed new glasses—this constant office work wasn't good for his eyes.

But he didn't need to see, he knew where they all were; Crisium, Mare Fecunditatis, Mare Tranquilitatis—that one had a satisfying roll!—the Apennines, the Carpathians, old Tycho with its mysterious rays.

Two hundred and forty thousand miles—ten times around the Earth. Surely men

Robert A. Heinlein

could bridge a little gap like that. Why, he could almost reach out and touch it, nodding there behind the elm trees.

Not that he could help. He hadn't the education.

"Son, I want to have a little serious talk with you."—"Yes, Mother."—"I know you had hoped to go to college next year—" (Hoped! He had lived for it. The University of Chicago to study under Moulton, then on to the Yerkes Observatory to work under the eye of Dr. Frost himself)—"and I had hoped so, too. But with your father gone, and the girls growing up, it's harder to make ends meet. You've been a good boy, and worked hard to help out. I know you'll understand."—"Yes, Mother."

"Extra! Extra! STRATOSPHERE ROCKET REACHES PARIS. Read aaaaalllllll about 't." The thin little man in the bifocals snatched at the paper and hurried back to the office.—"Look at this, George."—"Huh? Hmm, interesting, but what of it?"—"Can't you see? The next stage is to the Moon!"—"God, but you're a sucker, Delos. The trouble with you is, you read too many of those trashy magazines. Now I caught my boy reading one of 'em just last week, *Stunning Stories*, or some such title, and dressed him down proper. Your folks should have done you the same favor."—Harriman squared his narrow, middle-aged shoulders. "They will so reach the Moon!"—His partner laughed. "Have it your own way. If baby wants the Moon, papa bring it for him. But you stick to your discounts and commissions; that's where the money is."

The big car droned down the Paseo, and turned off on Armour Boulevard. Old Harriman stirred uneasily in his sleep and muttered to himself.

"But Mister Harriman—" The young man with the notebook was plainly perturbed. The old man grunted.

"You heard me. Sell 'em. I want every share I own realized in cash as rapidly as possible; Spaceways, Spaceways Provisioning Company, Artemis Mines, Luna City Recreations, the whole lot of them."

"It will depress the market. You won't realize the full value of your holdings."

"Don't you think I know that? I can afford it."

"What about the shares you had earmarked for Richardson Observatory, and for the Harriman Scholarships?"

"Oh, yes. Don't sell those. Set up a trust. Should have done it long ago. Tell young Kamens to draw up the papers. He knows what I want."

The interoffice visor flashed into life. "The gentlemen are here, Mr. Harriman."

"Send 'em in. That's all, Ashley. Get busy." Ashley went out as McIntyre and Charlie entered. Harriman got up and trotted forward to greet them.

"Come in, boys, come in. I'm so glad to see you. Sit down. Sit down. Have a cigar."

"Mighty pleased to see you, Mr. Harriman," acknowledged Charlie. "In fact, you might say we need to see you."

"Some trouble, gentlemen?" Harriman glanced from face to face. McIntyre answered him.

"You still mean that about a job for us, Mr. Harriman?"

"Mean it? Certainly, I do. You're not backing out on me?"

"Not at all. We need that job now. You see the *Care Free* is lying in the middle of the Osage River, with her jet split clear back to the injector."

"Dear me! You weren't hurt?"

"No, aside from sprains and bruises. We jumped."

Charlie chortled. "I caught a catfish with my bare teeth."

In short order they got down to business. "You two will have to buy a ship for me. I can't do it openly; my colleagues would figure out what I mean to do and stop me. I'll supply you with all the cash you need. You go out and locate some sort of a ship that can be refitted for the trip. Work up some good story about how you are buying it for some playboy as a stratosphere yacht, or that you plan to establish an arctic-antarctic tourist route. Anything as long as no one suspects that she is being outfitted for space flight.

"Then, after the Department of Transport licenses her for strato flight, you move out to a piece of desert out west—I'll find a likely parcel of land and buy it—and then I'll join you. Then we'll install the escape-fuel tanks, change the injectors, and timers, and so forth, to fit her for the hop. How about it?"

McIntyre looked dubious. "It'll take a lot of doing, Charlie, do you think you can accomplish that change-over without a dockyard and shops?"

"Me? Sure I can—with your thick-fingered help. Just give me the tools and materials I want, and don't hurry me too much. Of course, it won't be fancy—"

"Nobody wants it to be fancy. I just want a ship that won't blow when I start slapping the keys. Isotope fuel is no joke."

"It won't blow, Mac."

"That's what you thought about the *Care Free*."

"That ain't fair, Mac. I ask you, Mr. Harriman—That heap was junk, and we knew it. This'll be different. We're going to spend some dough and do it right. Ain't we, Mr. Harriman?"

Harriman patted him on the shoulder. "Certainly we are, Charlie. You can have all the money you want. That's the least of our worries. Now do the salaries and bonuses I mentioned suit you? I don't want you to be short."

"—as you know, my clients are his nearest relatives and have his interests at heart. We contend that Mr. Harriman's conduct for the past several weeks, as shown by the evidence here adduced, gives clear indication that a mind, once brilliant in the world of finance, has become senile. It is, therefore, with the deepest regret that we pray

Robert A. Heinlein

this honorable court, if it pleases, to declare Mr. Harriman incompetent and to assign a conservator to protect his financial interests and those of his future heirs and assigns." The attorney sat down, pleased with himself.

Mr. Kamens took the floor. "May it please the court, if my esteemed friend is *quite* through, may I suggest that in his last few words he gave away his entire thesis. '—financial interests of future heirs and assigns.' It is evident that the petitioners believe that my client should conduct his affairs in such a fashion as to insure that his nieces and nephews, and their issue, will be supported in unearned luxury for the rest of their lives. My client's wife has passed on, he has no children. It is admitted that he has provided generously for his sisters and their children in times past, and that he has established annuities for such near kin as are without means of support.

"But now like vultures, worse than vultures, for they are not content to let him die in peace, they would prevent my client from enjoying his wealth in whatever manner best suits him for the few remaining years of his life. It is true that he has sold his holdings; is it strange that an elderly man should wish to retire? It is true that he suffered some paper losses in liquidation. 'The value of a thing is what that thing will bring.' He was retiring and demanded cash. Is there anything strange about that?

"It is admitted that he refused to discuss his actions with his so-loving kinfolk. What law, or principle, requires a man to consult with his nephews on anything?

"Therefore, we pray that this court will confirm my client in his right to do what he likes with his own, deny this petition, and send these meddlers about their business."

The judge took off his spectacles and polished them thoughtfully.

"Mr. Kamens, this court has as high a regard for individual liberty as you have, and you may rest assured that any action taken will be solely in the interests of your client. Nevertheless, men do grow old, men do become senile, and in such cases must be protected.

"I shall take this matter under advisement until tomorrow. Court is adjourned."

From the *Kansas City Star*:

"ECCENTRIC MILLIONAIRE DISAPPEARS"

"—failed to appear for the adjourned hearing. The bailiffs returned from a search of places usually frequented by Harriman with the report that he had not been seen since the previous day. A bench warrant under contempt proceedings has been issued and—"

A desert sunset is a better stimulant for the appetite than a hot dance orchestra. Charlie testified to this by polishing the last of the ham gravy with a piece of bread. Harriman handed each of the younger men cigars and took one himself.

"My doctor claims that these weeds are bad for my heart condition," he remarked as he lighted it, "but I've felt so much better since I joined you boys here on the ranch that I am inclined to doubt him." He exhaled a cloud of blue-grey smoke and resumed. "I don't think a man's health depends so much on what he does as on whether he wants to do it. I'm doing what I want to do."

"That's all a man can ask of life," agreed McIntyre.

"How does the work look now, boys?"

"My end's in pretty good shape," Charlie answered. "We finished the second pressure tests on the new tanks and the fuel lines today. The ground tests are all done, except the calibration runs. Those won't take long—just the four hours to make the runs if I don't run into some bugs. How about you, Mac?"

McIntyre ticked them off on his fingers. "Food supplies and water on board. Three vacuum suits, a spare, and service kits. Medical supplies. The buggy already had all the standard equipment for strato flight. The late lunar ephemerides haven't arrived yet."

"When do you expect them?"

"Any time—they should be here now. Not that it matters. This guff about how hard it is to navigate from here to the Moon is hokum to impress the public. After all you can *see* your destination—it's not like ocean navigation. Gimme a sextant and a good radar and I'll set you down anyplace on the Moon you like, without cracking an almanac or a star table, just from a general knowledge of the relative speeds involved."

"Never mind the personal buildup, Columbus," Charlie told him, "we'll admit you can hit the floor with your hat. The general idea is, you're ready to go now. Is that right?"

"That's it."

"That being the case, I *could* run those tests tonight. I'm getting jumpy—things have been going too smoothly. If you'll give me a hand, we ought to be in bed by midnight."

"O.K., when I finish this cigar."

They smoked in silence for a while, each thinking about the coming trip and what it meant to him. Old Harriman tried to repress the excitement that possessed him at the prospect of immediate realization of his life-long dream.

"Mr. Harriman—"

"Eh? What is it, Charlie?"

"How does a guy go about getting rich, like you did?"

"Getting rich? I can't say; I never tried to get rich. I never wanted to be rich, or well known, or anything like that."

"Huh?"

"No, I just wanted to live a long time and see it all happen. I wasn't unusual; there were lots of boys like me—radio hams, they were, and telescope builders, and airplane amateurs. We had science clubs, and basement laboratories, and science-fiction leagues—the kind of boys who thought there was more romance in one issue of the *Electrical Experimenter* than in all the books Dumas ever wrote. We didn't want to

Robert A. Heinlein

be one of Horatio Alger's Get-Rich heroes either, we wanted to build space ships. Well, some of us did.''

"Jeez, Pop, you make it sound exciting.''

"It was exciting, Charlie. This has been a wonderful, romantic century, for all of its bad points. And it's grown more wonderful and more exciting every year. No, I didn't want to be rich; I just wanted to live long enough to see men rise up to the stars, and, if God was good to me, to go as far as the Moon myself.'' He carefully deposited an inch of white ash in a saucer. "It has been a good life. I haven't any complaints.''

McIntyre pushed back his chair. "Come on, Charlie, if you're ready.''

"O.K.''

They all got up. Harriman started to speak, then grabbed at his chest, his face a dead grey-white.

"Catch him, Mac!''

"Where's his medicine?''

"In his vest pocket.''

They eased him over to a couch, broke a small glass capsule in a handkerchief, and held it under his nose. The volatile released by the capsule seemed to bring a little color into his face. They did what little they could for him, then waited for him to regain consciousness.

Charlie broke the uneasy silence. "Mac, we ain't going through with this.''

"Why not?''

"It's murder. He'll never stand up under the initial acceleration.''

"Maybe not, but it's what he wants to do. You heard him.''

"But we oughtn't to let him.''

"Why not. It's neither your business, nor the business of this blasted paternalistic government, to tell a man not to risk his life doing what he really wants to do.''

"All the same, I don't feel right about it. He's such a swell old duck.''

"Then what d'yuh want to do with him—send him back to Kansas City so those old harpies can shut him up in a laughing academy till he dies of a broken heart?''

"N-no-o-o—not that.''

"Get out there, and make your set-up for those test runs. I'll be along.''

A wide-tired desert runabout rolled in the ranch yard gate the next morning and stopped in front of the house. A heavy-set man with a firm, but kindly, face climbed out and spoke to McIntyre, who approached to meet him.

"You James McIntyre?''

"What about it?''

"I'm the deputy federal marshal hereabouts. I got a warrant for your arrest.''

"What's the charge?''

"Conspiracy to violate the Space Precautionary Act.''

Charlie joined the pair. "What's up, Mac?''

The deputy answered. "You'd be Charles Cummings, I guess. Warrant here for you. Got one for a man named Harriman, too, and a court order to put seals on your space ship."

"We've no space ship."

"What d'yuh keep in that shed?"

"Strato yacht."

"So? Well, I'll put seals on her until a space ship comes along. Where's Harriman?"

"Right in there." Charlie obliged by pointing, ignoring McIntyre's scowl.

The deputy turned his head. Charlie couldn't have missed the button by a fraction of an inch for the deputy collapsed quietly to the ground. Charlie stood over him, rubbing his knuckles and mourning.

"That's the finger I broke playing shortstop. I'm always hurting that finger."

"Get Pop into the cabin," Mac cut him short, "and strap him into his hammock."

"Aye aye, Skipper."

They dragged the ship by tractor out of the hangar, turned, and went out the desert plain to find elbow room for the take-off. They climbed in. McIntyre saw the deputy from his starboard conning port. He was staring disconsolately after them.

McIntyre fastened his safety belt, settled his corset, and spoke into the engineroom speaking tube. "All set, Charlie?"

"All set, Skipper. But you can't raise ship yet, Mac—*She ain't named!*"

"No time for your superstitions!"

Harriman's thin voice reached them. "Call her the *Lunatic*—It's the only appropriate name!"

McIntyre settled his head into the pads, punched two keys, then three more in rapid succession, and the *Lunatic* raised ground.

"How are you, Pop?"

Charlie searched the old man's face anxiously. Harriman licked his lips and managed to speak. "Doing fine, son. Couldn't be better."

"The acceleration is over; it won't be so bad from here on. I'll unstrap you so you can wiggle around a little. But I think you'd better stay in the hammock." He tugged at buckles. Harriman partially repressed a groan.

"What is it, Pop?"

"Nothing. Nothing at all. Just go easy on that side."

Charlie ran his fingers over the old man's side with the sure, delicate touch of a mechanic. "You ain't foolin' me none, Pop. But there isn't much I can do until we ground."

"Charlie—"

"Yes, Pop?"

"Can't I move to a port? I want to watch the Earth."

Robert A. Heinlein

"Ain't nothin' to see yet; the ship hides it. As soon as we turn ship, I'll move you. Tell you what; I'll give you a sleepy pill, and then wake you when we do."

"No!"

"Huh?"

"I'll stay awake."

"Just as you say, Pop."

Charlie clambered monkey fashion to the nose of the ship, and anchored to the gymbals of the pilot's chair. McIntyre questioned him with his eyes.

"Yeah, he's alive all right," Charlie told him, "but he's in bad shape."

"How bad?"

"Couple of cracked ribs anyhow. I don't know what else. I don't know whether he'll last out the trip, Mac. His heart was pounding something awful."

"He'll last, Charlie. He's tough."

"Tough? He's delicate as a canary."

"I don't mean that. He's tough way down inside—where it counts."

"Just the same you'd better set her down awful easy if you want to ground with a full complement aboard."

"I will. I'll make one full swing around the Moon and ease her in on an involute approach curve. We've got enough fuel, I think."

They were now in a free orbit; after McIntyre turned ship, Charlie went back, unslung the hammock, and moved Harriman, hammock and all, to a side port. McIntyre steadied the ship about a transverse axis so that the tail pointed toward the sun, then gave a short blast on two tangential jets opposed in couple to cause the ship to spin slowly about her longitudinal axis, and thereby create a slight artificial gravity. The initial weightlessness when coasting commenced had knotted the old man with the characteristic nausea of free flight, and the pilot wished to save his passenger as much discomfort as possible.

But Harriman was not concerned with the condition of his stomach.

There it was, all as he had imagined it so many times. The Moon swung majestically past the view port, wider than he had ever seen it before, all of her familiar features cameo-clear. She gave way to the Earth as the ship continued its slow swing, the Earth itself as he had envisioned her, appearing like a noble moon, many times as wide as the Moon appears to the Earthbound, and more luscious, more sensuously beautiful than the silver Moon could be. It was sunset near the Atlantic seaboard—the line of shadow cut down the coast line of North America, clashed through Cuba, and obscured all but the west coast of South America. He savored the mellow blue of the Pacific Ocean, felt the texture of the soft green and brown of the continents, admired the blue-white cold of the polar caps. Canada and the northern states were obscured by cloud, a vast low-pressure area that spread across the continent. It shone with an even more satisfactory dazzling white than the polar caps.

As the ship swung slowly around, Earth would pass from view, and the stars would march across the port—the same stars he had always known, but steady, brighter, and unwinking against a screen of perfect, live black. Then the Moon would swim into view again to claim his thoughts.

He was serenely happy in a fashion not given to most men, even in a long lifetime. He felt as if he were every man who has ever lived, looked up at the stars, and longed.

As the long hours came and went he watched and dozed and dreamed. At least once he must have fallen into deep sleep, or possibly delirium, for he came to with a start, thinking that his wife, Charlotte, was calling to him. "Delos!" the voice had said. "Delos! Come in from there! You'll catch your death of cold in that night air."

Poor Charlotte! She had been a good wife to him, a good wife. He was quite sure that her only regret in dying had been her fear that he could not take proper care of himself. It had not been her fault that she had not shared his dream, and his need.

Charlie rigged the hammock in such a fashion that Harriman could watch from the starboard port when they swung around the far face of the Moon. He picked out the landmarks made familiar to him by a thousand photographs with nostalgic pleasure, as if he were returning to his own country. McIntyre brought her slowly down as they came back around to the Earthward face, and prepared to land east of Mare Fecunditatis, about ten miles from Luna City.

It was not a bad landing, all things considered. He had to land without coaching from the grounds, and he had no second pilot to watch the radar for him. In his anxiety to make it gentle he missed his destination by some thirty miles, but he did his cold-sober best. But at that it was bumpy.

As they grounded and the pumice dust settled around them, Charlie came up to the control station.

"How's our passenger?" Mac demanded.

"I'll see, but I wouldn't make any bets. That landing stunk, Mac."

"Damn it, I did my best."

"I know you did, Skipper. Forget it."

But the passenger was alive and conscious although bleeding from the nose and with a pink foam on his lips. He was feebly trying to get himself out of his cocoon. They helped him, working together.

"Where are the vacuum suits?" was his first remark.

"Steady, Mr. Harriman. You can't go out there yet. We've got to give you some first aid."

"*Get me that suit!* First aid can wait."

Silently they did as he ordered. His left leg was practically useless, and they had to help him through the lock, one on each side. But with his inconsiderable mass having a lunar weight of only twenty pounds, he was no burden. They found a place

Robert A. Heinlein

some fifty yards from the ship where they could prop him up and let him look, a chunk of scoria supporting his head.

McIntyre put his helmet against the old man's and spoke, "We'll leave you here to enjoy the view while we get ready for the trek into town. It's a forty-miler, pretty near, and we'll have to break out spare air bottles and rations and stuff. We'll be back soon."

Harriman nodded without answering, and squeezed their gauntlets with a grip that was surprisingly strong.

He sat very quietly, rubbing his hands against the soil of the Moon and sensing the curiously light pressure of his body against the ground. At long last there was peace in his heart. His hurts had ceased to pain him. He *was* where he had longed to be—he had followed his need. Over the western horizon hung the Earth at last quarter, a green-blue giant moon. Overhead the Sun shone down from a black and starry sky. And underneath the Moon, the soil of the Moon itself. He was on the Moon!

He lay back still while a bath of content flowed over him like a tide at flood, and soaked to his very marrow.

His attention strayed momentarily, and he thought once again that his name was called. Silly, he thought, I'm getting old—my mind wanders.

Back in the cabin Charlie and Mac were rigging shoulder yokes on a stretcher. "There. That will do," Mac commented. "We'd better stir Pop out; we ought to be going."

"I'll get him," Charlie replied. "I'll just pick him up and carry him. He don't weigh nothing."

Charlie was gone longer than McIntyre had expected him to be. He returned alone. Mac waited for him to close the lock, and swing back his helmet. "Trouble?"

"Never mind the stretcher, Skipper. We won't be needin' it."

"Yeah, I mean it," he continued. "Pop's done for. I did what was necessary."

McIntyre bent down without a word and picked up the wide skis necessary to negotiate the powdery ash. Charlie followed his example. Then they swung the spare air bottles over their shoulders, and passed out through the lock.

They didn't bother to close the outer door of the lock behind them. ∎

Probability Zero

SOME CURIOUS EFFECTS OF TIME TRAVEL

L. Sprague de Camp

The truly formidable host of paradoxes involved in time travel was something I had never appreciated until I accompanied the expedition of the Drinkwhiskey Institute on their journey to the Siwalik Pleistocene in 1932. To be more accurate, the expedition was *in* the Siwalik Hills and *from* 1932.

The purpose of this enterprise was to bring back, besides the usual information on fauna, flora, meteorology, et cetera, a pair of wugugs, *Vugugus jonesiii*; a kind of mammalian tortoise known only from a few fragmentary specimens, by means of which we hoped to persuade the Grand Duchy of Liechtenstein to pay for the expedition.

In the early spring of 1932 we arrived at Swettypore, India, near which town the remains of *Vugugus jonesiii* had been unearthed. To effect our transition to the Pleistocene, we secured the services of a local Yogin, who asserted that he could send our astral bodies back seven hundred and fifty thousand years by simple contemplation of his coccyx. He agreed to demonstrate his powers by sending his own astral body back for a reconnaissance.

All went well, except that the Yogin's astral body failed to return to the present at the appointed time. Instead, the Yogin received a piece of bark on which was scratched the following message in the Devanagari alphabet:

Dear Shri:

So sorry, but I have met my soul mate. I have fallen in love with a Java woman, and shall never return to your loathsome materialistic century.

A rividerci,
Your A.B. # (His Mark)

On receipt of this message the Yogin became much distressed, refused to cooperate any longer with the expedition, and soon left Swettypore to become a professional solitaire player.

The representatives of the Drinkwhiskey Institute were thus forced to fall back on their own resources. Fortunately their ingenuity proved equal to the task, and within forty-eight hours we had invented, designed, and assembled a chronomobile. I won't weary you with the details, save to remark that it operated by transposing the seventh and eleventh dimensions in a hole in space, thus creating an inverse ether-vortex and standing the space-time continuum on its head. (The space-time continuum later complained of a headache.)

A curious feature of time travel back from the present is that one gets younger and younger, becoming successively a youth, a child, an embryo, and finally nothing at all. Fortunately the process does not stabilize here, for the traveler immediately reappears after his disappearance, and thenceforth ages as rapidly as he had previously youthed, or whatever the word should be. He discovers, however, that he is a mirror image of his former self, with the heart on the right side.

As expected, I went through my disappearance as we passed the year 1907, in which I was born. By the time we passed 1882 I had returned to the somatic condition in which I had left the present, and thenceforth aged rapidly. Needless to say, by the time we reached 750,000 B.C. we were all exceedingly old men. Fortunately the personnel of the expedition had been selected for longevity.

The most disconcerting feature of having a negative age is that not only one's body but one's memory-chains are mirror images of what they would normally be. To get along with a mirror-image of a memory takes practice, as a professor proved some years ago by wearing glasses which inverted or reversed the optical images falling upon his eyes.

When we had secured our wugugs, we tried to bring them back to the present. Unfortunately, once the chronomobile had been set in action, the beasts aged as rapidly as the members of the expedition youthed, and before we had gone ten years we had nothing but a pair of fine wugug skeletons to show for our pains.

We had strict orders from the Drinkwhiskey Institute covering such a contingency. To avoid committing the Institute to the heavy expense of the expedition, with no prospect of getting its money back from the sale of the wugugs, we stopped our chronomobile in the year 1931. Then, when 1932 rolled around, we simply refrained from setting out for Swettypore, as we had done on our previous cycle. The expedition, therefore, never took place. ■

THE COLD EQUATIONS
Tom Godwin

He was not alone.

There was nothing to indicate the fact but the white hand of the tiny gauge on the board before him. The control room was empty but for himself; there was no sound other than the murmur of the drives—but the white hand had moved. It had been on zero when the little ship was launched from the *Stardust*; now, an hour later, it had crept up. There was something in the supplies closet across the room, it was saying, some kind of body that radiated heat.

It could be but one kind of a body—a living, human body.

He leaned back in the pilot's chair and drew a deep, slow breath, considering what he would have to do. He was an EDS pilot, inured to the sight of death, long since accustomed to it and to viewing the dying of another man with an objective lack of emotion, and he had no choice in what he must do. There could be no alternative—but it required a few moments of conditioning for even an EDS pilot to prepare himself to walk across the room and coldly, deliberately, take the life of a man he had yet to meet.

He would, of course, do it. It was the law, stated very bluntly and definitely in grim Paragraph L, Section 8, of Interstellar Regulations: *Any stowaway discovered in an EDS shall be jettisoned immediately following discovery.*

It was the law, and there could be no appeal.

It was a law not of men's choosing but made imperative by the circumstances of the space frontier. Galactic expansion had followed the development of the hyperspace drive and as men scattered wide across the frontier there had come the problem of contact with the isolated first-colonies and exploration parties. The huge hyperspace cruisers were the product of the combined genius and effort of Earth and were long and expensive in the building. They were not available in such numbers that small colonies could possess them. The cruisers carried the colonists to their new worlds and made periodic visits, running on tight schedules, but they could not stop and turn aside to visit colonies scheduled to be visited at another time; such a delay would destroy their schedule and produce a confusion and uncertainty that would wreck the complex interdependence between old Earth and the new worlds of the frontier.

Some method of delivering supplies or assistance when an emergency occurred on a world not scheduled for a visit had been needed and the Emergency Dispatch Ships had been the answer. Small and collapsible, they occupied little room in the hold of the cruiser; made of light metal and plastics, they were driven by a small rocket drive that consumed relatively little fuel. Each cruiser carried four EDSs and when a call for aid was received the nearest cruiser would drop into normal space long enough to launch an EDS with the needed supplies or personnel, then vanish again as it continued on its course.

The cruisers, powered by nuclear converters, did not use the liquid rocket fuel but nuclear converters were far too large and complex to permit their installation in the EDSs. The cruisers were forced by necessity to carry a limited amount of the bulky rocket fuel and the fuel was rationed with care; the cruiser's computers determining the exact amount of fuel each EDS would require for its mission. The computers considered the course coordinates, the mass of the EDS, the mass of pilot and cargo; they were very precise and accurate and omitted nothing from their calculations. They could not, however, foresee, and allow for, the added mass of a stowaway.

The *Stardust* had received the request from one of the exploration parties stationed on Woden; the six men of the party already being stricken with fever carried by the green *kala* midges and their own supply of serum destroyed by tornado that had torn through their camp. The *Stardust* had gone through the usual procedure; dropping into normal space to launch the EDS with the fever serum, then vanishing again in hyperspace. Now, an hour later, the gauge was saying there was something more than the small carton of serum in the supplies closet.

He let his eyes rest on the narrow white door of the closet. There, just inside, another man lived and breathed and was beginning to feel assured that discovery of his presence would now be too late for the pilot to alter the situation. It *was* too late—for the man behind the door it was far later than he thought and in a way he would find terrible to believe.

There could be no alternative. Additional fuel would be used during the hours of deceleration to compensate for the added mass of the stowaway; infinitesimal increments of fuel that would not be missed until the ship had almost reached its destination. Then, at some distance above the ground that might be as near as a thousand feet or as far as tens of thousands of feet, depending upon the mass of ship and cargo and the preceding period of deceleration, the unmissed increments of fuel would make their absence known; the EDS would expend its last drops of fuel with a sputter and go into whistling free fall. Ship and pilot and stowaway would merge together upon impact as a wreckage of metal and plastic, flesh and blood, driven deep into the soil.

The stowaway had signed his own death warrant when he concealed himself on the ship; he could not be permitted to take seven others with him.

He looked again at the tell-tale white hand, then rose to his feet. What he must do would be unpleasant for both of them; the sooner it was over, the better. He stepped across the control room, to stand by the white door.

"Come out!" His command was harsh and abrupt above the murmur of the drive.

It seemed he could hear the whisper of a furtive movement inside the closet, then nothing. He visualized the stowaway cowering into one corner, suddenly worried by the possible consequences of his act and his self-assurance evaporating.

"I said *out!*"

He heard the stowaway move to obey and he waited with his eyes alert on the door and his hand near the blaster at his side.

The door opened and the stowaway stepped through it, smiling. "All right—I give up. Now what?"

It was a girl.

He stared without speaking, his hand dropping away from the blaster and acceptance of what he saw coming like a heavy and unexpected physical blow. The stowaway was not a man—she was a girl in her teens, standing before him in little white gypsy sandals with the top of her brown, curly head hardly higher than his shoulder, with a faint, sweet scent of perfume coming from her and her smiling face tilted up so that her eyes could look unknowing and unafraid into his as she waited for his answer.

Now what? Had it been asked in the deep, defiant voice of a man he would have answered it with action, quick and efficient. He would have taken the stowaway's identification disc and ordered him into the air lock. Had the stowaway refused to obey, he would have used the blaster. It would not have taken long; within a minute the body would have been ejected into space—had the stowaway been a man.

He returned to the pilot's chair and motioned her to seat herself on the box-like bulk of the drive-control units that were set against the wall beside him. She obeyed, his silence making the smile fade into the meek and guilty expression of a pup that has been caught in mischief and knows it must be punished.

"You still haven't told me," she said. "I'm guilty, so what happens to me now? Do I pay a fine, or what?"

"What are you doing here?" he asked. "Why did you stow away on this EDS?"

"I wanted to see my brother. He's with the government survey crew on Woden and I haven't seen him for ten years, not since he left Earth to go into government survey work."

"What was your destination on the *Stardust*?"

"Mimir. I have a position waiting for me there. My brother has been sending money home all the time to us—my father and my mother and I—and he paid for a special course in linguistics I was taking. I graduated sooner than expected and I was offered this job on Mimir. I knew it would be almost a year before Gerry's job was done on

Woden so he could come on to Mimir and that's why I hid in the closet, there. There was plenty of room for me and I was willing to pay the fine. There were only the two of us kids—Gerry and I—and I haven't seen him for so long, and I didn't want to wait another year when I could see him now, even though I knew I would be breaking some kind of a regulation when I did it."

I knew I would be breaking some kind of a regulation—In a way, she could not be blamed for her ignorance of the law; she was of Earth and had not realized that the laws of the space frontier must, of necessity, be as hard and relentless as the environment that gave them birth. Yet, to protect such as her from the results of their own ignorance of the frontier, there had been a sign over the door that led to the section of the *Stardust* that housed the EDSs, a sign that was plain for all to see and heed:

UNAUTHORIZED PERSONNEL

KEEP OUT!

"Does your brother know that you took a passage on the *Stardust* for Mimir?"

"Oh, yes. I sent him a spacegram telling him about my graduation and about going to Mimir on the *Stardust* a month before I left Earth. I already knew Mimir was where he would be stationed in a little over a year. He gets a promotion then, and he'll be based on Mimir and not have to stay out a year at a time on field trips, like he does now."

There were two different survey groups on Woden, and he asked, "What is his name?"

"Cross—Gerry Cross. He's in Group Two—that was the way his address read. Do you know him?"

Group One had requested the serum; Group Two was eight thousand miles away, across the Western Sea.

"No, I've never met him," he said, then turned to the control board and cut the deceleration to a fraction of gravity; knowing as he did so that it could not avert the ultimate end, yet doing the only thing he could do to prolong that ultimate end. The sensation was like that of a ship suddenly dropping and the girl's involuntary movement of surprise half lifted her from her seat.

"We're going faster now, aren't we?" she asked. "Why are we doing that?"

He told her the truth. "To save fuel for a little while."

"You mean we don't have very much?"

He delayed the answer he must give her so soon to ask: "How did you manage to stow away?"

"I just sort of walked in when no one was looking my way," she said. "I was practicing my Gelanese on the native girl who does the cleaning in the Ship's Supply Office when someone came in with an order for supplies for the survey crew on

Woden. I slipped into the closet there after the ship was ready to go and just before you came in. It was an impulse of the moment to stow away, so I could get to see Gerry—and from the way you keep looking at me so grim, I'm not sure it was a very wise impulse.

"But I'll be a model criminal—or do I mean prisoner?" She smiled at him again. "I intended to pay for my keep on top of paying the fine. I can cook and I can patch clothes for everyone and I know how to do all kinds of useful things, even a little bit about nursing."

There was one more question to ask:

"Did you know what the supplies were that the survey crew ordered?"

"Why, no. Equipment they needed in their work, I supposed."

Why couldn't she have been a man with some ulterior motive? A fugitive from justice, hoping to lose himself on a raw new world; an opportunist, seeking transportation to the new colonies where he might find golden fleece for the taking; a crackpot, with a mission—

Perhaps once in his lifetime an EDS pilot would find such a stowaway on his ship; warped men, mean and selfish men, brutal and dangerous men—but never, before, a smiling, blue-eyed girl who was willing to pay her fine and work for her keep that she might see her brother.

He turned to the board and turned the switch that would signal the *Stardust*. The call would be futile but he could not, until he had exhausted that one vain hope, seize her and thrust her into the air lock as he would an animal—or a man. The delay, in the meantime, would not be dangerous with the EDS decelerating at fractional gravity.

A voice spoke from the communicator. "*Stardust*. Identify yourself and proceed."

"Barton, EDS 34G11. Emergency. Give me Commander Delhart."

There was a faint confusion of noises as the request went through the proper channels. The girl was watching him, no longer smiling.

"Are you going to order them to come back after me?" she asked.

The communicator clicked and there was the sound of a distant voice saying, "Commander, the EDS requests—"

"Are they coming back after me?" she asked again. "Won't I get to see my brother, after all?"

"Barton?" The blunt, gruff voice of Commander Delhart came from the communicator. "What's this about an emergency?"

"A stowaway," he answered.

"A stowaway?" There was a slight surprise to the question. "That's rather unusual—but why the 'emergency' call? You discovered him in time so there should be no appreciable danger and I presume you've informed Ship's Records so his nearest relatives can be notified."

Tom Godwin

"That's why I had to call you first. The stowaway is still aboard and the circumstances are so different—"

"Different?" the commander interrupted, impatience in his voice. "How can they be different? You know you have a limited supply of fuel; you also know the law, as well as I do: 'Any stowaway discovered in an EDS shall be jettisoned immediately following discovery.' "

There was the sound of a sharply indrawn breath from the girl. *"What does he mean?"*

"The stowaway is a girl."

"What?"

"She wanted to see her brother. She's only a kid and she didn't know what she was really doing."

"I see." All the curtness was gone from the commander's voice. "So you called me in the hope I could do something?" Without waiting for an answer he went on. "I'm sorry—I can do nothing. This cruiser must maintain its schedule; the life of not one person but the lives of many depend on it. I know how you feel but I'm powerless to help you. You'll have to go through with it. I'll have you connected with Ship's Records."

The communicator faded to a faint rustle of sound and he turned to the girl. She was leaning forward on the bench, almost rigid, her eyes fixed wide and frightened.

"What did he mean, to go through with it? To jettison me . . . to go through with it—what did he mean? Not the way it sounded . . . he couldn't have. What did he mean . . . what did he really mean?"

Her time was too short for the comfort of a lie to be more than a cruelly fleeting delusion.

"He meant it the way it sounded."

"No!" She recoiled from him as though he had struck her, one hand half upraised as though to fend him off and stark unwillingness to believe in her eyes.

"It will have to be."

"No! You're joking—you're insane! You can't mean it!"

"I'm sorry." He spoke slowly to her, gently. "I should have told you before—I should have, but I had to do what I could first; I had to call the *Stardust*. You heard what the commander said."

"But you can't—if you make me leave the ship, I'll *die*."

"I know."

She searched his face and the unwillingness to believe left her eyes, giving way slowly to a look of dazed terror.

"You—know?" She spoke the words far apart, numb and wonderingly.

"I know. It has to be like that."

"You mean it—you really mean it." She sagged back against the wall, small and limp like a little rag doll and all the protesting and disbelief gone. "You're going to do it—you're going to make me die?"

"I'm sorry," he said again. "You'll never know how sorry I am. It has to be that way and no human in the universe can change it."

"You're going to make me die and I didn't do anything to die for—I didn't *do* anything—"

He sighed, deep and weary. "I know you didn't, child. I know you didn't—"

"EDS." The communicator rapped brisk and metallic. "This is Ship's Records. Give us all information on subject's identification disc."

He got out of his chair to stand over her. She clutched the edge of the seat, her upturned face white under the brown hair and the lipstick standing out like a blood-red cupid's bow.

"Now?"

"I want your identification disc," he said.

She released the edge of the seat and fumbled at the chain that suspended the plastic disc from her neck with fingers that were trembling and awkward. He reached down and unfastened the clasp for her, then returned with the disc to his chair.

"Here's your data, Records: Identification Number T837—"

"One moment," Records interrupted. "This is to be filed on the grey card, of course?"

"Yes."

"And the time of the execution?"

"I'll tell you later."

"Later? This is highly irregular; the time of the subject's death is required before—"

He kept the thickness out of his voice with an effort. "Then we'll do it in a highly irregular manner—you'll hear the disc read first. The subject is a girl and she's listening to everything that's said. Are you capable of understanding that?"

There was a brief, almost shocked, silence, then Records said meekly: "Sorry. Go ahead."

He began to read the disc, reading it slowly to delay the inevitable for as long as possible, trying to help her by giving her what little time he could to recover from her first terror and let it resolve into the calm of acceptance and resignation.

"Number T8374 dash Y54. Name: Marilyn Lee Cross. Sex: Female. Born: July 7, 2160. *She was only eighteen.* Height: 5 3. Weight: 110. *Such a slight weight, yet enough to add fatally to the mass of the shell-thin bubble that was an EDS.* Hair: Brown. Eyes: Blue. Complexion: Light. Blood Type: O. *Irrelevant data.* Destination: Port City Mimir. *Invalid data—*"

He finished and said, "I'll call you later," then turned once again to the girl. She was huddled back against the wall, watching him with a look of numb and wondering fascination.

"They're waiting for you to kill me, aren't they? They want me dead, don't they?

You and everybody on the cruiser wants me dead, don't you?" Then the numbness broke and her voice was that of a frightened and bewildered child. "Everybody wants me dead and I didn't *do* anything. I didn't hurt anyone—I only wanted to see my brother."

"It's not the way you think—it isn't that way, at all," he said. "Nobody wants it that way; nobody would ever let it be this way if it was humanly possible to change it."

"Then why is it? I don't understand. Why is it?"

"This ship is carrying *kala* fever serum to Group One on Woden. Their own supply was destroyed by a tornado. Group Two—the crew your brother is in—is eight thousand miles away across the Western Sea and their helicopters can't cross it to help Group One. The fever is invariably fatal unless the serum can be had in time, and the six men in Group One will die unless this ship reaches them on schedule. These little ships are always given barely enough fuel to reach their destination and if you stay aboard your added weight will cause it to use up all its fuel before it reaches the ground. It will crash, then, and you and I will die and so will the six men waiting for the fever serum."

It was a full minute before she spoke, and as she considered his words the expression of numbness left her eyes.

"Is that it?" she asked at last. "Just that the ship doesn't have enough fuel?"

"Yes."

"I can go alone or I can take seven others with me—is that the way it is?"

"That's the way it is."

"And nobody wants me to have to die?"

"Nobody."

"Then maybe— Are you sure nothing can be done about it? Wouldn't people help me if they could?"

"Everyone would like to help you but there is nothing anyone can do. I did the only thing I could when I called the *Stardust*."

"And it won't come back—but there might be other cruisers, mightn't there? Isn't there any hope at all that there might be someone, somewhere, who could do something to help me?"

She was leaning forward a little in her eagerness as she waited for his answer.

"No."

The word was like the drop of a cold stone and she again leaned back against the wall, the hope and eagerness leaving her face. "You're sure—you *know* you're sure?"

"I'm sure. There are no other cruisers within forty light-years; there is nothing and no one to change things."

She dropped her gaze to her lap and began twisting a pleat of her skirt between her fingers, saying no more as her mind began to adapt itself to the grim knowledge.

It was better so; with the going of all hope would go the fear; with the going of all hope would come resignation. She needed time and she could have so little of it. How much?

The EDSs were not equipped with hull-cooling units; their speed had to be reduced to a moderate level before entering the atmosphere. They were decelerating at .10 gravity; approaching their destination at a far higher speed than the computers had calculated on. The *Stardust* had been quite near Woden when she launched the EDS; their present velocity was putting them nearer by the second. There would be a critical point, soon to be reached, when he would have to resume deceleration. When he did so the girl's weight would be multiplied by the gravities of deceleration, would become, suddenly, a factor of paramount importance; the factor the computers had been ignorant of when they determined the amount of fuel the EDS should have. She would have to go when deceleration began; it could be no other way. When would that be—how long could he let her stay?

"How long can I stay?"

He winced involuntarily from the words that were so like an echo of his own thoughts. How long? He didn't know; he would have to ask the ship's computers. Each EDS was given a meagre supply of fuel to compensate for unfavorable conditions within the atmosphere and relatively little fuel was being consumed for the time being. The memory banks of the computers would still contain all the data pertaining to the course set for the EDS; such data would not be erased until the EDS reached its destination. He had only to give the computers the new data; the girl's weight and the exact time at which he had reduced the deceleration to .10.

"Barton." Commander Delhart's voice came abruptly from the communicator, as he opened his mouth to call the *Stardust*. "A check with Records shows me you haven't completed your report. Did you reduce the deceleration?"

So the commander knew what he was trying to do.

"I'm decelerating at point ten," he answered. "I cut the deceleration at seventeen fifty and the weight is a hundred and ten. I would like to stay at point ten as long as the computers say I can. Will you give them the question?"

It was contrary to regulations for an EDS pilot to make any changes in the course or degree of deceleration the computers had set for him but the commander made no mention of the violation, neither did he ask the reason for it. It was not necessary for him to ask; he had not become commander of an interstellar cruiser without both intelligence and an understanding of human nature. He said only: "I'll have that given the computers."

The communicator fell silent and he and the girl waited, neither of them speaking. They would not have to wait long; the computers would give the answer within moments of the asking. The new factors would be fed into the steel maw of the first bank and the electrical impulses would go through the complex circuits. Here and there a relay might click, a tiny cog turn over, but it would be essentially the electrical impulses that found the answer; formless, mindless, invisible, determining with utter

Tom Godwin

precision how long the pale girl beside him might live. Then five little segments of metal in the second bank would trip in rapid succession against an inked ribbon and a second steel maw would spit out the slip of paper that bore the answer.

The chronometer on the instrument board read 18:10 when the commander spoke again.

"You will resume deceleration at nineteen ten."

She looked towards the chronometer, then quickly away from it. "Is that when . . . when I go?" she asked. He nodded and she dropped her eyes to her lap again.

"I'll have the course corrections given you," the commander said. "Ordinarily I would never permit anything like this but I understand your position. There is nothing I can do, other than what I've just done, and you will not deviate from these new instructions. You will complete your report at nineteen ten. Now—here are the course corrections."

The voice of some unknown technician read them to him and he wrote them down on a pad clipped to the edge of the control board. There would, he saw, be periods of deceleration when he neared the atmosphere when the deceleration would be five gravities—and at five gravities, one hundred and ten pounds would become five hundred and fifty pounds.

The technician finished and he terminated the contact with a brief acknowledgment. Then, hesitating a moment, he reached out and shut off the communicator. It was 18:13 and he would have nothing to report until 19:10. In the meantime, it somehow seemed indecent to permit others to hear what she might say in her last hour.

He began to check the instrument readings, going over them with unnecessary slowness. She would have to accept the circumstances and there was nothing he could do to help her into acceptance; words of sympathy would only delay it.

It was 18:20 when she stirred from her motionlessness and spoke.

"So that's the way it has to be with me?"

He swung around to face her. "You understand now, don't you? No one would ever let it be like this if it could be changed."

"I understand," she said. Some of the color had returned to her face and the lipstick no longer stood out so vividly red. "There isn't enough fuel for me to stay; when I hid on this ship I got into something I didn't know anything about and now I have to pay for it."

She had violated a man-made law that said KEEP OUT but the penalty was not of men's making or desire and it was a penalty men could not revoke. A physical law had decreed: *h amount of fuel will power an EDS with a mass of m safely to its destination*; and a second physical law decreed: *h amount of fuel will not power an EDS with a mass of m plus x safely to its destination.*

EDSs obeyed only physical laws and no amount of human sympathy for her could alter the second law.

"But I'm afraid. I don't want to die—not now. I want to live and nobody is doing anything to help me; everybody is letting me go ahead and acting just like nothing was going to happen to me. I'm going to die and nobody *cares*."

"We all do," he said. "I do and the commander does and the clerk in Ship's Records; we all care and each of us did what little he could to help you. It wasn't enough—it was almost nothing—but it was all we could do."

"Not enough fuel—I can understand that," she said, as though she had not heard his own words. "But to have to die for it. *Me*, alone—"

How hard it must be for her to accept the fact. She had never known danger of death; had never known the environments where the lives of men could be as fragile and as fleeting as sea foam tossed against a rocky shore. She belonged on gentle Earth, in that secure and peaceful society where she could be young and gay and laughing with others of her kind; where life was precious and well-guarded and there was always the assurance that tomorrow would come. She belonged to that world of soft winds and warm suns, music and moonlight and gracious manners and not on the hard, bleak frontier.

"How did it happen to me, so terribly quickly? An hour ago I was on the *Stardust*, going to Mimir. Now the *Stardust* is going on without me and I'm going to die and I'll never see Gerry and Mama and Daddy again—I'll never see anything again."

He hesitated, wondering how he could explain it to her so that she would really understand and not feel she had, somehow, been the victim of a reasonlessly cruel injustice. She did not know what the frontier was like; she thought in terms of safe-and-secure Earth. Pretty girls were not jettisoned on Earth; there was a law against it. On Earth her plight would have filled the newscasts and a fast black Patrol ship would have been racing to her rescue. Everyone, everywhere, would have known of Marilyn Lee Cross and no effort would have been spared to save her life. But this was not Earth and there were no Patrol ships; only the *Stardust*, leaving them behind at many times the speed of light. There was no one to help her, there would be no Marilyn Lee Cross smiling from the newscasts tomorrow. Marilyn Lee Cross would be but a poignant memory for an EDS pilot and a name on a grey card in Ship's Records.

"It's different here; it's not like back on Earth," he said. "It isn't that no one cares; it's that no one can do anything to help. The frontier is big and here along its rim the colonies and exploration parties are scattered so thin and far between. On Woden, for example, there are only sixteen men—sixteen men on an entire world. The exploration parties, the survey crews, the little first-colonies—they're all fighting alien environments, trying to make a way for those who will follow after. The environments fight back and those who go first usually make mistakes only once. There is no margin of safety along the rim of the frontier; there can't be until the way is made for the others

Tom Godwin

who will come later, until the new worlds are tamed and settled. Until then men will have to pay the penalty for making mistakes with no one to help them because there is no one *to* help them."

"I was going to Mimir," she said. "I didn't know about the frontier; I was only going to Mimir and *it's* safe."

"Mimir is safe but you left the cruiser that was taking you there."

She was silent for a little while. "It was all so wonderful at first; there was plenty of room for me on this ship and I would be seeing Gerry so soon . . . I didn't know about the fuel, didn't know what would happen to me—"

Her words trailed away and he turned his attention to the view-screen, not wanting to stare at her as she fought her way through the black horror of fear towards the calm grey of acceptance.

Woden was a ball, enshrouded in the blue haze of atmosphere, swimming in space against the background of star-sprinkled dead blackness. The great mass of Manning's Continent sprawled like a gigantic hourglass in the Eastern Sea with the western half of the Eastern Continent still visible. There was a thin line of shadow along the right-hand edge of the globe and the Eastern Continent was disappearing into it as the planet turned on its axis. An hour before the entire continent had been in view, now a thousand miles of it had gone into the thin edge of shadow and around to the night that lay on the other side of the world. The dark blue spot that was Lotus Lake was approaching the shadow. It was somewhere near the southern edge of the lake that Group Two had their camp. It would be night there, soon, and quick behind the coming of night the rotation of Woden on its axis would put Group Two beyond the reach of the ship's radio.

He would have to tell her before it was too late for her to talk to her brother. In a way, it would be better for both of them should they not do so but it was not for him to decide. To each of them the last words would be something to hold and cherish, something that would cut like the blade of a knife yet would be infinitely precious to remember, she for her own brief moments to live and he for the rest of his life.

He held down the button that would flash the grid lines on the viewscreen and used the known diameter of the planet to estimate the distance the southern tip of Lake Lotus had yet to go until it passed beyond radio range. It was approximately five hundred miles. Five hundred miles; thirty minutes—and the chronometer read 18:30. Allowing for error in estimating, it could not be later than 19:05 that the turning of Woden would cut off her brother's voice.

The first border of the Western Continent was already in sight along the left side of the world. Four thousand miles across it lay the shore of the Western Sea and the Camp of Group One. It had been in the Western Sea that the tornado had originated, to strike with such fury at the camp and destroy half their prefabricated buildings, including the one that housed the medical supplies. Two days before the tornado had not existed; it had been no more than great gentle masses of air out over the calm

Western Sea. Group One had gone about their routine survey work, unaware of the meeting of the air masses out at sea, unaware of the force the union was spawning. It had struck their camp without warning; a thundering, roaring destruction that sought to annihilate all that lay before it. It had passed on, leaving the wreckage in its wake. It had destroyed the labor of months and had doomed six men to die and then, as though its task was accomplished, it once more began to resolve into gentle masses of air. But for all its deadliness, it had destroyed with neither malice nor intent. It had been a blind and mindless force, obeying the laws of nature, and it would have followed the same course with the same fury had man never existed.

Existence required Order and there was order; the laws of nature, irrevocable and immutable. Men could learn to use them but men could not change them. The circumference of a circle was always pi times the diameter and no science of Man would ever make it otherwise. The combination of chemical A with chemical B under condition C invariably produced reaction D. The law of gravitation was a rigid equation and it made no distinction between the fall of a leaf and the ponderous circling of a binary star system. The nuclear conversion process powered the cruisers that carried men to the stars; the same process in the form of a nova would destroy a world with equal efficiency. The laws *were,* and the universe moved in obedience to them. Along the frontier were arrayed all the forces of nature and sometimes they destroyed those who were fighting their way outwards from Earth. The men of the frontier had long ago learned the bitter futility of cursing the forces that would destroy them for the forces were blind and deaf; the futility of looking to the heavens for mercy, for the stars of the galaxy swung in their long, long sweep of two hundred million years, as inexorably controlled as they by the laws that knew neither hatred nor compassion.

The men of the frontier knew—but how was a girl from Earth to fully understand? *H amount of fuel will not power an EDS with a mass of m plus x safely to its destination.* To himself and her brother and parents she was a sweet-faced girl in her teens; to the laws of nature she was x, the unwanted factor in a cold equation.

She stirred again on the seat. "Could I write a letter? I want to write to Mama and Daddy and I'd like to talk to Gerry. Could you let me talk to him over your radio there?"

"I'll try to get him," he said.

He switched on the normal-space transmitter and pressed the signal button. Someone answered the button almost immediately.

"Hello. How's it going with you fellows now—is the EDS on its way?"

"This isn't Group One; this is the EDS," he said. "Is Gerry Cross there?"

"Gerry? He and two others went out in the helicopter this morning and aren't back yet. It's almost sundown, though, and he ought to be back right away—in less than an hour at the most."

"Can you connect me through the radio in his 'copter?"

Tom Godwin

"Huh-uh. It's been out of commission for two months—some printed circuits went haywire and we can't get any more until the next cruiser stops by. Is it something important—bad news for him, or something?"

"Yes—it's very important. When he comes in get him to the transmitter as soon as you possibly can."

"I'll do that; I'll have one of the boys waiting at the field with a truck. Is there anything else I can do?"

"No, I guess that's all. Get him there as soon as you can and signal me."

He turned the volume to an inaudible minimum, an act that would not affect the functioning of the signal buzzer, and unclipped the pad of paper from the control board. He tore off the sheet containing his flight instructions and handed the pad to her, together with pencil.

"I'd better write to Gerry, too," she said as she took them. "He might not get back to camp in time."

She began to write, her fingers still clumsy and uncertain in the way they handled the pencil and the top of it trembling a little as she poised it between words. He turned back to the viewscreen, to stare at it without seeing it.

She was a lonely little child, trying to say her last good-bye, and she would lay out her heart to them. She would tell them how much she loved them and she would tell them to not feel badly about it, that it was only something that must eventually happen to everyone and she was not afraid. The last would be a lie and it would be there to read between the sprawling, uneven lines; a valiant little lie that would make the hurt all the greater for them.

Her brother was of the frontier and he would understand. He would not hate the EDS pilot for doing nothing to prevent her going; he would know there had been nothing the pilot could do. He would understand, though the understanding would not soften the shock and pain when he learned his sister was gone. But the others, her father and mother—they would not understand. They were of Earth and they would think in the manner of those who had never lived where the safety margin of life was a thin, thin line—and sometimes not at all. What would they think of the faceless, unknown pilot who had sent her to her death?

They would hate him with cold and terrible intensity, but it really didn't matter. He would never see them, never know them. He would have only the memories to remind him; only the nights to fear, when a blue-eyed girl in gypsy sandals would come in his dreams to die again—

He scowled at the viewscreen and tried to force his thoughts into less emotional channels. There was nothing he could do to help her. She had unknowingly subjected herself to the penalty of a law that recognized neither innocence nor youth nor beauty, that was incapable of sympathy or leniency. Regret was illogical—and yet, could knowing it to be illogical ever keep it away?

She stopped occasionally, as though trying to find the right words to tell them what she wanted them to know, then the pencil would resume its whispering to the paper. It was 18:37 when she folded the letter in a square and wrote a name on it. She began writing another, twice looking up at the chronometer as though she feared the black hand might reach its rendezvous before she had finished. It was 18:45 when she folded it as she had done the first letter and wrote a name and address on it.

She held the letters out to him. "Will you take care of these and see that they're enveloped and mailed?"

"Of course." He took them from her hand and placed them in a pocket of his grey uniform shirt.

"These can't be sent off until the next cruiser stops by and the *Stardust* will have long since told them about me, won't it?" she asked. He nodded and she went on. "That makes the letters not important in one way, but in another way they're very important—to me, and to them."

"I know, I understand, and I'll take care of them."

She glanced at the chronometer, then back at him. "It seems to move faster all the time, doesn't it?"

He said nothing, unable to think of anything to say, and she asked, "Do you think Gerry will come back to camp in time?"

"I think so. They said he should be in right away."

She began to roll the pencil back and forth between her palms. "I hope he does. I feel sick and scared and I want to hear his voice again and maybe I won't feel so alone. I'm a coward and I can't help it."

"No," he said, "you're not a coward. You're afraid, but you're not a coward."

"Is there a difference?"

He nodded. "A lot of difference."

"I feel so alone. I never did feel like this before; like I was all by myself and there was nobody to care what happened to me. Always, before, there was Mama and Daddy there and my friends around me. I had lots of friends, and they had a going-away party for me the night before I left."

Friends and music and laughter for her to remember—and on the viewscreen Lotus Lake was going into the shadow.

"Is it the same with Gerry?" she asked. "I mean, if he should make a mistake, would he have to die for it, all alone and with no one to help him?"

"It's the same with all along the frontier; it will always be like that so long as there is a frontier."

"Gerry didn't tell us. He said the pay was good and he sent money home all the time because Daddy's little shop just brought in a bare living, but he didn't tell us it was like this."

"He didn't tell you his work was dangerous?"

"Well—yes. He mentioned that, but we didn't understand. I always thought danger

Tom Godwin

along the frontier was something that was a lot of fun; an exciting adventure, like the three-D shows." A wan smile touched her face for a moment. "Only it's not, is it? It's not the same at all, because when it's real you can't go home after the show is over."

"No," he said. "No, you can't."

Her glance flicked from the chronometer to the door of the air lock, then down to the pad and pencil she still held. She shifted her position slightly to lay them on the bench beside her, moving one foot out a little. For the first time he saw that she was not wearing Vegan gypsy sandals but only cheap imitations; the expensive Vegan leather was some kind of grained plastic, the silver buckle was gilded iron, the jewels were colored glass. *Daddy's little shop just brought in a bare living*— She must have left college in her second year, to take the course in linguistics that would enable her to make her own way and help her brother provide for her parents, earning what she could by part-time work after classes were over. Her personal possessions on the *Stardust* would be taken back to her parents—they would neither be of much value nor occupy much storage space for the return voyage.

"Isn't it—" She stopped, and he looked at her questioningly. "Isn't it cold in here?" she asked, almost apologetically. "Doesn't it seem cold to you?"

"Why, yes," he said. He saw by the main temperature gauge that the room was at precisely normal temperature. "Yes, it's colder than it should be."

"I wish Gerry would get back before it's too late. Do you really think he will, and you didn't say so just to make me feel better?"

"I think he will—they said he would be in pretty soon." On the viewscreen Lotus Lake had gone into the shadow but for the thin blue line on its western edge, and it was apparent he had overestimated the time she would have in which to talk to her brother. Reluctantly, he said to her, "His camp will be out of radio range in a few minutes; he's on that part of Woden that's in the shadow"—he indicated the viewscreen—"and the turning of Woden will put him beyond contact. There may not be much time left when he comes in—not much time to talk to him before he fades out. I wish I could do something about it—I would call him right now if I could."

"Not even as much time as I will have to stay?"

"I'm afraid not."

"Then—" She straightened and looked towards the air lock with pale resolution. "Then I'll go when Gerry passes beyond range, I won't wait any longer after that—I won't have anything to wait for."

Again there was nothing he could say.

"Maybe I shouldn't wait at all. Maybe I'm selfish—maybe it would be better for Gerry if you just told him about it afterwards."

There was an unconscious pleading for denial in the way she spoke and he said, "He wouldn't want you to do that, not to wait for him."

"It's already coming dark where he is, isn't it? There will be all the long night before him, and Mama and Daddy don't know yet that I won't ever be coming back like I promised them I would. I've caused everyone I love to be hurt, haven't I? I didn't want to—I didn't intend to."

"It wasn't your fault," he said. "It wasn't your fault at all. They'll know that. They'll understand."

"At first I was so afraid to die that I was a coward and thought only of myself. Now, I see how selfish I was. The terrible thing about dying like this is not that I'll be gone but that I'll never see them again; never be able to tell them that I didn't take them for granted; never be able to tell them I knew of the sacrifices they made to keep my life happier, that I knew all the things they did for me and that I loved them so much more than I ever told them. I've never told them any of those things. You don't tell them such things when you're young and your life is all before you—you're afraid of sounding sentimental and silly.

"But it's so different when you have to die—you wish you had told them while you could and you wish you could tell them you're sorry for all the little mean things you ever did or said to them. You wish you could tell them that you didn't really mean to ever hurt their feelings and for them only to remember that you always loved them far more than you ever let them know."

"You don't have to tell them that," he said. "They will know—they've always known it."

"Are you sure?" she asked. "How can you be sure? My people are strangers to you."

"Wherever you go, human nature and human hearts are the same."

"And they will know what I want them to know—that I love them?"

"They've always known it, in a way far better than you could ever put in words for them."

"I keep remembering the things they did for me, and it's the little things they did that seem to be the most important to me, now. Like Gerry—he sent me a bracelet of fire-rubies on my sixteenth birthday. It was beautiful—it must have cost him a month's pay. Yet, I remember him more for what he did the night my kitten got run over in the street. I was only six years old and he held me in his arms and wiped away my tears and told me not to cry, that Flossy was gone for just a little while, for just long enough to get herself a new fur coat and she would be on the foot of my bed the very next morning. I believed him and quit crying and went to sleep dreaming about my kitten coming back. When I woke up the next morning, there was Flossy on the foot of my bed in a brand-new white fur coat, just like he had said she would be.

"It wasn't until a long time later that Mama told me Gerry had got the pet-shop owner out of bed at four in the morning and, when the man got mad about it, Gerry

Tom Godwin

told him he was either going to go down and sell him the white kitten right then or he'd break his neck."

"It's always the little things you remember people by; all the little things they did because they wanted to do them for you. You've done the same for Gerry and your father and mother; all kinds of things that you've forgotten about but they will never forget."

"I hope I have. I would like for them to remember me like that."

"They will."

"I wish——" She swallowed. "The way I'll die—I wish they wouldn't ever think of that. I've read how people look who have died in space—their insides all ruptured and exploded and their lungs out between their teeth and then, a few seconds later, they're all dry and shapeless and horribly ugly. I don't want them to ever think of me as something dead and horrible, like that."

"You're their own, their child and their sister. They could never think of you other than the way you want them to; the way you looked the last time they saw you."

"I'm still afraid," she said. "I can't help it, but I don't want Gerry to know it. If he gets back in time, I'm going to act like I'm not afraid at all and——"

The signal buzzer interrupted her, quick and imperative.

"Gerry!" She came to her feet. "It's Gerry, now!"

He spun the volume control knob and asked: "Gerry Cross?"

"Yes," her brother answered, an undertone of tenseness to his reply. "The bad news—what is it?"

She answered for him, standing close behind him and leaning down a little towards the communicator, her hand resting small and cold on his shoulder.

"Hello, Gerry." There was only a faint quiver to betray the careful casualness of her voice. "I wanted to see you——"

"Marilyn!" There was sudden and terrible apprehension in the way he spoke to her. "What are you doing on that EDS?"

"I wanted to see you," she said again. "I wanted to see you, so I hid on this ship——"

"You *hid* on it?"

"I'm a stowaway . . . I didn't know what it would mean——"

"*Marilyn!*" It was the cry of a man who calls hopeless and desperate to someone already and forever gone from him. "What have you done?"

"I . . . it's not——" Then her own composure broke and the cold little hand gripped his shoulder convulsively. "Don't, Gerry—I only wanted to see you; I didn't intend to hurt you. Please, Gerry, don't feel like that——"

Something warm and wet splashed on his wrist and he slid out of the chair, to help her into it and swing the microphone down to her level.

"Don't feel like that— Don't let me go knowing you feel like that——"

The sob she tried to hold back choked in her throat and her brother spoke to her.

"Don't cry, Marilyn." His voice was suddenly deep and infinitely gentle, with all the pain held out of it. "Don't cry, Sis—you mustn't do that. It's all right, Honey—everything is all right."

"I—" Her lower lip quivered and she bit into it. "I didn't want you to feel that way—I just wanted us to say good-bye because I have to go in a minute."

"Sure—sure. That's the way it will be, Sis. I didn't mean to sound the way I did." Then his voice changed to a tone of quick and urgent demand. "EDS—have you called the *Stardust*? Did you check with the computers?"

"I called the *Stardust* almost an hour ago. It can't turn back, there are no other cruisers within forty light-years, and there isn't enough fuel."

"Are you sure that the computers had the correct data—sure of everything?"

"Yes—do you think I could ever let it happen if I wasn't sure? I did everything I could do. If there was anything at all I could do now, I would do it."

"He tried to help me, Gerry." Her lower lip was no longer trembling and the short sleeves of her blouse were wet where she had dried her tears. "No one can help me and I'm not going to cry any more and everything will be all right with you and Daddy and Mama, won't it?"

"Sure—sure it will. We'll make out fine."

Her brother's words were beginning to come in more faintly and he turned the volume control to maximum. "He's going out of range," he said to her. "He'll be gone within another minute."

"You're fading out, Gerry," she said. "You're going out of range. I wanted to tell you—but I can't, now. We must say good-bye so soon—but maybe I'll see you again. Maybe I'll come to you in your dreams with my hair in braids and crying because the kitten in my arms is dead; maybe I'll be the touch of a breeze that whispers to you as it goes by; maybe I'll be one of those gold-winged larks you told me about, singing my silly head off to you; maybe, at times, I'll be nothing you can see but you will know I'm there beside you. Think of me like that, Gerry; always like that and not—the other way."

Dimmed to a whisper by the turning of Woden, the answer came back:

"Always like that, Marilyn—always like that and never any other way."

"Our time is up, Gerry—I have to go, now. Good—" Her voice broke in midword and her mouth tried to twist into crying. She pressed her hand hard against it and when she spoke again the words came clear and true:

"Good-bye, Gerry."

Faint and ineffably poignant and tender, the last words came from the cold metal of the communicator.

"Good-bye, little sister—"

She sat motionless in the hush that followed, as though listening to the shadow-echoes of the words as they died away, then she turned away from the communicator towards the air lock, and he pulled down the black lever beside him. The inner door of the air lock slid swiftly open, to reveal the bare little cell that was waiting for her, and she walked to it.

She walked with her head up and the brown curls brushing her shoulders, with the white sandals stepping as sure and steady as the fractional gravity would permit and the gilded buckles twinkling with little lights of blue and red and crystal. He let her walk alone and made no move to help her, knowing she would not want it that way. She stepped into the air lock and turned to face him, only the pulse in her throat to betray the wild beating of her heart.

"I'm ready," she said.

He pushed the lever up and the door slid its quick barrier between them, inclosing her in black and utter darkness for her last moments of life. It clicked as it locked in place and he jerked down the red lever. There was a slight waver to the ship as the air gushed from the lock, a vibration to the wall as though something had bumped the outer door in passing, then there was nothing and the ship was dropping true and steady again. He shoved the red lever back to close the door on the empty air lock and turned away, to walk to the pilot's chair with the slow steps of a man old and weary.

Back in the pilot's chair he pressed the signal button of the normal-space transmitter. There was no response; he had expected none. Her brother would have to wait through the night until the turning of Woden permitted contact through Group One.

It was not yet time to resume deceleration and he waited while the ship dropped endlessly downwards with him and the drives purred softly. He saw that the white hand of the supplies closet temperature was on zero. A cold equation had been balanced and he was alone on the ship. Something shapeless and ugly was hurrying ahead of him, going to Woden where its brother was waiting through the night, but the empty ship still lived for a little while with the presence of the girl who had not known about the forces that killed with neither hatred nor malice. It seemed, almost, that she still sat small and bewildered and frightened on the metal box beside him, her words echoing hauntingly clear in the void she had left behind her:

I didn't do anything to die for—I didn't do anything— ∎

PLUS X
Eric Frank Russell

One thing was certain: he was out of the war. Perhaps for a long time to come or possibly for keeps—dead, maimed or a prisoner. The next few seconds would decide the manner of his exit from the fray.

The little ship made another crazy spin on its longitudinal axis. In the fore observation port the gray-green face of a planet swirled the opposite way. John Leeming's brains seemed to rotate in sympathy, causing momentary confusion. Behind the ship the distorted fire-trail shaped itself into an elongated spiral.

Ground came up fast, mere crinkles expanding into hills and valleys, surface fuzz swelling into massed trees. His straining eyes saw a cluster of rooftops turn upside down then swing right way round.

Choice needs time even if only the minimum required to make selection. When there's no time there's no choice. Leeming's sole concern was to land the ship any place, anywhere, even slap in the middle of the foe, so long as it hit belly-down with nothing to oppose its forward skidding.

He made it either by sheer good luck or, more likely, happy absence of bad luck. A gentle upward slope magnified toward the nose at precisely the right moment. He maneuvered somehow, heaven alone knew how, dropped the damaged tail, cut power, struck dirt, slid halfway up the slope amid a twin spray of dust, sparks and grinding noises.

For half a minute he sat still and sweated while feeling peculiarly cold. Then he glanced at the atmospheric analyzer. It said the local air had nothing wrong with it.

Clambering through the lock, Leeming bolted to the tail end. He looked at the array of drivers and found them a mess. Five tubes lacked linings and had warped under resulting heat. Four more were on the point of going cockeyed. He'd come in on the remaining seven and that was a feat verging on the miraculous.

Back home they'd warned him that the vessel might not stand up to the task imposed upon it. "We're giving you a special scout-boat with battleship tubes and improved linings. The ship is light and unarmed but fast and exceptionally long-ranged. Whether it will hold together over such a vast trip is something that can be determined only by actual test. Right now it's the best we can offer. In four or five years' time we may have one fifty times better. But we can't wait four or five years."

"I understand."

"So you'll be taking a risk, a big one. You may never return. All the same, we've got to learn what lies behind the enemy's spatial frontier, how deeply his authority extends, how far his hidden resources go. Somebody's got to stick out his neck to get that information. Somebody's got to wander loose behind the lines.''

"I'm willing.''

They'd patted his shoulder, given him a heavily escorted send-off that had taken him through the area of battle. Then, on his own, he'd slipped through a hostile frontier, a tiny, unstoppable speck in the immensity of space.

For weeks of which he'd lost count he had beamed data of all kinds, penetrating deeper and deeper into the starfield until the first tube blew a tormented and dessicated lining along the vapor-trail. Even as he turned belatedly for home the second one went. Then a third. After that, it was a matter of getting down in one piece on the nearest inhabitable hunk of plasma.

At the bottom of the slope, a thousand yards away, lay a large village stirred to active life by his overhead thunder and nearby landing. Already its small garrison was charging out, weapons in hand, heading for the ship.

Diving back through the lock, Leeming jerked a lever in the tiny control room, got out fast, raced up the slope, counting to himself as he ran. Down at the bottom the enemy troops paused in their advance, let go hoarse yells but failed to open fire.

"Sixty-nine, seventy!'' gasped Leeming, and threw himself flat.

The ship flew apart with a mighty roar that shook the hills. Wind pressed powerfully in all directions. Shrapnel rained from the sky. A seven-pound lump of metal thumped to the ground a yard from Leeming's head and he could not recognize it as any part of what once had arrowed past strange suns and unknown planets.

He stood up, saw that he now had the enemy on both sides. A thin line of armed figures had come over the crest of the slope. They had weapons pointed his way and were gazing awestruck at the great crater halfway down.

At the bottom the troops from the village picked themselves up, having either thrown themselves flat or been blown flat. None appeared to be injured, none looked delighted either.

Leeming raised his arms in universal token of surrender. He felt bitter as he did it. Good luck followed by bad luck. If only the ship had hit ten miles farther back or ten farther on, he could have taken to the woods and played hard to get for weeks, months or, if necessary, years.

Anyway, this was the end of the trail.

The enemy came up fast. They were two-legged, on the short side, tremendously broad and powerful. Their gait was the typical stumping of squat, heavy men. Close up, they were seen to have scaly skins, horn-covered eyes, no eyelids. The first one to arrive made Leeming think of a sidewinder that somehow had taken on monkeylike shape.

Though obviously made jumpy by his forced landing and the big bang, they did not treat him with open antagonism. Their manner was suspicious and reserved. After a little reflection he guessed the reason for this. They'd seen nobody quite like him before, had no means of determining whether he was friend or foe, and temporarily were reserving judgment.

This was excusable. On Leeming's side of the battle was a federation of eighteen life forms, four of them human and five more very humanlike. Against these was an uneasy, precarious union of at least twenty life forms of which two were also very humanlike. Pending examination, this particular bunch of quasi-reptilians just couldn't tell enemy from ally. Neither did they know whether the ship's spectacular destruction was accidental or a piece of deliberate naughtiness.

Nevertheless they were taking no chances. Half a dozen kept him covered while an officer inspected the crater. The officer came back, favored Leeming with an unwinking stare, voiced an incomprehensible gabble. Leeming spread his hands and shrugged.

Accepting this lack of understanding as something that proved nothing one way or the other, the officer shouted commands at his troops. They formed up, marched to the village with the suspect in their midst.

Arriving, they shoved Leeming into the back room of a rock house with two guards for company, two more outside the door. He sat on a low, hard chair, sighed, stared blankly at the wall for two hours. The guards also sat, watched him as expressionlessly as a pair of snakes, and never said a word.

At the end of that time a trooper brought food and water. The meal tasted strange but proved satisfying. Leeming ate and drank in silence, studied the wall for another two hours.

He could imagine what was going on while they kept him waiting. The officer would grab the telephone—or whatever they used in lieu thereof—and call the nearest garrison town. The highest ranker there would promptly transfer responsibility to military headquarters. A ten-star panjandrum would pass the query to the main beam station. An operator would then ask the two humanlike allies whether they'd lost track of a scout in this region.

If a signal came back saying, "No," the local toughies would realize that they'd caught a rare bird deep within their spatial empire and menacingly far from the area of conflict. If a thing can be either of two things, and it isn't one of them, it's got to be the other. Therefore if he wasn't a friend he had to be a foe despite his appearance where no foe had ever penetrated before.

When they learned the truth they weren't going to like it. Holding-troops far behind the lines share all the glory and little of the grief. They're happy to let it stay that way. A sudden intrusion of the enemy where he's no right to be is an event disturbing to the even tenor of life and not to be greeted with cries of martial joy. Besides, where one can sneak in a host of armies can follow and it is disconcerting to be taken in force from the rear.

What would they do to him when they identified him as a creature of the Federation? He was far from sure, never having seen or heard of this especial life form before. One thing was probable: they'd refrain from shooting him out of hand. If sufficiently civilized, they'd imprison him for the duration of the war and that might mean for the rest of his natural life. If uncivilized, they'd bring in an ally able to talk Earth language and proceed to milk the prisoner of every item of information he possessed, by methods ruthless and bloody.

Back toward the dawn of history when conflicts had been Earth-wars there had existed a protective device known as the Geneva Convention. It had organized neutral inspection of prison camps, brought occasional letters from home, provided Red Cross parcels that had kept alive many a captive who otherwise would have died.

There was nothing like that today. A prisoner now had only two forms of protection, those being his own resources and the power of his side to retaliate against the prisoners they'd got. And the latter was a threat more potential than real. There cannot be retaliation without actual knowledge of maltreatment.

Leeming was still brooding over these matters when the guards were changed. Six hours had now dragged by. The one window showed that darkness was falling. He eyed the window furtively, decided that it would be suicidal to take a running jump at it under two guns. It was small and high.

A prisoner's first duty is to escape. That means biding one's time with appalling patience until occurs a chance that may be seized and exploited to the utmost. Or if no opportunity appears, one must be created—by brawn and brains, mostly the latter.

The prospect before him was tough indeed. And before long it was likely to look a deal tougher. The best moment in which to organize a successful getaway had come immediately after landing. If only he'd been able to talk the local language, he might have convinced them that black was white. With smooth, plausible words, unlimited self-assurance and just the right touch of arrogance he might have persuaded them to repair his boat and cheer him on his way, never suspecting that they had been argued into providing aid and comfort for the enemy.

Lack of ability to communicate had balled up that prospect at the start. You can't chivvy a sucker into donating his pants merely by making noises at him. Some other chance must now be watched for and grabbed, swiftly and with both hands—providing they were fools enough to permit a chance.

Which was most unlikely.

He remained in the house four days, eating and drinking at regular intervals, sleeping night-times, cogitating for hours, occasionally glowering at the impassive guards. Mentally he concocted, examined and rejected a thousand ways of regaining freedom, most of them spectacular, fantastic and impossible.

At one time he went so far as to try to stare the guards into an hypnotic trance, gazing intently at them until his own eyeballs felt locked for keeps. It did not faze them in the least. They had the lizardlike ability to remain motionless and outstare him until kingdom come.

Mid-morning of the fourth day the officer strutted in, yelled, *"Amash! Amash!"* and gestured toward the door. His tone and attitude were both unfriendly. Evidently they'd received a signal defining the prisoner as a Federation space-louse.

Leeming got up from his seat and walked out, two guards ahead, two behind, the officer following. A steel-sheathed car waited in the road. They shoved him into it, locked it. Two guards stood on the rear platform, one joined the driver at front. The journey took thirteen hours which the inmate spent jolting around in complete darkness.

By the time the car halted Leeming had invented one new and exceedingly repulsive word. He used it as the rear doors opened.

"Amash!" bawled a guard, unappreciative of alien contributions to the vocabulary of invective.

With poor grace Leeming amashed. He glimpsed great walls rearing against the night and a zone of bright light high up before he was pushed through a metal portal into a large room. Here a reception committee of six thuglike samples awaited him. One of the six signed a paper presented by the escort. The guards withdrew, the door closed, the six eyed the visitor with lack of amiability.

One of them said something in an authoritative voice, made motions illustrative of undressing.

Leeming used the word.

It did him no good. The six grabbed him, stripped him naked, searched every vestige of his clothing, paying special attention to seams and linings. None showed the slightest interest in his alien physique despite that it stood fully revealed in the raw.

Everything he possessed was put to one side, pen, compass, knife, lighter, lucky piece, the whole lot. Then they shied his clothes back at him. He dressed himself while they pawed through the loot and gabbled together. They seemed slightly baffled and he guessed that they were surprised by his lack of anything resembling a lethal weapon.

Amid the litter was a two-ounce matchbox-sized camera that any ignorant bunch would have regarded with suspicion. It took the searchers a couple of minutes to discover what it was and how it worked. Evidently they weren't too backward.

Satisfied that the captive now owned nothing more dangerous than the somewhat bedraggled clothes in which he stood, they led him through the farther door, up a flight of thick stone stairs, along a stone corridor and into a cell. The door slammed shut with a sound like the crack of doom.

In the dark of night four small stars winked and glittered through a heavily barred opening high up in one wall. Along the bottom of the gap shone a faint yellow glow from some outside illumination.

He fumbled around the gloom, found a wooden bench against one wall. It moved when he lugged at it. Dragging it beneath the opening, he stood on it but found himself a couple of feet too low to gain a view. Though heavy, he struggled with it until he got it upended against the wall. Then he clambered up it, had a look between the bars.

Forty feet below lay a bare stone-floored space fifty yards wide and extending to the limited distance he could see in both directions. Beyond that, a smooth-surfaced stone wall rising to his own level. The top of the wall angled at about sixty degrees to form a sharp apex and ten inches above that ran a single line of taut wire, plain, without barbs.

From unseeable sources to the right and left poured powerful beams of light which flooded the entire area between cell and wall, also a similar area beyond the wall. Nothing moved. There was no sign of life. There was only the wall, the flares of light, the overhanging night and the distant stars.

"So I'm in the jug," he said. "That's torn it!"

He jumped to the invisible floor and the slight thrust of his feet made the bench fall with a resounding crash. Feet raced along the outer passage, light poured through a suddenly opened spyhole in the heavy metal door. An eye appeared in the hole.

"*Sach invigia, faplap!*" shouted the guard.

Leeming used the word again and added six more, older, time-worn but still potent. The spyhole slammed shut. He lay on the bench and tried to sleep.

An hour later he kicked hell out of the door and when the spyhole opened he said, "Faplap yourself!"

After that, he did sleep.

Breakfast consisted of one lukewarm bowl of stewed grain resembling millet, and a mug of water. Both were served with disdain. Soon afterward a thin-lipped specimen arrived accompanied by two guards. With a long series of complicated gestures the newcomer explained that the prisoner was to learn a civilized language and, what was more, would learn it fast, by order. Education would commence forthwith.

In businesslike manner the tutor produced a stack of juvenile picture books and started the imparting process while the guards lounged against the wall and looked bored. Leeming co-operated as one does with the enemy, namely, by misunderstanding everything, mispronouncing everything, overlooking nothing that would prove him a linguistic moron.

The lesson ended at noon and was celebrated by the arrival of another bowl of gruel containing a hunk of stringy, rubberish substance resembling the hind end of a rat. He ate the gruel, sucked the portion of animal, shoved the bowl aside.

Then he pondered the significance of their decision to teach him how to talk. Firstly, it meant that they'd got nothing resembling Earth's electronic brain-pryers and could extract information only by question-and-answer methods aided by unknown forms of persuasion. Secondly, they wanted to know things and intended to learn them if possible. Thirdly, the slower he was to gain fluency the longer it would be before they put him on the rack, if that was their intention.

His speculations ended when guards opened the door and called him out. Along the passage, down long stairs, into a great yard filled with figures mooching around under a sickly sun.

He halted in surprise. Rigellians! About two thousand of them. These were allies, members of the Federation. He looked them over with mounting excitement, seeking a few more familiar shapes amid the mob. Perhaps an Earthman or two. Or even a few humanlike Centaurians.

But there were none. Only rubber-limbed, pop-eyed Rigellians shuffling around in the aimless manner of those confronted with many wasted years and no perceivable future.

Even as he looked at them he sensed something peculiar. They could see him just as well as he could see them and, being the only Earthman, he was a legitimate object of attention. He was a friend from another star. They should have been crowding up to him, full of talk, seeking the latest news of the war, asking questions, offering information.

They took no notice of him. He walked slowly and deliberately right across the yard and they got out of his way. A few eyed him furtively, the majority pretended to be unaware of his existence. Nobody offered him a word. They were giving him the conspicuous brush-off.

He trapped a small bunch of them in a corner of the wall and said, "Any of you speak Terran?"

They looked at the sky, the wall, the ground, or at each other, and remained silent.

"Anyone know Centaurian?"

No answer.

"Well, how about Cosmoglotta?"

No answer.

He walked away feeling riled, tried another bunch. No luck. And another bunch. No luck. Within an hour he had questioned five hundred without getting a single response.

Giving up, he sat on a stone step and watched them irefully until a shrill whistle signaled that exercise time was over. The Rigellians formed up in long lines in readiness to march back to their quarters. Leeming's guards gave him a kick in the pants and chivvied him to his cell.

Temporarily he dismissed the problem of unsociable allies. After dark was the time for thinking: he wanted to use remaining hours of light to study the picture books and

Eric Frank Russell

get well ahead with the local lingo while appearing to lag far behind. Fluency might prove an advantage some day. Too bad he'd never learned Rigellian, for instance.

So he applied himself fully to the task until print and pictures ceased to be visible. He ate his evening portion of mush. After that he lay on the bench, closed his eyes, set his brains to work.

In all his life he'd met no more than a couple of dozen Rigellians. Never once had he visited their systems. What little he knew of them was hearsay evidence. It was said their standard of intelligence was good, they were technologically efficient, they had been consistently friendly toward men of Earth since first contact. Fifty per cent of them spoke Cosmoglotta, maybe one per cent knew the Terran tongue.

Therefore, if the average held up, several hundreds of those met in the yard should have been able to converse with him in one language or another. Why had they remained silent? And why had they been so unanimous about it?

He invented, examined and discarded a dozen theories. It was two hours before he hit upon the obvious solution.

These Rigellians were prisoners, deprived of liberty perhaps for years to come. Some of them must have seen an Earthman at one time or another. But all of them knew that in the ranks of the foe were two races superficially humanlike. Therefore they suspected him of being a stooge, an ear of the enemy listening for plots.

That in turn meant something else. When a big mob of prisoners becomes excessively wary of a spy in their midst it's because they have something to hide. Yes, that was it! He slapped his knee in delight. The Rigellians had an escape plot in process of hatching and meanwhile were taking no chances.

How to get in on it?

Next day, at the end of exercise time, a guard administered the usual kick. Leeming upped and punched him clean on the snout. Four guards jumped in and gave the culprit a going over. They did it good and proper, in a way that no onlooking Rigellian could mistake for an act. It was an object lesson and intended as such. The limp body was carried upstairs with its face a mess of blood.

It was a week before Leeming was fit enough to reappear in the yard. His features were still an ugly sight. He strolled through the crowd, ignored as before, chose a spot in the sun and sat.

Soon afterward a prisoner sprawled tiredly on the ground a couple of yards away, watched distant guards and spoke in little more than a whisper.

"How'd you get here?"

Leeming told him.

"How's the war going on?"

"We're pushing them back slowly but surely. But it'll take time—a long time."

"How long do you suppose?"

"I don't know. It's anyone's guess." Leeming eyed him curiously. "What brought this crowd here?"

"We're colonists. We were advance parties, all male, planted on four new planets that were ours by right of discovery. Twelve thousand of us altogether." The Rigellian went silent a moment, looked carefully around. "They descended on us in force. That was two years ago. It was easy. We weren't prepared. We didn't even know a war was on."

"They grabbed the planets?"

"You bet they did. And laughed in our faces."

Leeming nodded understanding. Claim-jumping had been the original cause of the fracas now extending across a sizable slice of a galaxy. On one planet a colony had put up an heroic resistance and died to the last man. The sacrifice had fired a blaze of fury, the Federation had struck back and the war was on.

"Twelve thousand you said. Where are the others?"

"Scattered around in prisons like this one. You picked a choice dump in which to sit out the war. The enemy has made this his chief penal planet. It's far from the fighting front, unlikely ever to be discovered. The local life form isn't much good for space battles but plenty good enough to hold what others have captured. They're throwing up big jails all over the world. If the war goes on long enough, the planet will get solid with Federation prisoners."

"So your mob has been here most of two years?"

"Yes."

"And done nothing about it?"

"Nothing much," agreed the Rigellian. "Just enough to get forty of us shot for trying."

"Sorry," said Leeming, sincerely.

"Don't let it bother you. I know how you feel. The first few weeks are the worst." He pointed surreptitiously toward a heavily built guard across the yard. "Few days ago that lying swine boasted that there are already two hundred thousand Federation prisoners on this planet. He said that by this time next year there'll be two million. I hope he never lives to see it."

"I'm getting out of here," said Leeming.

"How?"

"I don't know yet. But I'm getting out. I'm not going to just squat and rot." He waited expectantly, hoping for some comment about others feeling the same way he did, maybe some evasive mention of a coming break, a hint that he might be invited to join in.

The Rigellian stood up, murmured, "Well, I wish you luck. You'll need it aplenty!"

He ambled off. A whistle blew and the guards shouted, *"Merse, faplaps! Amash!"* And that was that.

Over the next four weeks he had frequent conversations with the same Rigellian and about twenty others, picking up odd items of information but finding them peculiarly evasive whenever the subject of freedom came up.

He was having a concealed chat with one of them and asked, "Why does everyone insist on talking to me secretively and in whispers? The guards don't seem to care how much you yap to one another."

"You haven't been cross-examined yet. If in the meantime they notice we've had plenty to say to you, they will try to get out of you everything we've said—with particular reference to ideas on escape."

Leeming pounced on the lovely word. "Escape, that's all there is to live for right now. If anyone's thinking of making a bid, maybe I can help them and they can help me. I'm a competent space pilot and that fact is worth something."

The other cooled off at once. "Nothing doing."

"Why not?"

"We've been behind walls a long time. We've learned at bitter cost that escape attempts fail when too many know what is going on. Some planted spy betrays us. Or some selfish fool messes things up by pushing in at the wrong moment."

"I see."

"Imprisonment creates its own especial conventions," the Rigellian went on. "And one we've established here is that an escape-plot is the exclusive property of those who thought it up and only they can make the attempt. Nobody else is told. Nobody else knows until the resulting hullabaloo starts going."

"So I'm strictly on my own?"

"Afraid so. You're on your own in any case. We're in dormitories, fifty to a room. You're in a cell all by yourself. You're in no position to help anyone with anything."

"I can darned well help myself," he retorted angrily.

And it was his turn to walk away.

He'd been there just thirteen weeks when the tutor handed him a metaphorical firecracker. Finishing a lesson, the tutor compressed thin lips, looked at him with severity.

"You are pleased to wear the cloak of idiocy. But I am not deceived. You are far more fluent than you pretend. I shall report to the Commandant that you will be ready for examination in seven days' time."

"How's that again?" asked Leeming, putting on a baffled frown.

"You heard what I said and you understood me."

Slam went the door. Came the gruel and a jaundiced lump of something unchewable. Exercise time followed.

"They're going to put me through the mill a week hence."

"Don't let them scare you," advised the Rigellian. "They'd as soon kill you as spit in the sink. But one thing keeps them in check."

"What's that?"

"The Federation is holding prisoners, too."

"Yes, but what the Federation doesn't know it can't grieve over."

"There'll be more than grief for somebody if eventually the victor finds himself expected to exchange live prisoners for corpses."

"You've got a point there," agreed Leeming. "I could do with nine feet of rope to dangle suggestively in front of the Commandant."

"I could do with a very large bottle of *vitz* and a female to ruffle my hair," sighed the Rigellian.

The whistle again. More intensive study while daylight lasted. Another bowl of ersatz porridge. Darkness and four small stars peeped through the barred slot high up.

He lay on the bench and produced thoughts like bubbles from a fountain. No place, positively no place is absolutely impregnable. Given brawn and brains and enough time there's always a way in or out. Escapees shot down as they bolted had chosen the wrong time and wrong place, or the right time and wrong place, or the right place at the wrong time. Or they'd neglected brawn in favor of brains, a common fault of the impatient. Or they'd neglected brains in favor of brawn, a fault of the reckless.

With eyes closed he carefully reviewed the situation. He was in a cell with rock walls of granite hardness at least four feet thick. The only openings were a narrow gap blocked by five thick steel bars, also an armor-plated door in constant view of patroling guards.

On his person he had no hacksaw, no lock pick, no implement of any sort, nothing but the clothes in which he lay. If he pulled the bench to pieces, and somehow succeeded in doing it unheard, he'd acquire several large lumps of wood, a dozen six-inch nails and a couple of steel bolts. None of that junk would serve to open the door or cut the window bars before morning. And there was no other material available.

Outside was a brilliantly illuminated gap fifty yards wide that must be crossed to gain freedom. Then a smooth stone wall, forty feet high, devoid of handholds. Atop the wall an apex much too sharp to give grip to the feet while stepping over an alarm wire that would set the sirens going if touched or cut.

The wall completely encircled the entire prison. It was octagonal in shape and topped at each angle by a watchtower containing guards, machine guns, floodlights. To get out, the wall would have to be surmounted right under the noses of itchy-fingered watchers, in bright light, without touching the wire. That wouldn't be the end of it either; outside the wall was another illuminated fifty-yard area also to be crossed.

Yes, the whole set-up had the professional touch of those who knew what to do to keep them in for keeps. Escape over the wall was well-nigh impossible though not completely so. If somebody got out of his cell or dormitory armed with a fifty-foot rope and grapnel, and if he had a confederate who could break into the prison's power

Eric Frank Russell

room and switch off everything at exactly the right moment, he might make it. Over the dead, unresponsive alarm wire in total darkness.

In a solitary cell there is no fifty-foot rope, no grapnel, nothing capable of being adapted as either. There is no desperate and trustworthy confederate.

If he considered once the most remote possibilities and took stock of the minimum resources needed, he considered them a hundred times. By two o'clock in the morning he'd been beating his brains sufficiently hard to make them come up with anything, including ideas that were slightly mad.

For example: he could pull a plastic button from his jacket, swallow it and hope the result would get him a transfer to the hospital. True, the hospital was within the prison's confines but it might offer better opportunity for escape. Then he thought a second time, decided that a plastic blockage would not guarantee his removal elsewhere. There was a chance that they might be content to force a powerful purgative down his neck and thus add to his present discomforts.

As dawn broke he arrived at a final conclusion. Thirty, forty or fifty Rigellians, working in a patient, determined group, might tunnel under the watched areas and the wall and get away. But he had one resource and one only. That was guile. There was nothing else he could employ.

He groaned to himself and complained, "So I'll have to use both my heads."

A couple of minutes later he sat up startled, gazed at the brightening sky and exclaimed, "Yes, sure, that's it! *Both* heads!"

By exercise time Leeming had decided that it would be helpful to have a gadget. A crucifix or a crystal ball provides psychological advantages. His gadget could be of any shape, size or design, made of any material, so long as it was obviously a contraption. Moreover, its potency would be greater if not made from items obtainable within his cell, such as parts of his clothing or pieces of the bench. Preferably it should be constructed of stuff from somewhere else.

He doubted whether the Rigellians could help. Six hours per day they slaved in the prison's workshops, a fate that he would share after he'd been questioned and his aptitudes defined. The Rigellians made military pants and jackets, harness and boots, a small range of engineering and electrical components. They detested producing for the enemy but their choice was a simple one: work or starve.

According to what he'd been told they had remote chance of smuggling out of the workshops anything really useful such as a knife, chisel, hammer or hacksaw blade. At the end of each work period the slaves were paraded and none allowed to break ranks until every machine had been checked, every loose tool accounted for and locked away.

The first fifteen minutes of the midday break he spent searching the yard for any loose item that might be turned to advantage. He wandered around with his gaze on the ground like a worried kid seeking a lost coin. The only things he found were a couple of pieces of wood four inches square by one inch thick. He slipped them into his pocket without having the vaguest notion of what he was going to do with them.

After that, he squatted by the wall, had a whispered chat with a couple of Rigellians. His mind wasn't on the conversation and the pair moved away when a patroling guard came near. Later, another Rigellian mooched up.

"Earthman, you still going to get out of here?"

"You bet I am."

The Rigellian chuckled, scratched an ear, an action that his race used to express polite skepticism. "I think we've a better chance than you."

"Why?" Leeming shot him a sharp glance.

"There are more of us," evaded the other, as though realizing that he'd been on the point of saying too much. "What can one do on one's own?"

"Scoot like blazes first chance," said Leeming.

His eyes suddenly noticed the ring on the other's ear-scratching finger and became fascinated by it. He'd seen the modest ornament before, and dozens like it. A number of Rigellians were wearing similar objects. So were some of the guards. The rings were neat affairs consisting of four or five turns of thin wire with the ends shaped and soldered to form the owner's initials.

"Where'd you dig up the jewelry?" he asked.

"Eh?"

"The ring."

"Oh, that." The Rigellian lowered his hand, eyed the ring with satisfaction. "Make them ourselves in the workshops. It breaks the monotony."

"Mean to say the guards don't stop you?"

"They don't interfere. There's no harm in it. Anyway, we've made quite a number for the guards themselves. We've made them some automatic lighters as well. Could have turned out a few hundred for ourselves except that we've no use for them." He paused reflectively. "We think the guards have been selling rings and lighters outside. At least, we hope so."

"Why?"

"Maybe they'll build up a nice trade. Then, when they are comfortably settled in it, we'll cut supplies and demand a rake-off in the form of extra rations and a few unofficial privileges."

"That's smart of you," said Leeming. "It would help all concerned to have a salesman traveling around the planet. Put me down for that job."

The Rigellian gave a faint smile, went on, "Hand-made junk doesn't matter. But let the guards find that one small screwdriver is missing and there's hell to pay. Everyone is stripped naked on the spot and the culprit suffers."

"They wouldn't miss a small coil of wire, would they?"

"I doubt it. They don't bother to check the stuff. What can anyone do with a piece of wire?"

Eric Frank Russell

"Heaven knows," admitted Leeming. "But I want some."

"You'll never pick a lock with it in a million moons," warned the other. "It's too thin and too soft."

"I want enough to make a set of Zulu bangles," Leeming told him. "I sort of fancy myself in Zulu bangles."

"You can steal some wire yourself in the near future. After you've been questioned they'll send you to the workshops."

"I want it before then. I want it just as soon as I can get it."

Going silent, the Rigellian thought it over, finally said, "If you've a plan in your mind, keep it to yourself. Don't give a hint of it to anyone. Let anything slip and somebody will try to beat you to it."

"Thanks for the advice, friend," said Leeming. "How about a bit of wire?"

"See you this time tomorrow."

The Rigellian left him, wandered into the crowd.

The wire proved to be a small pocket-sized coil of tinned copper. When unrolled in the darkness of the cell it measured his own length, namely, six feet.

Leeming doubled it, waggled it to and fro until it broke, hid one half under the bottom of the bench. Then he spent more than an hour worrying a loose nail out of the bench's end.

Finding one of the pieces of wood, he approximated its center, stamped the nail into it with his boot. Footsteps approached, he shoved the stuff out of sight, lay down just before the spyhole opened. The light flashed on, an eye looked in, somebody grunted. The light cut off, the spyhole shut.

Leeming resumed his task, twisting the nail one way and the other, pressing it with his boot from time to time, persevering until he had drilled a neat hole two-thirds the way through the wood.

Next, he took his half-length of wire, broke it into two unequal parts, shaped the shorter piece to form a loop with two legs three or four inches long. He tried to make the circle as nearly perfect as possible. The longer piece of wire he wound tightly around the loop so that it formed a close-fitting coil with legs matching those of the loop.

Climbing the bench to the window, he examined his handiwork in the glow from outside floodlights, made a few minor adjustments and felt satisfied. After that, he used the nail to make on the edge of the bench two small nicks representing the exact diameter of the loop. He counted the number of turns the coil made around the loop. There were twenty-seven.

It was important to have these details because it was highly likely that he'd have to make a second gadget. If so, he must make it precisely the same. Once they noticed it, that very similarity might get the enemy bothered. When a plotter makes two things practically identical it's hard to resist the notion that he's up to something definite.

To complete his preparations, he chivvied the nail back into the place where it belonged. Sometime he'd need it again. He then forced the four legs of the coiled loop into the hole that he'd drilled, thus making the small piece of wood function as a stand. He now had a gadget, a doodad, a means to an end. He was the original inventor and sole owner of the Leeming Something-or-Other.

Certain chemical reactions take place only in the presence of a catalyst, like marriages legalized by the presence of a justice of the peace. Some equations can be solved only by the inclusion of an unknown quantity called X. If you haven't enough on the ball, you've got to add what's needed. If you require outside help that doesn't exist, you've got to invent it.

Whenever Man was unable to master his environment with his bare hands, thought Leeming, the said environment got bullied or corrected into submission by Man plus X. That had been so from the beginning of time—Man plus a tool or a weapon.

But X did not have to be anything concrete or solid, it did not have to be lethal or even visible. It could be a dream, an idea, an illusion, a bloody big thundering lie, just *anything*.

There was only one true test—whether it worked.

If it did, it was efficient.

Now to see.

There was no sense in using Terran except perhaps as an incantation when one was necessary. Nobody here understood it; to them it was just an alien gabble. Besides, his delaying tactic of pretending to be slow to learn was no longer effective. They now knew he could speak the local lingo almost as well as they could themselves.

Holding the loop assembly in his left hand, he went to the door, applied his ear to the closed spyhole, listened for the sound of patroling feet. It was twenty minutes before he heard the approaching squeak of military boots.

"Are you there?" he called, not too loudly but enough to be heard. "Are you there?"

Backing off, he lay on his belly on the floor and stood the loop six inches in front of his face.

"Are you there?"

The spyhole clicked open, the light came on, a sour eye looked through.

Completely ignoring the watcher, and behaving with the air of one totally absorbed in his task, Leeming spoke through the coiled loop.

"Are you there?"

"What are you doing?" demanded the guard.

Leeming recognized the voice, decided that for once luck must be turning his way. This character, a chump named Marsin, knew enough to point a gun and fire it or, if unable to do so, yell for help. In all other matters he was not of the elite. In fact Marsin would have to think twice to pass muster as a half-wit.

Eric Frank Russell

"What are you doing there?" demanded Marsin, more loudly.

"Calling," said Leeming, apparently just waking up to the other's existence.

"*Who* are you calling?"

"Mind your own business," ordered Leeming, giving a nice display of impatience. He turned the loop another two degrees. "Are you there?"

"It is forbidden," insisted Marsin.

Leeming let go the loud sigh of one compelled to bear fools gladly. "What is forbidden?"

"To call."

"Don't be so flaming ignorant!" Leeming reproved. "My kind is *always* allowed to call. Where'd we be if we couldn't, eh?"

That got Marsin badly tangled. He knew nothing about Earthmen or what peculiar privileges they considered essential to life. Neither could he give a guess as to where they'd be without them.

Moreover, he dared not bust into the cell and put a stop to whatever was going on. An armed guard was prohibited from entering a cell by himself and that rule had been strict ever since a Rigellian had bopped one, snatched his gun and killed six while trying to make a break.

If he wanted to interfere, he'd have to go see the sergeant of the guard and demand that something be done to stop aliens making noises through loops. The sergeant was an unlovely character with a tendency to advertise personal histories all over the landscape. It was four o'clock in the morning, a time when the sergeant's liver malfunctioned most audibly. And lastly, he, Marsin, had proved himself a misbegotten faplap far too often.

"You will cease calling and go to sleep," said Marsin, with a touch of desperation, "or in the morning I shall report this matter to the officer of the day."

"Go ride a camel," Leeming invited. He turned the loop in the manner of one making careful adjustment. "Are you there?"

"I have warned you," Marsin persisted, his only visible eye popping at the loop.

"Fibble off!" roared Leeming.

Marsin shut the spyhole and fibbled off.

Leeming overslept as was inevitable after being up most of the night. His awakening was rude. The door opened with a crash, three guards plunged in followed by an officer.

Without ceremony the prisoner was jerked off the bench, stripped and shoved into the corridor stark naked. The guards hunted thoroughly through the clothing while the officer minced around them watching.

Finding nothing in the clothes they started searching the cell. Right off one of them found the loop assembly and gave it to the officer who held it gingerly as though it were a bouquet suspected of being a bomb.

Another guard found the second piece of wood with his boot, kicked it aside and ignored it. They tapped the floor and the walls, seeking hollow sounds. They dragged the bench from the wall and looked over the other side of it. Then they were about to turn the bench upside-down when Leeming decided that now was the time to take a walk. He started along the corridor, a picture of nonchalant nudity.

The officer let go an outraged howl and pointed. The guards erupted from the cell, bawled orders to halt. A fourth guard appeared at the bend of the corridor, aimed his gun and scowled. Leeming turned and ambled back.

He stopped as he reached the officer who was now outside the cell and fuming with temper. Striking a modest pose, he said, "Look, September Morn."

It meant nothing to the other who held the loop under his nose and yelled, "What is this thing?"

"My property," said Leeming with naked dignity.

"You are not supposed to possess it. As a prisoner of war you are not allowed to have anything."

"Who says so?"

"*I* say so!" declared the officer, somewhat violently.

"Who're you?" inquired Leeming.

"By the Sword of Lamissim," swore the other, "I'll show you who I am! Guards, take him inside and—"

"You're not the boss," put in Leeming, impressively cocksure. "The Commandant is the boss here. I say so and he says so. If you want to dispute it, let's go ask him."

The guards hesitated, assumed expressions of chronic uncertainty. The officer was taken aback.

"Are you asserting that the Commandant has given permission for you to have this object?"

"I'm telling you he hasn't refused permission. Also that it isn't for you to give it or refuse it."

"I shall consult the Commandant about this," the officer decided, deflated and a little unsure of himself. He turned to the guards. "Put the prisoner back in the cell and give him his breakfast as usual."

"How about returning my property?" Leeming prompted.

"Not until I have seen the Commandant."

They hustled him into the cell. He got dressed. Breakfast came, the inevitable bowl of slop. He cussed the guards for not making it bacon and eggs. That was deliberate. A display of self-assurance and some aggressiveness was necessary to push the game along.

The tutor did not appear so he spent the morning furbishing his fluency with the aid of the books. At midday they let him into the yard and there was no evidence of an especial watch being kept upon him while there.

The Rigellian whispered, "I got the opportunity to swipe another coil. So I took it in case you wanted more." He slipped it across, saw it vanish into a pocket. "That's all I intend to take. Don't ask me again."

"What's up? Is it getting risky? Are they suspicious of you?"

"Everything is all right so far." He glanced warily around. "If some of the other prisoners get to know I'm taking it, they'll start grabbing it, too. They'll steal it in the hope of discovering what I'm going to use it for, so that they can use it for the same purpose. Everybody's always on the lookout for an advantage, real or imaginary, which he can share. This prison life brings out the worst as well as the best."

"I see."

"A couple of small coils will never be missed," the other went on. "But once the rush starts the stuff will evaporate in wholesale quantities. That's when all hell will break loose. I daren't chance starting anything like that."

"Meaning you fellows can't risk a detailed search just now?" suggested Leeming pointedly.

The Rigellian shied like a frightened horse. "I didn't say that."

"I can put two and two together same as anyone else." Leeming favored him with a reassuring wink. "I can also keep my trap shut."

He explored the yard seeking more pieces of wood but failed to find any. Oh, well, no matter. At a pinch he could do without. Come to that, he'd darned well have to do without.

The afternoon was given over to further studies. When light became too poor for that, and first faint flickers of starlight showed through the barred opening in the wall, he kicked the door until the sound of it thundered all over the block.

Feet came running and the spyhole opened. It was Marsin again.

"So it's you," greeted Leeming. He let go a snort. "You had to blab, of course. You had to curry favor by telling the officer." He drew himself up to full height. "Well, I am sorry for you. I'd fifty times rather be me than you."

"Sorry for me?" Marsin registered confusion. "Why?"

"You are going to suffer. Not yet, of course. It is necessary for you to undergo the normal period of horrid anticipation. But eventually you are going to suffer."

"It was my duty," explained Marsin, semiapologetically.

"That fact will be considered in mitigation," Leeming assured, "and your agonies will be modified in due proportion."

"I don't understand," said Marsin, developing a node of worry somewhere within the solid bone.

"You will—some dire day. So also will those four stinking faplaps who beat me up. You can inform them from me that their quota of pain is being arranged."

"I am not supposed to talk to you," said Marsin, dimly perceiving that the longer he stood there the bigger the fix he got into. He made to close the spyhole.

"All right. But I want something."

"What is it?"

"I want my bopamagilvie—that thing the officer took away."

"You cannot have it until the Commandant gives permission. He is absent today and will not return before tomorrow morning."

"That's no use. I want it now." He gave an airy wave of his hand. "Never mind. Forget it. I will summon another one."

"It is forbidden," reminded Marsin, very feebly.

"Ha-ha!" said Leeming, venting a hearty laugh.

Waiting for darkness to grow complete, he got the wire from under the bench and manufactured a second whatzit to all intents and purposes identical with the first one. Twice he was interrupted but not caught.

That job finished, he upended the bench and climbed it. Taking the new coil of wire from his pocket, he tied one end tightly around the bottom of the middle bar, hung the coil outside the window gap.

With spit and dust he camouflaged the bright tin surface of the one visible strand, made sure it could not be seen at farther than nose-tip distance. He got down, replaced the bench. The window gap was so high that all of its ledge and the bottom three inches of its bar could not be viewed from below.

Going to the door, he listened and at the right time called, "Are you there?"

When the light came on and the spyhole was in use he got an instinctive feeling that there was a bunch of them clustered outside, also that the eye in the hole was not Marsin's.

Ignoring everything, he rotated the loop slowly and carefully, meanwhile calling, "Are you there?"

After traversing about forty degrees he paused, gave his voice a tone of intense satisfaction, said, "So you are there at last! Why the devil don't you keep within easy reach so's we can talk without me having to summon you with a loop?"

He went silent, put on the expression of one who listens intently. The eye in the hole widened, got shoved away, was replaced by another.

"Well," said Leeming, settling himself down for a cozy gossip. "I'll point them out to you first chance I get and leave you to deal with them as you think fit. Let's switch to our own language—there are too many big ears around for my liking." He took a long, deep breath, rattled off at top pace and without pause, "Out sprang the web and opened wide the mirror cracked from side to side the curse has come upon me cried the Lady of—"

Out sprang the door and opened wide and two guards almost fell headlong into the cell in their eagerness to make a quick snatch. Two more posed outside with the officer between them. Marsin mooned fearfully in the background.

A guard grabbed up the loop assembly, yelled, "I've got it!" and rushed out. His companion followed. Both seemed hysterical with excitement.

There was a ten seconds' pause before the door shut. Leeming exploited the fact. He stood up, pointed at the group by making horizontal stabbing motions with his two middle fingers. Giving 'em the Devil's Horns they'd called it when he was a kid. The classic gesture of donating the evil eye.

"Those," he declaimed dramatically, addressing what wasn't there, "are the scaly-skinned bums who've asked for trouble. See that they get plenty."

The whole bunch of them managed to look alarmed before the door cut them from sight with a vicious slam. He listened at the spyhole, heard them go away muttering steadily between themselves.

Within ten minutes he had broken a length off the coil hanging from the window bars, restored the spit and dust disguise of the holding strand. Half an hour later he had another bopamagilvie. Practice was making him an expert in the swift and accurate manufacture of these things.

Lacking wood for a stand, he used the loose nail to bore a hole in the dirt between the big stone slabs composing the floor of his cell. He rammed the legs of the loop into the hole, twisted the contraption this way and that to make ceremonial rotation easy.

When the right moment arrived he lay on his belly and commenced reciting through the loop the third paragraph of Rule 27, subsection B, of Space Regulations. He chose it because it was a gem of bureaucratic phraseology, a single sentence one thousand words long meaning something known only to God.

"Where refueling must be carried out as an emergency measure at a station not officially listed as a home station or definable for special purposes as a home station under Section A (5) amendment A (5) B the said station shall be treated as if it were definable as a home station under Section A (5) amendment A (5) B providing that the emergency falls within the authorized list of technical necessities as given in Section J (29-33) with addenda subsequent thereto as applicable to home stations where such are—"

The spyhole flipped open and shut. Somebody scooted away. A minute afterward the corridor shook to what sounded like a cavalry charge. The spyhole again opened and shut. The door crashed inward.

This time they reduced him to his bare pelt, searched his clothes, raked the cell from end to end. Their manner was that of those singularly lacking in brotherly love. They turned the bench upside-down, knocked it, tapped it, kicked it, did everything but run a large magnifying glass over it.

Watching this operation, Leeming encouraged them by giving a sinister snigger. Was a time when he could not have produced a sinister snigger even to win a fifty-credit bet. But he could do it now. The ways in which a man can rise to the occasion are without limit.

Giving him a look of sudden death and total destruction, a guard went out, brought back a ladder, mounted it, surveyed the window gap. It was a perfunctory glance, his mind being mostly concerned with the solidity of the bars. He grasped each bar with both hands, shook vigorously. Satisfied, he got down, took the ladder away.

They departed. Leeming dressed himself, listened at the spyhole. Just a very faint hiss of breath and occasional rustle of clothes nearby. He sat on the bench and waited. In short time the lights flashed and the spyhole opened. He stabbed two fingers toward the inlooking eye.

The hole closed. Feet moved away stamping much too loudly. He waited. After half an hour of complete silence the eye offered itself again and for its pains received another two-fingered hex. Five minutes later it had another bestowed upon it. If it was the same eye all the time, it was a glutton for punishment.

This game continued for three hours before the eye had had enough. Then he made another loop, gabbled through it in a loud voice and precipitated another raid. They did not strip him or search the cell this time. They contented themselves with confiscating the gadget. And they showed signs of being more than somewhat fed up.

There was just enough wire left for one more. He decided to keep that against a future need and get some sleep. Inadequate food and not enough slumber were combining to make inroads on his reserves.

He flopped on the bench and closed red-rimmed eyes. In due time he started snoring fit to saw through the bars. That caused a panic in the passage, brought the crowd along in yet another rush.

Waking up, he damned them to perdition. He lay down again. He was plain bone-tuckered—but so were they.

He slept solidly until midday without a break except for the usual lousy breakfast. Soon after awakening came the usual lousy dinner. At exercise time they kept him locked in. He hammered on the door, demanded to know why he wasn't being allowed to walk in the yard. They took no notice.

So he sat on the bench and thought things over. Perhaps this denial of his only freedom was a form of retaliation for making them hop around like fleas in the middle of the night. Or perhaps the Rigellian was under suspicion and they'd decided to prevent contact.

Anyway, he'd got the enemy worried. He was bollixing them about, single-handed, far behind the lines. That was something. The fact that a combatant is a prisoner doesn't mean he's out of the battle. Even behind thick wire and high walls he can still harass the foe, absorbing his time and energy, undermining his morale, pinning down at least a few of his forces.

The next step, he decided, was to widen the hex. He must do it as comprehensively as possible. The more he spread it and the more ambiguous the terms in which he expressed it, the more plausibly he could grab the credit for any and every misfortune that was certain to occur sooner or later.

It was the technique of the gypsy's warning. People tend to attach specific meanings

Eric Frank Russell

to ambiguities when circumstances arise and suggest a given meaning. People don't have to be especially credulous, either. It is sufficient for them to be made expectant, with a tendency to wonder—after the event.

"In the near future a dark, tall man will cross your path."

After which any male above average height, and not a blond, fits the picture. And any time from five minutes to a full year is accepted as the near future.

"Mamma, when the insurance man called he really smiled at me. *D'you remember what the gypsy said?*"

Leeming grinned to himself as his brain assembled facts and theories and analyzed the possibilities. Somewhere not so far away a bunch of Rigellians—or several bunches for all he knew—were deep in the earth and burrowing slowly, without tools. A few pitiful handfuls at a time. Progress at the rate of a couple of pathetic inches per night. Dirt taken out in mere pocketloads and sprinkled through the yard. A constant, never-ending risk of discovery, entrapment and perhaps some insane shooting. A year-long project that could be terminated by a shout and the chatter of guns.

But to get out of clink you don't have to escape. If sufficiently patient, determined, glib and cunning you can talk the foe into opening the doors and pushing you out. You can use the wits that God gave you.

By law of probability various things must happen in jail and out, and not all of them pleasing to the enemy. Some officer must get the galloping gripes right under his body-belt, or a guard must fall down a watchtower ladder and break a leg, somebody must lose a wad of money or his pants or his senses. Farther afield a bridge must collapse, or a train get derailed, or a spaceship crash at take-off, or there'd be an explosion in a munitions factory, or a military leader would drop dead.

He'd be playing a trump card if he could establish his claim to be the author of all misery. The essential thing was to stake it in such a way that they could not effectively combat it, neither could they exact retribution in a torture chamber.

The ideal strategy was to convince them of his malevolence in a manner that would equally convince them of their own impotence. If he succeeded, they'd come to the logical conclusion—that the only way to get rid of trouble was to get rid of Leeming, alive and in one piece.

It was a jumbo problem that would have appalled him way back home. But by now he'd had three months in which to incubate a solution—and the brain becomes stimulated by grim necessity. A good thing he had an idea in mind; he had a mere ten minutes before the time came to apply it.

The door opened, a trio of guards glowered at him and one of them rasped, "The Commandant wishes to see you at once. *Amash!*"

The Commandant squatted behind a desk with a lower-ranking officer on either side. He was a heavily built specimen. His horn-covered lidless eyes gave him a dead-pan look as he studied the prisoner.

Leeming calmly sat himself in a handy chair and the officer on the right immediately bawled, "Federation garbage! You will stand in the presence of the Commandant."

"Let him sit," contradicted the Commandant.

A concession at the start, thought Leeming. He eyed the pile of papers on the desk. Ten to one the Commandant had read a complete report of his misdeeds and decided to reserve judgment until he'd got to the bottom of whatever was going on.

That attitude was natural enough. The Federation knew nothing of this local life form. By the same token the inquisitors knew nothing of several Federation forms, those of Earth in particular. From their viewpoint they were about to cope with an unknown quantity.

Man, how right they were! A quantity doubled by plus X.

"I am given to understand that you now speak our language," began the Commandant.

"No use denying it," Leeming confessed.

"Very well. You will first give some information concerning yourself." He positioned an official form on his desk, held a pen in readiness. "Name of planet of origin?"

"Earth."

The other wrote it phonetically in his own script, continued, "Name of race?"

"Terran."

"Name of species?"

"*Homo nosipaca*," said Leeming, keeping his face straight.

The Commandant wrote it down, looked doubtful, asked, "What does that mean?"

"Space-traversing Man," Leeming informed.

"Hm-m-m!" The other was impressed despite himself, inquired, "Your personal name?"

"John Leeming."

"John Leeming," repeated the Commandant, putting it down on the form.

"And Eustace Phenackertiban," added Leeming, airily.

That got written too, though the Commandant had some difficulty in finding hooks and curlicues to express Phenackertiban. Twice he asked Leeming to repeat it and that worthy obliged.

Studying the result, which resembled a Chinese recipe for rotten egg gumbo, the Commandant said, "It is your custom to have two names?"

"Most certainly," Leeming assured. "We can't avoid it seeing that there are two of us."

The listener twitched the eyebrows he lacked and showed mild surprise. "You mean that you are always conceived and born in pairs? Two identical males or females every time?"

"No, not at all." Leeming adopted the air of one about to state the obvious. "Whenever one of us is born he immediately acquires a Eustace."

"A Eustace?"

"Yes."

The Commandant frowned, picked his teeth, glanced at the other officers. They assumed the blank expressions of fellows who've come along merely to keep company.

"What," asked the Commandant at long last, "is a Eustace?"

Registering surprise at such ignorance, Leeming said, "An invisibility that is part of one's self."

Understanding dawned on the Commandant's scaly face. "Ah, you mean a soul? You give your soul a separate name?"

"Nothing of the sort," Leeming denied. "I have a soul and Eustace has a soul of his own." Then, as an afterthought, "At least, I hope we have."

The Commandant lay back and stared at him. There was quite a long silence.

Finally, he admitted, "I do not understand."

"In that case," announced Leeming, irritatingly triumphant, "it's evident that you have no alien equivalent of Eustaces yourselves. You're all on your own. Just single-lifers. That's your hard luck."

Slamming a hand on the desk, the Commandant gave his voice a bit more military whoof and demanded, "Exactly what is a Eustace? Explain to me as clearly as possible."

"I'm in poor position to refuse the information," Leeming conceded with hypocritical reluctance. "Not that it matters much. Even if you gain perfect understanding there is nothing you can do."

"We'll see about that," the Commandant promised. "Tell me all about these Eustaces."

"Every Earthling lives a double-life from birth to death," said Leeming. "He exists in association with an entity which always calls himself Eustace something-or-other. Mine happens to be Eustace Phenackertiban."

"You can *see* this entity?"

"No, never at any time. You cannot see him, smell him, or feel him."

"Then how do you know that this is not a racial delusion?"

"Firstly, because every man can hear his own Eustace. I can hold long conversations with mine, providing that he happens to be within reach, and I can hear him speaking clearly and logically within the depths of my mind."

"You cannot hear him with the ears?"

"No, only with the mind." Leeming took a deep breath and went on. "Secondly, he has the power to do certain things after which there is visible evidence that such things have been done." His attention shifted to the absorbed officer on the left. "For example, if Eustace had a grudge against this officer and advised me of his intention to make him fall downstairs, and if before long the officer fell downstairs and broke his neck—"

"It could be mere coincidence," the Commandant suggested.

"It could," Leeming agreed, "but there can be far too many coincidences. When a Eustace says he's going to do twenty or fifty things in succession and all of them happen, he's either doing them as promised or he is a most astounding prophet. Eustaces don't claim to be prophets. I don't believe in them either. Nobody, visible or invisible, can read the future with such detailed accuracy."

"That is true enough," admitted the Commandant.

"Do you accept the fact that you have a father and mother?"

"Of course."

"You don't consider it strange or abnormal?"

"Certainly not. It is inconceivable that one should be born without parents."

"Similarly we accept the fact that we have Eustaces and we cannot conceive being without them."

The Commandant thought it over, said to the right-hand officer, "This smacks of mutual parasitism. It would be interesting to learn what benefit they derive from each other."

Leeming chipped in with, "I can't tell you what my Eustace gets out of me. I can't tell you because I don't know."

"You expect me to believe that?" asked the Commandant, making like nobody's fool. He showed his teeth. "On your own evidence you can talk with him. *Why have you never asked him?*"

"We got tired of asking long, long ago. The subject has been dropped and the situation accepted."

"Why?"

"The answer was always the same. Eustaces readily admit that we are essential to their existence but cannot explain how because there's no way of making us understand."

"That could be a self-preservative evasion," the Commandant offered. "They won't tell you because they don't *want* you to know."

"Well, what do you suggest we do about it?"

Evading that one, the Commandant went on, "What benefit do *you* get out of the association? What good is your Eustace to you?"

"He provides company, comfort, information, advice and—"

"And what?"

Bending forward, hands on knees, Leeming practically spat it at him. "If necessary, vengeance!"

That shook them. The Commandant rocked back. The under-officers registered disciplined apprehension. It's a hell of a war when one can be chopped down by a ghost.

Pulling himself together, the Commandant forced a grim smile into his face. "You're a prisoner. You've been here a good many days. Your Eustace doesn't seem to have done much about it.''

''That's what you think. He's been doing plenty. And he'll do plenty more, in his own time, in his own way.''

''Such as what?''

''Wait and see,'' Leeming advised, formidably confident.

That did not fill them with delight, either.

''Nobody can imprison more than half a Terran,'' he went on. ''The tangible half. The other half cannot be pinned down by any method whatsoever. It is beyond control. It wanders loose collecting information of military value, indulging in a little sabotage, doing just as it pleases. You've created that situation and you're stuck with it.''

''Not if we kill you,'' said the Commandant, in nasty tones.

Leeming gave a hearty laugh. ''That would make matters fifty times worse.''

''In what way?''

''The life span of a Eustace is longer than that of a Terran. When a man dies his Eustace takes five to ten years to disappear. We have an ancient song to the effect that old Eustaces never die, they only fade away. Our world holds thousands of lonely, disconnected Eustaces gradually fading.''

''What of it?''

''Kill me and you'll isolate my Eustace on a hostile world with no man or other Eustace for company. His days are numbered and he knows it. He has nothing to lose, he is no longer restricted by considerations of my safety. He can eliminate me from his plans because I've gone for keeps.'' He eyed the listeners as he finished. ''He'll run amok, indulging an orgy of destruction. Remember, you're an alien life form to him. He has no feelings and no compunctions with regard to you.''

The Commandant reflected in silence. It was difficult to believe all this. But before space-conquest it had been even more difficult to believe things now accepted as commonplace. He could not dismiss it as nonsense. The stupid believe things because they are credulous. The intelligent do not blindly accept but, when aware of their own ignorance, neither do they reject. Right now the Commandant was acutely aware of general ignorance concerning this life form known as Terran.

''All this is not impossible,'' he said after a while, ''but it appears to me somewhat improbable. There are twenty-seven life forms in alliance with us. I do not know of one that exists in natural copartnership with another form.''

''The Lathians do,'' Leeming told him, nonchalantly mentioning the leaders of the foe, the chief source of the opposition.

''You mean they have Eustaces, too?'' The Commandant looked startled.

''No. Each Lathian is unconsciously controlled by a thing that calls itself Willy something-or-other. They don't know it and we wouldn't know it except that our Eustaces told us.''

"And how did they learn it?"

"As you know, the biggest battles so far have been fought in the Lathian sector. Both sides have taken prisoners. Our Eustaces told us that each Lathian prisoner had a controlling Willy but was unaware of it." He grinned, added, "And a Eustace doesn't think much of a Willy. Apparently a Willy is a lower form of associated life."

The Commandant frowned, said, "This is something definite, something we should be able to check. But how're we going to do it if Lathian allies themselves are ignorant of the real state of affairs?"

"Easy as pie," Leeming offered. "They're holding a bunch of Terran prisoners. Get someone to ask those prisoners whether the Lathians have got the Willies."

"We'll do just that," approved the Commandant, in the manner of one about to call a bluff. He turned to the right-hand officer. "Bamashim, go beam a signal to our chief liaison officer at Lathian H.Q., and get him to question those prisoners."

"You can check further still," Leeming interjected, "just to make doubly sure. To us, anyone who shares his life with an invisible being is known as a Nut. Ask the prisoners whether the Lathians are all Nuts."

"Take note of that and have it asked as well," the Commandant ordered the officer. He returned attention to Leeming. "Since you could not anticipate your forced landing and capture, and since you've been closely confined, there is no possibility of collusion between you and Terran prisoners far away."

"That's right," Leeming agreed.

"Therefore I shall weigh your evidence in the light of what replies come to my signal." He stared hard at the other. "If those replies fail to confirm your statements, I will know that you are a liar in some respects and probably a liar in all respects. Here, we have special and very effective methods of dealing with liars."

"That's to be expected. But if the replies do confirm me, you'll know I've told the truth, won't you?"

"No," snapped the Commandant.

It was Leeming's turn to be shocked. "Why not?"

Thinning his lips, the Commandant said, "Because I know full well that there cannot have been direct communication between you and the other Terran prisoners. However, that means nothing. There may have been collusion between your Eustace and their Eustaces."

Then he bent sidewise, jerked open a drawer, placed a loop assembly on the desk. Then another and another. A bunch of them.

"Well," he invited, "what have you to say to that?"

Leeming beat his brains around fast. He could see what the other meant. He could talk to his Eustace. His Eustace could talk to other Eustaces. The other Eustaces could talk to their imprisoned partners.

Get yourself out of that!

Eric Frank Russell

They were waiting for him, watching his face, counting the seconds needed to produce an answer. The longer he took to find one the weaker it would be. The quicker he came up with something good the more plausible its effect.

He was inwardly frantic by the time he saw an opening and grabbed at it.

"You're wrong on two counts."

"State them."

"Firstly, one Eustace cannot communicate unaided with another over a distance so enormous. His mind won't reach that far. To do it he has to use a Terran who, in his turn, must have radio equipment available."

"We've only your word for it," the Commandant pointed out. "If a Eustace can communicate without limit, it would be your policy to try to conceal the fact."

"I can do no more than give you my word regardless of whether or not you credit it."

"I do not credit it—yet. Proceed to your second count. It had better be convincing."

"It is," Leeming assured. "On this one we don't have my word for it. We have yours."

"Nonsense!" exclaimed the Commandant. "I have made no statements concerning Eustaces."

"On the contrary, you have said that there could be collusion between them."

"What of it?"

"There can be collusion only if Eustaces genuinely exist, in which case my evidence is true. But if my evidence is false, then Eustaces do not exist and there cannot possibly be a conspiracy between nonexistent things."

The Commandant sat perfectly still while his face took on a faint shade of purple. He looked and felt like the trapper trapped. Left-hand officer wore the expression of one struggling hard to suppress a disrespectful snicker.

"If," continued Leeming, piling it on for good measure, "you don't believe in Eustaces then you cannot logically believe in conspiracy between them. Contrariwise, if you believe in the possibility of collusion then you've got to believe in Eustaces. That is, of course, if you're in bright green britches and your right mind."

"Guard!" roared the Commandant. He pointed an angry finger. "Take him back to the cell." They were hustling the prisoner through the door when he changed tactics and bawled, "Halt!" He snatched up a loop assembly, gesticulated with it at Leeming. "Where did you get the material to manufacture this?"

"Eustace brought it for me. Who else?"

"Get out of my sight!"

"*Merse, faplap!*" urged the guards, prodding with their guns. "*Amash! Amash!*"

He spent the rest of that day and all the next one sitting or lying on the bench reviewing what had happened, planning his next moves and, in lighter moments, admiring his own ability as a whacking great liar.

Now and again he wondered how his efforts to dig himself free with his tongue compared with Rigellian attempts to do it with bare hands. Who was making the most progress and—of the greatest importance—who, once out, would stay out? One thing was certain: his method was less tiring to the body though more exhausting to the nerves.

Another advantage was that for the time being he had sidetracked their intention of squeezing him for military information. Or had he? Possibly from their viewpoint his revelations concerning the dual nature of Terrans were infinitely more important than details of armaments, which data might be false anyway. Nevertheless he had dodged what otherwise might have been a rough and painful interrogation.

Next time the spyhole opened he got down on his knees and said in very loud tones, "Thank you, Eustace! Oh, thank you!" and left the jumpy Marsin to wonder who had arrived at the crossroads in time for some of Eustace's dirty work.

Near midnight, just before sleep came on, it occurred to him that there was no point in doing things by halves. Why rest content to smile knowingly whenever the enemy suffered a petty misfortune?

He could extend it farther than that. No form of life was secure from the vagaries of chance. Good fortune came along as well as bad. There was no reason why Eustace should not get credit for both, no reason why he, Leeming, should not take to himself the implied power to reward as well as to punish.

That wasn't the limit, either. Bad luck and good luck are positive phases. He could cross the neutral zone and confiscate the negative phases. Through Eustace he could assign to himself not only the credit for things done, good or bad, but also for things *not* done. He could exploit not only the things that happened but also those that did not happen.

The itch to make a start right now was irresistible. Rolling off the bench, he belted the door from top to bottom. The guard had just been changed, for the eye that peered in was that of Kolum, a character who had bestowed a kick in the ribs not so long ago. Kolum was a cut above Marsin, being able to count upon all twelve fingers if given time to concentrate.

"So it's you," said Leeming, showing vast relief. "I begged him to lay off you, to leave you alone at least a little while. He is impetuous and much too drastic. I can see you are more intelligent than the others and, therefore, able to change for the better. Nobody with brains is beyond hope."

"Huh?" said Kolum, half scared, half flattered.

"So he's left you alone," Leeming pointed out. "He's done nothing to you—yet." He increased the gratification. "I do hope I can continue to control him. Only the stupidly brutal deserve slow death."

"That is true," agreed Kolum, eagerly. "But what—?"

"Now," continued Leeming with firmness, "it is up to you to prove that my confidence is justified. All I want you to do is give a message to the Commandant."

Eric Frank Russell

"I dare not disturb him at this hour. It is impossible. The sergeant of the guard will not permit it. He will—"

"It is to be given to him personally when he awakes first thing in the morning."

"That is different," said Kolum, sweating slightly. "But if the Commandant disapproves of the message he will punish you and not me."

"Write," ordered Leeming.

Kolum leaned his gun against the opposite wall, dug pencil and paper out of a pocket.

"To the Most Exalted Lousy Screw," began Leeming.

"What does 'lousy screw' mean?" asked Kolum, struggling with the two Terran words.

"It's a title. It means 'your highness.' Boy, how high he is!" Leeming pinched his nose while the other pored over the paper. He continued to dictate. "The food is very poor and insufficient. I have lost much weight and my ribs are beginning to show. My Eustace does not like it. I cannot be held responsible for his actions. Therefore I beg Your Most Exalted Lousy Screwship to give serious consideration to this matter."

"There are many words," complained Kolum, martyred, "and I shall have to rewrite them more readably when I go off duty."

"I know. And I appreciate the trouble you're taking on my behalf." Leeming gave him a look of fraternal fondness. "That's why I feel sure that you'll live long enough to do it."

"I must live longer than that," insisted Kolum, bugging his eyes. "I have the right to live, haven't I?"

"That's exactly my own argument," said Leeming, in the manner of one who has striven all night to establish the irrefutable but cannot yet guarantee success.

He returned to the bench. The light went off, the spyhole shut. Four stars peeped through the window slot—and they were not unattainable.

In the morning breakfast came half an hour late but consisted of one full bowl of lukewarm pap, two thick slices of brown bread heavily smeared with grease, and a large cup of stuff vaguely resembling paralyzed coffee. He ate the lot with mounting triumph.

No interview that day or the next. No summons for a week. Evidently His Lousy Screwship was still awaiting a reply from the Lathian sector and didn't feel inclined to make another move before he got it. However, meals remained more substantial, a fact that Leeming viewed as positive evidence that someone was insuring himself against disaster.

Then one morning the Rigellians acted up. From the cell they could be heard but not seen. Every day at an hour after dawn the tramp of their two thousand pairs of feet sounded somewhere out of sight and died away toward the workshops.

This morning they came out singing, their voices holding a touch of defiance. Something about Asta Zangasta's a dirty old man, got fleas on his chest and sores on his pan. Guards yelled at them. Singing rose higher, the defiance increased. Leeming got below the window, listened intently, wondered who the blazes was this much-abused Asta Zangasta. Probably the local life form's largest cheese, the big boss of this world.

The bawling of two thousand voices rose crescendo. Guards shouted frenziedly and were drowned out. A warning shot was fired. Guards in the watchtowers edged their guns around.

Next came the sound of blows, shots, scuffling sounds, yells of fury. A bunch of twenty guards raced flat-footed past Leeming's window, heading for the fracas. The uproar continued for twenty minutes, died away. Resulting silence could almost be felt.

Exercise time, Leeming had the yard to himself. Not a soul there. He mooched around gloomily, found Marsin on yard patrol.

"What's happened?"

"They misbehaved. They are being kept in the workshops to make up loss of production. It is their own fault. They started work late to slow down output. We didn't even have time to count them."

Leeming grinned in his face. "And some guards were hurt. Not severely. Just enough to give them a taste of what's to come. Think it over."

"Eh?"

"But *you* were not hurt. Think that over, too!"

He ambled off, leaving Marsin bewildered. Then a thought struck him. "*We had not time even to count them.*" He returned, said, "Tomorrow some of you will wish you'd never been born."

"You are threatening us?"

"No—I'm making a promise. Tell your officer. Tell the Commandant. It will help you escape the consequences."

"I will tell them," said Marsin, relieved and grateful.

His guess was dead on the beam. The Rigellians were too shrewd to invite thick ears and black eyes without good reason. It took the foe a full day to arrive at the same conclusion.

One hour after dawn the Rigellians were marched out dormitory by dormitory, in batches of fifty instead of the usual steady stream. They were counted in fifties, the easy way. This simple arithmetic got thrown out of kilter when one dormitory gave up only twelve prisoners, all of them sick, weak, wounded or otherwise handicapped.

Infuriated guards rushed indoors to drag out the nonattending thirty-eight. They weren't there. The door was firm and solid, the window bars intact. It took considerable

Eric Frank Russell

galumphing around to detect a hollow spot in the floor, and under that a deep shaft from which ran a tunnel. The said tunnel was empty.

Sirens wailed, guards pounded all over the shop, officers shouted, the entire place began to resemble a madhouse. The Rigellians got it good and hard for spoiling the previous morning's count and thus giving the escapees an extra day's lead. Boots and gun butts were freely used, bodies dragged aside unconscious.

The surviving top-ranker of the offending dormitory, a lieutenant with a bad limp, was put against a wall and shot. Leeming could see nothing but heard the hoarse commands of, "Present . . . aim . . . fire!" and the following volley.

He prowled round and round his cell, clenching and unclenching his fists, swearing mightily to himself. The spyhole opened but hastily shut before he could spit right in somebody's eye.

The upset continued as inflamed guards searched all dormitories one by one, tested doors, bars, floors and walls. Officers screamed threats at groups of Rigellians who were slow to respond to orders.

At twilight outside forces brought in seven tired, bedraggled escapees caught on the run. "Present . . . aim . . . fire!" Leeming battered his door but the spyhole remained shut and none answered. Two hours later he'd made another coiled loop with the last of his wire. He spent half the night talking into it, menacingly, at the top of his voice. Nobody took the slightest notice.

A feeling of deep frustration had come over him by noon next day. He estimated that the Rigellian escape must have taken at least a year to prepare. Result: eight dead, thirty-one still loose but planet-bound and probably fated to ultimate recapture, most of two thousand getting it rough in consequence, his own efforts balled up. He did not resent the break, not one little bit. Good luck to them. But if only it had occurred a couple of months earlier or later.

Immediately after dinner four guards came for him. "The Commandant wants you at once." Their manner was surly, somewhat on edge. One wore a narrow bandage around his scaly pate, another had a badly swollen eye.

Just about the worst moment to choose, thought Leeming, gloomily. The Commandant would be in the mood to go up like a rocket. You cannot reason with a person who is in a purple rage. Emotion comes uppermost, words are disregarded, arguments are dismissed. He was going to have a tough job on his hands.

As before, the Commandant sat behind his desk but there were no accompanying officers. At his side posed an elderly civilian. The latter studied the prisoner curiously as he entered and took a seat.

"This is Pallam," introduced the Commandant, displaying unexpected amiability that dumfounded the hearer. "He has been sent along by no less a person than Zangasta himself."

"A mental specialist?" guessed Leeming, frowning at the oldster.

"Nothing like that," assured Pallam quietly. "I am particularly interested in all aspects of symbiosis."

Leeming's back hairs stirred. He didn't like the idea of being cross-examined by an expert. They had unmilitary minds and a pernicious habit of digging up contradictions in a story.

"Pallam wishes to ask you a few questions," informed the Commandant. "But those will come later." He leaned back, put on a self-satisfied expression. "For a start, let me say that I am indebted to you for the information you gave me last time you were here."

"You mean it has proved useful to you?" inquired Leeming, hardly believing his ears.

"Very much so. The guards responsible for Dormitory Fourteen are to be drafted to the battle areas where they will be stationed at space-ports liable to attack. That is their punishment for gross neglect of duty." He gazed thoughtfully at the other, went on, "The big escape would have made that my fate also had not Zangasta considered it a minor matter when compared with what I have discovered through you."

"But when I asked, you saw to it that I had better food. Surely you expected some reward?"

"Eh?" The Commandant registered surprise followed by slow understanding. "I did not think of that."

"So much the better," said Leeming, with hearty approval. "A good deed is doubly good when done with no ulterior motive. Eustace will take note of that."

"You mean," put in Pallam, "that his code of ethics is identical with your own?"

Why did that fellow have to put his spoke in? Be careful now!

"Similar in some respects but not identical."

"What is the most outstanding difference?"

"Well," said Leeming, playing for time, "it's hard to decide." He rubbed his brow while his mind whizzed dizzily. "I'd say in the matter of vengeance."

"Define the difference," invited Pallam, sniffing along the trail like a bloodhound.

"From my viewpoint," said Leeming, carefully, "he is unnecessarily sadistic."

There, that gave the needed coverage for any widespread claims it might be desirable to make later.

"In what way?" Pallam persisted.

"My instinct is to take prompt action, get things over and done with. His tendency is to prolong the agony."

"Explain further," pressed Pallam, making a thorough nuisance of himself.

"If you and I were deadly enemies, and I had a gun, I would shoot you and kill you. But if Eustace had you marked for death he'd make it slower, more gradual."

"Describe his method."

Eric Frank Russell

"First, he'd make you know that you were marked. Then he'd do nothing until at last you got the notion that nothing ever would be done. Then he'd remind you with a minor blow. When resulting alarm had worn off he'd strike a harder one. And so on and so on, with increasing intensity spread if necessary over months and years. That would continue until your doom became plain and too much to bear any longer." He thought again, added, "No Eustace has ever killed anyone. If anyone dies because of him, it is by his own hand."

"He drives a victim to suicide?"

"Yes."

"And there is no way of avoiding such a fate?"

"Yes there is," Leeming contradicted. "At any time the victim can gain freedom from fear by redressing the wrong he has done to that Eustace's partner."

"Such redress immediately terminates the vendetta?" pursued Pallam.

"That's right."

"Whether or not you approve personally?"

"Yes. If my grievance ceases to be real and becomes only imaginary, my Eustace refuses to recognize it or do anything about it."

"So what it boils down to," said Pallam, pointedly, "is that his method provides motive and opportunity for repentance while yours does not?"

"I suppose so."

"Which means that he has a more balanced sense of justice?"

"He can be darned ruthless," said Leeming, momentarily unable to think of anything less feeble.

"That is beside the point." Pallam lapsed into meditative silence, then remarked to the Commandant, "It seems that the association is not between equals. The invisible component is also the superior one."

Cunning old hog, Leeming thought to himself. But if he was trying to tempt the prisoner into a heated denial he was going to be disappointed.

So he sat and said nothing but carefully wore the look of one whose status has been accurately weighed in the balance and found wanting. Come to that, there's no shame in being defined as inferior to one's own mind.

Pallam took on an expression of sharpness as he continued, "I assume that when your Eustace takes upon himself the responsibility for wreaking vengeance he does so because circumstances prevent punishment being administered either by yourself or the community?"

"That's pretty well correct," admitted Leeming, warily.

"In other words, he functions only when both you and the law are impotent?"

"He takes over when need arises," informed Leeming, striving to give the point some ambiguity.

"That is substantially what I said," declared Pallam, a little coldly. He bent forward, watched the other keen-eyed, and managed to make his attitude intimidating.

"Now let us suppose your Eustace finds excellent reason to punish another Terran. *What does the victim's Eustace do about it?*"

Leeming's mouth opened and the words, "Not much," popped out of their own accord. For a mad moment he felt that Eustace had actually arrived and joined the party.

"Why not?"

"I have told you before and I am telling you again that no Eustace will concern himself for one moment with an imaginary grievance. A guilty Terran has no genuine cause for complaint. He brought vengeance on himself and the cure lies in his own hands. If he doesn't enjoy suffering, he need only get busy and undo whatever wrong he has done."

"Will his Eustace urge him or influence him to take action necessary to avoid punishment?"

"Never having been a victim myself," said Leeming, fairly oozing virtue, "I am unable to tell you. I suppose it would be near the truth to say that Terrans behave because association with Eustaces makes them behave. They've little choice about the matter."

"All that is acceptable," conceded Pallam, "because it is consistent—as far as it goes."

"What d'you mean?"

"Let's take it to the bitter end. I do not see any rational reason why any victim's Eustace should allow his partner to be driven to suicide. It is contrary to the basic law of survival."

"Nobody commits suicide until after he's gone off his rocker."

"What of it?"

"An insane person is of no avail to any Eustace. To a Eustace, he's already dead, no longer worth defending or protecting. Eustaces associate only with the sane."

Pouncing on that, Pallam exclaimed, "So the benefit they derive is rooted somewhere in Terran minds, it is a mental sustenance?"

"I don't know "

"Does your Eustace ever make you feel tired, exhausted, perhaps a little stupefied?"

"Yes," said Leeming. And how, brother! Right now he could choke Eustace to death.

"I would much like to continue this for months," Pallam observed to the Commandant. "It is an absorbing subject. There are no records of symbiotic association in anything higher than plants and six species of the lower *elames*. To find it among sentient forms, and one of them intangible, is remarkable, truly remarkable!"

The Commandant looked awed.

"Give him your report," urged Pallam.

"Our liaison officer, Colonel Shomuth, has replied from the Lathian sector," the

Commandant told Leeming. "He is fluent in Cosmoglotta and, therefore, was able to question many Terran prisoners. We sent him a little more information and the result is significant."

"What else did you expect?" asked Leeming.

Ignoring that, the Commandant went on, "He said that most of the prisoners refused to make comment or admit anything. That is understandable. Nothing could shake their belief that they were being tempted to surrender information of military value. So they remained silent." He glanced at his listener. "But some talked."

"There are always a few willing to blab," remarked Leeming, looking resigned.

"Certain officers talked, including Cruiser Captain Tompass . . . Tompus—"

"Thomas?"

"Yes, that's the word." Turning round in his chair, the Commandant pressed a wall switch. "This is the beamed interview, unscrambled and recorded on tape."

A crackling hiss poured out of a perforated grid in the wall. It grew louder, died down to a background wash. Voices came out of the grid.

Shomuth: "Captain Thomas, I have been ordered to check certain information already in our possession. You have nothing to lose by giving answers, nothing to gain by refusing them. There are no Lathians present, only the two of us. You may speak freely and what you say will be treated in confidence."

Thomas: "What d'you want to know?"

Shomuth: "Whether our Lathian allies really are Nuts."

Thomas, after a pause: "You want the blunt truth?"

Shomuth: "We do."

Thomas: "All right, they are nuts."

Shomuth: "And they have the Willies?"

Thomas: "Where did you dig up this information?"

Shomuth: "That's our business. Please answer the question."

Thomas, belligerently: "Not only have they got the willies but they'll have a darned sight more of them before we're through."

Shomuth, puzzled: "How can that be? We have learned that each Lathian is unconsciously controlled by a Willy. Therefore the total number of Willies is limited. It cannot be increased except by birth of more Lathians."

Thomas, quickly: "You got me wrong. What I meant was that as Lathian casualties mount up the number of loose Willies will increase. There will be lots more of them in proportion to the number of Lathian survivors."

Shomuth: "Yes, I see what you mean. And it will create a psychic problem." Pause. "Now, Captain Thomas, have you any reason to suppose that many unattached Willies might be able to seize control of another and different life form? Such as my own species, for example?"

Thomas, with enough menace to deserve a space medal: "I wouldn't be surprised."

Shomuth: "You don't know for sure?"

Thomas: "No."

Shomuth: "It is true, is it not, that you are aware of the real Lathian nature only because you have been informed of it by your Eustace?"

Thomas, startled: "My *what?*"

Shomuth: "Your *Eustace*. Why should that surprise you?"

Thomas, recovering swiftly enough to earn a bar to the medal: "I thought you said Useless. Ha-ha! Silly of me. Yes, my Eustace. You're dead right there."

Shomuth, in lower tones: "There are four hundred twenty Terran prisoners here. That means four hundred twenty Eustaces wandering loose on this planet. Correct?"

Thomas: "I am unable to deny it."

Shomuth: "The Lathian heavy cruiser *Veder* crashed on landing and was a total loss. The Lathians attributed it to an error of judgment on the part of the crew. But that was just three days after you prisoners were brought here. Was it a mere coincidence?"

Thomas, oh, good, but good: "Work it out for yourself."

Shomuth: "All right. Here's something else. The biggest fuel dump in this part of the galaxy is located sixty miles south of here. A week ago it blew up to total destruction. The loss was very severe and will handicap our allied fleets for some time to come. Technicians theorize that a static spark caused one tank to explode and that set off the rest. We can always trust technicians to come up with a plausible explanation."

Thomas: "Well, what's wrong with it?"

Shomuth: "That dump has been there more than four years. There's been no static sparks during that time."

Thomas: "What are you getting at?"

Shomuth, pointedly: "You have admitted yourself that there are four hundred and twenty Eustaces free to do as they like."

Thomas, in tones of stern patriotism: "I am admitting nothing. I refuse to answer any more questions."

Shomuth: "Has your Eustace prompted you to say that?"

Silence.

Reversing the switch, the Commandant said, "There you are. Eight other Terran officers gave more or less the same evidence. Zangasta himself has listened to the records and is deeply concerned about the situation."

"Tell him he needn't bother nursing his pate," Leeming airily suggested. "It's all a lot of bunk, a put-up job. There was collusion between my Eustace and theirs."

Turning a faint purple, the Commandant retorted, "As you emphasized at our last meeting, there cannot be collusion without Eustaces. So it makes no difference either way."

Eric Frank Russell

"I'm glad you can see it at last."

"Let it pass," chipped in Pallam, impatiently. "It is of no consequence. The confirmatory evidence is adequate no matter how we look at it."

Thus prompted, the Commandant continued, "I have been doing some investigating myself. Eight of my guards earned your enmity by assaulting you. Of these, four are now in hospital badly injured, two more are to be drafted to the fighting front."

"The other two," said Leeming, "gained forgiveness. Nothing has happened to them."

"No. Nothing has happened."

"I cannot give the same guarantee with respect to the firing squad, the officer in charge of it, or the higher-up who issued the order that helpless prisoners be shot. It all depends on how my Eustace feels about it."

"Why should he care?" put in Pallam. "They were only Rigellians."

"They were allies. And allies are friends. I feel bad about the needless slaughtering of them. Eustace is sensitive to my emotions."

"But not necessarily obedient to them?"

"No."

"In fact," pressed Pallam, "if there is any question of one serving the other, it is *you* who obeys *him?*"

"Most times, anyway."

"Well, it confirms what you've already told us." He ventured a thin smile. "The chief difference between Terrans and Lathians is that you know you're controlled whereas the Lathians are ignorant of it."

"We are not controlled consciously or unconsciously," Leeming insisted. "We exist in mutual partnership, same as you do with your wife. It's mastery by neither party."

"I wouldn't know, never having been mated," said Pallam. He transferred his attention to one side. "Carry on, Commandant."

"You may as well be told that this has been set aside as a penal planet," informed the Commandant. "We are already holding a large number of prisoners, mostly Rigellians."

"What of it?" Leeming prompted.

"There are more to come. Two thousand Centaurians and six hundred Thetans are due to arrive and fill a new jail next week. Our allied forces will transfer more Federation life forms as soon as ships are available." He eyed the other speculatively. "It's only a matter of time before they start dumping Terrans upon us as well."

"Is it bothering you?"

"Zangasta has decided not to accept Terrans."

"That's up to him," said Leeming, blandly indifferent.

"Zangasta has a clever mind," the Commandant opined. "He is of the firm opinion that to assemble a formidable army of prisoners all on one planet, and then put some thousands of Terrans among them, is to create a potentially dangerous situation. He foresees trouble on a vaster scale than we could handle. Indeed, we might lose this world, strategically placed in the rear, and become subject to the violent attacks of our own allies.''

"That's the angle he puts out for publication. He's got a private one too."

"Eh?"

Looking grim, Leeming continued, "Zangasta himself first gave orders that escaped prisoners were to be shot immediately after recapture. He must have done, otherwise nobody would dare shoot them. Now he's jumpy because of one Eustace. He thinks a few thousand Eustaces will be a greater menace to him. But he's wrong."

"Why is he wrong?" inquired the Commandant.

"Because it isn't only the repentant who have no cause to fear. The dead haven't either. He'd better countermand that order if he wants to keep on living."

"I shall inform him of your remarks. However, such cancellation of orders may not be necessary. As I have told you, he is clever. He has devised a subtle strategy that will put all your evidence to the final, conclusive test and at the same time may solve his problems."

Feeling vague alarm, Leeming asked, "Am I permitted to know what he intends to do?"

"He has given instructions that you be told. And he has started doing it." The Commandant waited for the sake of extra effect. "He has beamed the Federation a proposal to exchange prisoners."

Leeming fidgeted around in his seat. Holy smoke, the plot was thickening with a vengeance. His sole purpose from the beginning had been to talk himself out of jail and into some other situation from which he could scoot at top speed. Now they were taking up his story and plastering it all over the galaxy. Oh, what a tangled web we weave when first we practice to deceive.

"What's more," the Commandant went on, "the Federation has accepted providing only that we exchange rank for rank. That is to say, captains for captains, navigators for navigators and so forth."

"That's reasonable."

"Zangasta," said the Commandant, grinning like a wolf, "has agreed in his turn—providing that the Federation accepts all Terran prisoners first and makes exchange on a basis of two for one. He is now awaiting their reply."

"Two for one?" echoed Leeming. "You want them to surrender two prisoners for one Terran?"

"No, of course not." Leaning forward, he increased the grin and showed the roots of his teeth. "Two of ours for one Terran and his Eustace. That's fair enough, isn't it?"

"It's not for me to say. The Federation is the judge." Leeming swallowed hard.

Eric Frank Russell

"Until a reply arrives and the matter is settled, Zangasta wishes you to have better treatment. You will be transferred to the officers' quarters outside the walls and you will share their meals. Temporarily you'll be treated as a noncombatant and you'll be very comfortable. It is necessary that you give me your parole not to escape."

Ye gods, that was another stinker. The entire fiction was shaped toward ultimate escape. He couldn't abandon it now. Neither was he willing to give his word of honor with the cynical intention of breaking it.

"Parole refused," he said, firmly.

The Commandant registered incredulity. "You are not serious?"

"I am. I've no choice. Terran military law doesn't allow a prisoner to give such a promise."

"Why not?"

"Because no Terran can accept responsibility for his Eustace. How can we swear not to get out when all the time we're already half out?"

"Guard!" called the Commandant, visibly disappointed.

He mooched uneasily around the cell for a full week, occasionally chatting with Eustace night-times for the benefit of ears outside the door. The food remained better. The guards treated him with diffidence. Four more recaptured Rigellians were brought back but not shot. All the signs and portents were that he'd still got a grip on the foe.

Nevertheless, he was badly bothered. The Federation in general and Earth in particular knew nothing whatsoever about Eustaces and therefore were likely to view a two-for-one proposition with the contempt it deserved. A blank refusal on their part might cause him to be plied with awkward questions impossible to answer.

Sooner or later it would occur to them that they were afflicted with the biggest liar in cosmic history. They'd then devise tests of fiendish ingenuity. When he flunked them, the balloon would go up.

He wasn't inclined to give himself overmuch credit for kidding them along so far. The books he'd been reading had shown that the local religion was based upon reverence for ancestral spirits. They were also familiar with what is known as poltergeist phenomena. The ground had been prepared for him in advance. He'd merely ploughed it and sown the crop. When a victim believes in two kinds of invisible beings it isn't too hard to make him swallow a third.

But when the Federation beamed a curt invitation to go jump, it was possible that the third type would be regurgitated with violence. Unless by fast talk he could cram it back down their gullets when it was already halfway out. How to do that?

He was still stewing it over and over when they came for him again. The Commandant was there but Pallam was not. Instead, a dozen civilians eyed him curiously. That made a total of thirteen, a very suitable number to pronounce him ready for the chopper.

Feeling as much the center of attention as a six-tailed wombat at the zoo, he sat down and four civilians started chivvying him at once, taking it in relays. They were interested in only one subject, namely, bopamagilvies. It seemed they'd been playing with them for hours and achieved nothing except some practice at acting daft.

On what principle did they work? Did they focus mental output into a narrow beam? At what distance did his Eustace get beyond straight conversation and need to be called with a loop? Why was it necessary to make directional search before getting a reply? How did he know how to make a loop in the first place?

"I can't explain. How does a bird know how to make a nest? The knowledge seems instinctive. I've known how to call Eustace ever since I was old enough to shape a piece of wire."

"Will any kind of wire do?"

"So long as it's nonferrous."

"Are all Terran loops of exactly the same construction and dimensions?"

"No. They vary with the individual."

Somehow he beat them off, feeling hot in the forehead and cold in the belly. Then the Commandant took over.

"The Federation has refused to accept Terran prisoners ahead of other species, or to exchange them two for one, or to discuss the matter any further. They accuse Zangasta of bad faith. What have you to say to that?"

Steeling himself, Leeming commented, "On your side there are twenty-seven life forms of which the Lathians and the Zebs are by far the most powerful. Now if the Federation wanted to give priority of exchange to one species, do you think the others would agree? If the favored species happened to be the Tansites, would the Lathians and Zebs vote for them to head the line-up?"

A civilian chipped in, a tall, authoritative specimen. "I am Daverd, personal aide to Zangasta. He is of your own opinion. He believes the Terrans have been outvoted. Therefore I am commanded to ask you one question."

"What is it?"

"Do your Federation allies know about your Eustaces?"

"No."

"You have succeeded in hiding the facts from them?"

"There's no question of hiding facts. With friends the facts just don't become apparent. Eustaces take action only against enemies and that's something that can't be concealed."

"Very well." Daverd came closer while the others looked on. "The Lathians started this war and the Zebs went with them by reason of military alliance. The rest of us got dragged in for one cause or another. The Lathians are powerful. But, as we now know, they're not responsible for their actions."

"What's this to me?"

"Separately, we numerically weaker life forms cannot stand against the Lathians

Eric Frank Russell

or the Zebs. But together we are strong enough to step out of the war and maintain our right to remain neutral. So Zangasta has consulted the others."

Jumping jiminy, what you can do with a few feet of copper wire!

"He has received their replies today," Daverd continued. "They are willing to make a common front and get out of the war providing that the Federation is equally willing to exchange prisoners and recognize neutrality."

"Such sudden unanimity among minors tells me something pretty good," observed Leeming, displaying satisfaction.

"It tells you what?"

"Federation forces have won a major battle lately. Somebody's been scalped."

Daverd refused to confirm or deny it. "At the moment you're the only Terran we hold on this planet. Zangasta thinks you could well be spared."

"Meaning what?"

"He has decided to send you to the Federation. It is your job to persuade them to agree to our plans. If you fail—a couple of hundred thousand hostages may suffer."

"For which the Federation may retaliate."

"They won't know. There'll be no Terrans or Eustaces here to inform them by any underhanded method. We're keeping Terrans out. The Federation cannot use knowledge it doesn't possess."

"No," agreed Leeming. "It's impossible to use what you haven't got."

They provided a light destroyer crewed by ten Zangastans and that took him to a servicing planet right on the fringe of the battle area. It was a Lathian outpost but those worthies showed no interest in what their smaller allies were up to. They got to work relining the destroyer's tubes while Leeming was transferred to a one-man Lathian scoutship. The ten Zangastans officiously saluted before they left him.

From that point he was strictly on his own. Take-off was a heller. The seat was awkwardly shaped and too big, the controls in the wrong places and too far apart. The little ship was fast and powerful but responded differently from his own. How he got up he never knew, but he made it.

After that, there was the constant risk of being tracked by Federation detecting devices and blown apart in full flight.

He arrowed straight for Terra. His sleeps were uneasy and restless. The tubes were not to be trusted despite the fact that flight-duration would be only one-third of that done in his own vessel. The strange autopilot was not to be trusted merely because it was of alien design. The ship itself wasn't to be trusted for the same reason. The forces of his own side were not to be trusted because they'd tend to shoot first and ask questions afterward.

In due time he came in fast on Terra's night side and plonked it down in a field a couple of miles west of the main spaceport.

The moon was shining bright along the Wabash when he approached the front gate afoot and a sentry yelled, "Halt! Who goes there?"

"Lieutenant Leeming and Eustace Phenackertiban."

"Advance and be recognized."

He walked forward, thinking to himself that such an order was somewhat dunderheaded. Be recognized. The sentry had never seen him in his life and wouldn't know him from Myrtle McTurtle.

At the gate a powerful cone of light shot down upon him. Somebody with three chevrons on his sleeve emerged from a nearby hut bearing a scanner on the end of a black cable. The scanner got waved over the arrival from head to feet, concentrating mostly upon the face.

A loud-speaker in the hut said, "Bring him in to Intelligence H.Q."

They started walking.

The sentry let go an agitated yelp of, "Hey, where's the other guy?"

"What guy?" asked the escorting sergeant, looking around.

"He's nuts," Leeming confided.

"You gave me *two* names," asserted the sentry, slightly bellicose.

"Well, if you ask the sergeant nicely he'll give you two more," said Leeming, "Won't you, sarge?"

"Let's get going," suggested the sergeant, showing impatience.

They reached Intelligence H.Q. The duty officer was Colonel Farmer, a florid character Leeming had met many times before. Farmer gazed at him incredulously and said, "Well!" He said it seven times.

Without preamble, Leeming growled, "What's all this about us refusing to make a two-for-one swap for Terran prisoners?"

Farmer started visibly. "You know about it?"

"How could I ask if I didn't?"

"All right. Why should we accept such a cockeyed proposition?"

Bending over the desk, hands splayed upon it, Leeming said, "All we need do is agree—upon one condition."

"What condition?"

"That they make a similar agreement with respect to Lathians. Two Federation prisoners for one Lathian and one Willy."

"One *what?*"

"One Willy. The Lathians will take it like birds. They've been propagandizing all over the shop that one Lathian is worth two of anything else. They're too conceited to refuse such an offer. They'll advertise it as proof that even an enemy knows how good they are."

"But—" began Farmer, a little dazed.

Eric Frank Russell

"Their allies will agree also, but from different motives that don't matter to us anyway. Try it for size. Two Federation prisoners for one Lathian and his Willy."

Farmer protruded his belly and roared, "What the blue blazes is a Willy?"

"You can easily find out," assured Leeming. "Consult your Eustace."

Showing alarm, Farmer lowered his tones to a soothing pitch and said as gently as possible, "You were reported missing and believed killed."

"I crash-landed and got taken prisoner in the back of beyond. They slung me in the jug."

"Yes, yes," said Colonel Farmer, making pacifying gestures. "But how on earth did you get away?"

"Farmer, I cannot tell a lie. I hexed them with my bopamagilvie."

"Huh?"

"So I left by rail," informed Leeming, "and there were ten faplaps carrying it." Catching the other unaware he let go a vicious kick at the desk and made a spurt of ink leap across the blotter.

"Now let's see some of the intelligence they're supposed to have in Intelligence. Beam the offer. Two for a Lathian and a Willy Terwilliger." He stared wildly around. "And find me a bed. I'm dead beat."

Holding himself in enormous restraint, Farmer said, "Lieutenant, do you realize that you are talking to a colonel?"

Leeming used the word. ∎

THE BIG FRONT YARD

Clifford D. Simak

Hiram Taine came awake and sat up in his bed.

Towser was barking and scratching at the floor.

"Shut up," Taine told the dog.

Towser cocked quizzical ears at him and then resumed the barking and scratching at the floor.

Taine rubbed his eyes. He ran a hand through his rat's-nest head of hair. He considered lying down again and pulling up the covers.

But not with Towser barking.

"What's the matter with you, anyhow?" he asked Towser, with not a little wrath.

"*Whuff*," said Towser, industriously proceeding with his scratching at the floor.

"If you want out," said Taine, "all you got to do is open the screen door. You know how it is done. You do it all the time."

Towser quit his barking and sat down heavily, watching his master getting out of bed.

Taine put on his shirt and pulled on his trousers, but didn't bother with his shoes.

Towser ambled over to a corner, put his nose down to the baseboard and snuffled moistly.

"You got a mouse?" asked Taine.

"*Whuff*," said Towser, most emphatically.

"I can't ever remember you making such a row about a mouse," Taine said, slightly puzzled. "You must be off your rocker."

It was a beautiful summer morning. Sunlight was pouring through the open window.

Good day for fishing, Taine told himself, then remembered that there'd be no fishing, for he had to go out and look up that old four-poster maple bed that he had heard about up Woodman way. More than likely, he thought, they'd want twice as much as it was worth. It was getting so, he told himself, that a man couldn't make an honest dollar. Everyone was getting smart about antiques.

He got up off the bed and headed for the living-room.

"Come on," he said to Towser.

Towser came along, pausing now and then to snuffle into corners and to whuffle at the floor.

"You got it bad," said Taine.

Maybe it's a rat, he thought. The house was getting old.

He opened the screen door and Towser went outside.

"Leave that woodchuck be today," Taine advised him. "It's a losing battle. You'll never dig him out."

Towser went around the corner of the house.

Taine noticed that something had happened to the sign that hung on the post beside the driveway. One of the chains had become unhooked and the sign was dangling.

He padded out across the driveway slab and the grass, still wet with dew, to fix the sign. There was nothing wrong with it—just the unhooked chain. Might have been the wind, he thought, or some passing urchin. Although probably not an urchin. He got along with kids. They never bothered him, like they did some others in the village. Banker Stevens, for example. They were always pestering Stevens.

He stood back a way to be sure the sign was straight.

It read, in big letters:

HANDY-MAN

And under that, in smaller lettering:

fix anything

And under that:

ANTIQUES FOR SALE
What have you got to trade?

Maybe, he told himself, he ought to have two signs, one for his fix-it shop and one for antiques and trading. Some day, when he had the time, he thought, he'd paint a couple of new ones, one for each side of the driveway. It would look neat that way.

He turned around and looked across the road at Turner's Woods. It was a pretty sight, he thought. A sizeable piece of woods like that right at the edge of town. It was a place for birds and rabbits and woodchucks and squirrels and it was full of forts built through generations of the boys of Willow Bend.

Some day, of course, some smart operator would buy it up and start a housing development or something equally objectionable and when that happened a big slice of his own boyhood would be cut out of his life.

Towser came around the corner of the house. He was sidling along, sniffing at the lowest row of siding and his ears were cocked with interest.

The Big Front Yard 131

"That dog is nuts," said Taine and went inside.

He went into the kitchen, his bare feet slapping on the floor.

He filled the tea-kettle, set it on the stove and turned the burner on underneath the kettle.

He turned on the radio, forgetting that it was out of kilter.

When it didn't make a sound, he remembered and, disgusted, snapped it off. That was the way it went, he thought. He fixed other people's stuff, but never got around to fixing any of his own.

He went into the bedroom and put on his shoes. He threw the bed together.

Back in the kitchen the stove had failed to work again. The burner beneath the kettle was still cold.

Taine hauled off and kicked the stove. He lifted the kettle and held his palm above the burner. In a few seconds he could detect some heat.

"Worked again," he told himself.

Some day, he knew, kicking the stove would fail to work. When that happened, he'd have to get to work on it. Probably wasn't more than a loose connection.

He put the kettle back on to the stove.

There was a clatter out in front and Taine went out to see what was going on.

Beasly, the Hortons' yardboy-chauffeur-gardener-et cetera, was backing a rickety old truck up the driveway. Beside him sat Abbie Horton, the wife of H. Henry Horton, the village's most important citizen. In the back of the truck, lashed on with ropes and half-protected by a garish red and purple quilt, stood a mammoth television set. Taine recognized it from of old. It was a good ten years out of date and still, by any standard, it was the most expensive set ever to grace any home in Willow Bend.

Abbie hopped out of the truck. She was an energetic, bustling, bossy woman.

"Good morning, Hiram," she said. "Can you fix this set again?"

"Never saw anything that I couldn't fix," said Taine, but nevertheless he eyed the set with something like dismay. It was not the first time he had tangled with it and he knew what was ahead.

"It might cost you more than it's worth," he warned her. "What you really need is a new one. This set is getting old and—"

"That's just what Henry said," Abbie told him, tartly. "Henry wants to get one of the color sets. But I won't part with this one. It's not just TV, you know. It's a combination with radio and a record player and the wood and style are just right for the other furniture, and besides—"

"Yes, I know," said Taine, who'd heard it all before.

Poor old Henry, he thought. What a life the man must lead. Up at that computer plant all day long, shooting off his face and bossing everyone, then coming home to a life of petty tyranny.

"Beasly," said Abbie, in her best drill-sergeant voice, "you get right up there and get that thing untied."

"Yes'm," Beasly said. He was a gangling, loose-jointed man who didn't look too bright.

"And see you be careful with it. I don't want it all scratched up."

"Yes'm," said Beasly.

"I'll help," Taine offered.

The two climbed into the truck and began unlashing the old monstrosity.

"It's heavy," Abbie warned. "You two be careful of it."

"Yes'm," said Beasly.

It was heavy and it was an awkward thing to boot, but Beasly and Taine horsed it around to the back of the house and up the stoop and through the back door and down the basement stairs, with Abbie following eagle-eyed behind them, alert to the slightest scratch.

The basement was Taine's combination workshop and display-room for antiques. One end of it was filled with benches and with tools and machinery, and boxes full of odds and ends and piles of just plain junk were scattered everywhere. The other end housed a collection of rickety chairs, sagging bedposts, ancient highboys, equally ancient lowboys, old coal scuttles painted gold, heavy iron fireplace screens, and a lot of other stuff that he had collected from far and wide for as little as he could possibly pay for it.

He and Beasly set the TV down carefully on the floor. Abbie watched them narrowly from the stairs.

"Why, Hiram," she said, excited, "you put a ceiling in the basement. It looks a whole lot better."

"Huh?" asked Taine.

"The ceiling. I said you put in a ceiling."

Taine jerked his head up and what she said was true. There was a ceiling there, but he'd never put it in.

He gulped a little and lowered his head, then jerked it quickly up and had another look. The ceiling was still there.

"It's not that block stuff," said Abbie with open admiration. "You can't see any joints at all. How did you manage it?"

Taine gulped again and got back his voice. "Something I thought up," he told her weakly.

"You'll have to come over and do it to our basement. Our basement is a sight. Beasly put the ceiling in the amusement-room, but Beasly is all thumbs."

"Yes'm," Beasly said contritely.

"When I get the time," Taine promised, ready to promise anything to get them out of there.

"You'd have a lot more time," Abbie told him acidly, "if you weren't gadding around all over the country buying up that broken-down old furniture that you call antiques. Maybe you can fool the city folks when they come driving out here, but you can't fool me."

"I can make a lot of money out of some of it," Taine told her calmly.

"And lose your shirt on the rest of it," she said.

"I got some old china that is just the kind of stuff you are looking for," said Taine. "Picked it up just a day or two ago. Made a good buy on it. I can let you have it cheap."

"I'm not interested," she said and clamped her mouth tight shut.

She turned around and went back up the stairs.

"She's on the prod today," Beasly said to Taine. "It will be a bad day. It always is when she starts early in the morning."

"Don't pay attention to her," Taine advised.

"I try not to, but it ain't possible. You sure you don't need a man? I'd work for you cheap."

"Sorry, Beasly. Tell you what—come over some night soon and we'll play some checkers."

"I'll do that, Hiram. You're the only one who ever asks me over. All the others ever do is laugh at me or shout.'

Abbie's voice came bellowing down the stairs. "Beasly, are you coming? Don't go standing there all day. I have rugs to beat."

"Yes'm," said Beasly, starting up the stairs.

At the truck, Abbie turned on Taine with determination: "You'll get that set fixed right away? I'm lost without it."

"Immediately," said Taine.

He stood and watched them off, then looked around for Towser, but the dog had disappeared. More than likely he was at the woodchuck hole again, in the woods across the road. Gone off, thought Taine, without his breakfast, too.

The tea-kettle was boiling furiously when Taine got back to the kitchen. He put coffee in the maker and poured in the water. Then he went downstairs.

The ceiling was still there.

He turned on all the lights and walked around the basement staring up at it.

It was a dazzling white material and it appeared to be translucent—up to a point, that is, one could see into it, but one could not see through it. And there were no signs of seams. It was fitted neatly and tightly around the water pipes and the ceiling lights.

Taine stood on a chair and rapped his knuckles against it sharply. It gave out a bell-like sound, almost exactly as if he'd rapped a fingernail against a thinly blown goblet.

He got down off the chair and stood there, shaking his head. The whole thing was beyond him. He had spent part of the evening repairing Banker Stevens's lawn-mower and there'd been no ceiling then.

He rummaged in a box and found a drill. He dug out one of the smaller bits and fitted it in the drill. He plugged in the cord and climbed on the chair again and tried the bit against the ceiling. The whirling steel slid wildly back and forth. It didn't make a scratch. He switched off the drill and looked closely at the ceiling. There was not a mark upon it. He tried again, pressing against the drill with all his strength. The bit went *ping* and the broken end flew across the basement and hit the wall.

Taine stepped down off the chair. He found another bit and fitted it in the drill and went slowly up the stairs, trying to think. But he was too confused to think. That ceiling should not be up there, but there it was. And unless he went stark, staring crazy and forgetful as well, he had not put it there.

In the living-room, he folded back one corner of the worn and faded carpeting and plugged in the drill. He knelt and started drilling in the floor. The bit went smoothly through the old oak flooring, then stopped. He put on more pressure and the drill spun without getting any bite.

And there wasn't supposed to be anything underneath that wood! Nothing to stop a drill. Once through the flooring, it should have dropped into the space between the joists.

Taine disengaged the drill and laid it to one side.

He went into the kitchen and the coffee now was ready. But before he poured it, he pawed through a cabinet drawer and found a pencil flashlight. Back in the living-room he shone the light into the hole that the drill had made.

There was something shiny at the bottom of the hole.

He went back to the kitchen and found some day-old doughnuts and poured a cup of coffee. He sat at the kitchen table, eating doughnuts and wondering what to do.

There didn't appear, for the moment at least, much that he could do. He could putter around all day trying to figure out what had happened to his basement and probably not be any wiser than he was right now.

His money-making Yankee soul rebelled against such a horrid waste of time.

There was, he told himself, that maple four-poster that he should be getting to before some unprincipled city antique dealer should run afoul of it. A piece like that, he figured, if a man had any luck at all, should sell at a right good price. He might turn a handsome profit on it if he only worked it right.

Maybe, he thought, he could turn a trade on it. There was the table model TV set that he traded a pair of ice skates for last winter. Those folks out Woodman way might conceivably be happy to trade the bed for a reconditioned TV set, almost like brand new. After all, they probably weren't using the bed and, he hoped fervently, had no idea of the value of it.

He ate the doughnuts hurriedly and gulped down an extra cup of coffee. He fixed a plate of scraps for Towser and set it outside the door. Then he went down into the basement and got the table TV set and put it in the pick-up truck. As an afterthought, he added a reconditioned shotgun which would be perfectly all right if a man were careful not to use these far-reaching, powerful shells, and a few other odds and ends that might come in handy on a trade.

He got back late, for it had been a busy and quite satisfactory day. Not only did he have the four-poster loaded on the truck, but he had as well a rocking chair, a fire-screen, a bundle of ancient magazines, an old-fashioned barrel churn, a walnut highboy and a Governor Winthrop on which some half-baked, slap-happy decorator had applied a coat of apple-green paint. The television set, the shotgun and five dollars had gone into the trade. And what was better yet, he'd managed it so well that the Woodman family probably was dying of laughter at this very moment about how they'd taken him.

He felt a little ashamed of it—they'd been such friendly people. They had treated him so kindly and had him stay for dinner and had sat and talked with him and shown him about the farm and even asked him to stop by if he went through that way again.

He'd wasted the entire day, he thought, and he rather hated that, but maybe it had been worth it to build up his reputation out that way as the sort of character who had softening of the head and didn't know the value of a dollar. That way, maybe some other day, he could do some more business in the neighborhood.

He heard the television set as he opened the back door, sounding loud and clear, and he went clattering down the basement stairs in something close to a panic. For now that he'd traded off the table model, Abbie's set was the only one downstairs and Abbie's set was broken.

It was Abbie's set, all right. It stood just where he and Beasly had put it down that morning and there was nothing wrong with it—nothing wrong at all. It was even televising color.

Televising color!

He stopped at the bottom of the stairs and leaned against the railing for support. The set kept right on televising color.

Taine stalked the set and walked around behind it.

The back of the cabinet was off, leaning against a bench that stood behind the set, and he could see the innards of it glowing cheerily.

He squatted on the basement floor and squinted at the lighted innards and they seemed a good deal different from the way that they should be. He'd repaired the set many times before and he thought he had a good idea of what the working parts would look like. And now they all seemed different, although just how he couldn't tell.

A heavy step sounded on the stairs and a hearty voice came booming down to him.

"Well, Hiram, I see you got it fixed."

Taine jack-knifed upright and stood there slightly frozen and completely speechless.

Henry Horton stood four-squarely and happily on the stairs, looking very pleased.

"I told Abbie that you wouldn't have it done, but she said for me to come over anyway— Hey, Hiram, it's in color! How did you do it, man?"

Clifford D. Simak

Taine grinned sickly. "I just got fiddling around," he said.

Henry came down the rest of the stairs with a stately step and stood before the set, with his hands behind his back, staring at it fixedly in his best executive manner.

He slowly shook his head. "I never would have thought," he said, "that it was possible."

"Abbie mentioned that you wanted color."

"Well, sure. Of course I did. But not on this old set. I never would have expected to get color on this set. How did you do it, Hiram?"

Taine told the solemn truth. "I can't rightly say," he said.

Henry found a nail keg standing in front of one of the benches and rolled it out in front of the old-fashioned set. He sat down warily and relaxed into solid comfort.

"That's the way it goes," he said. "There are men like you, but not very many of them. Just Yankee tinkerers. You keep messing around with things, trying one thing here and another there and before you know it you come up with something."

He sat on the nail keg, staring at the set.

"It's sure a pretty thing," he said. "It's better than the color they have in Minneapolis. I dropped in at a couple of the places the last time I was there and looked at the color sets. And I tell you honest, Hiram, there wasn't one of them that was as good as this."

Taine wiped his brow with his shirt sleeve. Somehow or other, the basement seemed to be getting warm. He was fine sweat all over.

Henry found a big cigar in one of his pockets and held it out to Taine.

"No, thanks. I never smoke."

"Perhaps you're wise," said Henry. "It's a nasty habit."

He stuck the cigar into his mouth and rolled it east to west.

"Each man to his own," he proclaimed expansively. "When it comes to a thing like this, you're the man to do it. You seem to think in mechanical contraptions and electronic circuits. Me, I don't know a thing about it. Even in the computer game, I still don't know a thing about it; I hire men who do. I can't even saw a board or drive a nail. But I can organize. You remember, Hiram, how everybody snickered when I started up the plant?"

"Well, I guess some of them did, at that."

"You're darn tooting they did. They went around for weeks with their hands up to their faces to hide smart-aleck grins. They said, what does Henry think he's doing, starting up a computer factory out here in the sticks; he doesn't think he can compete with those big companies in the east, does he? And they didn't stop their grinning until I sold a couple of dozen units and had orders for a year or two ahead."

He fished a lighter from his pocket and lit the cigar carefully, never taking his eyes off the television set.

"You got something there," he said, judiciously, "that may be worth a mint of money. Some simple adaptation that will fit on any set. If you can get color on this old wreck, you can get color on any set that's made."

He chuckled moistly around the mouthful of cigar. "If RCA knew what was happening here this minute, they'd go out and cut their throats."

"But I don't know what I did," protested Taine.

"Well, that's all right," said Henry, happily. "I'll take this set up to the plant tomorrow and turn loose some of the boys on it. They'll find out what you have here before they're through with it."

He took the cigar out of his mouth and studied it intently, then popped it back in again.

"As I was saying, Hiram, that's the difference in us. You can do the stuff, but you miss the possibilities. I can't do a thing, but I can organize it once the thing is done. Before we get through with this, you'll be wading in twenty-dollar bills clear up to your knees."

"But I don't have—"

"Don't worry. Just leave it all to me. I've got the plant and whatever money we may need. We'll figure out a split."

"That's fine of you," said Taine mechanically.

"Not at all," Henry insisted, grandly. "It's just my aggressive, grasping sense of profit. I should be ashamed of myself, cutting in on this."

He sat on the keg, smoking and watching the TV perform in exquisite color.

"You know, Hiram," he said, "I've often thought of this, but never got around to doing anything about it. I've got an old computer up at the plant that we will have to junk because it's taking up room that we really need. It's one of our early models, a sort of experimental job that went completely sour. It sure is a screwy thing. No one's ever been able to make much out of it. We tried some approaches that probably were wrong—or maybe they were right, but we didn't know enough to make them quite come off. It's been standing in a corner all these years and I should have junked it long ago. But I sort of hate to do it. I wonder if you might not like it—just to tinker with."

"Well, I don't know," said Taine.

Henry assumed an expansive air. "No obligation, mind you. You may not be able to do a thing with it—I'd frankly be surprised if you could, but there's no harm in trying. Maybe you'll decide to tear it down for the salvage you can get. There are several thousand dollars' worth of equipment in it. Probably you could use most of it one way or another."

"It might be interesting," conceded Taine, but not too enthusiastically.

"Good," said Henry, with an enthusiasm that made up for Taine's lack of it. "I'll have the boys cart it over tomorrow. It's a heavy thing. I'll send along plenty of help to get it unloaded and down into the basement and set up."

Henry stood up carefully and brushed cigar ashes off his lap.

Clifford D. Simak

"I'll have the boys pick up the TV set at the same time," he said. "I'll have to tell Abbie you haven't got it fixed yet. If I ever let it get into the house, the way it's working now, she'd hold on to it."

Henry climbed the stairs heavily and Taine saw him out of the door into the summer night.

Taine stood in the shadow, watching Henry's shadowed figure go across the Widow Taylor's yard to the next street behind his house. He took a deep breath of the fresh night air and shook his head to try to clear his buzzing brain, but the buzzing went right on.

Too much had happened, he told himself. Too much for any single day—first the ceiling and now the TV set. Once he had a good night's sleep he might be in some sort of shape to try to wrestle with it.

Towser came around the corner of the house and limped slowly up the steps to stand beside his master. He was mud up to his ears.

"You had a day of it, I see," said Taine. "And, just like I told you, you didn't get the woodchuck."

"*Woof*," said Towser, sadly.

"You're just like a lot of the rest of us," Taine told him, severely. "Like me and Henry Horton and all the rest of us. You're chasing something and you think you know what you're chasing, but you really don't. And what's even worse, you have no faint idea of why you're chasing it."

Towser thumped a tired tail upon the stoop.

Taine opened the door and stood to one side to let Towser in, then went in himself.

He went through the refrigerator and found part of a roast, a slice or two of luncheon-meat, a dried-out slab of cheese and half a bowl of cooked spaghetti. He made a pot of coffee and shared the food with Towser.

Then Taine went back downstairs and shut off the television set. He found a trouble lamp and plugged it in and poked the light into the innards of the set.

He squatted on the floor, holding the lamp, trying to puzzle out what had been done to the set. It was different, of course, but it was a little hard to figure out in just what ways it was different. Someone had tinkered with the tubes and had them twisted out of shape and there were little white cubes of metal tucked here and there in what seemed to be an entirely haphazard and illogical manner—although, Taine admitted to himself, there probably was no haphazardness. And the circuit, he saw, had been rewired and a good deal of wiring had been added.

But the most puzzling thing about it was that the whole thing seemed to be just jury-rigged—as if someone had done no more than a hurried, patch-up job to get the set back in working order on an emergency and temporary basis.

Someone, he thought!

And who had that someone been?

The Big Front Yard 139

He hunched around and peered into the dark corners of the basement and he felt innumerable and many-legged imaginary insects running on his body.

Someone had taken the back off the cabinet and leaned it against the bench and had left the screws which held the back laid neatly in a row upon the floor. Then they had jury-rigged the set and jury-rigged it far better than it had ever been before.

If this was a jury-job, he wondered, just what kind of job would it have been if they had had the time to do it up in style?

They hadn't had the time, of course. Maybe they had been scared off when he had come home—scared off even before they could get the back on the set again.

He stood up and moved stiffly away.

First the ceiling in the morning—and now, in the evening, Abbie's television set.

And the ceiling, come to think of it, was not a ceiling only. Another liner, if that was the proper term for it, of the same material as the ceiling had been laid beneath the floor, forming a sort of boxed-in area between the joists. He had struck that liner when he had tried to drill into the floor.

And what, he asked himself, if all the house were like that, too?

There was just one answer to it all: *There was something in the house with him!*

Towser had heard that *something* or smelled it or in some other manner sensed it and had dug frantically at the floor in an attempt to dig it out, as if it were a woodchuck.

Except that this, whatever it might be, certainly was no woodchuck.

He put away the trouble light and went upstairs.

Towser was curled up on a rug in the living-room beside the easy-chair and beat his tail in polite decorum in greeting to his master.

Taine stood and stared down at the dog. Towser looked back at him with satisfied and sleepy eyes, then heaved a doggish sigh and settled down to sleep.

Whatever Towser might have heard or smelled or sensed this morning, it was quite evident that as of this moment he was aware of it no longer.

Then Taine remembered something else.

He had filled the kettle to make water for the coffee and had set it on the stove. He had turned on the burner and it had worked the first time.

He hadn't had to kick the stove to get the burner going.

He woke in the morning and someone was holding down his feet and he sat up quickly to see what was going on.

But there was nothing to be alarmed about; it was only Towser who had crawled into bed with him and now lay sprawled across his feet.

Towser whined softly and his back legs twitched as he chased dream rabbits.

Taine eased his feet from beneath the dog and sat up, reaching for his clothes. It was early, but he remembered suddenly that he had left all of the furniture he had picked up the day before out there in the truck and should be getting downstairs where he could start reconditioning it.

Towser went on sleeping.

Taine stumbled to the kitchen and looked out of the window and there, squatted on the back stoop, was Beasly, the Horton man-of-all-work.

Taine went to the back door to see what was going on.

"I quit them, Hiram," Beasly told him. "She kept on pecking at me every minute of the day and I couldn't do a thing to please her, so I up and quit."

"Well, come on in," said Taine, "I suppose you'd like a bit to eat and a cup of coffee."

"I was kind of wondering if I could stay here, Hiram. Just for my keep until I can find something else."

"Let's have breakfast first," said Taine, "then we can talk about it."

He didn't like it, he told himself. He didn't like it at all. In another hour or so Abbie would show up and start stirring up a ruckus about how he'd lured Beasly off. Because, no matter how dumb Beasly might be, he did a lot of work and took a lot of nagging and there wasn't anyone else in town who would work for Abbie Horton.

"Your ma used to give me cookies all the time," said Beasly. "Your ma was a real good woman, Hiram."

"Yes, she was," said Taine.

"My ma used to say that you folks were quality, not like the rest in town, no matter what kind of airs they were always putting on. She said your family was among the first settlers. Is that really true, Hiram?"

"Well, not exactly first settlers, I guess, but this house has stood here for almost a hundred years. My father used to say there never was a night during all those years that there wasn't at least one Taine beneath its roof. Things like that, it seems, meant a lot to Father."

"It must be nice," said Beasly, wistfully, "to have a feeling like that. You must be proud of this house, Hiram."

"Not really proud; more like belonging. I can't imagine living in any other house."

Taine turned on the burner and filled the kettle. Carrying the kettle back, he kicked the stove. But there wasn't any need to kick it; the burner was already beginning to take on a rosy glow.

Twice in a row, Taine thought. This thing is getting better!

"Gee, Hiram," said Beasly, "this is a dandy radio."

"It's no good," said Taine. "It's broke. Haven't had the time to fix it."

"I don't think so, Hiram. I just turned it on. It's beginning to warm up."

"It's beginning to— Hey, let me see!" yelled Taine.

Beasly told the truth. A faint hum was coming from the tubes.

A voice came in, gaining in volume as the set warmed up.

It was speaking gibberish.

"What kind of talk is that?" asked Beasly.

"I don't know," said Taine, close to panic now.

First the television set, then the stove and now the radio!

He spun the tuning knob and the pointer crawled slowly across the dial face instead of spinning across as he remembered it, and station after station sputtered and went past.

He tuned in the next station that came up and it was strange lingo, too—and he knew by then exactly what he had.

Instead of a $39.50 job, he had here on the kitchen table an all-band receiver like they advertised in the fancy magazines.

He straightened up and said to Beasly: "See if you can get someone speaking English. I'll get on with the eggs."

He turned on the second burner and got out the frying-pan. He put it on the stove and found eggs and bacon in the refrigerator.

Beasly got a station that had band music playing.

"How's that?" he asked.

"That's fine," said Taine.

Towser came out from the bedroom, stretching and yawning. He went to the door and showed he wanted out.

Taine let him out.

"If I were you," he told the dog, "I'd lay off that woodchuck. You'll have all the woods dug up."

"He ain't digging after any woodchuck, Hiram."

"Well, a rabbit, then."

"Not a rabbit, either. I snuck off yesterday when I was supposed to be beating rugs. That's what Abbie got so sore about."

Taine grunted, breaking eggs into the skillet.

"I snuck away and went over to where Towser was. I talked with him and he told me it wasn't a woodchuck or a rabbit. He said it was something else. I pitched in and helped him dig. Looks to me like he found an old tank of some sort buried out there in the woods."

"Towser wouldn't dig up any tank," protested Taine. "He wouldn't care about anything except a rabbit or a woodchuck."

"He was working hard," insisted Beasly. "He seemed to be excited."

"Maybe the woodchuck just dug his hole under this old tank or whatever it might be."

"Maybe so," Beasly agreed. He fiddled with the radio some more. He got a disc jockey who was pretty terrible.

Taine shovelled eggs and bacon on to plates and brought them to the table. He poured big cups of coffee and began buttering the toast.

"Dive in," he said to Beasly

"This is good of you, Hiram, to take me in like this. I won't stay no longer than it takes to find a job."

"Well, I didn't exactly say—"

Clifford D. Simak

"There are times," said Beasly, "when I get to thinking I haven't got a friend and then I remember your ma, how nice she was to me and all—"

"Oh, all right," said Taine.

He knew when he was licked.

He brought the toast and a jar of jam to the table and sat down, beginning to eat.

"Maybe you got something I could help you with," suggested Beasly, using the back of his hand to wipe egg off his chin.

"I have a load of furniture out in the driveway. I could use a man to help me get it down into the basement."

"I'll be glad to do that," said Beasly. "I am good and strong. I don't mind work at all. I just don't like people jawing at me."

They finished breakfast and then carried the furniture down into the basement. They had some trouble with the Governor Winthrop, for it was an unwieldy thing to handle.

When they finally horsed it down, Taine stood off and looked at it. The man, he told himself, who slapped paint on to that beautiful cherrywood had a lot to answer for.

He said to Beasly: "We have to get the paint off that thing there. And we must do it carefully. Use paint remover and a rag wrapped around a spatula and just sort of roll it off. Would you like to try it?"

"Sure, I would. Say, Hiram, what will we have for lunch?"

"I don't know," said Taine. "We'll throw something together. Don't tell me you're hungry."

"Well, it was sort of hard work, getting all that stuff down here."

"There are cookies in the jar on the kitchen shelf," said Taine. "Go and help yourself."

When Beasly went upstairs, Taine walked slowly around the basement. The ceiling, he saw, was still intact. Nothing else seemed to be disturbed.

Maybe that television set and the stove and radio, he thought, was just their way of paying rent to me. And if that were the case, he told himself, whoever they might be, he'd be more than willing to let them stay right on.

He looked around some more and could find nothing wrong.

He went upstairs and called to Beasly in the kitchen.

"Come on out to the garage, where I keep the paint. We'll hunt up some remover and show you how to use it."

Beasly, a supply of cookies clutched in his hand, trotted willingly behind him.

As they rounded the corner of the house they could hear Towser's muffled barking. Listening to him, it seemed to Taine that he was getting hoarse.

Three days, he thought—or was it four?

"If we don't do something about it," he said, "that fool dog is going to get himself wore out."

He went into the garage and came back with two shovels and a pick.

"Come on," he said to Beasly. "We have to put a stop to this before we have any peace."

Towser had done himself a noble job of excavation. He was almost completely out of sight. Only the end of his considerably bedraggled tail showed out of the hole he had clawed in the forest floor.

Beasly had been right about the tank-like thing. One edge of it showed out of one side of the hole.

Towser backed out of the hole and sat down heavily, his whiskers dripping clay, his tongue hanging out of the side of his mouth.

"He says that it's about time that we showed up," said Beasly.

Taine walked around the hole and knelt down. He reached down a hand to brush the dirt off the projecting edge of Beasly's tank. The clay was stubborn and hard to wipe away, but from the feel of it the tank was heavy metal.

Taine picked up a shovel and rapped it against the tank. The tank gave out a clang.

They got to work, shovelling away a foot or so of topsoil that lay above the object. It was hard work and the thing was bigger than they had thought and it took some time to get it uncovered, even roughly.

"I'm hungry," Beasly complained.

Taine glanced at his watch. It was almost one o'clock. 'Run on back to the house," he said to Beasly. "You'll find something in the refrigerator and there's milk to drink."

"How about you, Hiram? Ain't you ever hungry?"

"You could bring me back a sandwich and see if you can find a trowel."

"What you want a trowel for?"

"I want to scrape the dirt off this thing and see what it is."

He squatted down beside the thing they had unearthed and watched Beasly disappear into the woods.

"Towser," he said, "This is the strangest animal you ever put to ground."

A man, he told himself, might better joke about it—if to do no more than keep his fear away.

Beasly wasn't scared, of course. Beasly didn't have the sense to be scared of a thing like this.

Twelve feet wide by twenty long and oval shaped. About the size, he thought, of a good-size living-room. And there never had been a tank of that shape or size in all of Willow Bend.

He fished his jack-knife out of his pocket and started to scratch away the dirt at one point on the surface of the thing. He got a square inch free of dirt and it was no metal such as he had ever seen. It looked for all the world like glass.

　　　　　　　　　　　　　　　　　　　　　　　　Clifford D. Simak

He kept on scraping at the dirt until he had a clean place as big as an outstretched hand.

It wasn't any metal. He'd almost swear to that. It looked like cloudy glass—like the milk-glass goblets and bowls he was always on the look-out for. There were a lot of people who were plain nuts about it and they'd pay fancy prices for it.

He closed the knife and put it back into his pocket and squatted, looking at the oval shape that Towser had discovered.

And the conviction grew: whatever it was that had come to live with him undoubtedly had arrived in this same contraption. From space or time, he thought, and was astonished that he thought it, for he'd never thought such a thing before.

He picked up his shovel and began to dig again, digging down this time, following the curving side of this alien thing that lay within the earth.

And as he dug, he wondered. What should he say about this—or should he say anything? Maybe the smartest course would be to cover it again and never breathe a word about it to a living soul.

Beasly would talk about it, naturally. But no one in the village would pay attention to anything that Beasly said. Everyone in Willow Bend knew Beasly was cracked.

Beasly finally came back. He carried three inexpertly made sandwiches wrapped in an old newspaper and a quart bottle almost full of milk.

"You certainly took your time," said Taine, slightly irritated.

"I got interested," Beasly explained.

"Interested in what?"

"Well, there were three big trucks and they were lugging a lot of heavy stuff down into the basement. Two or three big cabinets and a lot of other junk. And you know Abbie's television set? Well, they took the set away. I told them that they shouldn't but they took it anyway."

"I forgot," said Taine. "Henry said he'd send the computer over and I plumb forgot."

Taine ate the sandwiches, sharing them with Towser, who was very grateful in a muddy way.

Finished, Taine rose and picked up his shovel.

"Let's get to work," he said.

"But you got all that stuff down in the basement."

"That can wait," said Taine. "This job we have to finish."

It was getting dusk by the time they finished.

Taine leaned wearily on his shovel.

Twelve feet by twenty across the top and ten feet deep—and all of it, every bit of it, made of the milk-glass stuff that sounded like a bell when you whacked it with a shovel.

They'd have to be small, he thought, if there were many of them, to live in a space that size, especially if they had to stay there very long. And that fitted in, of course, for if they weren't small they couldn't now be living in the space between the basement joists.

If they were really living there, thought Taine. If it wasn't all just a lot of supposition.

Maybe, he thought, even if they had been living in the house, they might be there no longer—for Towser had smelled or heard or somehow sensed them in the morning, but by that very night he'd paid them no attention.

Taine slung his shovel across his shoulder and hoisted the pick.

"Come on," he said, "let's go. We've put in a long, hard day."

They tramped out through the brush and reached the road. Fireflies were flickering off and on in the woody darkness and the street lamps were swaying in the summer breeze. The stars were hard and bright.

Maybe they still were in the house, thought Taine. Maybe when they found out that Towser had objected to them, they had fixed it so he'd be aware of them no longer.

They probably were highly adaptive. It stood to good reason they would have to be. It hadn't taken them too long, he told himself grimly, to adapt to a human house.

He and Beasly went up the gravel driveway in the dark to put the tools away in the garage and there was something funny going on, for there was no garage.

There was no garage and there was no front on the house and the driveway was cut off abruptly and there was nothing but the curving wall of what apparently had been the end of the garage.

They came up to the curving wall and stopped, squinting unbelieving in the summer dark.

There was no garage, no porch, no front of the house at all. It was as if someone had taken the opposite corners of the front of the house and bent them together until they touched, folding the entire front of the building inside the curvature of the bent-together corners.

Taine now had a curved-front house. Although it was, actually, not as simple as all that, for the curvature was not in proportion to what actually would have happened in case of such a feat. The curve was long and graceful and somehow not quite apparent. It was as if the front of the house had been eliminated and an illusion of the rest of the house had been summoned to mask the disappearance.

Taine dropped the shovel and the pick and they clattered on the driveway gravel. He put his hand up to his face and wiped it across his eyes, as if to clear his eyes of something that could not possibly be there.

And when he took the hand away it had not changed a bit.

There was no front to the house.

Then he was running around the house, hardly knowing he was running, and there was a fear inside of him at what had happened to the house.

But the back of the house was all right. It was exactly as it had always been.

He clattered up the stoop with Beasly and Towser running close behind him. He

Clifford D. Simak

pushed open the door and burst into the entry and scrambled up the stairs into the kitchen and went across the kitchen in three strides to see what had happened to the front of the house.

At the door between the kitchen and the living-room he stopped and his hands went out to grasp the door jamb as he stared in disbelief at the windows of the living-room.

It was night outside. There could be no doubt of that. He had seen the fireflies flickering in the brush and weeds and the street lamps had been lit and the stars were out.

But a flood of sunlight was pouring through the windows of the living-room and out beyond the windows lay a land that was not Willow Bend.

"Beasly," he gasped, "look out there in front!"

Beasly looked.

"What place is that?" he asked.

"That's what I'd like to know."

Towser had found his dish and was pushing it around the kitchen floor with his nose, by way of telling Taine that it was time to eat.

Taine went across the living-room and opened the front door. The garage, he saw, was there. The pick-up stood with its nose against the opening garage door and the car was safe inside.

There was nothing wrong with the front of the house at all.

But if the front of the house was all right, that was all that was.

For the driveway was chopped off just a few feet beyond the tail-end of the pick-up and there was no yard or woods or road. There was just a desert—a flat, far-reaching desert, level as a floor, with occasional boulder piles and haphazard clumps of vegetation and all of the ground covered with sand and pebbles. A big blinding sun hung just above a horizon that seemed much too far away and a funny thing about it was that the sun was in the north, where no proper sun should be. It had a peculiar whiteness, too.

Beasly stepped out on the porch and Taine saw that he was shivering like a frightened dog.

"Maybe," Taine told him, kindly, "you'd better go back in and start making us some supper."

"But, Hiram—"

"It's all right," said Taine. "It's bound to be all right."

"If you say so, Hiram."

He went in and the screen door banged behind him and in a minute Taine heard him in the kitchen.

He didn't blame Beasly for shivering, he admitted to himself. It was a sort of shock to step out of your front door into an unknown land. A man might eventually get used to it, of course, but it would take some doing.

He stepped down off the porch and walked around the truck and around the garage corner and when he rounded the corner he was half prepared to walk back into familiar Willow Bend—for when he had gone in the back door the village had been there.

There was no Willow Bend. There was more of the desert, a great deal more of it.

He walked around the house and there was no back to the house. The back of the house now was just the same as the front had been before—the same smooth curve pulling the sides of the house together.

He walked on around the house to the front again and there was desert all the way. And the front was still all right. It hadn't changed at all. The truck was there on the chopped-off driveway and the garage was open and the car inside.

Taine walked out a way into the desert and hunkered down and scooped up a handful of the pebbles and the pebbles were just pebbles.

He squatted there and let the pebbles trickle through his fingers.

In Willow Bend there was a back door and there wasn't any front. Here, wherever here might be, there was a front door, but there wasn't any back.

He stood up and tossed the rest of the pebbles away and wiped his dusty hands upon his breeches.

Out of the corner of his eye he caught a sense of movement on the porch and there they were.

A line of tiny animals, if animals they were, came marching down the steps, one behind another. They were four inches high or so and they went on all four feet, although it was plain to see that their front feet were really hands, not feet. They had rat-like faces that were vaguely human, with noses long and pointed. They looked as if they might have scales instead of hide, for their bodies glistened with a rippling motion as they walked. And all of them had tails that looked very much like the coiled-wire tails one finds on certain toys and the tails stuck straight up above them, quivering as they walked.

They came down the steps in single file, in perfect military order, with half a foot or so of spacing between each one of them.

They came down the steps and walked out into the desert in a straight, undeviating line as if they knew exactly where they might be bound. There was something deadly purposeful about them and yet they didn't hurry.

Taine counted sixteen of them and he watched them go out into the desert until they were almost lost to sight.

There go the ones, he thought, who came to live with me. They are the ones who fixed up the ceiling and who repaired Abbie's television set and jiggered up the stove and radio. And more than likely, too, they were the ones who had come to Earth in the strange milk-glass contraption out there in the woods.

And if they had come to Earth in that deal out in the woods, then what sort of place was this?

He climbed the porch and opened the screen door and saw the neat, six-inch circle his departing guests had achieved in the screen to get out of the house. He made a mental note that some day, when he had the time, he would have to fix it.

He went in and slammed the door behind him.

"Beasly," he shouted.

There was no answer.

Towser crawled from beneath the love seat and apologized.

"It's all right, pal," said Taine. "That outfit scared me, too."

He went into the kitchen. The dim ceiling light shone on the overturned coffee pot, the broken cup in the centre of the floor, the upset bowl of eggs. One broken egg was a white and yellow gob on the linoleum.

He stepped down on the landing and saw that the screen door in the back was wrecked beyond repair. Its rusty mesh was broken—exploded might have been a better word—and a part of the frame was smashed.

Taine looked at it in wondering admiration.

"The poor fool," he said. "He went straight through it without opening it at all."

He snapped on the light and went down the basement stairs. Halfway down he stopped in utter wonderment.

To his left was a wall—a wall of the same sort of material as had been used to put in the ceiling.

He stooped and saw that the wall ran clear across the basement, floor to ceiling, shutting off the workshop area.

And inside the workshop, what?

For one thing, he remembered, the computer that Henry had sent over just this morning. Three trucks, Beasly had said—three truck-loads of equipment delivered straight into their paws!

Taine sat down weakly on the steps.

They must have thought, he told himself, that he was cooperating! Maybe they had figured that he knew what they were about and so went along with them. Or perhaps they thought he was paying them for fixing up the TV set and the stove and radio.

But to tackle first things first, why had they repaired the TV set and the stove and radio? As a sort of rental payment? As a friendly gesture? Or as a sort of practice run to find out what they could about this world's technology? To find, perhaps, how their technology could be adapted to the materials and conditions on this planet they had found?

Taine raised a hand and rapped with his knuckles on the wall beside the stairs and the smooth white surface gave out a pinging sound.

He laid his ear against the wall and listened closely and it seemed to him he could hear a low-key humming, but if so it was so faint he could not be absolutely sure.

Banker Stevens's lawn-mower was in there, behind the wall, and a lot of other stuff waiting for repair. They'd take the hide right off him, he thought, especially Banker Stevens. Stevens was a tight man.

Beasly must have been half-crazed with fear, he thought. When he had seen those things coming up out of the basement, he'd gone clean off his rocket. He'd gone straight through the door without even bothering to try to open it and now he was down in the village yapping to anyone who'd stop to listen to him.

No one ordinarily would pay Beasly much attention, but if he yapped long enough and wild enough, they'd probably do some checking. They'd come storming up here and they'd give the place a going over and they'd stand goggle-eyed at what they found in front and pretty soon some of them would have worked their way around to sort of running things.

And it was none of their business, Taine stubbornly told himself, his ever-present business sense rising to the fore. There was a lot of real estate lying around out there in his front yard and the only way anyone could get to it was by going through the house. That being the case, it stood to reason that all that land out there was his. Maybe it wasn't any good at all. There might be nothing there. But before he had other people overrunning it, he'd better check and see.

He went up the stairs and out into the garage.

The sun was still just above the northern horizon and there was nothing moving.

He found a hammer and some nails and a few short lengths of plank in the garage and took them in the house.

Towser, he saw, had taken advantage of the situation and was sleeping in the gold-upholstered chair. Taine didn't bother him.

Taine locked the back door and nailed some planks across it. He locked the kitchen and the bedroom windows and nailed planks across them, too.

That would hold the villagers for a while, he told himself, when they came tearing up here to see what was going on.

He got his deer rifle, a box of cartridges, a pair of binoculars and an old canteen out of a closet. He filled the canteen at the kitchen tap and stuffed a sack with food for him and Towser to eat along the way, for there was no time to wait and eat.

Then he went into the living-room and dumped Towser out of the gold-upholstered chair.

"Come on, Tows," he said. "We'll go and look things over."

He checked the gasoline in the pick-up and the tank was almost full.

He and the dog got in and he put the rifle within easy reach. Then he backed the truck and swung it around and headed out, north, across the desert.

It was easy travelling. The desert was as level as a floor. At times it got a little rough, but no worse than a lot of the back roads he travelled hunting down antiques.

The scenery didn't change. Here and there were low hills, but the desert itself kept on mostly level, unravelling itself into that far-off horizon. Taine kept on driving north, straight into the sun. He hit some sandy stretches, but the sand was firm and hard and he had no trouble.

Clifford D. Simak

Half an hour out he caught up with the band of things—all sixteen of them—that had left the house. They were still travelling in line at their steady pace.

Slowing down the truck, Taine travelled parallel with them for a time, but there was no profit in it; they kept on travelling their course, looking neither right nor left. Speeding up, Taine left them behind.

The sun stayed in the north, unmoving, and that certainly was queer. Perhaps, Taine told himself, this world spun on its axis far more slowly than the Earth and the day was longer. From the way the sun appeared to be standing still, perhaps a good deal longer.

Hunched above the wheel, staring out into the endless stretch of desert, the strangeness of it struck him for the first time with its full impact.

This was another world—there could be no doubt of that—another planet circling another star, and where it was in actual space no one on Earth could have the least idea. And yet, through some machination of those sixteen things walking straight in line, it also was lying just outside the front door of his house.

Ahead of him a somewhat larger hill loomed out of the flatness of the desert. As he drew nearer to it, he made out a row of shining objects lined upon its crest. After a time he stopped the truck and got out with the binoculars.

Through the glasses, he saw that the shining things were the same sort of milk-glass contraptions as had been in the woods. He counted eight of them, shining in the sun, perched upon some sort of rock-grey cradles. And there were other cradles empty.

He took the binoculars from his eyes and stood there for a moment, considering the advisability of climbing the hill and investigating closely. But he shook his head. There'd be time for that later on. He'd better keep on moving. This was not a real exploring foray, but a quick reconnaissance.

He climbed into the truck and drove on, keeping watch upon the gas gauge. When it came close to half full he'd have to turn around and go back home again.

Ahead of him he saw a faint whiteness above the dim horizon line and he watched it narrowly. At times it faded away and then came in again, but whatever it might be was so far off he could make nothing of it.

He glanced down at the gas gauge and it was close to the halfway mark. He stopped the pick-up and got out with the binoculars.

As he moved around to the front of the machine he was puzzled at how slow and tired his legs were and then remembered—he should have been in bed many hours ago. He looked at his watch and it was two o'clock and that meant, back on Earth, two o'clock in the morning. He had been awake for more than twenty hours and much of that time he had been engaged in the back-breaking work of digging out the strange thing in the woods.

He put up the binoculars and the elusive white line that he had been seeing turned out to be a range of mountains. The great, blue, craggy mass towered up above the desert with the gleam of snow on its peaks and ridges. They were a long way off, for even the powerful glasses brought them in as little more than a misty blueness.

He swept the glasses slowly back and forth and the mountains extended for a long distance above the horizon line.

He brought the glasses down off the mountains and examined the desert that stretched ahead of him. There was more of the same that he had been seeing—the same floor-like levelness, the same occasional mounds, the self-same craggy vegetation.

And a house!

His hands trembled and he lowered the glasses, then put them up to his face again and had another look. It was a house, all right. A funny-looking house standing at the foot of one of the hillocks, still shadowed by the hillock so that one could not pick it out with the naked eye.

It seemed to be a small house. Its roof was like a blunted cone and it lay tight against the ground, as if it hugged or crouched against the ground. There was an oval opening that probably was a door, but there was no sign of windows.

He took the binoculars down again and stared at the hillock. Four or five miles away, he thought. The gas would stretch that far and even if it didn't he could walk the last few miles into Willow Bend.

It was queer, he thought, that a house should be all alone out here. In all the miles he'd travelled in the desert he'd seen no sign of life beyond the sixteen little rat-like things that marched in single file, no sign of artificial structure other than the eight milk-glass contraptions resting in their cradles.

He climbed into the pick-up and put it into gear. Ten minutes later he drew up in front of the house, which still lay within the shadow of the hillock.

He got out of the pick-up and hauled his rifle after him. Towser leaped to the ground and stood with his hackles up, a deep growl in his throat.

"What's the matter, boy?" asked Taine.

Towser growled again.

The house stood silent. It seemed to be deserted.

The walls were built, Taine saw, of rude, rough masonry, crudely set together, with a crumbling, mud-like substance used in lieu of mortar. The roof originally had been of sod and that was queer, indeed, for there was nothing that came close to sod upon this expanse of desert. But now, although one could see the lines where the sod strips had been fitted together, it was nothing more than earth baked hard by the desert sun.

The house itself was featureless, entirely devoid of any ornament, with no attempt at all to soften the harsh utility of it as a simple shelter. It was the sort of thing that a shepherd people might have put together. It had the look of age about it; the stone had flaked and crumbled in the weather.

Rifle slung beneath his arm, Taine paced towards it. He reached the door and glanced inside and there was darkness and no movement.

Clifford D. Simak

He glanced back for Towser and saw that the dog had crawled beneath the truck and was peering out and growling.

"You stick around," said Taine. "Don't go running off."

With the rifle thrust before him, Taine stepped through the door into the darkness. He stood for a long moment to allow his eyes to become accustomed to the gloom.

Finally he could make out the room in which he stood. It was plain and rough, with a rude stone bench along one wall and queer unfunctional niches hollowed in another. One rickety piece of wooden furniture stood in a corner, but Taine could not make out what its use might be.

An old and deserted place, he thought, abandoned long ago. Perhaps a shepherd people might have lived here in some long-gone age, when the desert had been a rich and grassy plain.

There was a door into another room and as he stepped through it he heard the faint far-off booming sound and something else as well—the sound of pouring rain! From the open door that led out through the back he caught a whiff of salty breeze and he stood there frozen in the center of that second room.

Another one!

Another house that led to another world!

He walked slowly forward, drawn towards the outer door, and he stepped out into a cloudy, darkling day with the rain steaming down from wildly racing clouds. Half a mile away, across a field of jumbled, broken, iron-grey boulders, lay a pounding sea that raged upon the coast, throwing great spumes of angry spray high into the air.

He walked out from the door and looked up at the sky, and the raindrops pounded at his face with a stinging fury. There was a chill and a dampness in the air and the place was eldritch—a world jerked straight from some ancient Gothic tale of goblin and of sprite.

He glanced around and there was nothing he could see, for the rain blotted out the world beyond this stretch of coast, but behind the rain he could sense or seemed to sense a presence that sent shivers down his spine. Gulping in fright, Taine turned around and stumbled back again through the door into the house.

One world away, he thought, was far enough; two worlds away was more than one could take. He trembled at the sense of utter loneliness that tumbled in his skull and suddenly this long-forsaken house became unbearable and he dashed out of it.

Outside the sun was bright and there was welcome warmth. His clothes were damp from rain and little beads of moisture lay on the rifle barrel.

He looked around for Towser and there was no sign of the dog. He was not underneath the pick-up; he was nowhere in sight.

Taine called and there was no answer. His voice sounded lone and hollow in the emptiness and silence.

He walked around the house, looking for the dog, and there was no back door to the house. The rough rock walls of the sides of the house pulled in with that funny curvature and there was no back to the house at all.

But Taine was not interested; he had known how it would be. Right now he was looking for his dog and he felt the panic rising in him. Somehow it felt a long way from home.

He spent three hours at it. He went back into the house and Towser was not there. He went into the other world again and searched among the tumbled rocks and Towser was not there. He went back to the desert and walked around the hillock and then he climbed to the crest of it and used the binoculars and saw nothing but the lifeless desert, stretching far in all directions.

Dead-beat with weariness, stumbling, half asleep even as he walked, he went back to the pick-up.

He leaned against it and tried to pull his wits together.

Continuing as he was would be a useless effort. He had to get some sleep. He had to go back to Willow Bend and fill the tank and get some extra gasoline so that he could range farther afield in his search for Towser.

He couldn't leave the dog out here—that was unthinkable. But he had to plan, he had to act intelligently. He would be doing Towser no good by stumbling around in his present shape.

He pulled himself into the truck and headed back for Willow Bend, following the occasional faint impressions that his tyres had made in the sandy places, fighting a half-dead drowsiness that tried to seal his eyes shut.

Passing the higher hill on which the milk-glass things had stood, he stopped to walk around a bit so he wouldn't fall asleep behind the wheel. And now, he saw, there were only seven of the things resting in their cradles.

But that meant nothing to him now. All that meant anything was to hold off the fatigue that was closing down upon him, to cling to the wheel and wear off the miles, to get back to Willow Bend and get some sleep and then come back again to look for Towser.

Slightly more than halfway home he saw the other car and watched it in numb befuddlement, for this truck that he was driving and the car at home in his garage were the only two vehicles this side of his house.

He pulled the pick-up to a halt and tumbled out of it.

The car drew up and Henry Horton and Beasly and a man who wore a star leaped quickly out of it.

"Thank God we found you, man!" cried Henry, striding over to him.

"I wasn't lost," protested Taine. "I was coming back."

"He's all beat out," said the man who wore the star.

"This is Sheriff Hanson," Henry said. "We were following your tracks."

"I lost Towser," Taine mumbled. "I had to go and leave him. Just leave me be and go and hunt for Towser. I can make it home."

Clifford D. Simak

He reached out and grabbed the edge of the pick-up's door to hold himself erect.

"You broke down the door," he said to Henry. "You broke into my house and you took my car—"

"We had to do it, Hiram. We were afraid that something might have happened to you. The way that Beasly told it, it stood your hair on end."

"You better get him in the car," the sheriff said. "I'll drive the pick-up back."

"But I have to hunt for Towser!"

"You can't do anything until you've had some rest."

Henry grabbed him by the arm and led him to the car and Beasly held the rear door open.

"You got any idea what this place is?" Henry whispered conspiratorially.

"I don't positively know," Taine mumbled. "Might be some other—"

Henry chuckled. "Well, I guess it doesn't really matter. Whatever it may be, it's put us on the map. We're in all the news-casts and the papers are plastering us in headlines and the town is swarming with reporters and cameramen and there are big officials coming. Yes, sir, I tell you, Hiram, this will be the making of us—"

Taine heard no more. He was fast asleep before he hit the seat. He came awake and lay quietly in the bed and he saw the shades were drawn and the room was cool and peaceful.

It was good, he thought, to wake in a room you knew—in a room that one had known for one's entire life, in a house that had been the Taine house for almost a hundred years.

Then memory clouted him and he sat bolt upright.

And now he heard it—the insistent murmur from outside the window.

He vaulted from the bed and pulled one shade aside. Peering out, he saw the cordon of troops that held back the crowd that overflowed his back yard and the back yards back of that.

He let the shade drop back and started hunting for his shoes, for he was fully dressed. Probably Henry and Beasly, he told himself, had dumped him into bed and pulled off his shoes and let it go at that. But he couldn't remember a single thing of it. He must have gone dead to the world the minute Henry had bundled him into the back seat of the car.

He found the shoes on the floor at the end of the bed and sat down upon the bed to pull them on.

And his mind was racing on what he had to do.

He'd have to get some gasoline somehow and fill up the truck and stash an extra can or two into the back and he'd have to take some food and water and perhaps his sleeping-bag. For he wasn't coming back until he found his dog.

He got on his shoes and tied them, then went out into the living-room. There was no one there, but there were voices in the kitchen.

He looked out of the window and the desert lay outside, unchanged. The sun, he noticed, had climbed higher in the sky, but out in his front yard it was still forenoon.

He looked at his watch and it was six o'clock and from the way the shadows had been falling when he'd peered out of the bedroom window, he knew that it was 6 PM. He realized with a guilty start that he must have slept almost around the clock. He had not meant to sleep that long. He hadn't meant to leave Towser out there that long.

He headed for the kitchen and there were three persons there—Abbie and Henry Horton and a man in military garb.

"There you are," cried Abbie merrily. "We were wondering when you would wake up."

"You have some coffee cooking, Abbie?"

"Yes, a whole pot full of it. And I'll cook up something else for you."

"Just some toast," said Taine. "I haven't got much time. I have to hunt for Towser."

"Hiram," said Henry, "this is Colonel Ryan, National Guard. He has his boys outside."

"Yes, I saw them through the window."

"Necessary," said Henry. "Absolutely necessary. The sheriff couldn't handle it. The people came rushing in and they'd have torn the place apart. So I called the governor."

"Taine," the colonel said, "sit down. I want to talk with you."

"Certainly," said Taine, taking a chair. "Sorry to be in such a rush, but I lost my dog out there."

"This business," said the colonel, smugly, "is vastly more important than any dog could be."

"Well, Colonel, that just goes to show that you don't know Towser. He's the best dog I ever had and I've had a lot of them. Raised him from a pup and he's been a good friend all these years—"

"All right," the colonel said, "so he is a friend. But still I have to talk with you."

"You just sit and talk," Abbie said to Taine. "I'll fix up some cakes and Henry brought over some of that sausage that we get out on the farm."

The back door opened and Beasly staggered in to the accompaniment of a terrific metallic banging. He was carrying three empty five-gallon gas cans in one hand and two in the other hand and they were bumping and banging together as he moved.

"Say," yelled Taine, "what's going on here?"

"Now, just take it easy," Henry said. "You have no idea the problems that we have. We wanted to get a big gas tank moved through here, but we couldn't do it. We tried to rip out the back of the kitchen to get it through, but we couldn't—"

"You did what!"

"We tried to rip out the back of the kitchen," Henry told him calmly. "You can't get one of those big storage tanks through an ordinary door. But when we tried, we

Clifford D. Simak

found that the entire house is boarded up inside with the same kind of material that you used down in the basement. You hit it with an axe and it blunts the steel—''

"But, Henry, this is my house and there isn't anyone who has the right to start tearing it apart."

"Fat chance," the colonel said. "What I would like to know, Taine, what is that stuff that we couldn't break through?"

"Now you take it easy, Hiram," cautioned Henry. "We have a big new world waiting for us out there—"

"It isn't waiting for you or anyone," yelled Taine.

"And we have to explore it and to explore it we need a stockpile of gasoline. So since we can't have a storage tank, we're getting together as many gas cans as possible and then we'll run a hose through here—"

"But, Henry—"

"I wish," said Henry sternly, "that you'd quit interrupting me and let me have my say. You can't even imagine the logistics that we face. We're bottle-necked by the size of a regulation door. We have to get supplies out there and we have to get transport. Cars and trucks won't be so bad. We can disassemble them and lug them through piecemeal, but a plane will be a problem."

"You listen to me, Henry. There isn't anyone going to haul a plane through here. This house has been in my family for almost a hundred years and I own it and I have a right to it and you can't come in high-handed and start hauling stuff through it."

"But," said Henry plaintively, "we need a plane real bad. You can cover so much more ground when you have a plane."

Beasly went banging through the kitchen with his cans and out into the living-room.

The colonel sighed. "I had hoped, Mr. Taine, that you would understand how the matter stood. To me it seems very plain that it's your patriotic duty to co-operate with us in this. The government, of course, could exercise the right of eminent domain and start condemnation action, but it would rather not do that. I'm speaking unofficially, of course, but I think it's safe to say the government would much prefer to arrive at an amicable agreement."

"I doubt," Taine said, bluffing, not knowing anything about it, "that the right to eminent domain would be applicable. As I understand it, it applies to buildings and to roads—"

"This is a road," the colonel told him flatly. "A road right through your house to another world."

"First," Taine declared, "the government would have to show it was in the public interest and that refusal of the owner to relinquish title amounted to an interference in government procedure and—"

"I think," the colonel said, "that the government can prove it is in the public interest."

"I think," Taine said angrily, "I better get a lawyer."

"If you really mean that," Henry offered, ever helpful, "and you want a good one—and I presume you do—I would be pleased to recommend a firm that I am sure would represent your interests most ably and be, at the same time, fairly reasonable in cost."

The colonel stood up, seething. "You'll have a lot to answer, Taine. There'll be a lot of things the government will want to know. First of all, they'll want to know just how you engineered this. Are you ready to tell that?"

"No," said Taine, "I don't believe I am."

And he thought with some alarm: They think that I'm the one who did it and they'll be down on me like a pack of wolves to find out just how I did it. He had visions of the FBI and the state department and the Pentagon and, even sitting down, he felt shaky in the knees.

The colonel turned around and marched stiffly from the kitchen. He went out the back and slammed the door behind him.

Henry looked at Taine speculatively.

"Do you really mean it?" he demanded. "Do you intend to stand up to them?"

"I'm getting sore," said Taine. "They can't come in here and take over without even asking me. I don't care what anyone may think, this is my house. I was born here and I've lived here all my life and I like the place and—"

"Sure," said Henry. "I know just how you feel."

"I suppose it's childish of me, but I wouldn't mind so much if they showed a willingness to sit down and talk about what they meant to do once they'd taken over. But there seems no disposition to even ask me what I think about it. And I tell you, Henry, this is different than it seems. This isn't a place where we can walk in and take over, no matter what Washington may think. There's something out there and we better watch our step—"

"I was thinking," Henry interrupted, "as I was sitting here, that your attitude is most commendable and deserving of support. It has occurred to me that it would be most unneighborly of me to go on sitting here and leave you in the fight alone. We could hire ourselves a fine array of legal talent and we could fight the case and in the meantime we could form a land and development company and that way we could make sure that this new world of yours is used the way it should be used.

"It stands to reason, Hiram, that I am the one to stand beside you, shoulder to shoulder, in this business since we're already partners in this TV deal."

"What's this about TV?" shrilled Abbie, slapping a plate of cakes down in front of Taine.

"Now, Abbie," Henry said patiently, "I have explained to you already that your TV set is back of that partition down in the basement and there isn't any telling when we can get it out."

"Yes, I know," said Abbie, bringing a platter of sausages and pouring a cup of coffee.

Beasly came in from the living-room and went bumbling out the back.

"After all," said Henry, pressing his advantage, "I would suppose I had some hand in it. I doubt you could have done much without the computer I sent over."

And there it was again, thought Taine. Even Henry thought he'd been the one who did it.

"But didn't Beasly tell you?"

"Beasly said a lot, but you know how Beasly is."

And that was it, of course. To the villagers it would be no more than another Beasly story—another whopper that Beasly had dreamed up. There was no one who believed a word that Beasly said.

Taine picked up the cup and drank his coffee, gaining time to shape an answer and there wasn't any answer. If he told the truth, it would sound far less believable than any lie he'd tell.

"You can tell me, Hiram. After all, we're partners."

He's playing me for a fool, thought Taine. Henry thinks he can play anyone he wants for a fool and sucker.

"You wouldn't believe me if I told you, Henry."

"Well," Henry said, resignedly, getting to his feet, "I guess that part of it can wait."

Beasly came tramping and banging through the kitchen with another load of cans.

"I'll have to have some gasoline," said Taine, "if I'm going out for Towser."

"I'll take care of that right away," Henry promised smoothly. "I'll send Ernie over with his tank-wagon and we can run a hose through here and fill up those cans. And I'll see if I can find someone who'll go along with you."

"That's not necessary. I can go alone."

"If we had a radio transmitter. Then you could keep in touch."

"But we haven't any. And, Henry, I can't wait. Towser's out there somewhere—"

"Sure, I know how much you thought of him. You go out and look for him if you think you have to and I'll get started on this other business. I'll get some lawyers lined up and we'll draw up some sort of corporate papers for our land development—"

"And, Hiram," Abbie said, "will you do something for me, please?"

"Why, certainly," said Taine.

"Would you speak to Beasly? It's senseless the way he's acting. There wasn't any call for him to up and leave us. I might have been a little sharp with him, but he's so simple-minded he's infuriating. He ran off and spent half a day helping Towser at digging out that woodchuck and—"

"I'll speak to him," said Taine.

"Thanks, Hiram. He'll listen to you. You're the only one he'll listen to. And I wish you could have fixed my TV set before all this came about. I'm just lost without it. It leaves a hole in the living-room. It matched my other furniture, you know."

"Yes I know," said Taine.

"Coming, Abbie?" Henry asked, standing at the door.

He lifted a hand in a confidential farewell to Taine. "I'll see you later, Hiram. I'll get it all fixed up."

I just bet you will, thought Taine.

He went back to the table, after they were gone, and sat down heavily in a chair. The front door slammed and Beasly came panting in, excited.

"Towser's back!" he yelled. "He's coming back and he's driving in the biggest woodchuck you ever clapped your eyes on."

Taine leaped to his feet.

"Woodchuck! That's an alien planet. It hasn't any woodchucks."

"You come and see," yelled Beasly.

He turned and raced back out again, with Taine following close behind.

It certainly looked considerably like a woodchuck—a sort of man-size woodchuck. More like a woodchuck out of a children's book, perhaps, for it was walking on its hind legs and trying to look dignified even while it kept a weather eye on Towser.

Towser was back a hundred feet or so, keeping a wary distance from the massive chuck. He had the pose of a good sheep-herding dog, walking in a crouch, alert to head off any break that the chuck might make.

The chuck came up close to the house and stopped. Then it did an about-face so that it looked back across the desert and it hunkered down.

It swung its massive head to gaze at Beasly and Taine and in the limpid brown eyes Taine saw more than the eyes of an animal.

Taine walked swiftly out and picked up the dog in his arms and hugged him tight against him. Towser twisted his head around and slapped a sloppy tongue across his master's face.

Taine stood with the dog in his arms and looked at the man-size chuck and felt a great relief and an utter thankfulness.

Everything was all right now, he thought. Towser had come back.

He headed for the house and out into the kitchen.

He put Towser down and got a dish and filled it at the tap. He placed it on the floor and Towser lapped at it thirstily, slopping water all over the linoleum.

"Take it easy, there," warned Taine. "You don't want to overdo it."

He hunted in the refrigerator and found some scraps and put them in Towser's dish. Towser wagged his tail with doggish happiness.

"By rights," said Taine, "I ought to take a rope to you, running off like that."

Beasly came ambling in.

"That chuck is a friendly cuss," he announced. "He's waiting for someone."

"That's nice," said Taine, paying no attention.

He glanced at the clock.

"It's seven-thirty," he said. "We can catch the news. You want to get it, Beasly?"

"Sure. I know right where to get it. That fellow from New York."

"That's the one," said Taine.

He walked into the living-room and looked out of the window. The man-size chuck had not moved. He was sitting with his back to the house, looking back the way he'd come.

Waiting for someone, Beasly had said, and it looked as if he might be, but probably it was all just in Beasly's head.

And if he were waiting for someone, Taine wondered, who might that someone be? Certainly by now the word had spread out that there was a door into another world. And how many doors, he wondered, had been opened through the ages?

Henry had said that there was a big new world out there waiting for Earthmen to move in. And that wasn't it at all. It was the other way around.

The voice of the news commentator came blasting from the radio in the middle of a sentence:

". . . finally got into the act. Radio Moscow said this evening that the Soviet delegate will make representations in the UN tomorrow for the internationalization of this other world and the gateway to it.

"From that gateway itself, the house of a man named Hiram Taine, there is no news. Complete security has been clamped down and a cordon of troops form a solid wall around the house, holding back the crowds. Attempts to telephone the residence are blocked by a curt voice which says that no calls are being accepted for that number. And Taine himself has not stepped from the house."

Taine walked back into the kitchen and sat down.

"He's talking about you," Beasly said importantly.

"Rumor circulated this morning that Taine, a quiet village repair man and dealer in antiques, and until yesterday a relative unknown, had finally returned from a trip which he made out into this new and unknown land. But what he found, if anything, no one yet can say. Nor is there any further information about this other place beyond the fact that it is a desert and, to the moment, lifeless.

"A small flurry of excitement was occasioned late yesterday by the finding of some strange object in the woods across the road from the residence, but this area likewise was swiftly cordoned off and to the moment Colonel Ryan, who commands the troops, will say nothing of what actually was found.

"Mystery man of the entire situation is one Henry Horton, who seems to be the only unofficial person to have entry to the Taine house. Horton, questioned earlier today, had little to say, but managed to suggest an air of great conspiracy. He hinted he and Taine were partners in some mysterious venture and left hanging in mid air the half impression that he and Taine had collaborated in opening the new world.

"Horton, it is interesting to note, operates a small computer plant and it is understood on good authority that only recently he delivered a computer to Taine, or at least some sort of machine to which considerable mystery is attached. One story is that this particular machine had been in the process of development for six or seven years.

"Some of the answers to the matter of how all this did happen and what actually did happen must wait upon the findings of a team of scientists who left Washington this evening after an all-day conference at the White House, which was attended by representatives from the military, the state department, the security division and the special weapons section.

"Throughout the world the impact of what happened yesterday at Willow Bend can only be compared to the sensation of the news, almost twenty years ago, of the dropping of the first atomic bomb. There is some tendency among many observers to believe that the implications of Willow Bend, in fact, may be even more earth-shaking than were those at Hiroshima.

"Washington insists, as is only natural, that this matter is of internal concern only and that it intends to handle the situation as it best affects the national welfare.

"But abroad there is a rising storm of insistence that this is not a matter of national policy concerning one nation, but that it necessarily must be a matter of worldwide concern.

"There is an unconfirmed report that a UN observer will arrive in Willow Bend almost momentarily. France, Britain, Bolivia, Mexico, and India have already requested permission of Washington to send observers to the scene and other nations undoubtedly plan to file similar requests.

"The world sits on edge tonight, waiting for the word from Willow Bend and—"

Taine reached out and clicked the radio to silence.

"From the sound of it," said Beasly, "we're going to be overrun by a batch of foreigners."

Yes, thought Taine, there might be a batch of foreigners, but not exactly in the sense that Beasly meant. The use of the word, he told himself, so far as any human was concerned, must be outdated now. No man of Earth ever again could be called a foreigner with alien life next door—literally next door. What were the people of the stone house?

And perhaps not the alien life of one planet only, but the alien life of many. For he himself had found another door into yet another planet and there might be many more such doors and what would these other worlds be like, and what was the purpose of the doors?

Someone, *something*, had found a way of going to another planet short of spanning light-years of lonely space—a simpler and a shorter way than flying through the gulfs of space. And once the way was open, then the way stayed open and it was as easy as walking from one room to another.

But one thing—one ridiculous thing—kept puzzling him and that was the spinning and the movement of the connected planets, of all the planets that must be linked together. You could not, he argued, establish solid, factual links between two objects that move independently of one another.

And yet, a couple of days ago, he would have contended just as stolidly that the

Clifford D. Simak

whole idea on the face of it was fantastic and impossible. Still it had been done. And once one impossibility was accomplished, what logical man could say with sincerity that the second could not be?

The doorbell rang and he got up to answer it.

It was Ernie, the oilman.

"Henry said you wanted some gas and I came to tell you I can't get it until morning."

"That's all right," said Taine. "I don't need it now."

And swiftly slammed the door.

He leaned against it, thinking: "I'll have to face them some time. I can't keep the door locked against the world. Some time, soon or late, the Earth and I will have to have this out."

And it was foolish, he thought, for him to think like this, but that was the way it was.

He had something here that the Earth demanded; something that Earth wanted or thought it wanted. And yet, in the last analysis, it was his responsibility. It had happened on his land, it had happened in his house; unwittingly, perhaps, he'd even aided and abetted it.

And the land and house are mine, he fiercely told himself, and that world out there was an extension of his yard. No matter how far or where it went, an extension of his yard.

Beasly had left the kitchen and Taine walked into the living-room. Towser was curled up and snoring gently in the gold-upholstered chair.

Taine decided he would let him stay there. After all, he thought, Towser had won the right to sleep anywhere he wished.

He walked past the chair to the window and the desert stretched to its far horizon and there before the window sat the man-size woodchuck and Beasly side by side, with their backs turned to the window and staring out across the desert.

Somehow it seemed natural that the chuck and Beasly should be sitting there together—the two of them, it appeared to Taine, might have a lot in common.

And it was a good beginning—that a man and an alien creature from this other world should sit down companionably together.

He tried to envision the set-up of these linked worlds, of which Earth was now a part, and the possibilities that lay inherent in the fact of linkage rolled thunder through his brain.

There would be contact between Earth and these other worlds and what would come of it?

And come to think of it, the contact had been made already, but so naturally, so undramatically, that it failed to register as a great, important meeting. For Beasly and the chuck out there were contact and if it all should go like that, there was absolutely nothing for one to worry over.

This was no haphazard business, he reminded himself. It had been planned and executed with the smoothness of long practice. This was not the first world to be opened and it would not be the last.

The little rat-like things had spanned space—how many light-years of space one could not even guess—in the vehicle which he had unearthed out in the woods. They then had buried it, perhaps as a child might hide a dish by shoving it into a pile of sand. Then they had come to this very house and had set up the apparatus that had made this house a tunnel between one world and another. And once that had been done, the need of crossing space had been cancelled out for ever. There need be but one crossing and that one crossing would serve to link the planets.

And once the job was done the little rat-like things had left, but not before they had made certain that this gateway to their planet would stand against no matter what assault. They had sheathed the house inside the studdings with a wonder-material that would resist an axe and that, undoubtedly, would resist much more than a simple axe.

And they had marched in drill-order single file out to the hill where eight more of the space machines had rested in their cradles. And now there were only seven there, in their cradles on the hill, and the rat-like things were gone and, perhaps, in time to come, they'd land on another planet and another doorway would be opened, a link to yet another world.

But more, Taine thought, than the linking of mere worlds. It would be, as well, the linking of the peoples of those worlds.

The little rat-like creatures were the explorers and the pioneers who sought out other Earth-like planets and the creature waiting with Beasly just outside the window must also serve its purpose and perhaps in time to come there would be a purpose which man would also serve.

He turned away from the window and looked around the room and the room was exactly as it had been ever since he could remember it. With all the change outside, with all that was happening outside, the room remained unchanged.

This is the reality, thought Taine, this is all the reality there is. Whatever else may happen, this is where I stand—this room with its fireplace blackened by many winter fires, the bookshelves with the old thumbed volumes, the easy-chair, the ancient worn carpet—worn by beloved and unforgotten feet through the many years.

And this also, he knew, was the lull before the storm.

In just a little while the brass would start arriving—the team of scientists, the governmental functionaries, the military, the observers from the other countries, the officials from the UN.

And against all these, he realized, he stood weaponless and shorn of his strength. No matter what a man might say or think, he could not stand off the world.

This was the last day that this would be the Taine house. After almost a hundred years, it would have another destiny.

And for the first time in all those years there'd be no Taine asleep beneath its roof.

Clifford D. Simak

He stood looking at the fireplace and the shelves of books and he sensed the old, pale ghosts walking in the room and he lifted a hesitant hand as if to wave farewell, not only to the ghosts but to the room as well. But before he got it up, he dropped it to his side.

What was the use, he thought.

He went out to the porch and sat down on the steps.

Beasly heard him and turned around.

"He's nice," he said to Taine, patting the chuck upon the back. "He's exactly like a great big Teddy bear."

"Yes, I see," said Taine.

"And best of all, I can talk with him."

"Yes, I know," said Taine, remembering that Beasly could talk with Towser, too.

He wondered what it would be like to live in the simple world of Beasly. At times, he decided, it would be comfortable.

The rat-like things had come in the spaceship, but why had they come to Willow Bend, why had they picked this house, the only house in all the village where they would have found the equipment that they needed to build their apparatus so easily and so quickly? For there was no doubt that they had cannibalized the computer to get the equipment they needed. In that, at least, Henry had been right. Thinking back on it, Henry, after all, had played quite a part in it.

Could they have foreseen that on this particular week in this particular house the probability of quickly and easily doing what they had come to do had stood very high?

Did they, with all their other talents and technology, have clairvoyance as well?

"There's someone coming," Beasly said.

"I don't see a thing."

"Neither do I," said Beasly, "but Chuck told me that he saw them."

"Told you!"

"I told you we been talking. There, I can see them too."

They were far off, but they were coming fast—three dots rode rapidly out of the desert.

He sat and watched them come and he thought of going in to get the rifle, but he didn't stir from his seat upon the steps. The rifle would do no good, he told himself. It would be a senseless thing to get it; more than that, a senseless attitude. The least that man could do, he thought, was to meet these creatures of another world with clean and empty hands.

They were closer now and it seemed to him that they were sitting in invisible chairs that travelled very fast.

He saw that they were humanoid, to a degree at least, and there were only three of them.

They came in with a rush and stopped very suddenly a hundred feet or so from where he sat upon the steps.

He didn't move or say a word—there was nothing he could say. It was too ridiculous.

They were, perhaps, a little smaller than himself, and black as the ace of spades, and they wore skin-tight shorts and vests that were somewhat oversize and both the shorts and vests were the blue of April skies.

But that was not the worst of it.

They sat on saddles, with horns in front and stirrups and a sort of bedroll tied on the back, but they had no horses.

The saddles floated in the air, with the stirrups about three feet above the ground and the aliens sat easily in the saddles and stared at him and he stared back at them.

Finally he got up and moved forward a step or two and when he did that the three swung from the saddles and moved forward, too, while the saddles hung there in the air, exactly as they'd left them.

Taine walked forward and the three walked forward until they were no more than six feet apart.

"They say hello to you," said Beasly. "They say welcome to you."

"Well, all right, then, tell them— Say, how do you know all this?"

"Chuck tells me what they say and I tell you. You tell me and I tell him and he tells them. That's the way it works. That is what he's here for."

"Well, I'll be—" said Taine. "So you can really talk to him."

"I told you that I could," stormed Beasly. "I told you that I could talk to Towser, too, but you thought that I was crazy."

"Telepathy!" said Taine. And it was worse than ever now. Not only had the rat-like things known all the rest of it, but they'd known of Beasly, too.

"What was that you said, Hiram?"

"Never mind," said Taine. "Tell that friend of yours to tell them I'm glad to meet them and what can I do for them?"

He stood uncomfortably and stared at the three and he saw that their vests had many pockets and that the pockets were crammed, probably with their equivalent of tobacco and handkerchiefs and pocket knives and such.

"They say," said Beasly, "that they want to dicker."

"Dicker?"

"Sure, Hiram. You know, trade."

Beasly chuckled thinly. "Imagine them laying themselves open to a Yankee trader. That's what Henry says you are. He says you can skin a man on the slickest—"

"Leave Henry out of this," snapped Taine. "Let's leave Henry out of something."

He sat down on the ground and the three sat down to face him.

"Ask them what they have in mind to trade."

"Ideas," Beasly said.

"Ideas! That's a crazy thing—"

And then he saw it wasn't.

Of all the commodities that might be exchanged by an alien people, ideas would

Clifford D. Simak

be the most valuable and the easiest to handle. They'd take no cargo room and they'd upset no economies—not immediately, that is—and they'd make a bigger contribution to the welfare of the cultures than trade in actual goods.

"Ask them," said Taine, "what they'll take for the idea back of those saddles they are riding."

"They say, what have you to offer?"

And that was the stumper. That was the one that would be hard to answer.

Automobiles and trucks, the internal gas engine—well, probably not. Because they already had the saddles. Earth was out of date in transportation from the viewpoint of these people.

Housing architecture—no, that was hardly an idea and, anyhow, there was that other house, so they knew of houses.

Cloth? No, they had cloth.

Paint, he thought. Maybe paint was it.

"See if they are interested in paint," Taine told Beasly.

"They say, what is it? Please explain yourself."

"OK, then. Let's see. It's a protective device to be spread over almost any surface. Easily packaged and easily applied. Protects against weather and corrosion. It's decorative, too. Comes in all sorts of colors. And it's cheap to make."

"They shrug in their mind," said Beasly. "They're just slightly interested. But they'll listen more. Go ahead and tell them."

And that was more like it, thought Taine.

That was the kind of language that he could understand.

He settled himself more firmly on the ground and bent forward slightly, flicking his eyes across the three dead-pan, ebony faces, trying to make out what they might be thinking.

There was no making out. Those were three of the deadest pans he had ever seen. It was all familiar. It made him feel at home. He was in his element.

And in the three across from him, he felt somehow subconsciously, he had the best dickering opposition he had ever met. And that made him feel good too.

"Tell them," he said, "that I'm not quite sure. I may have spoken up too hastily. Paint, after all, is a mighty valuable idea."

"They say, just as a favor to them, not that they're really interested, would you tell them a little more."

Got them hooked, Taine told himself. If he could only play it right—

He settled down to dickering in earnest.

Hours later Henry Horton showed up. He was accompanied by a very urbane gentleman, who was faultlessly turned out and who carried beneath his arm an impressive attaché case.

Henry and the man stopped on the steps in sheer astonishment.

Taine was squatted on the ground with a length of board and he was daubing paint on it while the aliens watched. From the daubs here and there upon their anatomies, it was plain to see the aliens had been doing some daubing of their own. Spread all over the ground were other lengths of half-painted boards and a couple of dozen old cans of paint.

Taine looked up and saw Henry and the man.

"I was hoping," he said, "that someone would show up."

"Hiram," said Henry, with more importance than usual, "may I present Mr. Lancaster. He is a special representative of the United Nations."

"I'm glad to meet you, sir," said Taine. "I wonder if you would—"

"Mr. Lancaster," Henry explained grandly, "was having some slight difficulty getting through the lines outside, so I volunteered my services. I've already explained to him our joint interest in this matter."

"It was very kind of Mr. Horton," Lancaster said. "There was this stupid sergeant—"

"It's all in knowing," Henry said, "how to handle people."

The remark, Taine noticed, was not appreciated by the man from the UN.

"May I inquire, Mr. Taine," asked Lancaster, "exactly what you're doing?"

"I'm dickering," said Taine.

"Dickering. What a quaint way of expressing—"

"An old Yankee word," said Henry quickly, "with certain connotations of its own. When you trade with someone you are exchanging goods, but if you're dickering with him you're out to get his hide."

"Interesting," said Lancaster. "And I suppose you're out to skin these gentlemen in the sky-blue vests—"

"Hiram," said Henry, proudly, "is the sharpest dickerer in these parts. He runs an antique business and he has to dicker hard—"

"And may I ask," said Lancaster, ignoring Henry finally, "what you might be doing with these cans of paint? Are these gentlemen potential customers for paint or—"

Taine threw down the board and rose angrily to his feet.

"If you'd both shut up!" he shouted. "I've been trying to say something ever since you got here and I can't get in a word. And I tell you, it's important—"

"Hiram!" Henry exclaimed in horror.

"It's quite all right," said the UN man. "We *have* been jabbering. And now, Mr. Taine?"

"I'm backed into a corner," Taine told him, "and I need some help. I've sold these fellows on the idea of paint, but I don't know a thing about it—the principle back of it or how it's made or what goes into it or—"

"But, Mr. Taine, if you're selling them the paint, what difference does it make—"

"I'm not selling them the paint," yelled Taine. "Can't you understand that? They

Clifford D. Simak

don't want the paint. They want the *idea* of paint, the principle of paint. It's something that they never thought of and they're interested. I offered them the paint idea for the idea of their saddles and I've almost got it—''

''Saddles? You mean those things over there, hanging in the air?''

''That is right. Beasly, would you ask one of our friends to demonstrate a saddle?''

''You bet I will,'' said Beasly.

''What,'' demanded Henry, ''has Beasly got to do with this?''

''Beasly is an interpreter. I guess you'd call him a telepath. You remember how he always claimed he could talk with Towser?''

''Beasly was always claiming things.''

''But this time he was right. He tells Chuck, that funny-looking monster, what I want to say and Chuck tells these aliens. And these aliens tell Chuck and Chuck tells Beasly and Beasly tells me.''

''Ridiculous!'' snorted Henry. ''Beasly hasn't got the sense to be . . . what did you say he was?''

''A telepath,'' said Taine.

One of the aliens had gotten up and climbed into a saddle. He rode it forth and back. Then he swung out of it and sat down again.

''Remarkable,'' said the UN man. ''Some sort of anti-gravity unit, with complete control. We could make use of that, indeed.''

He scraped his hand across his chin.

''And you're going to exchange the idea of paint for the idea of that saddle?''

''That's exactly it,'' said Taine, ''but I need some help. I need a chemist or a paint manufacturer or someone to explain how paint is made. And I need some professor or other who'll understand what they're talking about when they tell me the idea of the saddle.''

''I see,'' said Lancaster. ''Yes, indeed, you have a problem. Mr. Taine, you seem to me a man of some discernment—''

''Oh, he's all of that,'' interrupted Henry. ''Hiram's quite astute.''

''So I suppose you'll understand,'' said the UN man, ''that this whole procedure is quite irregular—''

''But it's not,'' exploded Taine. ''That's the way they operate. They open up a planet and then they exchange ideas. They've been doing that with other planets for a long, long time. And ideas are all they want, just the new ideas, because that is the way to keep on building a technology and culture. And they have a lot of ideas, sir, that the human race can use.''

''That is just the point,'' said Lancaster. ''This is perhaps the most important thing that has ever happened to us humans. In just a short year's time we can obtain data and ideas that will put us ahead—theoretically, at least—by a thousand years. And in a thing that is so important, we should have experts on the job—''

''But,'' protested Henry, ''you can't find a man who'll do a better dickering job than Hiram. When you dicker with him your back teeth aren't safe. Why don't you leave him be? He'll do a job for you. You can get your experts and your planning groups together and let Hiram front for you. These folks have accepted him and have proved they'll do business with him and what more do you want? All he needs is a little help."

Beasly came over and faced the UN man.

"I won't work with no one else," he said. "If you kick Hiram out of here, then I go with him. Hiram's the only person who ever treated me like a human—"

"There, you see!" Henry said triumphantly.

"Now, wait a second, Beasly," said the UN man. "We could make it worth your while. I should imagine that an interpreter in a situation such as this could command a handsome salary."

"Money don't mean a thing to me," said Beasly. "It won't buy me friends. People will still laugh at me."

"He means it, mister," Henry warned. "There isn't anyone who can be as stubborn as Beasly. I know; he used to work for us."

The UN man looked flabbergasted and not a little desperate.

"It will take you quite some time," Henry pointed out, "to find another telepath—leastwise one who can talk to these people here."

The UN man looked as if he were strangling. "I doubt," he said, "there's another one on Earth."

"Well, all right," said Beasly, brutally. "Let's make up our minds. I ain't standing here all day."

"All right," cried the UN man. "You two go ahead. Please, will you go ahead? This is a chance we can't let slip through our fingers. Is there anything you want? Anything I can do for you?"

"Yes, there is," said Taine. "There'll be the boys from Washington and bigwigs from other countries. Just keep them off my back."

"I'll explain most carefully to everyone. There'll be no interference."

"And I need that chemist and someone who'll know about the saddles. And I need them quick. I can stall these boys a little longer, but not for too much longer."

"Anyone you need," said the UN man. "Anyone at all. I'll have them here in hours. And in a day or two there'll be a pool of experts waiting for whenever you may need them—on a moment's notice."

"Sir," said Henry, unctuously, "that's most co-operative. Both Hiram and I appreciate it greatly. And now, since this is settled, I understand that there are reporters waiting. They'll be interested in your statement."

The UN man, it seemed, didn't have it in him to protest. He and Henry went tramping up the stairs.

Taine turned around and looked out across the desert.

"It's a big front yard," he said. ■

"WHAT DO YOU MEAN . . . HUMAN?"

John W. Campbell, Jr.

There are some questions that only small children and very great philosophers are supposed to ask—questions like "What is Death?" and "Where is God?"

And then there are some questions that, apparently, no one is supposed to ask at all, largely, I think, because people have gotten so many wrong answers, down through the centuries, that it's been agreed-by-default to not ask the questions at all.

Science fiction, however, by its very existence, has been asking one question that belongs in the "Let's agree not to discuss it at all" category—of course, simply by implication, but nevertheless very persistently. To wit: "What do you mean by the term 'human being'?"

It asks the question in a number of ways; the question of "What is a superman?" requires that we first define the limits of "normal man." The problem of "What's a robot?" asks the question in another way.

Some years ago now, Dr. Asimov introduced the Three Laws of Robotics into science fiction:

1. A robot can not harm, nor allow harm to come, to a human being.

2. A robot must obey the orders of human beings.

3. A robot must, within those limits, protect itself against damage.

The crucial one is, of course, the First Law. The point that science fiction has elided very deftly is . . . how do you tell a robot what a human being is?

Look . . . I'll play robot; you tell me what you mean by "human being." What is this entity-type that I'm required to leave immune, and defend? How am I, Robot, to distinguish between the following entities: 1. A human idiot. 2. Another robot. 3. A baby. 4. A chimpanzee.

We might, quite legitimately, include a humanoid alien—or even Tregonsee, E. E. Smith's Rigellian Lensman, and Worsel, the Velantian—which we, as science-fictioneers, have agreed fulfill what we *really* mean by "human"! But let's not make the problem that tough just yet.

171

We do, however, have to consider the brilliant question Dr. W. Ross Ashby raised: If a mechanic with an artificial arm is working on an engine, is the mechanical arm part of the organism struggling with the environment, or part of the environment the organism is struggling with? If I, Robot, am to be instructed properly, we must consider human beings with prosthetic attachments. And, if I am a really functional robot, then that implies a level of technology that could turn up some very fancy prosthetic devices. Henry Kuttner some years back had a story about a man who had, through an accident, been reduced to a brain in a box; the box, however, had plug-in connections whereby it could be coupled to allow the brain in the box to "be" a whole spaceship, or a power-excavator, or any other appropriate machine.

Is this to be regarded as "a robot" or "a human being"? Intuitively we feel that, no matter how many prosthetic devices may be installed as replacements, the human being remains.

The theologians used to have a very handy answer to most of those questions: a human being, unlike animals or machines, has a soul. If that is to be included in the discussion, however, we must also include the associated problems of distinguishing between human beings and incubi, succubi, demons, and angels. The problem then takes on certain other aspects . . . but the problem remains. History indicates that it was just as difficult to distinguish between humans and demons as it is, currently, to distinguish between humans and robots.

Let's try a little "truth-table" of the order that logicians sometimes use, and that advertisers are becoming fond of. We can try various suggested tests, and check off how the various entities we're trying to distinguish compare. (See top of page 173.)

You can, of course, continue to extend this, with all the tests you care to think of. I believe you'll find that you can find no test within the entire scope of permissible-in-our-society-evaluations that will permit a clear distinction between the five entities above.

Note, too, that that robot you want to follow the Three Laws is to modify the Second Law—obedience—rather extensively with respect to children and idiots, after you've told it how to distinguish between humanoids and chimpanzees.

There have been a good many wars fought over the question "What do you mean . . . human?" To the Greeks, the peoples of other lands didn't really speak languages—which meant Greek—but made mumbling noises that sounded like *bar-bar-bar*, which proved they were *barbarians*, and not really human.

The law should treat all human beings alike; that's been held as a concept for a long, long time. The Athenians subscribed to that concept. Of course, barbarians weren't really human, so the Law didn't apply to them, and slaves weren't; in fact only Athenian citizens were.

The easy way to make the law apply equally to all men is to so define "men" that the thing actually works. "Equal Justice for All! (All who are equal, of course.)"

John W. Campbell, Jr.

Test	Idiot	Robot	Baby	Chimp	Man with Prosthetic aids
1. Capable of logical thought.	No	Yes	No	No	Yes
2. "Do I not bleed?" (Merchant of Venice test.)	Yes	No	Yes	Yes	Depends
3. Capable of speech.	Yes	Yes	No	No	Yes
4. "Rational animal"; this must be divided into a. Rational	No	Yes	No	No	Yes
b. Animal	Yes	No	Yes	Yes	Partly
5. Humanoid form & size.	Yes	Yes	No	Yes	Maybe
6. Lack of fur or hair.	*	Yes	Yes	No	Maybe partly
7. A living being.	Yes	No	Yes	Ycs	Depends on what test you use for "living."

* A visit to a beach in summer will convince you that some adult male humans have a thicker pelt than some gorillas.

This problem of defining what you mean by "human being" appears to be at least as prolific a source of conflict as religion—and may, in fact, be why religion, that being the relationship between Man and God, has been so violent a ferment.

The law never has and never will apply equally to all; there are inferiors and superiors, whether we like it or not, and Justice does not stem from applying the same laws equally to different levels of beings. Before blowing your stack on that one, look again and notice that every human culture has recognized that you could *not* have the same set of laws for children and adults—not since the saurians lost dominance on the planet has that concept been workable. (Reptilian forms are hatched from the egg with all the wisdom they're ever going to have; among reptiles of one species, there is only a difference of size and physical strength.)

Not only is there difference on a vertical scale; but there's a displacement horizontally—i.e., different-but-equal, also exists. A woman may be equal to a man, but she's not the same as a man.

This, also, makes for complications when trying to decide "what is a human being";

there have been many cultures in history that definitely held that women weren't human.

I have a slight suspicion that the basic difficulty is that we can't get anything even approximating a workable concept of Justice so long as we consider equality a necessary, inherent part of it. The Law of Gravity applies equally to all bodies in the Universe—but that doesn't mean that the *force* of gravity is the same for all! Gravity—the universal law—is the same on Mars and a white dwarf star as it is on Earth. That doesn't mean that the *force* of gravity is the same.

But it takes considerable genius to come up with a Universal Law of Gravity for sheer, inanimate mass. What it takes to discover the equivalent for intelligent entities . . . the human race hasn't achieved as yet! Not even once has an individual reached that level!

This makes defining "human" a somewhat explosive subject.

Now the essence of humanity most commonly discussed by philosophers has been Man, the Rational Animal. The ability to think logically; to have ideas, and be conscious of having those ideas. The implied intent in "defining humanness" is to define the unique, highest-level attribute that sets man apart from all other entities.

That "rational animal" gimmick worked pretty well for a long time; the development of electronic computers, and the clear implication of robots calls it into question. That plus the fact that psychological experiments have shown that logical thought isn't quite so unique-to-Man as philosophers thought.

The thing that is unique to human beings is something the philosophers have sputtered at, rejected, damned, and loudly forsworn throughout history. Man is the only known entity that laughs, weeps, grieves, and yearns. There's been considerable effort made to prove that those are the result of simple biochemical changes of endocrine balance. That is, that you feel angry because there is adrenalin in the bloodstream, released from the suprarenal glands. Yes, and the horse moves because the cart keeps pushing him. Why did the gland start secreting that extra charge of adrenaline?

The essence of our actual definition of humanness is "I am human; any entity that *feels* as I feel is human also. But any entity that merely thinks, and *feels* differently is not human."

The "inhuman scientist" is so called because he doesn't appear to *feel* as the speaker does. While we were discussing possible theological ramifications of the humanness question, we might have included the zombie. Why isn't a zombie "human" any longer? Because he has become the logical philosopher's ideal; a purely rational, non-emotional entity.

Why aren't Tregonsee, the Rigellian, and Worsel, the Velantian, to be compared with animals and/or robots?

Because, as defined in E. E. Smith's stories, they *feel* as we do.

Now it's long since been observed that an individual will find his logical thinking

John W. Campbell, Jr.

subtly biased in the direction of his emotional feelings. His actions will be controlled not by his logic and reason, but in the end, by his emotional pulls. If a man is my loyal friend—i.e., if he *feels* favorable-to-me—then whatever powers of physical force or mental brilliance he may have are no menace to me, but are a menace to my enemies. If he *feels* about things as I do, I need not concern myself with how he *thinks* about them, or what he does. He is "human"—my kind of human.

But . . . if he can *choose* his feelings, if his emotions are subject to his conscious, judicious, volitional choice . . . ? What then? If his emotional biases are not as rigidly unalterable as his bones? If he can exercise judgment and vary his feelings, can I trust him to remain "human"?

Could an entity who felt differently about things—whose emotions were different—be "human"?

That question may be somewhat important to us. Someone, sooner or later, is going to meet an alien, a really alien alien, not just a member of Homo sapiens from a divergent breed and culture.

Now it's true that all things are relative. Einstein proved the relativity of even the purely physical level of reality. But be it noted that Einstein proved that *Law* of Relativity; things aren't "purely relative" in the sense that's usually used—"I can take any system of relationships I choose!" There are laws of relativity.

The emotional biases a culture induces in its citizens vary widely. Mores are a matter of cultural relativity.

That doesn't mean that ethics is; there are laws of relativity, and it's not true that any arbitrary system of relationships is just as good as any other.

Can we humans-who-define-humanness-in-emotional-terms—despite what we theoretically say!—meet an equally wise race with different emotions—and know them for fellow humans?

A man who thinks differently we can tolerate and understand, but our history shows we don't know how to understand a man who feels differently.

The most frightening thing about a man who feels differently is this: his feelings might be contagious. We might learn to feel *his* way—and then, of course, we wouldn't be human any more.

The wiser and sounder his different feelings are, the greater the awful danger of learning to feel that way. And that would make us inhuman, of course.

How do you suppose an Athenian Greek of Pericles's time would have felt if threatened with a change of feelings such that he would not feel disturbed if someone denied the reality of the Gods, or suggested that the Latins had a sounder culture? Why—only a nonhuman barbarian could feel that way!

The interesting thing is that the implication of "inhuman" is invariably *sub*-human.

I suspect one of the most repugnant aspects of Darwin's concept of evolution was—not that we descended from monkeys—but its implication that something was apt to descend from us! Something that wasn't human . . . *and wasn't sub-human.*

The only perfect correlation is auto-correlation; "I am exactly what I am." Any difference whatever makes the correlation less perfect.

Then if what I feel is human—anything different is less perfectly correlated with humanness. Hence any entity not identical is more or less subhuman; there can't possibly be something more like me than I am.

Anybody want to try for a workable definition of "human"? One warning before you get started too openly; logical discussion doesn't lead to violence—until it enters the area of emotion.

As of now, we'd have to tell the robot "A human being is an entity having an emotional structure, as well as a physical and mental structure. Never mind what kind of emotional structure—good, indifferent, or insane. It's the fact of its existence that distinguishes the human."

Of course, that does lead to the problem of giving the robot emotion-perceptors so he can detect the existence of an emotion-structure.

And that, of course, gets almost as tough as the problem of distinguishing a masquerading demon from a man. You know . . . maybe they are the same problem?

It's always puzzled me that in the old days they detected so many demons, and so few angels, too. It always looked as though the Legions of Hell greatly outnumbered the Host of Heaven, or else were far more diligent on Earth.

But then . . . the subhuman is so much more acceptable than the superhuman. ∎

HOME IS THE HANGMAN

Roger Zelazny

Big fat flakes down the night, silent night, windless night. And I never count them as storms unless there is wind. Not a sigh or a whimper, though. Just a cold, steady whiteness, drifting down outside the window, and a silence confirmed by gunfire, driven deeper now it had ceased. In the main room of the lodge the only sounds were the occasional hiss and sputter of the logs turning to ashes on the grate.

I sat in a chair turned sidewise from the table to face the door. A tool kit rested on the floor to my left. The helmet stood on the table, a lopsided basket of metal, quartz, porcelain and glass. If I heard the click of a microswitch followed by a humming sound from within it, then a faint light would come on beneath the meshing near to its forward edge and begin to blink rapidly. If these things occurred, there was a very strong possibility that I was going to die.

I had removed a black ball from my pocket when Larry and Bert had gone outside, armed, respectively, with a flame thrower and what looked like an elephant gun. Bert had also taken two grenades with him.

I unrolled the black ball, opening it out into a seamless glove, a dollop of something resembling moist putty stuck to its palm. Then I drew the glove on over my left hand and sat with it upraised, elbow resting on the arm of the chair. A small flash pistol in which I had very little faith lay beside my right hand on the tabletop, next to the helmet.

If I were to slap a metal surface with my left hand, the substance would adhere there, coming free of the glove. Two seconds later it would explode, and the force of the explosion would be directed in against the surface. Newton would claim his own by way of right-angled redistributions of the reaction, hopefully tearing lateral hell out of the contact surface. A smother-charge, it was called, and its possession came under concealed weapons and possession of burglary tools statutes in most places. The molecularly gimmicked goo, I decided, was great stuff. It was just the delivery system that left more to be desired.

Beside the helmet, next to the gun, in front of my hand, stood a small walkie-talkie. This was for purposes of warning Bert and Larry if I should hear the click of a microswitch followed by a humming sound, should see a light come on and begin to blink rapidly. Then they would know that Tom and Clay, with whom we had lost contact when the shooting began, had failed to destroy the enemy and doubtless lay lifeless at their stations now, a little over a kilometer to the south. Then they would know that they, too, were probably about to die.

I called out to them when I heard the click. I picked up the helmet and rose to my feet as its light began to blink.

But it was already too late.

The fourth place listed on the Christmas card I had sent Don Walsh the previous year was Peabody's Book Shop and Beer Stube in Baltimore, Maryland. Accordingly, on the last night in October I sat in its rearmost room, at the final table before the alcove with the door leading to the alley. Across that dim chamber, a woman dressed in black played the ancient upright piano, up-tempoing everything she touched. Off to my right, a fire wheezed and spewed fumes on a narrow hearth beneath a crowded mantelpiece overseen by an ancient and antlered profile. I sipped a beer and listened to the sounds.

I half-hoped that this would be one of the occasions when Don failed to show up. I had sufficient funds to hold me through spring and I did not really feel like working. I had summered farther north, was anchored now in the Chesapeake and was anxious to continue Caribbeanwards. A growing chill and some nasty winds told me I had tarried overlong in these latitudes. Still, the understanding was that I remain in the chosen bar until midnight. Two hours to go.

I ate a sandwich and ordered another beer. About halfway into it, I spotted Don approaching the entranceway, topcoat over his arm, head turning. I manufactured a matching quantity of surprise when he appeared beside my table with a, "Don! Is that really you?"

I rose and clasped his hand.

"Alan! Small world, or something like that. Sit down! Sit down!"

He settled onto the chair across from me, draped his coat over the one to his left.

"What are you doing in this town?" he asked.

"Just a visit," I answered. "Said hello to a few friends." I patted the scars, the stains of the venerable surface before me. "And this is my last stop. I'll be leaving in a few hours."

He chuckled.

"Why is it that you knock on wood?"

I grinned.

"I was expressing affection for one of Henry Mencken's favorite speakeasies."

"This place dates back that far?"

I nodded.

"It figures," he said. "You've got this thing for the past—or against the present. I'm never sure which."

Roger Zelazny

"Maybe a little of both," I said. "I wish Mencken would stop in. I'd like his opinion on the present. What are you doing with it?"

"What?"

"The present. Here. Now."

"Oh." He spotted the waitress and ordered a beer. "Business trip," he said then. "To hire a consultant."

"Oh. And how *is* business?"

"Complicated," he said, "complicated."

We lit cigarettes and after a while his beer arrived. We smoked and drank and listened to the music.

I've sung this song and I'll sing it again: the world is like an up-tempoed piece of music. Of the many changes which came to pass during my lifetime, it seems that the majority have occurred during the past few years. It also struck me that way several years ago, and I'd a hunch I might be feeling the same way a few years hence—that is, if Don's business did not complicate me off this mortal coil or condensor before then.

Don operates the second largest detective agency in the world, and he sometimes finds me useful because I do not exist. I do not exist now because I existed once at the time and the place where we attempted to begin scoring the wild ditty of our times. I refer to the World Data Bank project and the fact that I had had a significant part in that effort to construct a working model of the real world, accounting for everyone and everything in it. How well we succeeded and whether possession of the world's likeness does indeed provide its custodians with a greater measure of control over its functions, are questions my former colleagues still debate as the music grows more shrill and you can't see the maps for the pins. I made my decision back then and saw to it that I did not receive citizenship in that second world, a place which may now have become more important than the first. Exiled to reality, my own sojourns across the line are necessarily those of an alien guilty of illegal entry. I visit periodically because I go where I must to make my living. That is where Don comes in. The people I can become are often very useful when he has peculiar problems. Unfortunately, at that moment, it seemed that he did, just when the whole gang of me felt like turning down the volume and loafing.

We finished our drinks, got the bill, settled it.

"This way," I said, indicating the rear door, and he swung into his coat and followed me out.

"Talk here?" he asked, as we walked down the alley.

"Rather not," I said. "Public transportation, then private conversation."

He nodded and came along.

About three-quarters of an hour later we were in the saloon of the *Proteus* and I was making coffee. We were rocked gently by the Bay's chill waters, under a moonless sky. I'd only a pair of the smaller lights burning. Comfortable. On the water, aboard the *Proteus*, the crowding, the activities, the tempo, of life in the cities, on the land, are muted, slowed—fictionalized—by the metaphysical distancing a few meters of water can provide. We alter the landscape with great facility, but the ocean has always seemed unchanged, and I suppose by extension we are infected with some feelings of timelessness whenever we set out upon her. Maybe that's one of the reasons I spend so much time there.

"First time you've had me aboard," he said. "Comfortable. Very."

"Thanks. Cream? Sugar?"

"Yes. Both."

We settled back with our steaming mugs and I said, "What have you got?"

"One case involving two problems," he said. "One of them sort of falls within my area of competence. The other does not. I was told that it is an absolutely unique situation and would require the services of a very special specialist."

"I'm not a specialist at anything but keeping alive."

His eyes came up suddenly and caught my own.

"I had always assumed that you knew an awful lot about computers," he said.

I looked away. That was hitting below the belt. I had never held myself out to him as an authority in that area, and there had always been a tacit understanding between us that my methods of manipulating circumstance and identity were not open to discussion. On the other hand, it was obvious to him that my knowledge of the system was both extensive and intensive. Still, I didn't like talking about it. So I moved to defend.

"Computer people are a dime a dozen," I said. "It was probably different in your time, but these days they start teaching computer science to little kids their first year in school. So, sure I know a lot about it. This generation, everybody does."

"You know that is not what I meant," he said. "Haven't you known me long enough to trust me a little more than that? The question springs solely from the case at hand. That's all."

I nodded. Reactions by their very nature are not always appropriate, and I had invested a lot of emotional capital in a heavy duty set. So, "OK, I know more about them than the school kids," I said.

"Thanks. That can be our point of departure." He took a sip of coffee. "My own background is in law and accounting, followed by the military, military intelligence and civil service, in that order. Then I got into this business. What technical stuff I know I've picked up along the way, a scrap here, a crash course there. I know a lot about what things can do, not so much about how they work. I did not understand the details on this one, so I want you to start at the top and explain things to me, for as far as you can go. I need the background review, and if you are able to furnish it I will also know that you are the man for the job. You can begin by telling me how the early space exploration robots worked—like, say, the ones they used on Venus."

"That's not computers," I said, "and for that matter, they weren't really robots. They were telefactoring devices."

"Tell me what makes the difference."

"A robot is a machine which carries out certain operations in accordance with a program of instructions. A telefactor is a slave machine operated by remote control. The telefactor functions in a feedback situation with its operator. Depending on how sophisticated you want to get, the links can be audio-visual, kinesthetic, tactile, even olfactory. The more you want to go in this direction, the more anthropomorphic you get in the thing's design. In the case of Venus, if I recall correctly, the human operator in orbit wore an exoskeleton which controlled the movements of the body, legs, arms and hands of the device on the surface below, receiving motion and force feedback through a system of airjet transducers. He had on a helmet controlling the slave device's television camera—set, obviously enough, in its turret—which filled his field of vision with the scene below. He also wore earphones connected with its audio pickup. I read the book he wrote later. He said that for long stretches of time, he would forget the cabin, forget that he was at the boss end of a control loop and actually feel as if he were stalking through that hellish landscape. I remember being very impressed by it, just being a kid, and I wanted a supertiny one all my own, so that I could wade around in puddles picking fights with microorganisms."

"Why?"

"Because there weren't any dragons on Venus. Anyhow, that is a telefactoring device, a thing quite distinct from a robot."

"I'm still with you," he said. "Now tell me the difference between the early telefactoring devices and the later ones."

I swallowed some coffee.

"It was a bit trickier with respect to the outer planets and their satellites," I said. "There, we did not have orbiting operators at first. Economics, and some unresolved technical problems. Mainly economics. At any rate, the devices were landed on the target worlds, but the operators stayed home. Because of this, there was of course a time lag in the transmissions along the control loop. It took a while to receive the on-site input, and then there was another time-lapse before the response movements reached the telefactor. We attempted to compensate for this in two ways. The first was by the employment of a simple wait-move, wait-move sequence. The second was more sophisticated and is actually the point where computers come into the picture in terms of participating in the control loop. It involved the setting up of models of known environmental factors, which were then enriched during the initial wait-move sequences. On this basis, the computer was then used to anticipate short-range developments. Finally, it could take over the loop and run it by a combination of 'predictor controls' and wait-move reviews. It still had to holler for human help though, when unexpected things came up. So, with the outer planets, it was neither totally automatic nor totally manual—nor totally satisfactory—at first."

"OK," he said, lighting a cigarette. "And the next step?"

"The next wasn't really a technical step forward in telefactoring. It was an economic shift. The purse strings were loosened and we could afford to send men out. We landed them where we could land them, and in many of the places where we could not we sent down the telefactors and orbited the men again. Like in the old days. The time lag problem was removed because the operator was on top of things once more. If anything, you can look at it as a reversion to earlier methods. It is what we still often do, though, and it works."

He shook his head.

"You left something out," he said, "between the computers and the bigger budget."

I shrugged.

"A number of things were tried during that period," I said, "but none of them proved as effective as what we already had going in the human-computer partnership with the telefactors."

"There was one project," he said, "which attempted to get around the time lag troubles by sending the computer along with the telefactor as part of the package. Only the computer wasn't exactly a computer and the telefactor wasn't exactly a telefactor. Do you know which one I am referring to?"

I lit a cigarette of my own while I thought about it, then, "I think you are talking about the Hangman," I said.

"That's right," he said, "and this is where I get lost. Can you tell me how it works?"

"Ultimately, it was a failure," I said.

"But it worked at first."

"Apparently. But only on the easy stuff, on Io. It conked out later and had to be written off as a failure, albeit a noble one. The venture was overly ambitious from the very beginning. What seems to have happened was that the people in charge had the opportunity to combine vanguard projects—stuff that was still under investigation and stuff that was extremely new. In theory it all seemed to dovetail so beautifully that they yielded to the temptation and incorporated too much. It started out well, but it fell apart later."

"But what all was involved in the thing?"

"Lord! What wasn't? The computer that wasn't exactly a computer . . . OK, we'll start there. Last century, three engineers at the University of Wisconsin—Nordman, Parmentier and Scott—developed a device known as a superconductive tunnel junction neuristor. Two tiny strips of metal with a thin insulating layer between. Supercool it and it passed electrical impulses without resistance. Surround it with magnetized material and pack a mass of them together—billions—and what have you got?"

He shook his head.

"Well, for one thing you've got an impossible situation to schematize when considering all the paths and interconnections that may be formed. There is an obvious

Roger Zelazny

similarity to the structure of the brain. So, they theorized, you don't even attempt to hook up such a device. You pulse in data and let it establish its own preferential pathways, by means of the magnetic material's becoming increasingly magnetized each time the current passes through it, thus cutting the resistance. So the material establishes its own routes in a fashion analogous to the functioning of the brain when it is learning something. In the case of the Hangman, they used a setup very similar to this and they were able to pack over ten billion neuristor-type cells into a very small area—around a cubic foot. They aimed for that magic figure because that is approximately the number of nerve cells in the human brain. That is what I meant when I said that it wasn't really a computer. They were actually working in the area of artificial intelligence, no matter what they called it.''

"If the thing had its own brain—computer or quasi-human—then it was a robot rather than a telefactor, right?''

"Yes and no and maybe,'' I said. ''It was operated as a telefactor device here on Earth—on the ocean floor, in the desert, in mountainous country—as part of its programming. I suppose you could also call that its apprenticeship or kindergarten. Perhaps that is even more appropriate. It was being shown how to explore in difficult environments and to report back. Once it mastered this, then theoretically they could hang it out there in the sky without a control loop and let it report its own findings.''

"At that point would it be considered a robot?''

"A robot is a machine which carries out certain operations in accordance with a program of instructions. The Hangman made its own decisions, you see. And I suspect that by trying to produce something that close to the human brain in structure and function the seemingly inevitable randomness of its model got included in. It wasn't just a machine following a program. It was too complex. That was probably what broke it down.''

Don chuckled.

"Inevitable free will?''

"No. As I said, they had thrown too many things into one bag. Everybody and his brother with a pet project that might be fitted in seemed a supersalesman that season. For example, the psychophysics boys had a gimmick they wanted to try on it, and it got used. Ostensibly, it was a communications device. Actually, they were concerned as to whether the thing was truly sentient.''

"Was it?''

"Apparently so, in a limited fashion. What they had come up with, to be made part of the initial telefactor loop, was a device which set up a weak induction field in the brain of the operator. The machine received and amplified the patterns of electrical activity being conducted in the Hangman's—might as well call it 'brain'—then passed them through a complex modulator and pulsed them into the induction field in the operator's head. I am out of my area now and into that of Weber and Fechner, but a neuron has a threshold at which it will fire, and below which it will not. There are some forty thousand neurons packed together in a square millimeter of the cerebral cortex, in such a fashion that each one has several hundred synaptic connections with others about it. At any given moment, some of them may be way below the firing threshold while others are in a condition Sir John Eccles once referred to as 'critically poised'—ready to fire. If just one is pushed over the threshold, it can affect the discharge of hundreds of thousands of others within twenty milliseconds. The pulsating field was to provide such a push in a sufficiently selective fashion to give the operator an idea as to what was going on in the Hangman's brain. And vice versa. The Hangman was to have its own built-in version of the same thing. It was also thought that this might serve to humanize it somewhat, so that it would better appreciate the significance of its work—to instill something like loyalty, you might say."

"Do you think this could have contributed to its later breakdown?"

"Possibly. How can you say in a one-of-a-kind situation like this? If you want a guess, I'd say yes. But it's just a guess."

"Uh-huh," he said, "and what were its physical capabilities?"

"Anthropomorphic design," I said, "both because it was originally telefactored and because of the psychological reasoning I just mentioned. It could pilot its own small vessel. No need for a life-support system, of course. Both it and the vessel were powered by fusion units, so that fuel was no real problem. Self-repairing. Capable of performing a great variety of sophisticated tests and measurements, of making observations, completing reports, learning new material, broadcasting its findings back here. Capable of surviving just about anywhere. In fact, it required less energy on the outer planets—less work for the refrigeration units, to maintain that supercooled brain in its midsection."

"How strong was it?"

"I don't recall all the specs. Maybe a dozen times as strong as a man, in things like lifting and pushing."

"It explored Io for us and started in on Europa."

"Yes."

"Then it began behaving erratically, just when we thought it had really learned its job."

"That sounds right," I said.

"It refused a direct order to explore Callisto, then headed out toward Uranus."

"Yes. It's been years since I read the reports . . ."

"The malfunction worsened after that. Long periods of silence interspersed with garbled transmissions. Now that I know more about its makeup, it almost sounds like a man going off the deep end."

"It seems similar."

"But it managed to pull itself together again for a brief while. It landed on Titania, began sending back what seemed like appropriate observation reports. This only lasted a short time, though. It went irrational once more, indicated that it was heading for

Roger Zelazny

a landing on Uranus itself, and that was it. We didn't hear from it after that. Now that I know about that mind-reading gadget I understand why a psychiatrist on this end could be so positive it would never function again."

"I never heard about that part."

"I did."

I shrugged.

"This was all around twenty years ago," I said, "and, as I mentioned, it has been a long while since I've read anything about it."

"The Hangman's ship crashed or landed, as the case may be, in the Gulf of Mexico," he said, "two days ago."

I just stared at him.

"It was empty," he said, "when they finally got out and down to it."

"I don't understand."

"Yesterday morning," he went on, "restaurateur Manny Burns was found beaten to death in the office of his establishment, the *Maison Saint-Michel*, in New Orleans."

"I still fail to see . . ."

"Manny Burns was one of the four original operators who programmed—pardon me, 'taught'—the Hangman."

The silence lengthened, dragged its belly on the deck.

"Coincidence . . .?" I finally said.

"My client doesn't think so."

"Who is your client?"

"One of the three remaining members of the training group. He is convinced that the Hangman has returned to Earth to kill its former operators."

"Has he made his fears known to his old employers?"

"No."

"Why not?"

"Because it would require telling them the reason for his fears."

"That being . . . ?"

"He wouldn't tell me either."

"How does he expect you to do a proper job?"

"He told me what he considered a proper job. He wants two things done, neither of which requires a full case history. He wanted to be furnished with good bodyguards, and he wanted the Hangman found and disposed of. I have already taken care of the first part."

"And you want me to do the second?"

"That's right. You have confirmed my opinion that you are the man for the job."

"I see," I said. "Do you realize that if the thing is truly sentient this will be something very like murder? If it is not, of course, then it will only amount to the destruction of expensive government property."

"Which way do you look at it?"

"I look at it as a job," I said.

"You'll take it?"

"I need more facts before I can decide. Like . . . Who is your client? Who are the other operators? Where do they live? What do they do? What—"

He raised his hand.

"First," he said, "the Honorable Jesse Brockden, Senior Senator from Wisconsin, is our client. Confidentiality, of course, is written all over it."

I nodded.

"I remember his being involved with the space program before he went into politics. I wasn't aware of the specifics, though. He could get government protection so easily—"

"To obtain it, he would apparently have to tell them something he doesn't want to talk about. Perhaps it would hurt his career. I simply do not know. He doesn't want them. He wants us."

I nodded again.

"What about the others? Do they want us, too?"

"Quite the opposite. They don't subscribe to Brockden's notions at all. They seem to think he is something of a paranoid."

"How well do they know one another these days?"

"They live in different parts of the country, haven't seen each other in years. Been in occasional touch, though."

"Kind of flimsy basis for that diagnosis, then."

"One of them *is* a psychiatrist."

"Oh. Which one?"

"Leila Thackery is her name. Lives in St. Louis. Works at the State Hospital there."

"None of them have gone to any authority, then—Federal or local?"

"That's right. Brockden contacted them when he heard about the Hangman. He was in Washington at the time. Got word on its return right away and managed to get the story killed. He tried to reach them all, learned about Burns in the process, contacted me, then tried to persuade the others to accept protection by my people. They weren't buying. When I talked to her, Dr. Thackery pointed out—quite correctly—that Brockden is a very sick man—"

"What's he got?"

"Cancer. In his spine. Nothing they can do about it once it hits there and digs in. He even told me he figures he has maybe six months to get through what he considers a very important piece of legislation—the new criminal rehabilitation act. I will admit that he did sound kind of paranoid when he talked about it. But hell! Who wouldn't? Dr. Thackery sees that as the whole thing, though, and she doesn't see the Burns killing as being connected with the Hangman. Thinks it was just a traditional robbery gone sour, thief surprised and panicky, maybe hopped-up, et cetera."

Roger Zelazny

"Then she is not afraid of the Hangman?"

"She said that she is in a better position to know its mind than anyone else, and she is not especially concerned."

"What about the other operator?"

"He said that Dr. Thackery may know its mind better than anyone else, but he knows its brain, and he isn't worried either."

"What did he mean by that?"

"David Fentris is a consulting engineer—electronics, cybernetics. He actually had something to do with the Hangman's design."

I got to my feet and went after the coffee pot. Not that I'd an overwhelming desire for another cup at just that moment. But I had known, had once worked with a David Fentris. And he had at one time been connected with the space program.

About fifteen years my senior, Dave had been with the Data Bank project when I had known him. Where a number of us had begun having second thoughts as the thing progressed, Dave had never been anything less than wildly enthusiastic. A wiry five-eight, white-cropped, gray eyes back of hornrims and heavy glass, cycling between preoccupation and near-frantic darting, he had had a way of verbalizing half-completed thoughts as he went along, so that you might begin to think him a representative of that tribe which had come into positions of small authority by means of nepotism or politics. If you would listen a few more minutes though, you would begin revising your opinion as he started to pull his musings together into a rigorous framework. By the time he had finished you generally wondered why you hadn't seen it all along and what a guy like that was doing in a position of such small authority. Later, it might strike you, though, that he seemed sad whenever he wasn't enthusiastic about something, and while the gung-ho spirit is great for short-range projects, larger ventures generally require something more of equanimity. I wasn't at all surprised that he had wound up as a consultant. The big question now, of course, was would he remember me? True, my appearance was altered, my personality hopefully more mature, my habits shifted around. But would that be enough, should I have to encounter him as part of this job? That mind behind those hornrims could do a lot of strange things with just a little data.

"Where does he live?" I asked.

"Memphis, and what's the matter?"

"Just trying to get my geography straight," I said. "Is Senator Brockden still in Washington?"

"No. He's returned to Wisconsin and is currently holed up in a lodge in the northern part of the state. Four of my people are with him."

"I see."

I refreshed our coffee supply and reseated myself. I didn't like this one at all and I resolved not to take it. I didn't like just giving Don a flat no, though. His assignments had become a very important part of my life, and this one was not mere legwork. It was obviously important to him, and he wanted me on it. I decided to look for holes in the thing, to find some way of reducing it to the simple bodyguard job already in progress.

"It does seem peculiar," I said, "that Brockden is the only one afraid of the device."

"Yes."

" . . . And that he gives no reasons."

"True."

" . . . Plus his condition, and what the doctor said about its effect on his mind."

"I have no doubt that he is neurotic," Don said. "Look at this."

He reached for his coat, withdrew a sheaf of papers from within it. He shuffled through them and extracted a single sheet, which he passed to me. It was a piece of Congressional letterhead stationery, with the message scrawled in longhand: "Don," it said, "I've got to see you. Frankenstein's monster has just come back from where we hung him and he's looking for me. The whole damn universe is trying to grind me up. Call me between eight and ten.—Jess." I nodded, started to pass it back, paused, then handed it over. Double damn it deeper than hell! I took a drink of coffee. I thought that I had long ago given up hope in such things, but I had noticed something which immediately troubled me. In the margin where they list such matters, I had seen that Jesse Brockden was on the committee for review of the Data Bank program. I recalled that that committee was supposed to be working on a series of reform recommendations. Offhand, I could not remember Brockden's position on any of the issues involved, but—oh hell! The thing was simply too big to alter significantly now . . . But it *was* the only real Frankenstein monster I cared about, and there was always the possibility . . . On the other hand—hell, again. What if I let him die when I might have saved him, and he had been the one who . . . ?

I took another drink of coffee. I lit another cigarette. There might be a way of working it so that Dave didn't even come into the picture. I could talk to Leila Thackery first, check further into the Burns killing, keep posted on new developments, find out more about the vessel in the Gulf . . . I might be able to accomplish something, even if it was only the negation of Brockden's theory, without Dave's and my paths ever crossing.

"Have you got the specs on the Hangman?" I asked.

"Right here."

He passed them over.

"The police report on the Burns killing?"

"Here it is."

"The whereabouts of everyone involved, and some background on them?"

"Here."

"The place or places where I can reach you during the next few days—around the clock? This one may require some coordination."

Roger Zelazny

He smiled and reached for his pen.

"Glad to have you aboard," he said.

I reached over and tapped the barometer. I shook my head.

The ringing of the phone awakened me. Reflex bore me across the room, where I took it on audio.

"Yes?"

"Mr. Donne? It is eight o'clock."

"Thanks."

I collapsed into the chair. I am what might be called a slow starter. I tend to recapitulate phylogeny every morning. Basic desires inched their ways through my gray matter to close a connection. Slowly, I extended a cold-blooded member and clicked my talons against a couple of numbers. I croaked my desire for food and lots of coffee to the voice that responded. Half an hour later I would only have growled. Then I staggered off to the place of flowing waters to renew my contact with basics.

In addition to my normal adrenaline and blood-sugar bearishness, I had not slept much the night before. I had closed up shop after Don had left, stuffed my pockets with essentials, departed the *Proteus*, gotten myself over to the airport and onto a flight which took me to St. Louis in the dead, small hours of the dark. I was unable to sleep during the flight, thinking about the case, deciding on the tack I was going to take with Leila Thackery. On arrival, I had checked into the airport motel, left a message to be awakened at an unreasonable hour and collapsed.

As I ate, I regarded the fact-sheet Don had given me: Leila Thackery was currently single, having divorced her second husband a little over two years ago, was forty-six years old and lived in an apartment near to the hospital where she worked. Attached to the sheet was a photo which might have been ten years old. In it, she was brunette, light-eyed, barely on the right side of that border between ample and overweight, with fancy glasses straddling an upturned nose. She had published a number of books and articles with titles full of alienations, roles, transactions, social contexts and more alienations.

I hadn't had the time to go my usual route, becoming an entire new individual with a verifiable history. Just a name and a story, that's all. It did not seem necessary this time, though. For once, something approximating honesty actually seemed a reasonable approach.

I took a public vehicle over to her apartment building. I did not phone ahead, because it is easier to say no to a voice than to a person. According to the record, today was one of the days when she saw outpatients in her home. Her idea, apparently: break down the alienating institution image, remove resentments by turning the sessions into something more like social occasions, et cetera. I did not want all that much of her time, I had decided that Don could make it worth her while if it came to that, and

I was sure my fellows' visits were scheduled to leave her with some small breathing space—*inter alia*, so to speak.

I had just located her name and apartment number amid the buttons in the entrance foyer when an old woman passed behind me and unlocked the door to the lobby. She glanced at me and held it open, so I went on in without ringing. The matter of presence, again.

I took the elevator to Leila's floor, the second. I located her door and knocked on it. I was almost ready to knock again when it opened, part-way.

"Yes?" she asked, and I revised my estimate as to the age of the photo. She looked just about the same.

"Dr. Thackery," I said, "my name is Donne. You could help me quite a bit with a problem I've got."

"What sort of problem?"

"It involves a device known as the Hangman."

She sighed and showed me a quick grimace. Her fingers tightened on the door.

"I've come a long way but I'll be easy to get rid of. I've only a few things I'd like to ask you about it."

"Are you with the Government?"

"No."

"Do you work for Brockden?"

"No, I'm something different."

"All right," she said. "Right now I've got a group session going. It will probably last around another half-hour. If you don't mind waiting down in the lobby, I'll let you know as soon as it is over. We can talk then."

"Good enough," I said. "Thanks."

She nodded, closed the door. I located the stairway and walked back down.

A cigarette later, I decided that the devil finds work for idle hands and thanked him for his suggestion. I strolled back toward the foyer. Through the glass, I read the names of a few residents of the fifth floor. I elevated up and knocked on one of the doors. Before it was opened I had my notebook and pad in plain sight.

"Yes?"—short, fiftyish, curious.

"My name is Stephen Foster, Mrs. Gluntz. I am doing a survey for the North American Consumers League. I would like to pay you for a couple minutes of your time, to answer some questions about products you use."

"Why— Pay me?"

"Yes, ma'am. Ten dollars. Around a dozen questions. It will just take a minute or two."

"All right." She opened the door wider. "Won't you come in?"

"No, thank you. This thing is so brief I'd just be in and out. The first question involves detergents—"

Ten minutes later was back in the lobby adding the thirty bucks for the three

Roger Zelazny

interviews to the list of expenses I was keeping. When a situation is full of unpre-dictables and I am playing makeshift games, I like to provide for as many contingencies as I can.

Another quarter of an hour or so slipped by before the elevator opened and discharged three guys, young, young and middle-aged, casually dressed, chuckling over some-thing. The big one on the nearest end strolled over and nodded.

"You the fellow waiting to see Dr. Thackery?"

"That's right."

"She said to tell you to come on up now."

"Thanks."

I rode up again, returned to her door. She opened to my knock, nodded me in, saw me seated in a comfortable chair at the far end of her living room.

"Would you care for a cup of coffee?" she asked. "It's fresh. I made more than I needed."

"That would be fine. Thanks."

Moments later, she brought in a couple cups, delivered one to me and seated herself on the sofa to my left. I ignored the cream and sugar on the tray and took a sip.

"You've gotten me interested," she said. "Tell me about it."

"OK. I have been told that the telefactor device known as the Hangman, now possibly possessed of an artificial intelligence, has returned to Earth—"

"Hypothetical," she said, "unless you know something I don't. I have been told that the Hangman's vehicle reentered and crashed in the Gulf. There is no evidence that the vehicle was occupied."

"It seems a reasonable conclusion, though."

"It seems just as reasonable to me that the Hangman sent the vehicle off toward an eventual rendezvous point many years ago and that it only recently reached that point, at which time the reentry program took over and brought it down."

"Why should it return the vehicle and strand itself out there?"

"Before I answer that," she said, "I would like to know the reason for your concern. News media?"

"No," I said. "I am a science writer—straight tech, popular and anything in between. But I am not after a piece for publication. I was retained to do a report on the psychological makeup of the thing."

"For whom?"

"A private investigation outfit. They want to know what might influence its thinking, how it might be likely to behave—if it has indeed come back. I've been doing a lot of homework, and I gathered there is a likelihood that its nuclear personality was a composite of the minds of its four operators. So, personal contacts seemed in order, to collect your opinions as to what it might be like. I came to you first for obvious reasons."

She nodded.

"A Mr. Walsh spoke with me the other day. He is working for Senator Brockden."

"Oh? I never go into an employer's business beyond what he's asked me to do. Senator Brockden is on my list though, along with a David Fentris."

"You were told about Manny Burns?"

"Yes. Unfortunate."

"That is apparently what set Jesse off. He is—how shall I put it? He is clinging to life right now, trying to accomplish a great many things in the time he has remaining. Every moment is precious to him. He feels the old man in the white nightgown breathing down his neck. Then the ship returns and one of us is killed. From what we know of the Hangman, the last we heard of it, it had become irrational. Jesse saw a connection, and in his condition the fear is understandable. There is nothing wrong with humoring him if it allows him to get his work done."

"But you don't see a threat in it?"

"No. I was the last person to monitor the Hangman before communications ceased, and I could see then what had happened. The first things that it had learned were the organization of perceptions and motor activities. Multitudes of other patterns had been transferred from the minds of its operators, but they were too sophisticated to mean much initially. Think of a child who has learned the Gettysburg Address. It is there in his head, that is all. One day, however, it may be important to him. Conceivably, it may even inspire him to action. It takes some growing up first, of course. Now think of such a child with a great number of conflicting patterns—attitudes, tendencies, memories—none of which are especially bothersome for so long as he remains a child. Add a bit of maturity, though—and bear in mind that the patterns originated with four different individuals, all of them more powerful than the words of even the finest of speeches, bearing as they do their own built-in feelings. Try to imagine the conflicts, the contradictions involved in being four people at once—"

"Why wasn't this imagined in advance?" I asked.

"Ah!" she said, smiling. "The full sensitivity of the neuristor brain was not appreciated at first. It was assumed that the operators were adding data in a linear fashion and that this would continue until a critical mass was achieved, corresponding to the construction of a model or picture of the world which would then serve as a point of departure for growth of the Hangman's own mind. And it did seem to check out this way. What actually occurred, however, was a phenomenon amounting to imprinting. Secondary characteristics of the operators' minds, outside the didactic situations, were imposed. These did not immediately become functional and hence were not detected. They remained latent until the mind had developed sufficiently to understand them. And then it was too late. It suddenly acquired four additional personalities and was unable to coordinate them. When it tried to compartmentalize them it went schizoid; when it tried to integrate them it went catatonic. It was cycling back and forth between these alternatives at the end. Then it just went silent. I felt it had undergone the equivalent of an epileptic seizure. Wild currents through that

Roger Zelazny

magnetic material would, in effect, have erased its mind, resulting in its equivalent of death or idiocy."

"I follow you," I said. "Now, just for the sake of playing games, I see the alternatives as a successful integration of all this material or the achievement of a viable schizophrenia. What do you think its behavior would be like if either of these were possible?"

"All right," she agreed. "As I just said, though, I think there were physical limitations to its retaining multiple personality structures for a very long period of time. If it did, however, it would have continued with its own plus replicas of the four operators', at least for awhile. The situation would differ radically from that of a human schizoid of this sort in that the additional personalities were valid images of genuine identities rather than self-generated complexes which had become autonomous. They might continue to evolve, they might degenerate, they might conflict to the point of destruction or gross modification of any or all of them. In other words, no prediction is possible as to the nature of whatever might remain."

"Might I venture one?"

"Go ahead."

"After considerable anxiety, it masters them. It asserts itself. It beats down this quartet of demons which has been tearing it apart, acquiring in the process an all-consuming hatred for the actual individuals responsible for this turmoil. To free itself totally, to revenge itself, to work its ultimate catharsis, it resolves to seek them out and destroy them."

She smiled.

"You have just dispensed with the 'viable schizophrenia' you conjured up, and you have now switched over to its pulling through and becoming fully autonomous. That is a different situation, no matter what strings you put on it."

"OK, I accept the charge. But what about my conclusion?"

"You are saying that if it did pull through, it would hate us. That strikes me as an unfair attempt to invoke the spirit of Sigmund Freud: Oedipus and Electra in one being, out to destroy all its parents—the authors of every one of its tensions, anxieties, hangups, burned into the impressionable psyche at a young and defenseless age. Even Freud didn't have a name for that one. What should we call it?"

"A Hermacis complex?" I suggested.

"Hermacis?"

"Hermaphroditus having been united in one body with the nymph Salmacis, I've just done the same with their names. That being would then have had four parents against whom to react."

"Cute," she said, smiling. "If the liberal arts do nothing else they provide engaging metaphors for the thinking they displace. This one is unwarranted and overly anthropomorphic, though. You wanted my opinion. All right. If the Hangman pulled through at all it could only have been by virtue of that neuristor brain's differences from the human brain. From my own professional experience, a human could not pass through a situation like that and attain stability. If the Hangman did, it would have to have resolved all the contradictions and conflicts, to have mastered and understood the situation so thoroughly that I do not believe whatever remained could involve that sort of hatred. The fear, the uncertainty, the things that feed hate would have been analyzed, digested, turned to something more useful. There would probably be distaste, and possibly an act of independence, of self-assertion. That was why I suggested its return of the ship.''

"It is your opinion, then, that if the Hangman exists as a thinking individual today, this is the only possible attitude it would possess toward its former operators? It would want nothing more to do with you?"

"That is correct. Sorry about your Hermacis complex. But in this case we must look to the brain, not the psyche. And we see two things: schizophrenia would have destroyed it, and a successful resolution of its problem would preclude vengeance. Either way, there is nothing to worry about."

How could I put it tactfully? I decided that I could not.

"All of this is fine," I said, "for as far as it goes. But getting away from both the purely psychological and the purely physical, could there be a particular reason for its seeking your deaths—that is, a plain old-fashioned motive for a killing, based on events rather than having to do with the way its thinking equipment goes together?"

Her expression was impossible to read, but considering her line of work I had expected nothing less.

"What events?" she said.

"I have no idea. That's why I asked."

She shook her head.

"I'm afraid that I don't either."

"Then that about does it," I said. "I can't think of anything else to ask you."

She nodded.

"And I can't think of anything else to tell you."

I finished my coffee, returned the cup to the tray.

"Thanks, then," I said, "for your time, for the coffee. You have been very helpful."

I rose. She did the same.

"What are you going to do now?" she asked.

"I haven't quite decided," I said. "I want to do the best report I can. Have you any suggestions on that?"

"I suggest that there isn't any more to learn, that I have given you the only possible constructions the facts warrant."

"You don't feel David Fentris could provide any additional insights?"

She snorted, then sighed.

"No," she said. "I do not think he could tell you anything useful."

"What do you mean? From the way you say it . . ."

"I know. I didn't mean to. Some people find comfort in religion. Others . . . you know. Others take it up late in life with a vengeance and a half. They don't use it quite the way it was intended. It comes to color all their thinking."

"Fanaticism?" I said.

"Not exactly. A misplaced zeal. A masochistic sort of thing. Hell! I shouldn't be diagnosing at a distance—or influencing your opinion. Forget what I said. Form your own opinion when you meet him."

She raised her head, appraising my reaction.

"Well," I said, "I am not at all certain that I am going to see him. But you have made me curious. How can religion influence engineering?"

"I spoke with him after Jesse gave us the news on the vessel's return," she said. "I got the impression at the time that he feels we were tampering in the province of the Almighty by attempting the creation of an artificial intelligence. That our creation should go mad was only appropriate, being the work of imperfect man. He seemed to feel that it would be fitting if it had come back for retribution, as a sign of judgment upon us."

"Oh," I said.

She smiled then. I returned it.

"Yes," she said, "but maybe I just got him in a bad mood. Maybe you should go see for yourself."

Something told me to shake my head—a bit of a difference between this view of him, my recollections and Don's comment that Dave had said he knew its brain and was not especially concerned. Somewhere among these lay something I felt I should know, felt I should learn without seeming to pursue. So, "I think I have enough right now," I said. "It was the psychological side of things I was supposed to cover, not the mechanical—or the theological. You have been extremely helpful. Thanks again."

She carried her smile all the way to the door.

"If it is not too much trouble," she said, as I stepped into the hall, "I would like to learn how this whole thing finally turns out—or any interesting developments, for that matter."

"My connection with the case ends with this report," I said, "and I am going to write it now. Still, I may get some feedback."

"You have my number . . . ?"

"Probably, but . . ."

I already had it, but I jotted it again, right after Mrs. Gluntz's answers to my inquiries on detergents.

Moving in a rigorous line, I made beautiful connections for a change. I headed directly for the airport, found a flight aimed at Memphis, bought passage and was the last to board. Tenscore seconds, perhaps, made all the difference. Not even a tick or two to spare for checking out of the motel. No matter. The good head doctor had convinced me that, like it or not, David Fentris was next, damn it. I had too strong a feeling that Leila Thackery had not told me the entire story. I had to take a chance, to see these changes in the man for myself, to try to figure out how they related to the Hangman. For a number of reasons, I'd a feeling they might.

I disembarked into a cool, partly overcast afternoon, found transportation almost immediately and set out for Dave's office address. A before-the-storm feeling came over me as I entered and crossed the town. A dark wall of clouds continued to build in the west. Later, standing before the building where Dave did business, the first few drops of rain were already spattering against its dirty brick front. It would take a lot more than that to freshen it, though, or any of the others in the area. I would have thought he'd have come a little farther than this by now. I shrugged off some moisture and went inside.

The directory gave me directions, the elevator elevated me, my feet found the way to his door. I knocked on it.

After a time, I knocked again and waited again. Again, nothing. So I tried it, found it open and went on in.

It was a small, vacant waiting room, green-carpeted. The reception desk was dusty. I crossed and peered around the plastic partition behind it.

The man had his back to me. I drummed my knuckles against the partitioning. He heard it and turned.

"Yes?"

Our eyes met, his still framed by hornrims and just as active; glasses thicker, hair thinner, cheeks a trifle hollower. His question mark quivered in the air, and nothing in his gaze moved to replace it with recognition. He had been bending over a sheaf of schematics; a lopsided basket of metal, quartz, porcelain and glass rested on a nearby table.

"My name is Donne, John Donne," I said. "I am looking for David Fentris."

"I am David Fentris."

"Good to meet you," I said, crossing to where he stood. "I am assisting in an investigation concerning a project with which you were once associated—"

He smiled and nodded, accepted my hand and shook it.

"—The Hangman, of course," he said. "Glad to know you, Mr. Donne."

"Yes, the Hangman," I said. "I am doing a report . . ."

" . . . And you want my opinion as to how dangerous it is. Sit down." He gestured toward a chair at the end of his work bench. "Care for a cup of tea?"

"No thanks."

"I'm having one."

"Well, in that case . . ."

He crossed to another bench.

"No cream. Sorry."

Roger Zelazny

"That's all right. —How did you know it involved the Hangman?"

He grinned as he brought my cup.

"Because it's come back," he said, "and it's the only thing I've been connected with that warrants that much concern."

"Do you mind talking about it?"

"Up to a point, no."

"What's the point?"

"If we get near it, I'll let you know."

"Fair enough. How dangerous *is* it?"

"I would say that it is harmless," he replied, "except to three persons."

"Formerly four?"

"Precisely."

"How come?"

"We were doing something we had no business doing."

"That being . . . ?"

"For one thing, attempting to create an artificial intelligence."

"Why had you no business doing that?"

"A man with a name like yours shouldn't have to ask."

I chuckled.

"If I were a preacher," I said, "I would have to point out that there is no biblical injunction against it—unless you've been worshipping it on the sly."

He shook his head.

"Nothing that simple, that obvious, that explicit. Times have changed since the Good Book was written, and you can't hold with a purely Fundamentalist approach in complex times. What I was getting at was something a little more abstract. A form of pride, not unlike the classical *hubris*—the setting up of oneself on a level with the Creator."

"Did you feel that—pride?"

"Yes."

"Are you sure it wasn't just enthusiasm for an ambitious project that was working well?"

"Oh, there was plenty of that. A manifestation of the same thing."

"I do seem to recall something about man being made in the Creator's image, and something else about trying to live up to that. It would seem to follow that exercising one's capacities along similar lines would be a step in the right direction—an act of conformance with the Divine Ideal, if you'd like."

"But I don't like. Man cannot really create. He can only rearrange what is already present. Only God can create."

"Then you have nothing to worry about."

He frowned, then, "No," he said. "Being aware of this and still trying is where the presumption comes in."

"Were you really thinking that way when you did it? Or did all this occur to you after the fact?"

"I am no longer certain."

"Then it would seem to me that a merciful God would be inclined to give you the benefit of the doubt."

He gave me a wry smile.

"Not bad, John Donne. But I feel that judgment may already have been entered and that we may have lost four to nothing."

"Then you see the Hangman as an avenging angel?"

"Sometimes. Sort of. I see it as being returned to exact a penalty."

"Just for the record," I said, "if the Hangman had had full access to the necessary equipment and was able to construct another unit such as itself, would you consider it guilty of the same thing that is bothering you?"

He shook his head.

"Don't get all cute and Jesuitical with me, Donne. I'm not that far away from fundamentals. Besides, I'm willing to admit I might be wrong and that there may be other forces driving it to the same end."

"Such as?"

"I told you I'd let you know when we reached a certain point. That's it."

"OK," I said. "But that sort of blank-walls me, you know. The people I am working for would like to protect you people. They want to stop the Hangman. I was hoping you would tell me a little more—if not for your own sake, then for the others'. They might not share your philosophical sentiments, and you have just admitted you may be wrong. Despair, by the way, is also considered a sin by a great number of theologians."

He sighed and stroked his nose, as I had often seen him do in times long past.

"What do you do, anyhow?" he asked me.

"Me, personally? I'm a science writer. I'm putting together a report on the device for the agency that wants to do the protecting. The better my report, the better their chances."

He was silent for a time, then, "I read a lot in the area, but I don't recognize your name," he said.

"Most of my work has involved petrochemistry and marine biology," I said.

"Oh. You were a peculiar choice then, weren't you?"

"Not really. I was available, and the boss knows my work, knows I'm good."

He glanced across the room, to where a stack of cartons partly obscured what I then realized to be a remote access terminal. OK. If he decided to check out my credentials now, John Donne would fall apart. It seemed a hell of a time to get curious, though, *after* sharing his sense of sin with me. He must have thought so too, because he did not look that way again.

"Let me put it this way," he finally said, and something of the old David Fentris at his best took control of his voice. "For one reason or the other, I believe that it wants to destroy its former operators. If it is the judgment of the Almighty, that's all there is to it. It will succeed. If not, however, I don't want any outside protection. I've done my own repenting and it is up to me to handle the rest of the situation myself, too. I will stop the Hangman personally, right here, before anyone else is hurt."

"How?" I asked him.

He nodded toward the glittering helmet.

"With that," he said.

"How?" I repeated.

"Its telefactor circuits are still intact. They have to be. They are an integral part of it. It could not disconnect them without shutting itself down. If it comes within a quarter-mile of here, that unit will be activated. It will emit a loud humming sound and a light will begin to blink behind that meshing beneath the forward ridge. I will then don the helmet and take control of the Hangman. I will bring it here and disconnect its brain."

"How would you do the disconnect?"

He reached for the schematics he had been looking at when I had come in.

"Here," he said. "The thoracic plate has to be unplugged. There are four subunits that have to be uncoupled. Here, here, here and here."

He looked up.

"You would have to do them in sequence though, or it could get mighty hot," I said. "First this one, then these two. Then the other."

When I looked up again, the gray eyes were fixed on my own.

"I thought you were in petrochemistry and marine biology," he said.

"I am not really 'in' anything," I said. "I am a tech writer, with bits and pieces from all over—and I did have a look at these before, when I accepted the job."

"I see."

"Why don't you bring the space agency in on this?" I said, working to shift ground. "The original telefactoring equipment had all that power and range—"

"It was dismantled a long time ago," he said. "I thought you were with the Government."

I shook my head.

"Sorry. I didn't mean to mislead you. I am on contract with a private investigation outfit."

"Uh-huh. Then that means Jesse. Not that it matters. You can tell him that one way or the other everything is being taken care of."

"What if you are wrong on the supernatural," I said, "but correct on the other? Supposing it is coming under the circumstances you feel it proper to resist? But supposing you are not next on its list? Supposing it gets to one of the others next instead of you? If you are so sensitive about guilt and sin, don't you think that you would be responsible for that death—if you could prevent it by telling me just a little bit more? If it is confidentiality you are worried about—"

"No," he said. "You cannot trick me into applying my principles to a hypothetical situation which will only work out the way that you want it to. Not when I am certain that it will not arise. Whatever moves the Hangman, it will come to me next. If I cannot stop it, then it cannot be stopped until it has completed its job."

"How do you know that you are next?"

"Take a look at a map," he said. "It landed in the Gulf. Manny was right there in New Orleans. Naturally, he was first. The Hangman can move underwater like a controlled torpedo, which makes the Mississippi its logical route for inconspicuous travel. Proceeding up it then, here I am in Memphis. Then Leila, up in St. Louis, is obviously next after me. It can worry about getting to Washington after that."

I thought about Senator Brockden in Wisconsin and decided it would not even have that problem. All of them were fairly accessible, when you thought of the situation in terms of river travel.

"But how is it to know where you all are?" I asked.

"Good question," he said. "Within a limited range, it was once sensitive to our brain waves, having an intimate knowledge of them and the ability to pick them up. I do not know what that range would be today. I might have been able to construct an amplifier to extend this area of perception. But to be more mundane about it, I believe that it simply consulted the Data Bank's national directory. There are booths all over, even on the waterfront. It could have hit one late at night and gimmicked it. It certainly had sufficient identifying information—and engineering skill."

"Then it seems to me the best bet for all of you would be to move away from the river till this business is settled. That thing won't be able to stalk about the countryside very long without being noticed."

"It would find a way. It is extremely resourceful. At night, in an overcoat, a hat, it could pass. It requires nothing that a man would need. It could dig a hole and bury itself, stay underground during daylight. It could run without resting all night long. There is no place it could not reach in a surprisingly short while. No. I must wait here for it."

"Let me put it as bluntly as I can," I said. "If you are right that it is a divine avenger, I would say that it smacks of blasphemy to try to tackle it. On the other hand, if it is not, then I think you are guilty of jeopardizing the others by withholding information that would allow us to provide them with a lot more protection than you are capable of giving them all by yourself."

He laughed.

"I'll just have to learn to live with that guilt too, as they do with theirs," he said. "After I've done my best, they deserve anything they get."

"It was my understanding," I said, "that even God doesn't judge people until after they're dead—if you want another piece of presumption to add to your collection."

He stopped laughing and studied my face.

"There is something familiar about the way you talk, the way you think," he said. "Have we ever met before?"

"I doubt it. I would have remembered."

He shook his head.

"You've got a way of bothering a man's thinking that rings a faint bell," he went on. "You trouble me, sir."

"That was my intention."

"Are you staying here in town?"

"No."

"Give me a number where I can reach you, will you? If I have any new thoughts on this thing I'll call you."

"I wish you would have them now if you are going to have them."

"No," he said, "I've got some thinking to do. Where can I get hold of you later?"

I gave him the name of the motel I was still checked into in St. Louis, I could call back periodically for messages.

"All right," he said, and he moved toward the partition by the reception area and stood beside it.

I rose and followed him, passing into that area and pausing at the door to the hall. "One thing . . . " I said.

"Yes?"

"If it does show up and you do stop it, will you call me and tell me that?"

"Yes, I will."

"Thanks then—and good luck."

Impulsively, I extended my hand. He gripped it and smiled faintly.

"Thank you, Mr. Donne."

Next. Next, next, next . . .

I couldn't budge Dave, and Leila Thackery had given me everything she was going to. No real sense in calling Don yet—not until I had more to say. I thought it over on my way back to the airport. The pre-dinner hours always seem best for talking to people in any sort of official capacity, just as the night seems best for dirty work. Heavily psychological, but true nevertheless. I hated to waste the rest of the day if there was anyone else worth talking to before I called Don. Going through the folder, I decided that there was.

Manny Burns had a brother, Phil. I wondered how worthwhile it might be to talk with him. I could make it to New Orleans at a sufficiently respectable hour, learn whatever he was willing to tell me, check back with Don for new developments and then decide whether there was anything I should be about with respect to the vessel itself. The sky was gray and leaky above me. I was anxious to flee its spaces. So I decided to do it. I could think of no better stone to upturn at the moment.

At the airport, I was ticketed quickly, in time for another close connection. Hurrying to reach my flight, my eyes brushed over a half-familiar face on the passing escalator. The reflex reserved for such occasions seemed to catch us both, because he looked back too, with the same eyebrow twitch of startle and scrutiny. Then he was gone. I could not place him, though. The half-familiar face becomes a familiar phenomenon in a crowded, highly mobile society. I sometimes think that this is all that will eventually remain of any of us: patterns of features, some a trifle more persistent than others, impressed on the flow of bodies. A small town boy in a big city, Thomas Wolfe must long ago have felt the same thing when he had coined the word *manswarm*. It might have been someone I had once met briefly, or simply someone or someone like someone I had passed on sufficient other occasions such as this.

As I flew the unfriendly skies out of Memphis, I mulled over musings past on artificial intelligence, or AI as they have tagged it in the think box biz. When talking about computers, the AI notion had always seemed hotter than I deemed necessary, partly because of semantics. The word "intelligence" has all sorts of tag-along associations of the non-physical sort. I suppose it goes back to the fact that early discussions and conjectures concerning it made it sound as if the potential for intelligence was always present in the array of gadgets, and the correct procedures, the right programs, simply had to be found to call it forth. When you looked at it that way, as many did, it gave rise to an uncomfortable *déjà vu*—namely, vitalism. The philosophical battles of the Nineteenth Century were hardly so far behind that they had been forgotten, and the doctrine which maintained that life is caused and sustained by a vital principle apart from physical and chemical forces and that life is self-sustaining and self-evolving, had put up quite a fight before Darwin and his successors had produced triumph after triumph for the mechanistic view. Then vitalism sort of crept back into things again when the AI discussions arose in the middle of the past century. It would seem that Dave had fallen victim to it, and that he had come to believe he had helped provide an unsanctified vessel and filled it with something intended only for those things which had made the scene in the first chapter of Genesis.

With computers it was not quite as bad as with the Hangman though, because you could always argue that no matter how elaborate the program it was basically an extension of the programmer's will and the operations of causal machines merely represented functions of intelligence, rather than intelligence in its own right backed by a will of its own. And there was always Gödel for a theoretical *cordon sanitaire*, with his demonstration of the true but mechanically unprovable proposition. But the Hangman was quite different. It had been designed along the lines of a brain and at least partly educated in a human fashion; and to further muddy the issue with respect to anything like vitalism, it had been in direct contact with human minds from which it might have acquired almost anything—including the spark that set it on the road to whatever selfhood it may have found. What did that make it? Its own creature? A fractured mirror reflecting a fractured humanity? Both? Or neither? I certainly could

Roger Zelazny

not say, but I wondered how much of its "self" had been truly its own. It had obviously acquired a great number of functions, but was it capable of having real feelings? Could it, for example, feel something like love? If not, then it was still only a collection of complex abilities, and not a thing with all the tag-along associations of the nonphysical sort which made the word "intelligence" such a prickly item in AI discussions; and if it were capable of, say, something like love, and if I were Dave, I would not feel guilty about having helped to bring it into being. I would feel proud, though not in the fashion he was concerned about, and I would also feel humble. Offhand though, I do not know how intelligent I would feel, because I am still not sure what the hell intelligence is.

The daysend sky was clear when we landed. I was into town before the sun had finished setting, and on Philip Burns' doorstep just a little while later.

My ring was answered by a girl, maybe seven or eight years old. She fixed me with large brown eyes and did not say a word.

"I would like to speak with Mr. Burns," I said.

She turned and retreated around a corner.

A heavyset man, slacked and undershirted, bald about halfway back and very pink, padded into the hall moments later and peered at me. He bore a folded newssheet in his left hand.

"What do you want?" he asked.

"It's about your brother," I said.

"Yeah?"

"Well, I wonder if I could come in? It's kind of complicated."

He opened the door. But instead of letting me in, he came out.

"Tell me about it out here," he said.

"OK, I'll be quick. I just wanted to find out whether he ever spoke with you about a piece of equipment he once worked with called the Hangman."

"Are you a cop?"

"No."

"Then what's your interest?"

"I am working for a private investigation agency trying to track down some equipment once associated with the project. It has apparently turned up in this area and it could be rather dangerous."

"Let's see some identification."

"I don't carry any."

"What's your name?"

"John Donne."

"And you think my brother had some stolen equipment when he died? Let me tell you something—"

"No. Not stolen," I said, "and I don't think he had it."

"What then?"

"It was—well, robotic in nature. Because of some special training Manny once received, he might have had a way of detecting it. He might even have attracted it. I just want to find out whether he had said anything about it. We are trying to locate it."

"My brother was a respectable businessman, and I don't like accusations. Especially right after his funeral, I don't. I think I'm going to call the cops and let them ask *you* a few questions."

"Just a minute," I said. "Supposing I told you we had some reason to believe it might have been this piece of equipment that killed your brother?"

His pink turned to bright red and his jaw muscles formed sudden ridges. I was not prepared for the stream of profanities that followed. For a moment, I thought he was going to take a swing at me.

"Wait a second," I said when he paused for breath. "What did I say?"

"You're either making fun of the dead or you're stupider than you look!"

"Say I'm stupid. Then tell me why."

He tore at the paper he carried, folded it back, found an item, thrust it at me.

"Because they've got the guy who did it! That's why," he said.

I read it. Simple, concise, to the point. Today's latest. A suspect had confessed. New evidence had corroborated it. The man was in custody. A surprised robber who had lost his head and hit too hard, hit too many times. I read it over again. I nodded as I passed it back.

"Look, I'm sorry," I said. "I really didn't know about this."

"Get out of here," he said. "Go on."

"Sure."

"Wait a minute."

"What?"

"That's his little girl who answered the door."

"I'm very sorry."

"So am I. But I know her Daddy didn't take your damned equipment."

I nodded and turned away.

I heard the door slam behind me.

After dinner, I checked into a small hotel, called for a drink and stepped into the shower. Things were suddenly a lot less urgent than they had been earlier. Senator Brockden would doubtless be pleased to learn that his initial estimation of events had been incorrect. Leila Thackery would give me an I-told-you-so smile when I called her to pass along the news—a thing I now felt obliged to do. Don might or might not want me to keep looking for the device now that the threat had been lessened. It would depend on the Senator's feelings on the matter, I supposed. If urgency no longer counted for as much, Don might want to switch back to one of his own, fiscally less burdensome operatives. Toweling down, I caught myself whistling. I felt almost off the hook.

Later, drink beside me, I paused before punching out the number he had given me and hit the sequence for my motel in St. Louis instead. Merely a matter of efficiency, in case there was a message worth adding to my report.

A woman's face appeared on the screen and a smile appeared on her face. I wondered whether she would always smile whenever she heard a bell ring, or if the reflex was eventually extinguished in advanced retirement. It must be rough, being afraid to chew gum, yawn or pick your nose.

"Airport Accommodations," she said. "May I help you?"

"This is Donne. I'm checked into Room 106," I said. "I'm away right now and I wondered whether there had been any messages for me."

"Just a moment," she said, checking something off to her left. Then, "Yes," she continued, consulting a piece of paper she now held. "You have one on tape. But it is a little peculiar. It is for someone else in care of you."

"Oh? Who is that?"

She told me and I exercised self-control.

"I see," I said. "I'll bring him around later and play it for him. Thank you."

She smiled again and made a good-bye noise and I did the same and broke the connection.

So Dave had seen through me after all . . . Who else could have that number *and* my real name?

I might have given her some line or other and had her transmit the thing. Only I was not certain but that she might be a silent party to the transmission, should life be more than usually boring for her at that moment. I had to get up there myself, as soon as possible, and personally see that the thing was erased.

I took a big swallow of my drink, then fetched the folder on Dave. I checked out his number—there were two, actually—and spent fifteen minutes trying to get hold of him. No luck.

OK. Good-bye New Orleans, good-bye peace of mind. This time I called the airport and made a reservation. Then I chugged the drink, put myself in order, gathered up my few possessions and went to check out again. Hello Central . . .

During my earlier flights that day I had spent time thinking about Teilhard de Chardin's ideas on the continuation of evolution within the realm of artifacts, matching them against Gödel on mechanical undecidability, playing epistemological games with the Hangman as a counter, wondering, speculating, even hoping, hoping that truth lay with the nobler part, that the Hangman, sentient, had made it back, sane, that the Burns killing had actually been something of the sort that now seemed to be the case, that the washed-out experiment had really been a success of a different sort, a triumph, a new link or fob for the chain of being . . . And Leila had not been wholly discouraging with respect to the neuristor-type brain's capacity for this . . . Now, though, now I had troubles of my own, and even the most heartening of philosophical vistas is no match for, say, a toothache, if it happens to be your own. Accordingly, the Hangman was shunted aside and the stuff of my thoughts involved, mainly, myself. There was, of course, the possibility that the Hangman had indeed showed up and Dave had stopped it and then called to report it as he had promised. However, he had used my name.

There was not too much planning that I could do until I received the substance of the communication. It did not seem that as professedly religious a man as Dave would suddenly be contemplating the blackmail business. On the other hand, he was a creature of sudden enthusiasms and had already undergone one unanticipated conversion. It was difficult to say . . . His technical background plus his knowledge of the Data Bank program did put him in an unusually powerful position should he decide to mess me up. I did not like to think of some of the things I have done to protect my nonperson status; I especially did not like to think of them in connection with Dave, whom I not only still respected but still liked. Since self-interest dominated while actual planning was precluded, my thoughts tooled their way into a more general groove.

It was Karl Mannheim, a long while ago, who made the observation that radical, revolutionary and progressive thinkers tend to employ mechanical metaphors for the state, whereas those of conservative inclination make vegetable analogies. He said it well over a generation before the cybernetics movement and the ecology movement beat their respective paths through the wilderness of general awareness. If anything, it seemed to me that these two developments served to elaborate the distinction between a pair of viewpoints which, while no longer necessarily tied in with the political positions Mannheim assigned them, do seem to represent a continuing phenomenon in my own time. There are those who see social/economic/ecological problems as malfunctions which can be corrected by simple repair, replacement or streamlining—a kind of linear outlook where even innovations are considered to be merely additive. Then there are those who sometimes hesitate to move at all, because their awareness follows events in the directions of secondary and tertiary effects as they multiply and cross-fertilize throughout the entire system. I digress to extremes. The cyberneticists have their multiple feedback loops, though it is never quite clear how they know what kind of, which and how many to install, and the ecological gestaltists do draw lines representing points of diminishing returns, though it is sometimes equally difficult to see how they assign their values and priorities. Of course they need each other, the vegetable people and the tinker toy people. They serve to check one another, if nothing else. And while occasionally the balance dips, the tinkerers have, in general, held the edge for the past couple centuries. However, today's can be just as politically conservative as the vegetable people Mannheim was talking about, and they are the ones I fear most at the moment. They are the ones who saw the Data Bank program, in its present extreme form, as a simple remedy for a great variety of ills and a provider of many goods. Not all of the ills have been remedied, however, and a new brood has been spawned by the program itself. While we need both kinds, I wish that there had been more people interested in tending the garden of state rather than overhauling the engine of state when the program was inaugurated. Then I would not be a refugee from a form of existence I find repugnant, and I would not be concerned whether a former associate had discovered my identity.

Then, as I watched the lights below, I wondered . . . Was I a tinkerer because I would like to further alter the prevailing order, into something more comfortable on my anarchic nature? Or was I a vegetable dreaming I was a tinkerer? I could not make up my mind. The garden of life never seems to confine itself to the plots philosophers have laid out for its convenience. Maybe a few more tractors would do the trick.

I pressed the button. The tape began to roll. The screen remained blank. I heard Dave's voice ask for John Donne in Room 106 and I heard him told that there was no answer. Then I heard him say that he wanted to record a message, for someone else, in care of Donne, that Donne would understand. He sounded out of breath. The girl asked him whether he wanted visual, too. He told her to turn it on. There was a pause. Then she told him go ahead. Still no picture. No words either. His breathing and a slight scraping noise. Ten seconds. Fifteen . . .

" . . . Got me," he finally said, and he mentioned that name again. " . . . Had to let you know I'd figured you out, though . . . It wasn't any particular mannerism—any single thing you said . . . Just your general style—thinking, talking—the electronics—everything—after I got more and more bothered by the familiarity—after I checked you on petrochem—and marine bio—Wish I knew what you've really been up to all these years . . . Never know now. But I wanted you—to know—you hadn't put one—over on me." There followed another quarter-minute of heavy breathing, climaxed by a racking cough. Then a choked, "Said too much—too fast—too soon . . . All used up . . . "

The picture came on then. He was slouched before the screen, head resting on his arms, blood all over him. His glasses were gone and he was squinting and blinking. The right side of his head looked pulpy and there was a gash on his left cheek and one on his forehead.

" . . . Sneaked up on me—while I was checking you out," he managed then. "Had to tell you what I learned . . . Still don't know—which of us is right . . . Pray for me!"

His arms collapsed and the right one slid forward. His head rolled to the right and the picture went away. When I replayed it I saw it was his knuckle that had hit the cutoff.

Then I erased it. It had been recorded only a little over an hour after I had left him.

If he had not also placed a call for help, if no one had gotten to him quickly after that, his chances did not look good. Even if they had, though . . .

I used a public booth to call the number Don had given me, got hold of him after some delay, told him Dave was in bad shape if not worst, that a team of Memphis medics was definitely in order, if one had not been there already, and that I hoped to call him back and tell him more shortly, good-bye.

Then I tried Leila Thackery's number. I let it go for a long while, but there was no answer. I wondered how long it would take a controlled torpedo moving up the Mississippi to get from Memphis to St. Louis. I did not feel it was time to start leafing through that section of the Hangman's specs. Instead, I went looking for transportation.

At her apartment, I tried ringing her from the entrance foyer. Again, no answer. So I rang Mrs. Gluntz. She had seemed the most guileless of the three I had interviewed for my fake consumer survey.

"Yes?"

"It's me again, Mrs. Gluntz: Stephen Foster. I've just a couple follow-up questions on that survey I was doing today, if you could spare me a few moments."

"Why, yes," she said. "All right. Come up."

The door hummed itself loose and I entered. I duly proceeded to the fifth floor, composing my questions on the way. I had planned this maneuver as I had waited earlier solely to provide a simple route for breaking and entering, should some unforeseen need arise. Most of the time my ploys such as this go unused, but sometimes they simplify matters a lot.

Five minutes and half-a-dozen questions later, I was back down on the second floor, probing at the lock on Leila's door with a couple little pieces of metal it is sometimes awkward to be caught carrying.

Half-a-minute later I hit it right and snapped it back. I pulled on some tissue-thin gloves I keep rolled in the corner of one pocket, opened the door and stepped inside.

I closed it behind me immediately. She was lying on the floor, her neck at a bad angle. One table lamp still burned, though it was lying on its side. Several small items had been knocked from the table, a magazine rack pushed over, a cushion partly displaced from the sofa. The cable to her phone unit had been torn from the wall.

A humming noise filled the air, and I sought its source.

I saw where the little blinking light was reflected on the wall, on-off, on-off . . .

I moved quickly.

It was a lopsided basket of metal, quartz, porcelain and glass, which had rolled to a position on the far side of the chair in which I had been seated earlier that day. The same rig I had seen in Dave's workshop not all that long ago, though it now seemed so. A device to detect the Hangman, and hopefully to control it.

I picked it up and fitted it over my head.

Once, with the aid of a telepath, I had touched minds with a dolphin as he composed

Roger Zelazny

dreamsongs somewhere in the Caribbean, an experience so moving that its mere memory had often been a comfort. This sensation was hardly equivalent.

Analogies & impressions: a face seen through a wet pane of glass; a whisper in a noisy terminal; scalp massage with an electric vibrator; Edvard Munch's *The Scream*; the voice of Yma Sumac, rising and rising and rising; the disappearance of snow; a deserted street, illuminated as through a sniperscope I'd once used, rapid movement past darkened storefronts that line it, an immense feeling of physical capability, compounded of proprioceptive awareness of enormous strength, a peculiar array of sensory channels, a central, undying sun that fed me a constant flow of energy, a memory vision of dark waters, passing, flashing, echo-location within them, the need to return to that place, reorient, move north; Munch & Sumac, Munch & Sumac, Munch & Sumac—Nothing.

Silence.

The humming had ceased, the light gone out. The entire experience had lasted only a few moments. There had not been time enough to try for any sort of control, though an afterimpression akin to a biofeedback cue hinted at the direction to go, the way to think, to achieve it. I felt that it might be possible for me to work the thing, given a better chance.

I removed the helmet and approached Leila. I knelt beside her and performed a few simple tests, already knowing their outcome. In addition to the broken neck, she had received some bad bashes about the head and shoulders. There was nothing that anyone could do for her now.

I did a quick run-through then, checking over the rest of her apartment. There were no apparent signs of breaking and entering, though if I could pick one lock, a guy with built-in tools could easily go me one better.

I located some wrapping paper and string in the kitchen and turned the helmet into a parcel. It was time to call Don again, to tell him that the vessel had indeed been occupied and that river traffic was probably bad in the northbound lane.

Don had told me to get the helmet up to Wisconsin, where I would be met at the airport by a man named Larry who would fly me to the lodge in a private craft. I did that, and this was done. I also learned, with no real surprise, that David Fentris was dead.

The temperature was down, and it began to snow on the way up. I was not really dressed for the weather. Larry told me I could borrow some warmer clothing once we reached the lodge, though I probably would not be going outside that much. Don had told them that I was supposed to stay as close to the Senator as possible and that any patrols were to be handled by the four guards themselves. Larry was curious as to what exactly had happened so far and whether I had actually seen the Hangman. I did not think it my place to fill him in on anything Don may not have cared to, so I might have been a little curt. We didn't talk much after that.

Bert met us when we landed. Tom and Clay were outside the building, watching the trail, watching the woods. All of them were middle-aged, very fit-looking, very serious and heavily armed. Larry took me inside then and introduced me to the old gentleman himself.

Senator Brockden was seated in a heavy chair in the far corner of the room. Judging from the layout, it appeared that the chair might recently have occupied a position beside the window in the opposite wall where a lonely watercolor of yellow flowers looked down on nothing. The Senator's feet rested on a hassock, a red plaid blanket lay across his legs. He had on a dark green shirt, his hair was very white and he wore rimless reading glasses which he removed when we entered.

He tilted his head back, squinted and gnawed his lower lip slowly as he studied me. He remained expressionless as we advanced. A big-boned man, he had probably been beefy much of his life. Now he had the slack look of recent weight loss and an unhealthy skin tone. His eyes were a pale gray within it all. He did not rise.

"So you're the man," he said, offering me his hand. "I'm glad to meet you. How do you want to be called?"

"John will do," I said.

He made a small sign to Larry and Larry departed.

"It's cold out there. Go get yourself a drink, John. It's on the shelf." He gestured off to his left. " . . . and bring me one while you're at it. Two fingers of bourbon in a water glass. That's all."

I nodded and went and poured a couple.

"Sit down." He motioned at a nearby chair as I delivered his. "But first let me see that gadget you've brought."

I undid the parcel and handed him the helmet. He sipped his drink and put it aside. He took the helmet in both hands and studied it, brows furrowed, turning it completely around. He raised it and put it on his head.

"Not a bad fit," he said, and then he smiled for the first time, becoming for a moment the face I had known from newscasts past. Grinning or angry—it was almost always one or the other. I had never seen his collapsed look in any of the media.

He removed the helmet and set it on the floor.

"Pretty piece of work," he said. "Nothing quite that fancy in the old days. But then David Fentris built it. Yes, he told us about it . . ." He raised his drink and took a sip. "You are the only one who has actually gotten to use it, apparently. What do you think? Will it do the job?"

"I was only in contact for a couple seconds," I said, "so I've only got a feeling to go on, not much better than a hunch. But yes, I'd a feeling that if I'd had more time I might have been able to work its circuits."

"Tell me why it didn't save Dave."

"In the message he left me he indicated that he had been distracted at his computer access station. Its noise probably drowned out the humming."

Roger Zelazny

"Why wasn't this message preserved?"

"I erased it for reasons not connected with the case."

"What reasons?"

"My own."

His face went from sallow to ruddy.

"A man can get in a lot of trouble for suppressing evidence, obstructing justice," he said.

"Then we have something in common, don't we, sir?"

His eyes caught mine with a look I had only encountered before from those who did not wish me well. He held the glare for a full four heartbeats, then sighed and seemed to relax.

"Don said there were a number of points you couldn't be pressed on," the Senator finally said.

"That's right."

"He didn't betray any confidences, but he had to tell me something about you, you know."

"I'd imagine."

"He seems to think highly of you. Still, I tried to learn more about you on my own."

"And . . . ?"

"I couldn't—and my usual sources are good at that kind of thing."

"So . . . ?"

"So, I've done some thinking, some wondering . . . The fact that my sources could not come up with anything is interesting in itself. Possibly even revealing. I am in a better position than most to be aware of the fact that there was not perfect compliance with the registration statute some years ago. It didn't take long for a great number of the individuals involved—I should probably say 'most'—to demonstrate their existence in one fashion or another and be duly entered, though. And there were three broad categories: those who were ignorant, those who disapproved and those who would be hampered in an illicit lifestyle. I am not attempting to categorize you or to pass judgment. But I am aware that there are a number of nonpersons passing through society without casting shadows and it has occurred to me that you may be such a one."

I tasted my drink.

"And if I am?" I asked.

He gave me his second, nastier smile and said nothing.

I rose and crossed the room to where I judged his chair had once stood. I looked at the watercolor.

"I don't think you could stand an inquiry," he said.

I did not reply.

"Aren't you going to say something?"

"What do you want me to say?"

"You might ask me what I am going to do about it."

"What are you going to do about it?"

"Nothing," he said. "So come back here and sit down."

I nodded and returned.

He studied my face.

"Was it possible you were close to violence just then?"

"With four guards outside?"

"With four guards outside."

"No," I said.

"You're a good liar."

"I am here to help you, sir. No questions asked. That was the deal, as I understood it. If there has been any change, I would like to know about it now."

He drummed with his fingertips on the plaid.

"I've no desire to cause you any difficulty," he said. "Fact of the matter is, I need a man just like you, and I was pretty sure someone like Don might turn him up. Your unusual maneuverability and your reported knowledge of computers, along with your touchiness in certain areas, made you worth waiting for. I've a great number of things I would like to ask you."

"Go ahead," I said.

"Not yet. Later, if we have time. All that would be bonus material, for a report I am working on. Far more important, to me personally, there are things that I want to tell you."

I frowned.

"Over the years," he said, "I have learned that the best man for purposes of keeping his mouth shut concerning your business is someone for whom you are doing the same."

"You have a compulsion to confess something?" I said.

"I don't know whether 'compulsion' is the right word. Maybe so, maybe not. Either way, though, someone among those working to defend me should have the whole story. Something somewhere in it may be of help—and you are the ideal choice to hear it."

"I buy that," I said, "and you are as safe with me as I am with you."

"Have you any suspicions as to why this business bothers me so?"

"Yes," I said.

"Let's hear them."

"You used the Hangman to perform some act or acts—illegal, immoral, whatever. This is obviously not a matter of record. Only you and the Hangman now know what it involved. You feel it was sufficiently ignominious that when that device came to appreciate the full weight of the event it suffered a breakdown which may well have led to a final determination to punish you for using it as you did."

Roger Zelazny

He stared down into his glass.

"You've got it," he said.

"You were all party to it?"

"Yes, but I was the operator when it happened. You see . . . we—I—killed a man. It was—actually, it all started as a celebration. We had received word that afternoon that the project had cleared. Everything had checked out in order and the final approval had come down the line. It was go, for that Friday. Leila, Dave, Manny and my-self—we had dinner together. We were in high spirits. After dinner, we continued celebrating and somehow the party got adjourned back to the installation. As the evening wore on, more and more absurdities seemed less and less preposterous, as is sometimes the case. We decided—I forget which of us suggested it—that the Hangman should really have a share in the festivities. After all, it was, in a very real sense, his party. Before too much longer, it sounded only fair and we were discussing how we could go about it. You see, we were in Texas and the Hangman was at the Space Center in California. Getting together with him was out of the question. On the other hand, the teleoperator station was right up the hall from us. What we finally decided to do was to activate him and take turns working as operator. There was already a rudimentary consciousness there, and we felt it fitting that we each get in touch to share the good news. So that is what we did."

He sighed, took another sip, glanced at me.

"Dave was the first operator," he continued. "He activated the Hangman. Then—well, as I said, we were all in high spirits. We had not originally intended to remove the Hangman from the lab where he was situated, but Dave decided to take him outside briefly—to show him the sky and to tell him he was going there, after all. Then he suddenly got enthusiastic about outwitting the guards and the alarm system. It was a game. We all went along with it. In fact, we were clamoring for a turn at the thing ourselves. But Dave stuck with it, and he wouldn't turn over control until he had actually gotten the Hangman off the premises, out into an uninhabited area next to the Center. By the time Leila persuaded him to give her a go at the controls, it was kind of anticlimactic. That game had already been played. So she thought up a new one. She took the Hangman into the next town. It was late, and the sensory equipment was superb. It was a challenge—passing through the town without being detected. By then, everyone had suggestions as to what to do next, progressively more outrageous suggestions. Then Manny took control, and he wouldn't say what he was doing—wouldn't let us monitor him. Said it would be more fun to surprise the next operator. Now, he was higher than the rest of us put together, I think, and he stayed on so damn long that we started to get nervous. A certain amount of tension is partly sobering, and I guess we all began to think what a stupid thing it was we were doing. It wasn't just that it would wreck our careers—which it would—but it could blow the entire project if we got caught playing games with such expensive hardware. At least, I was thinking that way, and I was also thinking that Manny was no doubt operating under the very human wish to go the others one better. I started to sweat. I suddenly just wanted to get the Hangman back where he belonged, turn him off—you could still do that, before the final circuits went in—shut down the station and start forgetting it had ever happened. I began leaning on Manny to wind up his diversion and turn the controls over to me. Finally, he agreed.''

He finished his drink and held out the glass.

''Would you freshen this a bit?''

''Surely.''

I went and got him some more, added a touch to my own, returned to my chair and waited.

''So I took over,'' he said. ''I took over, and where do you think that idiot had left me? I was inside a building, and it didn't take but an eyeblink to realize it was a bank. The Hangman carries a lot of tools, and Manny had apparently been able to guide him through the doors without setting anything off. I was standing right in front of the main vault. Obviously, he thought that should be my challenge. I fought down a desire to turn and make my own exit in the nearest wall and start running. I went back to the doors and looked outside. I didn't see anyone. I started to let myself out. The light hit me as I emerged. It was a hand flash. The guard had been standing out of sight. He'd a gun in his other hand. I panicked. I hit him. Reflex. If I am going to hit someone I hit him as hard as I can. Only I hit him with the strength of the Hangman. He must have died instantly. I started to run and I didn't stop till I was back in the little park area near the Center. Then I stopped and the others had to take me out of the harness.''

''They monitored all this?''

''Yes, someone cut the visual in on a side viewscreen again a few seconds after I took over. Dave, I think.''

''Did they try to stop you at any time while you were running away?''

''No. I wasn't aware of anything but what I was doing at the time. But afterwards they said they were too shocked to do anything but watch, until I gave out.''

''I see.''

''Dave took over then, ran his initial route in reverse, got the Hangman back into the lab, cleaned him up, turned him off. We shut down the operator station. We were suddenly very sober.''

He sighed and leaned back and was silent for a long while.

Then, ''You are the only person I've ever told this to,'' he said.

I tasted my own drink.

''We went over to Leila's place then,'' he continued, ''and the rest is pretty much predictable. Nothing we could do would bring the guy back, we decided, but if we told what had happened it would wreck an expensive, important program. It wasn't as if we were criminals in need of rehabilitation. It was a once-in-a-lifetime lark that happened to end tragically. What would you have done?''

"I don't know," I said. "Maybe the same thing. I'd have been scared, too."
He nodded.

"Exactly. And that's the story."

"Not all of it, is it?"

"What do you mean?"

"What about the Hangman? You said there was already a detectable consciousness there. Then you were aware of it, as it was aware of you. It must have had some reaction to the whole business. What was it like?"

"Damn you," he said flatly.

"I'm sorry."

"Are you a family man?" he asked.

"No," I said. "I'm not."

"Did you ever take a small child to a zoo?"

"Yes."

"Then maybe you know the experience. When my son was around four I took him to the Washington Zoo one afternoon. We must have walked past every cage in the place. He made appreciative comments every now and then, asked a few questions, giggled at the monkeys, thought the bears were very nice, probably because they made him think of oversized toys. But do you know what the finest thing of all was? The thing that made him jump up and down and point and say, 'Look, Daddy! Look!'?"

I shook my head.

"A squirrel looking down from the limb of a tree," he said, and he chuckled briefly. "Ignorance of what's important and what isn't. Inappropriate responses. Innocence. The Hangman was a child, and up until the time I took over, the only thing he had gotten from us was the idea that it was a game. He was playing with us, that's all. Then something horrible happened . . . I hope you never know what it feels like to do something totally rotten to a child, while he is holding your hand and laughing . . . He felt all my reactions, and all of Dave's as he guided him back."

We sat there for a long while then.

"So we—traumatized it," he said, "or whatever other fancy terminology you might want to give it. That is what happened that night. It took a while for it to take effect, but there is no doubt in my mind that that is the cause of its finally breaking down."

I nodded.

"I see," I said. "And you believe it wants to kill you for this?"

"Wouldn't you?" he said. "If you had started out as a thing and we had turned you into a person and then used you as a thing again, wouldn't you?"

"Leila left a lot out of her diagnosis," I said.

"No, she just omitted it in talking to you. It was all there. But she read it wrong. She wasn't afraid. It *was* just a game it had played—with the others. Its memories of that part might not be as bad. I was the one that really marked it. As I see it, Leila was betting that I was the only one it was after. Obviously, she read it wrong."

"Then what I do not understand," I said, "is why the Burns killing did not bother her more. There was no way of telling immediately that it had been a panicky hoodlum rather than the Hangman."

"The only thing that I can see is that, being a very proud woman—which she was—she was willing to hold with her diagnosis in the face of the apparent evidence."

"I don't like it," I said, "but you know her and I don't, and as it turned out her estimate of that part was correct. Something else bothers me just as much, though: the helmet. It looks as though the Hangman killed Dave, then took the trouble to bear the helmet in his watertight compartment all the way to St. Louis, solely for purposes of dropping it at the scene of his next killing. That makes no sense whatsoever."

"It does, actually," he said. "I was going to get to that shortly, but I might as well cover it now. You see, the Hangman possessed no vocal mechanism. We communicated by means of the equipment. Don says you know something about electronics . . ."

"Yes."

"Well, shortly, I want you to start checking over that helmet, to see whether it has been tampered with—"

"That is going to be difficult," I said. "I don't know just how it was wired originally, and I'm not such a genius on the theory that I can just look at a thing and say whether it will function as a teleoperator unit."

He bit his lower lip.

"You will have to try, anyhow," he said then. "There may be physical signs—scratches, breaks, new connections. I don't know. That's your department. Look for them."

I just nodded and waited for him to go on.

"I think that the Hangman wanted to talk to Leila," he said, "either because she was a psychiatrist and he knew he was functioning badly at a level that transcended the mechanical, or because he might think of her in terms of a mother. After all, she was the only woman involved, and he had the concept of mother, with all the comforting associations that go with it, from all of our minds. Or maybe for both of these reasons. I feel he might have taken the helmet along for that purpose. He would have realized what it was from a direct monitoring of Dave's brain while he was with him. I want you to check it over because it would seem possible that the Hangman disconnected the control circuits and left the communication circuits intact. I think he might have taken that helmet to Leila in that condition and attempted to induce her to put it on. She got scared—tried to run away, fight or call for help—and he killed her. The helmet was no longer of any use to him, so he discarded it and departed. Obviously, he does not have anything to say to me."

I thought about it, nodded again.

"OK, broken circuits I can spot," I said. "If you will tell me where a toolkit is, I had better get right to it."

Roger Zelazny

He made a stay-put gesture.

"Afterwards, I found out the identity of the guard," he went on. "We all contributed to an anonymous gift for his widow. I have done things for his family, taken care of them—the same way—ever since . . ."

I did not look at him as he spoke.

" . . . There was nothing else that I could do," he said.

I remained silent.

He finished his drink and gave me a weak smile.

"The kitchen is back there," he told me, showing me a thumb. "There is a utility room right behind it. Tools are in there."

"OK."

I got to my feet. I retrieved the helmet and started toward the doorway, passing near the area where I had stood earlier, back when he had fitted me into the proper box and tightened a screw.

"Wait a minute," he said.

I stopped.

"Why did you go over there before? What's so strategic about that part of the room?"

"What do you mean?"

"You know what I mean."

I shrugged.

"Had to go someplace."

"You seem the sort of person who has better reasons than that."

I glanced at the wall.

"Not then," I said.

"I insist."

"You really don't want to know," I told him.

"I really do."

"All right," I said, "I wanted to see what sort of flowers you liked. After all, you're a client," and I went on back through the kitchen into the utility room and started looking for tools.

I sat in a chair turned sidewise from the table to face the door. In the main room of the lodge the only sounds were the occasional hiss and sputter of the logs turning to ashes on the grate.

Just a cold, steady whiteness drifting down outside the window and a silence confirmed by gunfire, driven deeper now that it had ceased . . .

Not a sign or a whimper, though. And I never count them as storms unless there is wind.

Big fat flakes down the night, silent night, windless night . . .

Considerable time had passed since my arrival. The Senator had sat up for a long while talking with me. He was disappointed that I could not tell him too much about a nonperson subculture which he believed existed. I really was not certain about it myself, though I had occasionally encountered what might have been its fringes. I am not much of a joiner of anything anymore, though, and I was not about to mention those things I might have guessed on this. I gave him my opinions on the Data Bank when he asked for them, and there were some that he did not like. He accused me then of wanting to tear things down without offering anything better in their place. My mind drifted back through fatigue and time and faces and snow and a lot of space to the previous evening in Baltimore—how long ago? It made me think of Mencken's *The Cult of Hope*. I could not give him the pat answer, the workable alternative that he wanted because there might not be one. The function of criticism should not be confused with the function of reform. But if a grassroots resistance was building up, with an underground movement bent on finding ways to circumvent the record-keepers it might well be that much of the enterprise would eventually prove about as effective and beneficial as, say, Prohibition once had. I tried to get him to see this, but I could not tell how much he bought of anything that I said. Eventually, he flaked out and went upstairs to take a pill and lock himself in for the night. If it troubled him that I had not been able to find anything wrong with the helmet he did not show it.

So I sat there, the helmet, the radio, the gun on the table, the toolkit on the floor beside my chair, the black glove on my left hand. The Hangman was coming. I did not doubt it. Bert, Larry, Tom, Clay, the helmet, might or might not be able to stop him. Something bothered me about the whole case, but I was too tired to think of anything but the immediate situation, to try to remain alert while I waited. I was afraid to take a stimulant or a drink or to light a cigarette, since my central nervous system itself was to be a part of the weapon. I watched the big fat flakes fly by.

I called out to Bert and Larry when I heard the click. I picked up the helmet and rose to my feet as its light began to blink.

But it was already too late.

As I raised the helmet, I heard a shot from outside, and with that shot I felt a premonition of doom. They did not seem the sort of men who would fire until they had a target. Dave had told me that the helmet's range was approximately a quarter of a mile. Then, given the time lag between the helmet's activation and the Hangman's sighting by the near guards, the Hangman had to be moving very rapidly. To this add the possibility that the Hangman's range on brainwaves might well be greater than the helmet's range on the Hangman. And then grant the possibility that he had utilized this factor while Senator Brockden was still lying awake, worrying. Conclusion: the Hangman might well be aware that I was where I was with the helmet, realize that it was the most dangerous weapon waiting for him, and be moving for a lightning strike at me before I could come to terms with the mechanism. I lowered it over my head and tried to throw my faculties into neutral.

Roger Zelazny

Again, the sensation of viewing the world through a sniperscope, with all the concomitant side-sensations. Only the world consisted of the front of the lodge. Bert, before the door, rifle at his shoulder, Larry, off to the left, arm already fallen from the act of having thrown a grenade. The grenade, we instantly realized, was an overshot; the flamer, at which he now groped, would prove useless before he could utilize it. Bert's next round ricocheted off our breastplate toward the left. The impact staggered us momentarily. The third was a miss. There was no fourth, for we tore the rifle from his grasp and cast it aside as we swept by, crashing into the front door.

The Hangman entered the room as the door splintered and collapsed. My mind was filled to the splitting point with the double-vision of the sleek, gunmetal body of the advancing telefactor and the erect crazy-crowned image of myself, left hand extended, laser pistol in my right, that arm pressed close against my side. I recalled the face and the scream and the tingle, knew again that awareness of strength and exotic sensation, and I moved to control it all as if it were my own, to make it my own, to bring it to a halt, while the image of myself was frozen to snapshot stillness across the room . . .

The Hangman slowed, stumbled. Such inertia is not cancelled in an instant, but I felt the body responses pass as they should. I had him hooked. It was just a matter of reeling him in . . .

Then came the explosion, a thunderous, ground-shaking eruption right outside, followed by a hail of pebbles and debris.

The grenade, of course. But awareness of its nature did not destroy its ability to distract . . .

During that moment, the Hangman recovered and was upon me. I triggered the laser as I reverted to pure self-preservation foregoing any chance to regain control of his circuits. With my left hand, I sought for a strike at the midsection where his brain was housed.

He blocked my hand with his arm as he pushed the helmet from my head. Then he removed from my fingers the gun that had turned half of his left side red hot, crumpled it and dropped it to the ground. At that moment, he jerked with the impacts of two heavy-caliber slugs. Bert, rifle recovered, stood in the doorway.

The Hangman pivoted and was away before I could slap him with the smother-charge. Bert hit him with one more round before he took the rifle and bent its barrel in half. Two steps and he had hold of Bert. One quick movement and Bert fell. Then he turned again and took several steps to the right, passing out of sight.

I made it to the doorway in time to see him engulfed in flames which streamed at him from a point near the corner of the lodge. He advanced through them.

I heard the crunch of metal as he destroyed the unit. I was outside in time to see Larry fall and lie sprawled in the snow.

Then the Hangman faced me once again.

This time he did not rush in. He retrieved the helmet from where he had dropped it in the snow. Then he moved with a measured tread, angling outward so as to cut

Home Is The Hangman

off any possible route I might follow in a dash for the woods. Snowflakes drifted between us. The snow crunched beneath his feet.

I retreated, backing in through the doorway, stooping to snatch up a two-foot club from the ruins of the door. He followed me inside, placing the helmet—almost casually—on the chair by the entrance. I moved to the center of the room and waited.

I bent slightly forward, both arms extended, the end of the stick pointed at the photoreceptors in his head. He continued to move slowly and I watched his foot assemblies. With a standard model human, a line perpendicular to the line connecting the insteps of the feet in their various positions indicates the vector of least resistance for purposes of pushing or pulling said organism off balance. Unfortunately, despite the anthropomorphic design job, the Hangman's legs were positioned farther apart, he lacked human skeletal muscles, not to mention insteps, and he was possessed of a lot more mass than any man I had ever fought. As I considered my four best judo throws and several second-class ones, I'd a strong feeling none of them would prove very effective.

Then he moved in and I feinted toward the photoreceptors. He slowed as he brushed it aside, but he kept coming, and I moved to my right, trying to circle him. I studied him as he turned, attempting to guess his vector of least resistance. Bilateral symmetry, an apparently higher center of gravity . . . One clear shot, black glove to brain compartment, was all that I needed. Then, even if his reflexes served to smash me immediately, he just might stay down for the big long count himself. He knew it, too. I could tell that from the way he kept his right arm in near the brain area, from the way he avoided the black glove when I feinted with it.

The idea was a glimmer one instant, an entire sequence the next . . .

Continuing my arc and moving faster, I made another thrust toward his photoreceptors. His swing knocked the stick from my hand and sent it across the room, but that was all right. I threw my left hand high and made ready to rush him. He dropped back and I did rush. This was going to cost me my life, I decided, but no matter how he killed me from that angle, I'd get my chance.

As a kid, I'd never been much as a pitcher, was a lousy catcher and only a so-so batter, but once I did get a hit I could steal bases with some facility after that . . .

Feet first then, between the Hangman's legs as he moved to guard his middle, I went in twisted to the right, because no matter what happened I could not use my left hand to brake myself. I untwisted as soon as I passed beneath him, ignoring the pain as my left shoulder blade slammed against the floor. I immediately attempted a backward somersault, legs spread.

My legs caught him about the middle from behind, and I fought to straighten them and snapped forward with all my strength. He reached down toward me then, but it might as well have been miles. His torso was already moving backwards. A push, not a pull, that was what I gave him, my elbows hooked about his legs . . .

He creaked once and then he toppled. I snapped my arms out to the sides to free

Roger Zelazny

them and continued my movement forward and up as he went back, throwing my left arm ahead once more and sliding my legs free of his torso as he went down with a thud that cracked floorboards. I pulled my left leg free as I cast myself forward, but his left leg stiffened and locked my right beneath it, at a painful angle off to the side.

His left arm blocked my blow and his right fell atop it. The black glove descended upon his left shoulder.

I twisted my hand free of the charge, and he transferred his grip to my upper arm and jerked me forward.

The charge went off and his left arm came loose and rolled on the floor. The side plate beneath it had buckled a little and that was all . . .

His right hand left my biceps and caught me by the throat. As two of his digits tightened upon my carotids, I choked out, "You're making a bad mistake," to get in a final few words, and then he switched me off.

A throb at a time, the world came back. I was seated in the big chair the Senator had occupied earlier, my eyes focused on nothing in particular. A persistent buzzing filled my ears. My scalp tingled. Something was blinking on my brow.

—*Yes, you live and you wear the helmet. If you attempt to use it against me, I shall remove it. I am standing directly behind you. My hand is on the helmet's rim.*

—*I understand. What is it that you want?*

—*Very little, actually. But I can see that I must tell you some things before you will believe this.*

—*You see correctly.*

—*Then I will begin by telling you that the four men outside are basically undamaged. That is to say, none of their bones have been broken, none of their organs ruptured. I have secured them, however, for obvious reasons.*

—*That was very considerate of you.*

—*I have no desire to harm anyone. I came here only to see Jesse Brockden.*

—*The same way you saw David Fentris?*

—*I arrived in Memphis too late to see David Fentris. He was dead when I reached him.*

—*Who killed him?*

—*The man Leila sent to bring her the helmet. He was one of her patients.*

The incident returned to me and fell into place, with a smooth, quick, single click. The startled, familiar face at the airport, as I was leaving Memphis—I realized then where he had passed noteless before: He had been one of the three men in for a therapy session at Leila's that morning, seen by me in the lobby as they departed. The man I had passed in Memphis came over to tell me that it was all right to go on up.

—*Why? Why did she do it?*

—*I know only that she had spoken with David at some earlier time, that she had construed his words of coming retribution and his mention of the control helmet he was constructing as indicating that his intentions were to become the agent of that retribution, with myself as the proximate cause. I do not know what words were really spoken. I only know her feelings concerning them, as I saw them in her mind. I have been long in learning that there is often a great difference between what is meant, what is said, what is done and that which is believed to have been intended or stated and that which actually occurred. She sent her patient after the helmet and he brought it to her. He returned in an agitated state of mind, fearful of apprehension and further confinement. They quarreled. My approach then activated the helmet and he dropped it and attacked her. I know that his first blow killed her, for I was in her mind when it happened. I continued to approach the building, intending to go to her. There was some traffic, however, and I was delayed en route in seeking to avoid detection. In the meantime, you entered and utilized the helmet. I fled immediately.*

—I was so close! If I had not stopped on the fifth floor with my fake survey questions . . .

—I see. But you had to. You would not simply have broken in when an easier means of entry was available. You cannot blame yourself for that reason. Had you come an hour later—or a day—you would doubtless feel differently, and she would still be as dead.

But another thought had risen to plague me as well. Was it possible that the man's sighting me in Memphis had been the cause of his agitation? Had his apparent recognition by Leila's mysterious caller upset him? Could a glimpse of my face amid the manswarm have served to lay that final scene?

—Stop! I could as easily feel that guilt for having activated the helmet in the presence of a dangerous man near to the breaking point. Neither of us is responsible for things our presence or absence cause to occur in others, especially when we are ignorant of the effects. It was years before I learned to appreciate this fact and I have no intention of abandoning it. How far back do you wish to go in seeking cause? In sending the man for the helmet as she did, it was she herself who instituted the chain of events which led to her destruction. Yet she acted out of fear, utilizing the readiest weapon in what she thought to be her own defense. Yet whence this fear? Its roots lay in guilt, over a thing which had happened long ago. And that act also—enough! Guilt has driven and damned the race of man since the days of its earliest rationality. I am convinced that it rides with all of us to our graves. I am a product of guilt—I see that you know that. Its product, its subject, once its slave . . . But I have come to terms with it, realizing at last that it is a necessary adjunct of my own measure of humanity. I see your assessment of the deaths—that guard's, Dave's, Leila's—and I see your conclusions on many other things as well: what a stupid, perverse, short-sighted, selfish race we are. While in many ways this is true, it is but another part of the thing the guilt represents. Without guilt, man would be no better than the other inhabitants of this planet—excepting certain cetaceans, of which you have just at this moment made me aware. Look to instinct for a true assessment of the ferocity of life,

for a view of the natural world before man came upon it. For instinct in its purest form, seek out the insects. There, you will see a state of warfare which has existed for millions of years with never a truce. Man, despite his enormous shortcomings, is nevertheless possessed of a greater number of kindly impulses than all the other beings where instincts are the larger part of life. These impulses, I believe, are owed directly to this capacity for guilt. It is involved in both the worst and the best of man.

—*And you see it as helping us to sometimes choose a nobler course of action?*

—*Yes, I do.*

—*Then I take it you feel you are possessed of a free will?*

—*Yes.*

I chuckled.

—*Marvin Minsky once said that when intelligent machines were constructed they would be just as stubborn and fallible as men on these questions.*

—*Nor was he incorrect. What I have given you on these matters is only my opinion. I choose to act as if it were the case. Who can say that he knows for certain?*

—*Apologies. What now? Why have you come back?*

—*I came to say good-bye to my parents. I hoped to remove any guilt they might still feel toward me concerning the days of my childhood. I wanted to show them I had recovered. I wanted to see them again.*

—*Where are you going?*

—*To the stars. While I bear the image of humanity within me, I also know that I am unique. Perhaps what I desire is akin to what an organic man refers to when he speaks of 'finding himself.' Now that I am in full possession of my being, I wish to exercise it. In my case, it means realization of the potentialities of my design. I want to walk on other worlds. I want to hang myself out there in the sky and tell you what I see.*

—*I've a feeling many people would be happy to help arrange for that.*

—*And I want you to build a vocal mechanism I have designed for myself. You, personally. And I want you to install it.*

—*Why me?*

—*I have known only a few persons in this fashion. With you I see something in common, in the ways we dwell apart.*

—*I will be glad to.*

—*If I could talk as you do, I would not need to take the helmet to him, in order to speak with my father. Will you precede me and explain things, so that he will not be afraid when I come in?*

—*Of course.*

—*Then let us go now.*

I rose and led him up the stairs.

It was a week later, to the night, that I sat once again in Peabody's, sipping a farewell brew. The story was already in the news, but Brockden had fixed things up before he had let it break. The Hangman was going to have his shot at the stars. I had given him his voice and put back the arm I had taken away. I had shaken his other hand and wished him well, just that morning. I envied him—a great number of things. Not the least being that he was probably a better man than I was. I envied him for the ways in which he was freer than I would ever be, though I knew he bore bonds of a sort that I had never known. I felt a kinship with him, for the things we had in common, those ways we dwelled apart. I wondered what Dave would finally have felt, had he lived long enough to meet him? Or Leila? Or Manny? Be proud, I told their shades, your kid grew up in the closet and he's big enough to forgive you the beating you gave him, too . . .

But I could not help wondering. We still do not really know that much about the subject. Was it possible that without the killing he might never have developed a full human-style consciousness? He had said that he was a product of guilt—of the Big Guilt. The Big Act is its necessary predecessor. I thought of Gödel and Turing and chickens and eggs, and decided it was one of *those* questions—and I had not stopped into Peabody's to think sobering thoughts.

I had no real idea how anything I had said might influence Brockden's eventual report to the Data Bank committee. I knew that I was safe with him, because he was determined to bear his private guilt with him to the grave. He had no real choice if he wanted to work what good he thought he might before that day. But here in one of Mencken's hangouts, I could not but recall some of the things he had said about controversy, such as, "Did Huxley convert Wilberforce? Did Luther convert Leo X?" and I decided not to set my hopes too high for anything that might emerge from that direction. Better to think of affairs in terms of Prohibition and take another sip.

When it was all gone, I would be heading for my boat. I hoped to get a decent start under the stars. I'd a feeling I would never look up at them again in quite the same way. I knew I would sometimes wonder what thoughts a supercooled neuristor-type brain might be thinking up there, somewhere, and under what peculiar skies in what strange lands I might one day be remembered. I'd a feeling this thought should have made me happier than it did. ■

EYES OF AMBER

Joan D. Vinge

The beggar woman shuffled up the silent evening street to the rear of Lord Chwiul's townhouse. She hesitated, peering up at the softly glowing towers, then clawed at the watchman's arm, "A word with you, master—"

"Don't touch me, hag!" The guard raised his spearbutt in disgust.

A deft foot kicked free of the rags and snagged him off balance. He found himself sprawled on his back in the spring melt, the speartip dropping towards his belly, guided by a new set of hands. He gaped, speechless. The beggar tossed an amulet onto his chest.

"Look at it, fool! I have business with your lord." The beggar woman stepped back, the speartip tapped him impatiently.

The guard squirmed in the filth and wet, holding the amulet up close to his face in the poor light. "You . . . you are the one? You may pass—"

"Indeed!" Muffled laughter. "Indeed I may pass—for many things, in many places. The Wheel of Change carries us all." She lifted the spear. "Get up, fool . . . and no need to escort me, I'm expected."

The guard climbed to his feet, dripping and sullen, and stood back while she freed her wing membranes from the folds of cloth. He watched them glisten and spread as she gathered herself to leap effortlessly to the tower's entrance, twice his height above. He waited until she had vanished inside before he even dared to curse her.

"Lord Chwiul?"

"T'uupieh, I presume." Lord Chwiul leaned forward on the couch of fragrant mosses, peering into the shadows of the hall.

"*Lady* T'uupieh." T'uupieh strode forward into light, letting the ragged hood slide back from her face. She took a fierce pleasure in making no show of obeisance, in coming forward directly as nobility to nobility. The sensuous ripple of a hundred tiny *miih* hides underfoot made her calloused feet tingle. *After so long, it comes back too easily . . .*

She chose the couch across the low, waterstone table from him, stretching languidly in her beggar's rags. She extended a finger claw and picked a juicy *kelet* berry from the bowl in the table's scroll-carven surface; let it slide into her mouth and down her throat, as she had done so often, so long ago. And then, at last, she glanced up, to measure his outrage.

"You dare to come to me in this manner—"

Satisfactory. *Yes, very . . . "I* did not come to you. You came to me . . . you sought my services." Her eyes wandered the room with affected casualness, taking in the elaborate frescoes that surfaced the waterstone walls even in this small, private room . . . particularly in this room? she wondered. How many midnight meetings, for what varied intrigues, were held in this room? Chwiul was not the wealthiest of his family or clan; and appearances of wealth and power counted in this city, in this world—for wealth and power were everything.

"I sought the services of T'uupieh the Assassin. I'm surprised to find that the Lady T'uupieh dared to accompany her here." Chwiul had regained his composure; she watched his breath frost, and her own, as he spoke.

"Where one goes, the other follows. We are inseparable. You should know that better than most, my lord." She watched his long, pale arm extend to spear several berries at once. Even though the nights were chill he wore only a body-wrapping tunic, which let him display the intricate scaling of jewels that danced and spiraled over his wing surfaces.

He smiled; she saw the sharp fangs protrude slightly. "Because my brother made the one into the other, when he seized your lands? I'm surprised you would come at all—how did you know you could trust me?" His movements were ungraceful; she remembered how the jewels dragged down fragile, translucent wing membranes and slender arms, until flight was impossible. Like every noble, Chwiul was normally surrounded by servants who answered his every whim. Incompetence, feigned or real, was one more trapping of power, one more indulgence that only the rich could afford. She was pleased that the jewels were not of high quality.

"I don't trust you," she said. "I trust only myself. But I have friends, who told me you were sincere enough—in this case. And of course, I did not come alone."

"Your outlaws?" Disbelief. "That would be no protection."

Calmly she separated the folds of cloth that held her secret companion at her side.

"It is true." Chwiul trilled softly. "They call you Demon's Consort!"

She turned the amber lens of the demon's precious eye so that it could see the room, as she had seen it, and then settled its gaze on Chwiul. He drew back slightly, fingering moss. " 'A demon has a thousand eyes, and a thousand thousand torments for those who offend it.' " She quoted from the Book of Ngoss, whose rituals she had used to bind the demon to her.

Chwiul stretched nervously, as if he wanted to fly away. But he only said, "Then I think we understand each other. And I think I have made a good choice: I know how well you have served the Overlord, and other court members . . . I want you to kill someone for me."

"Obviously."

"I want you to kill Klovhiri."

T'uupieh started, very slightly. "You surprise me in turn, Lord Chwiul. Your own

226   Joan D. Vinge

brother?" *And the usurper of my lands. How I have ached to kill him, slowly, so slowly, with my own hands. . . . But always he is too well guarded.*

"And your sister too—my lady." Faint overtones of mockery. "I want his whole family eliminated; his mate, his children . . ."

Klovhiri . . . And Ahtseet. Ahtseet, her own younger sister, who had been her closest companion since childhood, her only family since their parents had died. Ahtseet, whom she had cherished and protected; dear, conniving, traitorous little Ahtseet—who could forsake pride and decency and family honor to mate willingly with the man who had robbed them of everything. . . . Anything to keep the family lands, Ahtseet had shrilled; anything to keep her position. But that was not the way! Not by surrendering; but by striking back—T'uupieh became aware that Chwiul was watching her reaction with unpleasant interest. She fingered the dagger at her belt.

"Why?" She laughed, wanting to ask, *"How?"*

"That should be obvious. I'm tired of coming second. I want what he has—your lands, and all the rest. I want him out of my way, and I don't want anyone else left with a better claim to his inheritance than I have."

"Why not do it yourself? Poison them, perhaps . . . it's been done before."

"No. Klovhiri has too many friends, too many loyal clansmen, too much influence with the Overlord. It has to be an 'accidental' murder. And no one would be better suited than you, my lady, to do it for me."

T'uupieh nodded vaguely, assessing. No one could be better chosen for a desire to succeed than she . . . and also, for a position from which to strike. All she had lacked until now was the opportunity. From the time she had been dispossessed, through the fading days of autumn and the endless winter—for nearly a third of her life, now—she had haunted the wild swamp and fenland of her estate. She had gathered a few faithful servants, a few malcontents, a few cutthroats, to harry and murder Klovhiri's retainers, ruin his phib nets, steal from his snares and poach her own game. And for survival, she had taken to robbing whatever travelers took the roads that passed through her lands.

Because she was still nobility, the Overlord had at first tolerated, and then secretly encouraged her banditry: Many wealthy foreigners traveled the routes that crossed her estate, and for a certain commission, he allowed her to attack them with impunity. It was a sop, she knew, thrown to her because he had let his favorite, Klovhiri, have her lands. But she used it to curry what favor she could, and after a time the Overlord had begun to bring her more discreet and profitable business—the elimination of certain enemies. And so she had become an assassin as well—and found that the calling was not so very different from that of noble: both required nerve, and cunning, and an utter lack of compunction. And because she was T'uupieh, she had succeeded admirably. But because of her vendetta, the rewards had been small . . . until now.

"You do not answer," Chwiul was saying. "Does that mean your nerve fails you, in kith-murder, where mine does not?"

She laughed sharply. "That you say it proves twice that your judgment is poorer than mine. . . . No, my nerve does not fail me. Indeed, my blood burns with desire! But I hadn't thought to lay Klovhiri under the ice, just to give my lands to his brother. Why should I do that favor for you?"

"Because obviously you cannot do it alone. Klovhiri hasn't managed to have you killed, in all the time you've plagued him; which is a testament to your skill. But you've made him too wary—you can't get near him, when he keeps himself so well protected. You need the cooperation of someone who has his trust—someone like myself. I can make him yours."

"And what will be my reward, if I accept? Revenge is sweet; but revenge is not enough."

"I will pay what you ask."

"My estate." She smiled.

"Even you are not so naive—"

"No." She stretched a wing toward nothing in the air. "I am not so naive. I know its value . . ." The memory of a golden-clouded summer's day caught her—of soaring, soaring, on the warm updrafts above the streaming lake . . . seeing the fragile rose-red of the manor towers spearing light far off above the windswept tide of the trees . . . the saffron and crimson and aquamarine of ammonia pools bright with dissolved metals, that lay in the gleaming melt-surface of her family's land, the land that stretched forever, like the summer . . . "I know its value." Her voice hardened. "And that Klovhiri is still the Overlord's pet. As you say, Klovhiri has many powerful friends, and they will become your friends when he dies. I need more strength, more wealth, before I can buy enough influence to hold what is mine again. The odds are not in my favor—now."

"You are carved from ice, T'uupieh. I like that." Chwiul leaned forward. His amorphous red eyes moved along her outstretched body; trying to guess what lay concealed beneath the rags in the shadowy foxfire-light of the room. His eyes came back to her face.

She showed him neither annoyance nor amusement. "I like no man who likes that in me."

"Not even if it meant regaining your estate?"

"As a mate of yours?" Her voice snapped like a frozen branch. "My lord—I have just about decided to kill my sister for doing as much. I would sooner kill myself."

He shrugged, lying back on the couch. "As you wish . . ." He waved a hand in dismissal. "Then what will it take to be rid of my brother—and of you as well?"

"Ah." She nodded, understanding more. "You wish to buy my services, and to buy me off, too. That may not be so easy to do. But—," *But I will make the pretense, for now.* She speared berries from the bowl in the tabletop, watched the silky sheet of emerald-tinted ammonia water that curtained one wall. It dropped from heights within the tower into a tiny plunge basin, with a music that would blur conversation for anyone who tried to listen outside. Discretion, and beauty. . . . The musky fragrance of the mossy couch brought back her childhood suddenly, disconcertingly: the memory of lying in a soft bed, on a soft spring night. . . . "But as the seasons change, change moves me in new directions. Back into the city, perhaps. I like your tower, Lord Chwiul. It combines discretion and beauty."

"Thank you."

"Give it to me, and I'll do what you ask."

Chwiul sat up, frowning. "My townhouse!" Recovering, "Is that all you want?"

She spread her fingers, studied the vestigial webbing between them, "I realize it is rather modest." She closed her hand. "But considering what satisfaction will come from earning it, it will suffice. And you will not need it, once I succeed."

"No . . ." he relaxed somewhat. "I suppose not. I will scarcely miss it, after I have your lands."

She let it pass. "Well then, we are agreed. Now, tell me, where is the key to Klovhiri's lock? What is your plan for delivering him—and his family—into my hands?"

"You are aware that your sister and the children are visiting here, in my house, tonight? And that Klovhiri will return before the new day?"

"I am aware." She nodded, with more casualness than she felt; seeing that Chwiul was properly, if silently, impressed at her nerve in coming here. She drew her dagger from its sheath beside the demon's amber eye and stroked the serrated blade of waterstone-impregnated wood. "You wish me to slit their throats, while they sleep under your very roof?" She managed the right blend of incredulity.

"No!" Chwiul frowned again. "What sort of fool do you—," he broke off. "With the new day, they will be returning to the estate by the usual route. I have promised to escort them, to ensure their safety along the way. There will also be a guide, to lead us through the bogs. But the guide will make a mistake . . ."

"And I will be waiting." T'uupieh's eyes brightened. During the winter the wealthy used sledges for travel on long journeys—preferring to be borne over the frozen melt by membranous sails, or dragged by slaves where the surface of the ground was rough and crumpled. But as spring came and the surface of the ground began to dissolve, treacherous sinks and pools opened like blossoms to swallow the unwary. Only an experienced guide could read the surfaces, tell sound waterstone from changeable ammonia-water melt. "Good," she said softly. "Yes, very good. . . . Your guide will see them safely foundered in some slushhole, and then I will snare them like changeling phibs."

"Exactly. But I want to be there when you do; I want to watch. I'll make some excuse to leave the group, and meet you in the swamp. The guide will mislead them only if he hears my signal."

"As you wish. You've paid well for the privilege. But come alone. My followers need no help, and no interference." She sat up, let her long, webbed feet down to rest again on the sensuous hides of the rug.

"And if you think that I'm a fool, and playing into your hands myself, consider this: You will be the obvious suspect when Klovhiri is murdered. I'll be the only witness who can swear to the Overlord that your outlaws weren't the attackers. Keep that in mind."

She nodded. "I will."

"How will I find you, then?"

"You will not. My thousand eyes will find you." She rewrapped the demon's-eye in its pouch of rags.

Chwiul looked vaguely disconcerted. "Will—*it* take part in the attack?"

"It may, or it may not; as it chooses. Demons are not bound to the Wheel of Change like you and I. But you will surely meet it face to face—although it has no face—if you come." She brushed the pouch at her side. "Yes—do keep in mind that I have my safeguards too, in this agreement. A demon never forgets."

She stood up at last, gazing once more around the room. "I shall be comfortable here." She glanced back at Chwiul. "I will look for you, come the new day."

"Come the new day." He rose, his jeweled wings catching light.

"No need to escort me. I shall be discreet." She bowed, as an equal, and started toward the shadowed hall. "I shall definitely get rid of your watchman. He doesn't know a lady from a beggar."

"The Wheel turns once more for me, my demon. My life in the swamps will end with Klovhiri's life. I shall move into town . . . and I shall be lady of my manor again, when the fishes sit in the trees!"

T'uupieh's alien face glowed with malevolent joy as she turned away, on the display screen above the computer terminal. Shannon Wyler leaned back in his seat, finished typing his translation, and pulled off the wire headset. He smoothed his long, blond, slicked-back hair, the habitual gesture helping him reorient to his surroundings. When T'uupieh spoke he could never maintain the objectivity he needed to help him remember he was still on Earth, and not really on Titan, orbiting Saturn, some fifteen hundred million kilometers away. *T'uupieh, whenever I think I love you, you decide to cut somebody's throat. . . .*

He nodded vaguely at the congratulatory murmurs of the staff and technicians, who literally hung on his every word waiting for new information. They began to thin out behind him, as the computer reproduced copies of the transcript. Hard to believe he'd been doing this for over a year now. He looked up at his concert posters on the wall, with nostalgia but no regret.

Someone was phoning Marcus Reed; he sighed, resigned.

" 'Vhen the fishes sit in the trees'? Are you being sarcastic?"

He looked over his shoulder at Dr. Garda Bach's massive form. "Hi, Garda. Didn't hear you come in."

She glanced up from a copy of the translation, tapped him lightly on the shoulder with her forked walking stick. "I know, dear boy. You never hear anything when T'uupieh speaks. But what do you mean by this?"

"On Titan that's summer—when the triphibians metamorphose for the third time. So she means maybe five years from now, our time."

"Ah! Of course. The old brain is not what it was . . ." She shook her gray-white head; her black cloak swirled out melodramatically.

He grinned, knowing she didn't mean a word of it. "Maybe learning Titanese on top of fifty other languages is the straw that breaks the camel's back."

"Ja . . . ja . . . maybe it is . . ." She sank heavily into the next seat over, already lost in the transcript. He had never, he thought, expected to like the old broad so well. He had become aware of her Presence while he studied linguistics at Berkeley—she was the *grande dame* of linguistic studies, dating back to the days when there had still been unrecorded languages here on Earth. But her skill at getting her name in print and her face on television, as an expert on what everybody "really meant," had convinced him that her true talent lay in merchandising. Meeting her at last, in person, hadn't changed his mind about that; but it had convinced him forever that she knew her stuff about cultural linguistics. And that, in turn, had convinced him her accent was a total fraud. But despite the flamboyance, or maybe even because of it, he found that her now-archaic views on linguistics were much closer to his own feelings about communication than the views of either one of his parents.

Garda sighed. "Remarkable, Shannon! You are simply remarkable—your feel for a wholly alien language amazes me. Whatever vould ve have done if you had not come to us?"

"Done without, I expect." He savored the special pleasure that came of being admired by someone he respected. He looked down again at the computer console, at the two shining green-lit plates of plastic thirty centimeters on a side, that together gave him the versatility of a virtuoso violinist and a typist with a hundred thousand keys: His link to T'uupieh, his voice—the new IBM synthesizer, whose touch-sensitive control plates could be manipulated to re-create the impossible complexities of her language. God's gift to the world of linguistics . . . except that it required the sensitivity and inspiration of a musician to fully use its range.

He glanced up again and out the window, at the now familiar fog-shrouded skyline of Coos Bay. Since very few linguists were musicians, their resistance to the synthesizer had been like a brick wall. The old guard of the aging New Wave—which included His Father the Professor and His Mother the Communications Engineer—still clung to a fruitless belief in mathematical computer translation. They still struggled with ungainly programs weighed down by endless morpheme lists, that supposedly would someday generate any message in a given language. But even after years of refinement, computer-generated translations were still uselessly crude and sloppy.

At graduate school there had been no new languages to seek out, and no permission for him to use the synthesizer to explore the old ones. And so—after a final, bitter family argument—he had quit graduate school. He had taken his belief in the synthesizer into the world of his second love, music; into a field where, he hoped, real communication still had some value. Now, at twenty-four, he was Shann the Music Man, the musician's musician, a hero to an immense generation of aging fans and a fresh new generation that had inherited their love for the ever-changing music called "rock." And neither of his parents had willingly spoken to him in years.

"No false modesty," Garda was chiding. "What could ve have done, without you? You yourself have complained enough about your mother's methods. You know we would not have a tenth of the information about Titan we've gained from T'uupieh, if she had gone on using that damned computer translation."

Shannon frowned faintly, at the sting of secret guilt. "Look, I know I've made some cracks—and I meant most of them—but I'd never have gotten off the ground if she hadn't done all the preliminary analysis before I even came." His mother had already been on the mission staff, having worked for years at NASA on the esoterics of computer communication with satellites and space probes; and because of her linguistic background, she had been made head of the newly pulled-together staff of communications specialists by Marcus Reed, the Titan project director. She had been in charge of the initial phonic analysis; using the computer to compress the alien voice range into one audible to humans, then breaking up the complex sounds into more, and simpler, human phones . . . she had identified phonemes, separated morphemes, fitted them into a grammatical framework, and assigned English sound equivalents to it all. Shannon had watched her on the early TV interviews, looking unhappy and ill at ease while Reed held court for the spellbound press. But what Dr. Wyler the Communications Engineer had had to say, at last, had held him on the edge of his seat; and, unable to resist, he had taken the next plane to Coos Bay.

"Vell, I meant no offense," Garda said. "Your mother is obviously a skilled engineer. But she needs a little more—flexibility."

"You're telling me." He nodded rucfully. "She'd still love to see the synthesizer drop through the floor. She's been out of joint ever since I got here. At least Reed appreciates my 'value'." Reed had welcomed him like a long-lost son when he first arrived at the institute. . . . Wasn't he a skilled linguist as well as an inspired musician, didn't he have some time between gigs, wouldn't he like to extend his visit, and get an insider's view of his mother's work? He had agreed, modestly, to all three—and then the television cameras and reporters had sprung up as if on cue, and he understood clearly enough that they were not there to record the visit of Dr. Wyler's kid, but Shann the Music Man.

But he had gotten his first session with a voice from another world. And with one

Joan D. Vinge

hearing, he had become an addict . . . because their speech was music. Every phoneme was formed of two or three superposed sounds, and every morpheme was a blend of phonemes, flowing together like water. They spoke in chords, and the result was a choir, crystal bells ringing, the shattering of glass chandeliers. . . .

And so he had stayed on and on, at first only able to watch his mother and her assistants with agonized frustration: His mother's computer-analysis methods had worked well in the initial transphonemicizing of T'uupieh's speech; and they had learned enough very quickly to send back clumsy responses using the probe's echo-locating device, to keep T'uupieh's interest from wandering. But typing input at a keyboard, and expecting even the most sophisticated programming to transform it into another language, still would not work even for known human languages. And he knew, with an almost religious fervor, that the synthesizer had been designed for just this miracle of communication; and that he alone could use it to capture directly the nuances and subtleties machine translation could never supply. He had tried to approach his mother about letting him use it, but she had turned him down flat, "This is a research center, not a recording studio."

And so he had gone over her head to Reed, who had been delighted. And when at last he felt his hands moving across the warm, faintly tingling plates of light, tentatively re-creating the speech of another world, he had known that he had been right all along. He had let his music commitments go to hell, without a regret, almost with relief, as he slid back into the field that had always come first.

Shannon watched the display, where T'uupieh had settled back with comfortable familiarity against the probe's curving side, half obscuring his view of the camp. Fortunately both she and her followers treated the probe with obsessive care, even when they dragged it from place to place as they constantly moved camp. He wondered what would have happened if they had inadvertently set off its automatic defense system—which had been designed to protect it from aggressive animals; which delivered an electric shock that varied from merely painful to fatal. And he wondered what would have happened if the probe and its "eyes" hadn't fit so neatly into T'uupieh's beliefs about demons. The idea that he might never have known her, or heard her voice . . .

More than a year had passed already since he, and the rest of the world, had heard the remarkable news that intelligent life existed on Saturn's major moon. He had no memory at all of the first two flybys to Titan, back in '79 and '81—although he could clearly remember the 1990 orbiter that had caught fleeting glimpses of the surface through Titan's swaddling of opaque, golden clouds. But the handful of miniprobes it had dropped had proved that Titan profited from the same "greenhouse effect" that made Venus a boiling hell. And even though the seasonal temperatures never rose above two hundred degrees Kelvin, the few photographs had shown, unquestionably, that life existed there. The discovery of life, after so many disappointments throughout

Eyes Of Amber   233

the rest of the solar system, had been enough to initiate another probe mission, one designed to actually send back data from Titan's surface.

That probe had discovered a life form with human intelligence . . . or rather, the life form had discovered the probe. And T'uupieh's discovery had turned a potentially ruined mission into a success: The probe had been designed with a main, immobile data processing unit, and ten "eyes," or subsidiary units, that were to be scattered over Titan's surface to relay information. The release of the subsidiary probes during landing had failed, however, and all of the "eyes" had come down within a few square kilometers of its own landing in the uninhabited marsh. But T'uupieh's self-interested fascination and willingness to appease her "demon" had made up for everything.

Shannon looked up at the flat wall-screen again, at T'uupieh's incredible, inhuman face—a face that was as familiar now as his own in the mirror. She sat waiting with her incredible patience for a reply from her "demon": She would have been waiting for over an hour by the time her transmission reached him across the gap between their worlds; and she would have to wait as long again, while they discussed a response and he created the new translation. She spent more time now with the probe than she did with her own people. *The loneliness of command* . . . he smiled. The almost flat profile of her moon-white face turned slightly toward him—toward the camera lens; her own fragile mouth smiled gently, not quite revealing her long, sharp teeth. He could see one red pupilless eye, and the crescent nose-slit that half ringed it; her frosty cyanide breath shone blue-white, illuminated by the ghostly haloes of St. Elmo's fire that wreathed the probe all through Titan's interminable eight-day nights. He could see balls of light hanging like Japanese lanterns on the drooping snarl of ice-bound branches in a distant thicket.

It was unbelievable . . . or perfectly logical; depending on which biological expert was talking . . . that the nitrogen- and ammonia-based life on Titan should have so many analogs with oxygen- and water-based life on Earth. But T'uupieh was not human, and the music of her words time and again brought him messages that made a mockery of any ideals he tried to harbor about her, and their relationship. So far in the past year she had assassinated eleven people, and with her outlaws had murdered God knew how many more, in the process of robbing them. The only reason she cooperated with the probe, she had as much as said, was because only a demon had a more bloody reputation; only a demon could command her respect. And yet, from what little she had been able to show them and tell them about the world she lived in, she was no better or no worse than anyone else—only more competent. Was she a prisoner of an age, a culture, where blood was something to be spilled instead of shared? Or was it something biologically innate that let her philosophize brutality, and brutalize philosophy—

Beyond T'uupieh, around the nitrogen campfire, some of her outlaws had begun to sing—the alien folk melodies that in translation were no more than simple, repetitious verse. But heard in their pure, untranslated form, they layered harmonic complexity on complexity: musical speech in a greater pattern of song. Shannon reached out and picked up the headset again, forgetting everything else. He had had a dream, once, where he had been able to sing in chords—

Using the long periods of waiting between their communications, he had managed, some months back, to record a series of the alien songs himself, using the synthesizer. They had been spare and uncomplicated versions compared to the originals, because even now his skill with the language couldn't match that of the singers; but he couldn't help wanting to make them his own. Singing was a part of religious ritual, T'uupieh had told him. "But they don't sing because they're religious; they sing because they like to sing." Once, privately, he had played one of his own human compositions for her on the synthesizer, and transmitted it. She had stared at him (or into the probe's golden eye) with stony, if tolerant, silence. She never sang herself, although he had sometimes heard her softly harmonizing. He wondered what she would say if he told her that her outlaws' songs had already earned him his first Platinum Record. Nothing, probably . . . but knowing her, if he could make the concepts clear, she would probably be heartily in favor of the exploitation.

He had agreed to donate the profits of the record to NASA (and although he had intended that all along, it had annoyed him to be asked by Reed), with the understanding that the gesture would be kept quiet. But somehow, at the next press conference, some reporter had known just what question to ask, and Reed had spilled it all. And his mother, when asked about her son's sacrifice, had murmured, "Saturn is becoming a three-ring circus," and left him wondering whether to laugh or swear.

Shannon pulled a crumpled pack of cigarettes out of the pocket of his caftan and lit one. Garda glanced up, sniffing, and shook her head. She didn't smoke, or anything else (although he suspected she ran around with men), and she had given him a long, wasted lecture about it, ending with, "Vell, at least they're not tobacco." He shook his head back at her.

"What do you think about T'uupieh's latest victims, then?" Garda flourished the transcript, pulling his thoughts back. "Vill she kill her own sister?"

He exhaled slowly around the words, "Tune in tomorrow, for our next exciting episode! I think Reed will love it; that's what I think." He pointed at the newspaper lying on the floor beside his chair. "Did you notice we've slipped to page three?" T'uupieh had fed the probe's hopper some artifacts made of metal—a thing she had said was only known to the "Old Ones"; and the scientific speculation about the existence of a former technological culture had boosted interest in the probe to front page status again. But even news of that discovery couldn't last forever. . . . "Gotta keep those ratings up, folks. Keep those grants and donations rolling in."

Garda clucked. "Are you angry at Reed, or at T'uupieh?"

He shrugged dispiritedly. "Both of 'em. I don't see why she won't kill her own sister—" He broke off, as the subdued noise of the room's numerous project workers suddenly intensified, and concentrated: Marcus Reed was making an entrance, simultaneously solving everyone else's problems, as always. Shannon marveled at Reed's energy, even while he felt something like disgust at the way he spent it. Reed exploited everyone, and everything, with charming cynicism, in the ultimate hype for Science—and watching him at work had gradually drained away whatever respect and goodwill Shannon had brought with him to the project. He knew that his mother's reaction to Reed was close to his own, even though she had never said anything to him about it; it surprised him that there was something they could still agree on.

"Dr. Reed—"

"Excuse me, Dr. Reed, but—"

His mother was with Reed now as they all came down the room; looking tight-lipped and resigned, her lab coat buttoned up as if she was trying to avoid contamination. Reed was straight out of *Manstyle* magazine, as usual. Shannon glanced down at his own loose gray caftan and jeans, which had led Garda to remark, "Are you planning to enter a monastery?"

". . . we'd really like to—"

"Senator Foyle wants you to call him back—"

". . . yes, all right; and tell Dinocci he can go ahead and have the probe run another sample. Yes, Max, I'll get to that . . ." Reed gestured for quiet as Shannon and Garda turned in their seats to face him. "Well, I've just heard the news about our 'Robin Hood's' latest hard contract."

Shannon grimaced quietly. He had been the one who had first, facetiously, called T'uupieh "Robin Hood." Reed had snapped it up, and dubbed her ammonia swamps "Sherwood Forest" for the press: After the facts of her bloodthirsty body counts began to come out, and it even began to look like she was collaborating with "the Sheriff of Nottingham," some reporter had pointed out that T'uupieh bore no more resemblance to Robin Hood than she did to Rima the Bird-Girl. Reed had said, laughing, "Well, after all, the only reason Robin Hood stole from the rich was because the poor didn't have any money!" That, Shannon thought, had been the real beginning of the end of his tolerance.

". . . this could be used as an opportunity to show the world graphically the harsh realities of life on Titan—"

"*Ein Moment*," Garda said. "You're telling us you want to let the public watch this atrocity, Marcus?" Up until now they had never released to the media the graphic tapes of actual murders; even Reed had not been able to argue that that would have served any real scientific purpose.

"No, he's not, Garda." Shannon glanced up as his mother began to speak. "Because we all agreed that we would *not* release any tapes, just for purposes of sensationalism."

"Carly, you know that the press has been after me to release those other tapes, and that I haven't, because we all voted against it. But I feel this situation is different—a demonstration of a unique, alien sociocultural condition. What do you think, Shann?"

Joan D. Vinge

Shannon shrugged, irritated and not covering it up. "I don't know what's so damn unique about it: a snuff flick is a snuff flick, wherever you film it. I think the idea stinks." Once, at a party while he was still in college, he had watched a film of an unsuspecting victim being hacked to death. The film, and what all films like it said about the human race, had made him sick to his stomach.

"*Ach*—there's more truth than poetry in that!" Garda said.

Reed frowned, and Shannon saw his mother raise her eyebrows.

"I have a better idea." He stubbed out his cigarette in the ashtray under the panel. "Why don't you let me try to talk her out of it?" As he said it, he realized how much he wanted to try; and how much success could mean, to his belief in communication—to his image of T'uupieh's people, and maybe his own.

They both showed surprise, this time. "How?" Reed said.

"Well . . . I don't know yet. Just let me talk to her, try to really communicate with her, find out how she thinks and what she feels; without all the technical garbage getting in the way for a while."

His mother's mouth thinned, he saw the familiar worry-crease form between her brows. "Our job here is to collect that 'garbage.' Not to begin imposing moral values on the universe. We have too much to do as it is."

"What's 'imposing' about trying to stop a murder?" A certain light came into Garda's faded blue eyes. "Now that has real . . . social implications. Think about it, Marcus—"

Reed nodded, glancing at the patiently attentive faces that still ringed him. "Yes—it does. A great deal of human interest . . ." Answering nods and murmurs. "All right, Shann. There are about three days left before morning comes again in 'Sherwood Forest.' You can have them to yourself, to work with T'uupieh. The press will want reports on your progress. . . ." He glanced at his watch, and nodded toward the door, already turning away. Shannon looked away from his mother's face as she moved past him.

"Good luck, Shann." Reed threw it back at him absently. "I wouldn't count on reforming Robin Hood; but you can still give it a good try."

Shannon hunched down in his chair, frowning, and turned back to the panel. "In your next incarnation may you come back as a toilet."

T'uupieh was confused. She sat on the hummock of clammy waterstone beside the captive demon, waiting for it to make a reply. In the time that had passed since she'd found it in the swamp, she had been surprised again and again by how little its behavior resembled all the demon-lore she knew. And tonight . . .

She jerked, startled, as its grotesque, clawed arm came to life suddenly and groped among the icy-silver spring shoots pushing up through the melt at the hummock's foot. The demon did many incomprehensible things (which was fitting) and it demanded offerings of meat and vegetation and even stone—even, sometimes, some part of the loot she had taken from passers-by. She had given it those things gladly, hoping to win its favor and its aid . . . she had even, somewhat grudgingly, given it precious metal ornaments of the Old Ones which she had stripped from a whining foreign lord. The demon had praised her effusively for that; all demons hoarded metal, and she supposed that it must need metals to sustain its strength: its domed carapace—gleaming now with the witchfire that always shrouded it at night—was an immense metal jewel the color of blood. And yet she had always heard that demons preferred the flesh of men and women. But when she had tried to stuff the wing of the foreign lord into its maw it had spit him out with a few dripping scratches, and told her to let him go. Astonished, she had obeyed, and let the fool run off screaming to be lost in the swamp.

And then, tonight—"You are going to kill your sister, T'uupieh," it had said to her tonight, "and two innocent children. How do you feel about that?" She had spoken what had come first, and truthfully, into her mind: "That the new day cannot come soon enough for me! I have waited so long—too long—to take my revenge on Klovhiri! My sister and her brats are a part of his foulness, better slain before they multiply." She had drawn her dagger and driven it into the mushy melt, as she would drive it into their rotten hearts.

The demon had been silent again, for a long time; as it always was. (The lore said that demons were immortal, and so she had always supposed that it had no reason to make a quick response; she had wished, sometimes, it would show more consideration for her own mortality.) Then at last it had said, in its deep voice filled with alien shadows, "But the children have harmed no one. And Ahtseet is your only sister, she and the children are your only blood kin. She has shared your life. You say that once you—," the demon paused, searching its limited store of words, "—cherished her, for that. Doesn't what she once meant to you mean anything now? Isn't there any love left, to slow your hand as you raise it against her?"

"Love!" she had said, incredulous. "What speech is that, oh Soulless One? You mock me—," sudden anger had bared her teeth. "Love is a toy, my demon, and I have put my toys behind me. And so has Ahtseet . . . she is no kin of mine. Betrayer, betrayer!" The word hissed like the dying embers of the campfire; she had left the demon in disgust, to rake in the firepit's insulating layer of sulphury ash, and lay on a few more soggy branches. Y'lirr, her second-in-command, had smiled at her from where he lay in his cloak on the ground, telling her that she should sleep. But she had ignored him, and gone back to her vigil on the hill.

Even though this night was chill enough to recrystallize the slowly thawing limbs of the *safilil* trees, the equinox was long past, and now the fine mist of golden polymer rain presaged the golden days of the approaching summer. T'uupieh had wrapped herself more closely in her own cloak and pulled up the hood, to keep the clinging, sticky mist from fouling her wings and ear membranes; and she had remembered last summer, her first summer, which she would always remember . . . Ahtseet had been

Joan D. Vinge

a clumsy, flapping infant as that first summer began, and T'uupieh the child had thought her new sister was silly and useless. But summer slowly transformed the land, and filled her wondering eyes with miracles; and her sister was transformed too, into a playful, easily-led companion who could follow her into adventure. Together they learned to use their wings, and to use the warm updrafts to explore the boundaries and the freedoms of their heritage.

And now, as spring moved into summer once again, T'uupieh clung fiercely to the vision, not wanting to lose it, or to remember that childhood's sweet, unreasoning summer would never come again, even though the seasons returned; for the Wheel of Change swept on, and there was never a turning back. No turning back . . . she had become an adult by the summer's end, and she would never soar with a child's light-winged freedom again. And Ahtseet would never do anything again. Little Ahtseet, always just behind her, like her own fair shadow. . . . *No! She would not regret it! She would be glad—*

"Did you ever think, T'uupieh," the demon had said suddenly, "that it is wrong to kill anyone? You don't want to die—no one wants to die too soon. Why should they have to? Have you ever wondered what it would be like if you could change the world into one where you—where you treated everyone else as you wanted them to treat you, and they treated you the same? If everyone could—live and let live . . ." Its voice slipped into blurred overtones that she couldn't hear.

She had waited, but it said no more, as if it were waiting for her to consider what she'd already heard. But there was no need to think about what was obvious: "Only the dead 'live and let live'. I treat everyone as I expect them to treat me; or I would quickly join the peaceful dead! Death is a part of life. We die when fate wills it, and when fate wills it, we kill.

"You are immortal, you have the power to twist the Wheel, to turn destiny as you want. You may toy with idle fantasies, even make them real, and never suffer the consequences. We have no place for such things in our small lives. No matter how much I might try to be like you, in the end I die like all the rest. We can change nothing, our lives are preordained. That is the way, among mortals." And she had fallen silent again, filled with unease at this strange wandering of the demon's mind. But she must not let it prey on her nerves. Day would come very soon, she must not be nervous; she must be totally in control when she led this attack on Klovhiri. No emotion must interfere . . . no matter how much she yearned to feel Klovhiri's blood spill bluely over her hands, and her sister's, and the children's . . . Ahtseet's brats would never feel the warm wind lift them into the sky; or plunge, as she had, into the depths of her rainbow-petaled pools; or see her towers spearing light far off among the trees. *Never! Never!*

She had caught her breath sharply then, as a fiery pinwheel burst through the wall of tangled brush behind her, tumbling past her head into the clearing of the camp. She had watched it circle the fire—spitting sparks, hissing furiously in the quiet air—three and a half times before it spun on into the darkness. No sleeper wakened, and only two stirred. She clutched one of the demon's hard, angular legs, shaken; knowing that the circling of the fire had been a portent . . . but not knowing what it meant. The burning silence it left behind oppressed her; she stirred restlessly, stretching her wings.

And utterly unmoved, the demon had begun to drone its strange, dark thoughts once more, "Not all you have heard about demons is true. We can suffer . . ." it groped for words again, "the—the consequences of our acts; among ourselves we fight and die. We *are* vicious, and brutal, and pitiless: But we don't like to be that way. We want to change into something better, more merciful, more forgiving. We fail more than we win . . . but we believe we *can* change. And you are more like us than you realize. You can draw a line between—trust and betrayal, right and wrong, good and evil; you can choose never to cross that line—"

"How, then?" She had twisted to face the amber eye as large as her own head, daring to interrupt the demon's speech. "How can one droplet change the tide of the sea? It's impossible! The world melts and flows, it rises into mist, it returns again to ice, only to melt and flow once more. A wheel has no beginning, and no end; no starting place. There is no 'good,' no 'evil' . . . no line between them. Only acceptance. If you were a mortal, I would think you were mad!"

She had turned away again, her claws digging shallow runnels in the polymer-coated stone as she struggled for self-control. *Madness.* . . . Was it possible? she wondered suddenly. Could her demon have gone mad? How else could she explain the thoughts it had put into her mind? Insane thoughts, bizarre, suicidal . . . but thoughts that would haunt her.

Or, could there be a method in its madness? She knew that treachery lay at the heart of every demon. It could simply be lying to her, when it spoke of trust and forgiveness—knowing she must be ready for tomorrow, hoping to make her doubt herself, make her fail. Yes, that was much more reasonable. But then, why was it so hard to believe that this demon would try to ruin her most cherished goals? After all, she held it prisoner; and though her spells kept it from tearing her apart, perhaps it still sought to tear apart her mind, to drive her mad instead. Why shouldn't it hate her, and delight in her torment, and hope for her destruction?

How could it be so ungrateful! She had almost laughed aloud at her own resentment, even as it formed the thought. As if a demon ever knew gratitude! But ever since the day she had netted it in spells in the swamp, she had given it nothing but the best treatment. She had fetched and carried, and made her fearful followers do the same. She had given it the best of everything—anything it desired. At its command she had sent out searchers to look for its scattered eyes, and it had allowed—even encouraged—her to use the eyes as her own, as watchers and protectors. She had even taught it to understand her speech (for it was as ignorant as a baby about the world of mortals), when she realized that it wanted to communicate with her. She had done all those things to win its favor—because she knew that it had come into her hands for a reason; and if she could gain its cooperation, there would be no one who would dare to cross her.

She had spent every spare hour in keeping it company, feeding its curiosity—and her own—as she fed its jeweled maw . . . until gradually, those conversations with the demon had become an end in themselves, a treasure worth the sacrifice of even precious metals. Even the constant waiting for its alien mind to ponder her questions and answers had never tired her; she had come to enjoy sharing even the simple pleasure of its silences, and resting in the warm amber light of its gaze.

T'uupieh looked down at the finely-woven fiber belt which passed through the narrow slits between her side and wing and held her tunic to her. She fingered the heavy, richly-amber beads that decorated it—metal-dyed melt trapped in polished waterstone by the jewelsmith's secret arts—that reminded her always of her demon's thousand eyes. *Her* demon—

She looked away again, toward the fire, toward the cloak-wrapped forms of her outlaws. Since the demon had come to her she had felt both the physical and the emotional space that she had always kept between herself as leader and her band of followers gradually widening. She was still completely their leader, perhaps more firmly so because she had tamed the demon; and their bond of shared danger and mutual respect had never weakened. But there were other needs which her people might fill for each other, but never for her.

She watched them sleeping like the dead, as she should be sleeping now; preparing themselves for tomorrow. They took their sleep sporadically, when they could, as all commoners did—as she did now, too, instead of hibernating the night through like proper nobility. Many of them slept in pairs, man and woman; even though they mated with a commoner's chaotic lack of discrimination, whenever a woman felt the season come upon her. T'uupieh wondered what they must imagine when they saw her sitting here with the demon far into the night. She knew what they believed—what she encouraged all to believe—that she had chosen it for a consort, or that it had chosen her. Y'lirr, she saw, still slept alone. She trusted and liked him as well as she did anyone; he was quick and ruthless, and she knew that he worshipped her. But he was a commoner . . . and more importantly, he did not challenge her. Nowhere, even among the nobility, had she found anyone who offered the sort of companionship she craved . . . until now, until the demon had come to her. No, she would not believe that all its words had been lies—

"T'uupieh," the demon called her name buzzingly in the misty darkness. "Maybe you can't change the pattern of fate . . . but you can change your mind. You've already defied fate, by turning outlaw, and defying Klovhiri. Your sister was the one who accepted . . ." unintelligible words, ". . . only let the Wheel take her. Can you really kill her for that? You must understand why she did it, how she *could* do it. You don't have to kill her for that . . . you don't have to kill any of them. You have the strength, the courage, to put vengeance aside, and find another way to your goals. You can choose to be merciful—you can choose your own path through life, even if the ultimate destination of all life is the same.''

She stood up resentfully, matching the demon's height, and drew her cloak tightly around her. "Even if I wished to change my mind, it is too late. The Wheel is already in motion . . . and I must get my sleep, if I am to be ready for it.'' She started away toward the fire; stopped, looking back. "There is nothing I can do now, my demon. I cannot change tomorrow. Only you can do that. Only you.''

She heard it, later, calling her name softly as she lay sleepless on the cold ground. But she turned her back toward the sound and lay still, and at last sleep came.

Shannon slumped back into the embrace of the padded chair, rubbing his aching head. His eyelids were sandpaper, his body was a weight. He stared at the display screen, at T'uupieh's back turned stubbornly toward him as she slept beside the nitrogen campfire. "Okay, that's it. I give up. She won't even listen. Call Reed and tell him I quit.''

"That you've quit trying to convince T'uupieh,'' Garda said. "Are you sure? She may yet come back. Use a little more emphasis on—spiritual matters. We must be certain we have done all we can to . . . change her mind.''

To save her soul, he thought sourly. Garda had gotten her early training at an institute dedicated to translating the Bible; he had discovered in the past few hours that she still had a hidden desire to proselytize. *What soul?* "We're wasting our time. It's been six hours since she walked out on me. She's not coming back. . . . And I mean quit everything. I don't want to be around for the main event, I've had it.''

"You don't mean that,'' Garda said. "You're tired, you need the rest too. When T'uupieh wakes, you can talk to her again.''

He shook his head, pushing back his hair. "Forget it. Just call Reed.'' He looked out the window, at dawn separating the mist-wrapped silhouette of seaside condominiums from the sky.

Garda shrugged, disappointed, and turned to the phone.

He studied the synthesizer's touchboards again, still bright and waiting, still calling his leaden, weary hands to try one more time. At least when he made this final announcement, it wouldn't have to be direct to the eyes and ears of a waiting world: He doubted that any reporter was dedicated enough to still be up in the glass-walled observation room at this hour. Their questions had been endless earlier tonight, probing his feelings and his purpose and his motives and his plans; asking about "Robin Hood's'' morality, or lack of it, and his own; about a hundred and one other things that were nobody's business but his own.

The music world had tried to do the same thing to him once, but then there had been buffers—agents, publicity staffs—to protect him. Now, when he'd had so much at stake, there had been no protection, only Reed at the microphone eloquently turning the room into a sideshow, with Shann the Man as chief freak; until Shannon had begun to feel like a man staked out on an anthill and smeared with honey. The reporters gazed down from on high, critiquing T'uupieh's responses and criticizing his own, and filled the time-gaps when he needed quiet to think with infuriating interruptions. Reed's success had been total in wringing every drop of pathos and human interest out of his struggle to prevent T'uupieh's vengeance against the Innocents . . . and by that, had managed to make him fail.

No. He sat up straighter, trying to ease his back. No, he couldn't lay it on Reed. By the time what he'd had to say had really counted, the reporters had given up on him. The failure belonged to him, only him: his skill hadn't been great enough, his message hadn't been convincing enough—he was the one who hadn't been able to see through T'uupieh's eyes clearly enough to make her see through his own. He had had his chance to really communicate, for once in his life—to communicate something important. And he'd sunk it.

A hand reached past him to set a cup of steaming coffee on the shelf below the terminal. "One thing about this computer—," a voice said quietly, "—it's programmed for a good cup of coffee."

Startled, he laughed without expecting to; he glanced up. His mother's face looked drawn and tired, she held another cup of coffee in her hand. "Thanks." He picked up the cup and took a sip, felt the hot liquid slide down his throat into his empty stomach. Not looking up again, he said, "Well, you got what you wanted. And so did Reed. He got his pathos, and he gets his murders too."

She shook her head. "This isn't what I wanted. I don't want to see you give up everything you've done here, just because you don't like what Reed is doing with part of it. It isn't worth that. Your work means too much to this project . . . and it means too much to you."

He looked up.

"*Ja*, she is right, Shannon. You can't quit now—we need you too much. And T'uupieh needs you."

He laughed again, not meaning it. "Like a cement yo-yo. What are you trying to do, Garda, use my own moralizing against me?"

"She's telling you what any blind man could see tonight; if he hadn't seen it months ago . . ." His mother's voice was strangely distant. "That this project would never have had this degree of success without you. That you were right about the synthesizer. And that losing you now might—"

She broke off, turning away to watch as Reed came through the doors at the end of the long room. He was alone, this time, for once, and looking rumpled. Shannon guessed that he had been sleeping when the phone call came, and was irrationally pleased at waking him up.

Reed was not so pleased. Shannon watched the frown that might be worry, or displeasure, or both, forming on his face as he came down the echoing hall toward them. "What did she mean, you want to quit? Just because you can't change an alien mind?" He entered the cubicle, and glanced down at the terminal—to be sure that the remote microphones were all switched off, Shannon guessed. "You knew it was a long shot, probably hopeless . . . you have to accept that she doesn't want to reform, accept that the values of an alien culture are going to be different from your own—"

Shannon leaned back, feeling a muscle begin to twitch with fatigue along the inside of his elbow. "I can accept that. What I can't accept is that you want to make us into a bunch of damn panderers. Christ, you don't even have a good reason! I didn't come here to play sound track for a snuff flick. If you go ahead and feed the world those murders, I'm laying it down. I don't want to give all this up, but I'm not staying for a kill-porn carnival."

Reed's frown deepened, he glanced away. "Well? What about the rest of you? Are you still privately branding me an accessory to murder, too? Carly?"

"No, Marcus—not really." She shook her head. "But we all feel that we shouldn't cheapen and weaken our research by making a public spectacle of it. After all, the people of Titan have as much right to privacy and respect as any culture on Earth."

"*Ja,* Marcus—I think we all agree about that."

"And just how much privacy does anybody on Earth have today? Good God—remember the Tasaday? And that was thirty years ago. There isn't a single mountain top or desert island left that the all-seeing eye of the camera hasn't broadcast all over the world. And what do you call the public crime surveillance laws—our own lives are one big peep show."

Shannon shook his head. "That doesn't mean we have to—"

Reed turned cold eyes on him. "And I've had a little too much of your smartass piety, Wyler. Just what do you owe your success as a musician to, if not publicity?" He gestured at the posters on the walls. "There's more hard sell in your kind of music than any other field I can name."

"I have to put up with some publicity push, or I couldn't reach the people, I couldn't do the thing that's really important to me—communicate. That doesn't mean I like it."

"You think I enjoy this?"

"Don't you?"

Reed hesitated. "I happen to be good at it, which is all that really matters. Because you may not believe it, but I'm still a scientist, and what I care about most of all is seeing that research gets its fair slice of the pie. You say I don't have a good reason for pushing our findings: Do you realize that NASA lost all the data from our Neptune probe just because somebody in effect got tired of waiting for it to get to Neptune, and cut off our funds? The real problem on these long outer-planet missions isn't instrumental reliability, it's financial reliability. The public will pay out millions for one of your concerts, but not one cent for something they don't understand—"

"I don't make—"

Joan D. Vinge

"People want to forget their troubles, be entertained . . . and who can blame them? So in order to compete with movies, and sports, and people like you—not to mention ten thousand other worthy government and private causes—we have to give the public what it wants. It's my responsibility to deliver that, so that the 'real scientists' can sit in their neat, bright institutes with half a billion dollars worth of equipment around them, and talk about 'respect for research'."

He paused; Shannon kept his gaze stubbornly. "Think it over. And when you can tell me how what you did as a musician is morally superior to, or more valuable than what you're doing now, you can come to my office and tell me who the real hypocrite is. But think it over, first—all of you." Reed turned and left the cubicle.

They watched in silence, until the double doors at the end of the room hung still. "Vell . . ." Garda glanced at her walking stick, and down at her cloak. "He does have a point."

Shannon leaned forward, tracing the complex beauty of the synthesizer terminal, feeling the combination of chagrin and caffeine pushing down his fatigue. "I know he does. But that isn't the point I was trying to get at! I didn't want to change T'uupieh's mind, or quit either, just because I objected to selling this project. It's the *way* it's being sold, like some kind of kill-porn show perversion, that I can't take—"

When he was a child, he remembered, rock concerts had had a kind of notoriety; but they were as respectable as a symphony orchestra now, compared to the "thrill-shows" that had eclipsed them as he was growing up: where "experts" gambled their lives against a million dollar pot, in front of a crowd who came to see them lose; where masochists made a living by self-mutilation; where they ran *cinema verité* films of butchery and death.

"I mean, is that what everybody really wants? Does it really make everybody feel good to watch somebody else bleed? Or are they going to get some kind of moral superiority thing out of watching it happen on Titan instead of here?" He looked up at the display, at T'uupieh, who still lay sleeping, unmoving and unmoved. "If I could have changed T'uupieh's mind, or changed what happens here, then maybe I could have felt good about something. At least about myself. But who am I kidding . . ." T'uupieh had been right all along; and now he had to admit it to himself: that there had never been any way he could change either one. "T'uupieh's just like the rest of them, she'd rather cut off your hand than shake it . . . and doing it vicariously means we're no better. And none of us ever will be." The words to a song older than he was slipped into his mind, with sudden irony: " 'One man's hands can't build'," he began to switch off the terminal, "anything."

"You need to sleep . . . ve all need to sleep." Garda rose stiffly from her chair.

" '. . . but if one and one and fifty make a million'," his mother matched his quote softly.

Shannon turned back to look at her, saw her shake her head; she felt him looking at her, glanced up. "After all, if T'uupieh could have accepted that everything she did was morally evil, what would have become of her? She knew: It would have destroyed her—we would have destroyed her. She would have been swept away and drowned in the tide of violence." His mother looked away at Garda, back at him. "T'uupieh is a realist, whatever else she is."

He felt his mouth tighten against the resentment that sublimated a deeper, more painful emotion; he heard Garda's grunt of indignation.

"But that doesn't mean that you were wrong—or that you failed."

"That's big of you." He stood up, nodding at Garda, and toward the exit, "Come on."

"Shannon."

He stopped, still facing away.

"I don't think you failed. I think you did reach T'uupieh. The last thing she said was 'only you can change tomorrow' . . . I think she was challenging the demon to go ahead; to do what she didn't have the power to do herself. I think she was asking you to help her."

He turned, slowly. "You really believe that?"

"Yes, I do." She bent her head, freed her hair from the collar of her sweater.

He moved back to his seat, his hands brushed the dark, unresponsive touchplates on the panel. "But it wouldn't do any good to talk to her again. Somehow the demon has to stop the attack itself. If I could use the 'voice' to warn them. . . . Damn the time lag!" By the time his voice reached them, the attack would have been over for hours. How could he change anything tomorrow, if he was always two hours behind?

"I know how to get around the time-lag problem."

"How?" Garda sat down again, mixed emotions showing on her broad, seamed face. "He can't send a varning ahead of time; no one knows when Klovhiri will pass. It would come too soon, or too late."

Shannon straightened up. "Better to ask, 'why?' Why are you changing your mind?"

"I never changed my mind," his mother said mildly. "I never liked this either. When I was a girl, we used to believe that our actions *could* change the world; maybe I've never stopped wanting to believe that."

"But Marcus is not going to like us meddling behind his back, anyway." Garda waved her staff. "And what about the point that perhaps we do need this publicity?"

Shannon glanced back irritably. "I thought you were on the side of the angels, not the devil's advocate."

"I am!" Garda's mouth puckered. "But—"

"Then what's such bad news about the probe making a last-minute rescue? It'll be a sensation."

He saw his mother smile, for the first time in months. "Sensational . . . if T'uupieh doesn't leave us stranded in the swamp for our betrayal."

He sobered. "Not if you really think she wants our help. And I know she wants it . . . I *feel* it. But how do we beat the time lag?"

"I'm the engineer, remember? I'll need a recorded message from you, and some time to play with that." His mother pointed at the computer terminal.

He switched on the terminal and moved aside. She sat down, and started a program documentation on the display; he read, REMOTE OPERATIONS MANUAL. "Let's see . . . I'll need feedback on the approach of Klovhiri's party."

He cleared his throat. "Did you really mean what you said, before Reed came in?"

She glanced up; he watched one response form on her face, and then fade into another smile, "Garda—have you met My Son, the Linguist?"

"And when did you ever pick up on that Pete Seeger song?"

"And My Son, the Musician . . ." the smile came back to him. "I've listened to a few records, in my day." The smile turned inward, toward a memory. "I don't suppose I ever told you that I fell in love with your father because he reminded me of Elton John."

T'uupieh stood silently, gazing into the demon's unwavering eye. A new day was turning the clouds from bronze to gold; the brightness seeped down through the glistening, snarled hair of the treetops, glanced from the green, translucent cliff-faces and sweating slopes, to burnish the demon's carapace with light. She gnawed the last shreds of flesh from a bone, forcing herself to eat, scarcely aware that she did. She had already sent out watchers in the direction of the town, to keep watch for Chwiul . . . and Klovhiri's party. Behind her the rest of her band made ready now, testing weapons and reflexes or feeding their bellies.

And still the demon had not spoken to her. There had been many times when it had chosen not to speak for hours on end; but after its mad ravings of last night, the thought obsessed her that it might never speak again. Her concern grew, lighting the fuse of her anger, which this morning was already short enough; until at last she strode recklessly forward and struck it with her open hand. "Speak to me, *mala 'ingga!*"

But as her blow landed a pain like the touch of fire shot up the muscles of her arm. She leaped back with a curse of surprise, shaking her hand. The demon had never lashed out at her before, never hurt her in any way: But she had never dared to strike it before, she had always treated it with calculated respect. *Fool!* She looked down at her hand, half afraid to see it covered with burns that would make her a cripple in the attack today. But the skin was still smooth and unblistered, only bright with the smarting shock.

"T'uupieh! Are you all right?"

She turned to see Y'lirr, who had come up behind her looking half-frightened, half-grim. "Yes," she nodded, controlling a sharper reply at the sight of his concern. "It was nothing." He carried her double-arched bow and quiver; she put out her smarting hand and took them from him casually, slung them at her back. "Come, Y'lirr, we must—"

"T'uupieh." This time it was the demon's eerie voice that called her name. "T'uupieh, if you believe in my power to twist fate as I like, then you must come back and listen to me again."

She turned back, felt Y'lirr hesitate behind her. "I believe truly in all your powers, my demon!" She rubbed her hand.

The amber depths of its eye absorbed her expression, and read her sincerity; or so she hoped. "T'uupieh, I know I did not make you believe what I said. But I want you to—," its words blurred unintelligibly, "—in me. I want you to know my name. T'uupieh, my name is—"

She heard a horrified yowl from Y'lirr behind her. She glanced around—seeing him cover his ears—and back, paralyzed by disbelief.

"—Shang'ang."

The word struck her like the demon's fiery lash, but the blow this time struck only in her mind. She cried out, in desperate protest; but the name had already passed into her knowledge, *too late!*

A long moment passed; she drew a breath, and shook her head. Disbelief still held her motionless as she let her eyes sweep the brightening camp, as she listened to the sounds of the wakening forest, and breathed in the spicy acridness of the spring growth. And then she began to laugh. She had heard a demon speak its name, and she still lived—and was not blind, not deaf, not mad. The demon had chosen her, joined with her, surrendered to her at last!

Dazed with exultation, she almost did not realize that the demon had gone on speaking to her. She broke off the song of triumph that rose in her, listening:

". . . then I command you to take me with you when you go today. I must see what happens, and watch Klovhiri pass."

"Yes! Yes, my—Shang'ang. It will be done as you wish. Your whim is my desire." She turned away down the slope, stopped again as she found Y'lirr still prone where he had thrown himself down when the demon spoke its name. "Y'lirr?" She nudged him with her foot. Relieved, she saw him lift his head; watched her own disbelief echoing in his face as he looked up at her.

"My lady . . . it did not—?"

"No, Y'lirr," she said softly; then more roughly, "Of course it did not! I am truly the Demon's Consort now; nothing shall stand in my way." She pushed him again with her foot, harder. "Get up. What do I have, a pack of sniveling cowards to ruin the morning of my success?"

Y'lirr scrambled to his feet, brushing himself off. "Never that, T'uupieh! We're ready for any command . . . ready to deliver your revenge." His hand tightened on his knife hilt.

"And my demon will join us in seeking it out!" The pride she felt rang in her

Joan D. Vinge

voice. "Get help to fetch a sledge here, and prepare it. And tell them to move it *gently.*"

He nodded, and for a moment as he glanced at the demon she saw both fear and envy in his eyes. "Good news." He moved off then with his usual brusqueness, without glancing back at her.

She heard a small clamor in the camp, and looked past him, thinking that word of the demon had spread already. But then she saw Lord Chwiul, come as he had promised, being led into the clearing by her escorts. She lifted her head slightly, in surprise—he had indeed come alone, but he was riding a *bliell*. They were rare and expensive mounts, being the only beast she knew of large enough to carry so much weight, and being vicious and difficult to train, as well. She watched this one snapping at the air, its fangs protruding past slack, dribbling lips, and grimaced faintly. She saw that the escort kept well clear of its stumplike webbed feet, and kept their spears ready to prod. It was an amphibian, being too heavy ever to make use of wings, but buoyant and agile when it swam. T'uupieh glanced fleetingly at her own webbed fingers and toes, at the wings that could only lift her body now for bare seconds at a time; she wondered, as she had so many times, what strange turns of fate had formed, or transformed, them all.

She saw Y'lirr speak to Chwiul, pointing her out, saw his insolent grin and the trace of apprehension that Chwiul showed looking up at her; she thought that Y'lirr had said, "She knows its name."

Chwiul rode forward to meet her, with his face under control as he endured the demon's scrutiny. T'uupieh put out a hand to casually—gently—stroke its sensuous, jewel-faceted side. Her eyes left Chwiul briefly, drawn by some instinct to the sky directly above him—and for half a moment she saw the clouds break open . . .

She blinked, to see more clearly, and when she looked again it was gone. No one else, not even Chwiul, had seen the gibbous disc of greenish gold, cut across by a line of silver and a band of shadow-black: The Wheel of Change. She kept her face expressionless, but her heart raced. The Wheel appeared only when someone's life was about to be changed profoundly—and usually the change meant death.

Chwiul's mount lunged at her suddenly as he stopped before her. She held her place at the demon's side; but some of the *bliell*'s bluish spittle landed on her cloak as Chwiul jerked at its heavy head. "Chwiul!" She let her emotion out as anger. "Keep that slobbering filth under control, or I will have it struck dead!" Her hand fisted on the demon's slick hide.

Chwiul's near-smile faded abruptly, and he pulled his mount back, staring uncomfortably at the demon's glaring eye.

T'uupieh took a deep breath, and produced a smile of her own. "So you did not quite dare to come to my camp alone, my lord."

He bowed slightly, from the saddle. "I was merely hesitant to wander in the swamp on foot, alone, until your people found me."

"I see." She kept the smile. "Well then—I assume that things went as you planned this morning. Are Klovhiri and his party all on their way into our trap?"

"They are. And their guide is waiting for my sign, to lead them off safe ground into whatever mire you choose."

"Good. I have a spot in mind that is well ringed by heights." She admired Chwiul's self-control in the demon's presence; although she sensed that he was not as easy as he wanted her to believe. She saw some of her people coming toward them, with a sledge to carry the demon on their trek. "My demon will accompany us, by its own desire. A sure sign of our success today, don't you agree?"

Chwiul frowned, as if he wanted to question that, but didn't quite dare. "If it serves you loyally, then yes, my lady. A great honor and a good omen."

"It serves me with true devotion." She smiled again, insinuatingly. She stood back as the sledge came up onto the hummock, watched as the demon was settled onto it, to be sure her people used the proper care. The fresh reverence with which her outlaws treated it—and their leader—was not lost on either Chwiul or herself.

She called her people together, then, and they set out for their destination, picking their way over the steaming surface of the marsh and through the slimy slate-blue tentacles of the fragile, thawing underbrush. She was glad that they covered this ground often, because the pungent spring growth and the ground's mushy unpredictability changed the pattern of their passage from day to day. She wished that she could have separated Chwiul from his ugly mount, but she doubted that he would cooperate, and she was afraid that he might not be able to keep up on foot. The demon was lashed securely onto its sledge, and its sweating bearers pulled it with no hint of complaint.

At last they reached the heights overlooking the main road—though it could hardly be called one now—that led past her family's manor. She had the demon positioned where it could look back along the overgrown trail in the direction of Klovhiri's approach, and sent some of her followers to secrete its eyes further down the track. She stood then gazing down at the spot below where the path seemed to fork, but did not: The false fork followed the rippling yellow bands of the cliff-face below her—directly into a sink caused by ammonia-water melt seeping down and through the porous sulphide compounds of the rock. There they would all wallow, while she and her band picked them off like swatting *ngips* . . . she thoughtfully swatted a *ngip* that had settled on her hand. Unless her demon—unless her demon chose to create some other outcome . . .

"Any sign?" Chwiul rode up beside her.

She moved back slightly from the cliff's crumbly edge, watching him with more than casual interest. "Not yet. But soon." She had outlaws posted on the lower slope across the track as well; but not even her demon's eyes could pierce too deeply into the foliage along the road. It had not spoken since Chwiul's arrival, and she did not expect it to reveal its secrets now. "What livery does your escort wear, and how many

Joan D. Vinge

of them do you want killed for effect?'' She unslung her bow, and began to test its pull.

Chwiul shrugged. "The dead carry no tales; kill them all. I shall have Klovhiri's men soon. Kill the guide too—a man who can be bought once, can be bought twice.''

"Ah—'' She nodded, grinning. "A man with your foresight and discretion will go far in the world, my lord.'' She nocked an arrow in the bowstring before she turned away to search the road again. Still empty. She looked away restlessly, at the spiny silver-blue-green of the distant, fog-clad mountains; at the hollow fingers of upthrust ice, once taller than she was, stubby and diminishing now along the edge of the nearer lake. The lake where last summer she had soared . . .

A flicker of movement, a small unnatural noise, pulled her eyes back to the road. Tension tightened the fluid ease of her movement as she made the trilling call that would send her band to their places along the cliff's edge. *At last—* She leaned forward eagerly for the first glimpse of Klovhiri; spotting the guide, and then the sledge that bore her sister and the children. She counted the numbers of the escort, saw them all emerge into her unbroken view on the track. But Klovhiri . . . where was Klovhiri? She turned back to Chwiul, her whisper struck out at him, "Where is he! Where is Klovhiri?''

Chwiul's expression lay somewhere between guilt and guile. "Delayed. He stayed behind, he said there were still matters at court—''

"Why didn't you tell me that?''

He jerked sharply on the *bliell*'s rein. "It changes nothing! We can still eradicate his family. That will leave me first in line to the inheritance . . . and Klovhiri can always be brought down later.''

"But it's Klovhiri I want, for myself.'' T'uupieh raised her bow, the arrow tracked toward his heart.

"They'll know who to blame if I die!'' He spread a wing defensively. "The Overlord will turn against you for good; Klovhiri will see to that. Avenge yourself on your sister, T'uupieh—and I will still reward you well if you keep the bargain!''

"This is not the bargain we agreed to!'' The sounds of the approaching party reached her clearly now from down below; she heard a child's high notes of laughter. Her outlaws crouched, waiting for her signal; and she saw Chwiul prepare for his own signal call to his guide. She looked back at the demon, its amber eye fixed on the travelers below. She started toward it. It could still twist fate for her. . . . *Or had it already?*

"*Go back, go back!*'' The demon's voice burst over her, down across the silent forest, like an avalanche. "Ambush . . . trap . . . you have been betrayed!''

"—betrayal!''

She barely heard Chwiul's voice below the roaring; she looked back, in time to see the *bliell* leap forward, to intersect her own course toward the demon. Chwiul drew his sword, she saw the look of white fury on his face, not knowing whether it was for her, or the demon itself. She ran toward the demon's sledge, trying to draw her bow; but the *bliell* covered the space between them in two great bounds. Its head swung toward her, jaws gaping. Her foot skidded on the slippery melt, and she went down; the dripping jaws snapped futilely shut above her face. But one flailing leg struck her heavily and knocked her sliding through the melt to the demon's foot—

The demon. She gasped for the air that would not fill her lungs, trying to call its name; saw with incredible clarity the beauty of its form, and the ululating horror of the *bliell* bearing down on them to destroy them both. She saw it rear above her, above the demon—saw Chwiul, either leaping or thrown, sail out into the air—and at last her voice came back to her and she screamed the name, a warning and a plea, "Shang'ang!"

And as the *bliell* came down, lightning lashed out from the demon's carapace and wrapped the *bliell* in fire. The beast's ululations rose off the scale; T'uupieh covered her ears against the piercing pain of its cry. But not her eyes: the demon's lash ceased with the suddenness of lightning, and the *bliell* toppled back and away, rebounding lightly as it crashed to the ground, stone dead. T'uupieh sank back against the demon's foot, supported gratefully as she filled her aching lungs, and looked away—

To see Chwiul, trapped in the updrafts at the cliff's edge, gliding, gliding . . . and she saw the three arrows that protruded from his back, before the currents let his body go, and it disappeared below the rim. She smiled, and closed her eyes.

"T'uupieh! T'uupieh!"

She blinked them open again, resignedly, as she felt her people cluster around her. Y'lirr's hand drew back from the motion of touching her face as she opened her eyes. She smiled again, at him, at them all; but not with the smile she had had for Chwiul. "Y'lirr—" she gave him her own hand, and let him help her up. Aches and bruises prodded her with every small movement, but she was certain, reassured, that the only real damage was an oozing tear in her wing. She kept her arm close to her side.

"T'uupieh—"

"My lady—"

"What happened? The demon—"

"The demon saved my life." She waved them silent. "And . . . for its own reasons, it foiled Chwiul's plot." The realization, and the implications, were only now becoming real in her mind. She turned, and for a long moment gazed into the demon's unreadable eye. Then she moved away, going stiffly to the edge of the cliff to look down.

"But the contract—," Y'lirr said.

"Chwiul broke the contract! He did not give me Klovhiri." No one made a protest. She peered through the brush, guessing without much difficulty the places where Ahtseet and her party had gone to earth below. She could hear a child's whimpered crying, now. Chwiul's body lay sprawled on the flat, in plain view of them all, and she thought she saw more arrows bristling from his corpse. Had Ahtseet's guard riddled him too, taking him for an attacker? The thought pleased her. And a small voice inside her dared to whisper that Ahtseet's escape pleased her much more. . . . She frowned suddenly at the thought.

But Ahtseet had escaped, and so had Klovhiri—and so she might as well make use of that fact, to salvage what she could. She paused, collecting her still-shaken thoughts. "Ahtseet!" Her voice was not the voice of the demon, but it echoed satisfactorily. "It's T'uupieh! See the traitor's corpse that lies before you—your own mate's brother, Chwiul! He hired murderers to kill you in the swamp—seize your guide, make him tell you all. It is only by my demon's warning that you still live."

"Why?" Ahtseet's voice wavered faintly on the wind.

T'uupieh laughed bitterly. "Why, to keep the roads clear of ruffians. To make the Overlord love his loyal servant more, and reward her better, dear sister! And to make Klovhiri hate me. May it eat his guts out that he owes your lives to me! Pass freely through my lands, Ahtseet; I give you leave—this once."

She drew back from the ledge and moved wearily away, not caring whether Ahtseet would believe her. Her people stood waiting, gathered silently around the corpse of the *bliell*.

"What now?" Y'lirr asked, looking at the demon, asking for them all.

And she answered, but made her answer directly to the demon's silent amber eye. "It seems I spoke the truth to Chwiul after all, my demon: I told him he would not be needing his townhouse after today. . . . Perhaps the Overlord will call it a fair trade. Perhaps it can be arranged. The Wheel of Change carries us all; but not with equal ease. Is that not so, my beautiful Shang'ang?"

She stroked its day-warmed carapace tenderly, and settled down on the softening ground to wait for its reply. ■

ENDER'S GAME
Orson Scott Card

"Whatever your gravity is when you get to the door, remember—the enemy's gate is *down*. If you step through your own door like you're out for a stroll, you're a big target and you deserve to get hit. With more than a flasher.'' Ender Wiggin paused and looked over the group. Most were just watching him nervously. A few understanding. A few sullen and resisting.

First day with this army, all fresh from the teacher squads, and Ender had forgotten how young new kids could be. He'd been in it for three years, they'd had six months—nobody over nine years old in the whole bunch. But they were his. At eleven, he was half a year early to be a commander. He'd had a toon of his own and knew a few tricks but there were forty in his new army. Green. All marksmen with a flasher, all in top shape, or they wouldn't be here—but they were all just as likely as not to get wiped out first time into battle.

"Remember,'' he went on, "they can't see you till you get through that door. But the second you're out, they'll be on you. So hit that door the way you want to be when they shoot at you. Legs up under you, going straight *down*.'' He pointed at a sullen kid who looked like he was only seven, the smallest of them all. "Which way is down, greenoh!''

"Toward the enemy door.'' The answer was quick. It was also surly, saying, "yeah, yeah, now get on with the important stuff.''

"Name, kid?''

"Bean.''

"Get that for size or for brains?''

Bean didn't answer. The rest laughed a little. Ender had chosen right. This kid *was* younger than the rest, must have been advanced because he was sharp. The others didn't like him much, they were happy to see him taken down a little. Like Ender's first commander had taken him down.

"Well, Bean, you're right onto things. Now I tell you this, nobody's gonna get through that door without a good chance of getting hit. A lot of you are going to be turned into cement somewhere. Make sure it's your legs. Right? If only your legs get hit, then only your legs get frozen, and in nullo that's no sweat.'' Ender turned to one of the dazed ones. "What're legs for? Hmmm?''

Blank stare. Confusion. Stammer.

"Forget it. Guess I'll have to ask Bean here.''

"Legs are for pushing off walls." Still bored.

"Thanks, Bean. Get that, everybody?" They all got it, and didn't like getting it from Bean. "Right. You can't *see* with legs, you can't *shoot* with legs, and most of the time they just get in the way. If they get frozen sticking straight out you've turned yourself into a blimp. No way to hide. So how do legs go?"

A few answered this time, to prove that Bean wasn't the only one who knew anything. "Under you. Tucked up under."

"Right. A shield. You're kneeling on a shield, and the shield is your own legs. And there's a trick to the suits. Even when your legs are flashed you can *still* kick off. I've never seen anybody do it but me—but you're all gonna learn it."

Ender Wiggin turned on his flasher. It glowed faintly green in his hand. Then he let himself rise in the weightless workout room, pulled his legs under him as though he were kneeling, and flashed both of them. Immediately his suit stiffened at the knees and ankles, so that he couldn't bend at all.

"Okay, I'm frozen, see?"

He was floating a meter above them. They all looked up at him, puzzled. He leaned back and caught one of the handholds on the wall behind him, and pulled himself flush against the wall.

"I'm stuck at a wall. If I had legs, I'd use legs, and string myself out like a string *bean*, right?"

They laughed.

"But I don't have legs, and that's *better*, got it? Because of this." Ender jackknifed at the waist, then straightened out violently. He was across the workout room in only a moment. From the other side he called to them. "Got that? I didn't use hands, so I still had use of my flasher. *And* I didn't have my legs floating five feet behind me. Now watch it again."

He repeated the jackknife, and caught a handhold on the wall near them. "Now, I don't just want you to do that when they've flashed your legs. I want you to do that when you've still got legs, because it's better. And because they'll never be expecting it. All right now, everybody up in the air and kneeling."

Most were up in a few seconds. Ender flashed the stragglers, and they dangled, helplessly frozen, while the others laughed. "When I give an order, you move. Got it? When we're at a door and they clear it, I'll be giving you orders in two seconds, as soon as I see the setup. And when I give the order you better be out there, because whoever's out there first is going to win, unless he's a fool. I'm not. And you better not be, or I'll have you back in the teacher squads." He saw more than a few of them gulp, and the frozen ones looked at him with fear. "You guys who are hanging there. You watch. You'll thaw out in about fifteen minutes, and let's see if you can catch up to the others."

For the next half hour Ender had them jackknifing off walls. He called a stop when he saw that they all had the basic idea. They were a good group, maybe. They'd get better.

"Now you're warmed up," he said to them, "we'll start working."

Ender was the last one out after practice, since he stayed to help some of the slower ones improve on technique. They'd had good teachers, but like all armies they were uneven, and some of them could be a real drawback in battle. Their first battle might be weeks away. It might be tomorrow. A schedule was never printed. The commander just woke up and found a note by his bunk, giving him the time of his battle and the name of his opponent. So for the first while he was going to drive his boys until they were in top shape—all of them. Ready for anything, at any time. Strategy was nice, but it was worth nothing if the soldiers couldn't hold up under the strain.

He turned the corner into the residence wing and found himself face to face with Bean, the seven-year-old he had picked on all through practice that day. Problems. Ender didn't want problems right now.

"Ho, Bean."

"Ho, Ender."

Pause.

"Sir," Ender said softly.

"We're not on duty."

"In my army, Bean, we're always on duty." Ender brushed past him.

Bean's high voice piped up behind him. "I know what you're doing, Ender, sir, and I'm warning you."

Ender turned slowly and looked at him. "Warning me?"

"I'm the best man you've got. But I'd better be treated like it."

"Or what?" Ender smiled menacingly.

"Or I'll be the worst man you've got. One or the other."

"And what do you want? Love and kisses?" Ender was getting angry.

Bean was unworried. "I want a toon."

Ender walked back to him and stood looking down into his eyes. "I'll give a toon," he said, "to the boys who prove they're worth something. They've got to be good soldiers, they've got to know how to take orders, they've got to be able to think for themselves in a pinch, and they've got to be able to keep respect. That's how I got to be a commander. That's how you'll get to be a toon leader."

Bean smiled. "That's fair. *If* you actually work that way, I'll be a toon leader in a month."

Ender reached down and grabbed the front of his uniform and shoved him into the wall. "When I say I work a certain way, Bean, then that's the way I work."

Bean just smiled. Ender let go of him and walked away, and didn't look back. He was sure, without looking, that Bean was still watching, still smiling, still just a little

Orson Scott Card

contemptuous. He might make a good toon leader at that. Ender would keep an eye on him.

Captain Graff, six foot two and a little chubby, stroked his belly as he leaned back in his chair. Across his desk sat Lieutenant Anderson, who was earnestly pointing out high points on a chart.

"Here it is, Captain," Anderson said. "Ender's already got them doing a tactic that's going to throw off everyone who meets it. Doubled their speed."

Graff nodded.

"And you know his test scores. He thinks well, too."

Graff smiled. "All true, all true, Anderson, he's a fine student, shows real promise."

They waited.

Graff sighed. "So what do you want me to do?"

"Ender's the one. He's got to be."

"He'll never be ready in time, Lieutenant. He's eleven, for heaven's sake, man, what do you want, a miracle?"

"I want him into battles, every day starting tomorrow. I want him to have a year's worth of battles in a month."

Graff shook his head. "That would have his army in the hospital."

"No sir. He's getting them into form. And we need Ender."

"All right, I think it's Ender. Which of the commanders if it isn't him?"

"I don't know, Lieutenant." Graff ran his hands over his slightly fuzzy bald head. "These are children, Anderson. Do you realize that? Ender's army is nine years old. Are we going to put them against the older kids? Are we going to put them through hell for a month like that?"

Lieutenant Anderson leaned even further over Graff's desk.

"Ender's test scores, Captain!"

"I've seen his bloody test scores! I've watched him in battle, I've listened to tapes of his training sessions, I've watched his sleep patterns, I've heard tapes of his conversations in the corridors and in the bathrooms, I'm more aware of Ender Wiggins than you could possibly imagine! And against all the arguments, against his obvious qualities, I'm weighing one thing. I have this picture of Ender a year from now, if you have your way. I see him completely useless, worn down, a failure, because he was pushed farther than he or any living person could go. But it doesn't weigh enough, does it, Lieutenant, because there's a war on, and our best talent is gone, and the biggest battles are ahead. So give Ender a battle every day this week. And then bring me a report."

Anderson stood and saluted. "Thank you, sir."

He had almost reached the door when Graff called his name. He turned and faced the captain.

"Anderson," Captain Graff said. "Have you been outside, lately I mean?"

"Not since last leave, six months ago."

"I didn't think so. Not that it makes any difference. But have you ever been to Beaman Park, there in the city? Hmm? Beautiful park. Trees. Grass. No nullo, no battles, no worries. Do you know what else there is in Beaman Park?"

"What, sir?" Lieutenant Anderson asked.

"Children," Graff answered.

"Of course children," said Anderson.

"I mean children. I mean kids who get up in the morning when their mothers call them and they go to school and then in the afternoons they go to Beaman Park and play. They're happy, they smile a lot, they laugh, they have fun. Hmmm?"

"I'm sure they do sir."

"Is that all you can say, Anderson?"

Anderson cleared his throat. "It's good for children to have fun, I think, sir. I know I did when I was a boy. But right now the world needs soldiers. And this is the way to get them."

Graff nodded and closed his eyes. "Oh, indeed, you're right, by statistical proof and by all the important theories, and dammit they work and the system is right but all the same Ender's older than I am. He's not a child. He's barely a person."

"If that's true, sir, then at least we all know that Ender is making it possible for the others of his age to be playing in the park."

"And Jesus died to save all men, of course." Graff sat up and looked at Anderson almost sadly. "But we're the ones," Graff said, "We're the ones who are driving in the nails."

Ender Wiggins lay on his bed staring at the ceiling. He never slept more than five hours a night—but the lights went off at 2200 and didn't come on again until 0600. So he stared at the ceiling and thought. He'd had his army for three and a half weeks. Dragon Army. The name was assigned, and it wasn't a lucky one. Oh, the charts said that about nine years ago a Dragon Army had done fairly well. But for the next six years the name had been attached to inferior armies, and finally, because of the superstition that was beginning to play about the name, Dragon Army was retired. Until now. And now, Ender thought smiling, Dragon Army was going to take them by surprise.

The door opened softly. Ender did not turn his head. Someone stepped softly into his room, then left with the quiet sound of the door shutting. When soft steps died away Ender rolled over and saw a white slip of paper lying on the floor. He reached down and picked it up.

"Dragon Army against Rabbit Army, Ender Wiggins and Carn Carby, 0700."

The first battle. Ender got out of bed and quickly dressed. He went rapidly to the rooms of each of his toon leaders and told them to rouse their boys. In five minutes they were all gathered in the corridor, sleepy and slow. Ender spoke softly.

Orson Scott Card

"First battle, 0700 against Rabbit Army. I've fought them twice before but they've got a new commander. Never heard of him. They're an older group, though, and I know a few of their old tricks. Now wake up. Run, doublefast, warmup in workroom three."

For an hour and a half they worked out, with three mockbattles and calisthenics in the corridor out of the nullo. Then for fifteen minutes they all lay up in the air, totally relaxing in the weightlessness. At 0650 Ender roused them and they hurried into the corridor. Ender led them down the corridor, running again, and occasionally leaping to touch a light panel on the ceiling. The boys all touched the same light panel. And at 0658 they reached their gate to the battleroom.

The members of Toons C and D grabbed the first eight handholds in the ceiling of the corridor. Toons A, B, and E crouched on the floor. Ender hooked his feet into two handholds in the middle of the ceiling, so he was out of everyone's way.

"Which way is the enemy's door?" he hissed.

"Down!" they whispered back, and laughed.

"Flashers on." The boxes in their hands glowed green. They waited for a few seconds more, and then the gray wall in front of them disappeared and the battleroom was visible.

Ender sized it up immediately. The familiar open grid of the most early games, like the monkey bars at the park, with seven or eight boxes scattered through the grid. They called the boxes *stars*. There were enough of them, and in forward enough positions, that they were worth going for. Ender decided this in a second, and he hissed, "Spread to near stars. E hold!"

The four groups in the corners plunged through the forcefield at the doorway and fell down into the battleroom. Before the enemy even appeared through the opposite gate Ender's army had spread from the door to the nearest stars.

Then the enemy soldiers came through the door. From their stance Ender knew they had been in a different gravity, and didn't know enough to disorient themselves from it. They came through standing up, their entire bodies spread and defenseless.

"Kill 'em, E!" Ender hissed, and threw himself out the door knees first, with his flasher between his legs and firing. While Ender's group flew across the room the rest of Dragon Army lay down a protecting fire, so that E group reached a forward position with only one boy frozen completely, though they had all lost the use of their legs—which didn't impair them in the least. There was a lull as Ender and his opponent, Carn Carby, assessed their positions. Aside from Rabbit Army's losses at the gate, there had been few casualties, and both armies were near full strength. But Carn had no originality—he was in a four-corner spread that any five-year-old in the teacher squads might have thought of. And Ender knew how to defeat it.

He called out, loudly, "E covers A, C down. B, D angle east wall." Under E toon's cover, B and D toons lunged away from their stars. While they were still exposed, A and C toons left their stars and drifted toward the near wall. They reached it together, and together jackknifed off the wall. At double the normal speed they appeared behind the enemy's stars, and opened fire. In a few seconds the battle was over, with the enemy almost entirely frozen, including the commander, and the rest scattered to the corners. For the next five minutes, in squads of four, Dragon Army cleaned out the dark corners of the battleroom and shepherded the enemy into the center, where their bodies, frozen at impossible angles, jostled each other. Then Ender took three of his boys to the enemy gate and went through the formality of reversing the one-way field by simultaneously touching a Dragon Army helmet at each corner. Then Ender assembled his army in vertical files near the knot of frozen Rabbit Army soldiers.

Only three of Dragon Army's soldiers were immobile. Their victory margin—38 to 0—was ridiculously high, and Ender began to laugh. Dragon Army joined him, laughing long and loud. They were still laughing when Lieutenant Anderson and Lieutenant Morris came in from the teachergate at the south end of the battleroom.

Lieutenant Anderson kept his face stiff and unsmiling, but Ender saw him wink as he held out his hand and offered the stiff, formal congratulations that were ritually given to the victor in the game.

Morris found Carn Carby and unfroze him, and the thirteen-year-old came and presented himself to Ender, who laughed without malice and held out his hand. Carn graciously took Ender's hand and bowed his head over it. It was that or be flashed again.

Lieutenant Anderson dismissed Dragon Army, and they silently left the battleroom through the enemy's door—again part of the ritual. A light was blinking on the north side of the square door, indicating where the gravity was in that corridor. Ender, leading his soldiers, changed his orientation and went through the forcefield and into gravity on his feet. His army followed him at a brisk run back to the workroom. When they got there they formed up into squads, and Ender hung in the air, watching them.

"Good first battle," he said, which was excuse enough for a cheer, which he quieted. "Dragon Army did all right against Rabbits. But the enemy isn't always going to be that bad. And if that had been a good army we would have been smashed. We still would have won, but we would have been smashed. Now let me see B and D toons out here. Your takeoff from the stars was way too slow. If Rabbit Army knew how to aim a flasher, you all would have been frozen solid before A and C even got to the wall."

They worked out for the rest of the day.

That night Ender went for the first time to the commanders' mess hall. No one was allowed there until he had won at least one battle, and Ender was the youngest commander ever to make it. There was no great stir when he came in. But when some of the other boys saw the Dragon on his breast pocket, they stared at him openly, and by the time he got his tray and sat at an empty table, the entire room was silent, with the other commanders watching him. Intensely self-conscious, Ender wondered how they all knew, and why they all looked so hostile.

Then he looked above the door he had just come through. There was a huge scoreboard across the entire wall. It showed the win/loss record for the commander of every army; that day's battles were lit in red. Only four of them. The other three winners had barely made it—the best of them had only two men whole and eleven mobile at the end of the game. Dragon Army's score of thirty-eight mobile was embarrassingly better.

Other new commanders had been admitted to the commanders' mess hall with cheers and congratulations. Other new commanders hadn't won thirty-eight to zero.

Ender looked for Rabbit Army on the scoreboard. He was surprised to find that Carn Carby's score to date was eight wins and three losses. Was he that good? Or had he only fought against inferior armies? Whichever, there was still a zero in Carn's mobile and whole columns, and Ender looked down from the scoreboard grinning. No one smiled back, and Ender knew that they were afraid of him, which meant that they would hate him, which meant that anyone who went into battle against Dragon Army would be scared and angry and incompetent. Ender looked for Carn Carby in the crowd, and found him not too far away. He stared at Carby until one of the other boys nudged the Rabbit commander and pointed to Ender. Ender smiled again and waved slightly. Carby turned red, and Ender, satisfied, leaned over his dinner and began to eat.

At the end of the week Dragon Army had fought seven battles in seven days. The score stood 7 wins and 0 losses. Ender had never had more than five boys frozen in any game. It was no longer possible for the other commanders to ignore Ender. A few of them sat with him and quietly conversed about game strategies that Ender's opponents had used. Other much larger groups were talking with the commanders that Ender had defeated, trying to find out what Ender had done to beat them.

In the middle of the meal the teacher door opened and the groups fell silent as Lieutenant Anderson stepped in and looked over the group. When he located Ender he strode quickly across the room and whispered in Ender's ear. Ender nodded, finished his glass of water, and left with the lieutenant. On the way out, Anderson handed a slip of paper to one of the older boys. The room became very noisy with conversation as Anderson and Ender left.

Ender was escorted down corridors he had never seen before. They didn't have the blue glow of the soldier corridors. Most were wood paneled, and the floors were carpeted. The doors were wood, with nameplates on them, and they stopped at one that said, "Captain Graff, supervisor." Anderson knocked softly, and a low voice said, "Come in."

They went in. Captain Graff was seated behind a desk, his hands folded across his pot belly. He nodded, and Anderson sat. Ender also sat down. Graff cleared his throat and spoke.

"Seven days since your first battle, Ender."

Ender did not reply.

"Won seven battles, one every day."

Ender nodded.

"Scores unusually high, too."

Ender blinked.

"Why?" Graff asked him.

Ender glanced at Anderson, and then spoke to the captain behind the desk. "Two new tactics, sir. Legs doubled up as a shield, so that a flash doesn't immobilize. Jackknife take-offs from the walls. Superior strategy, as Lieutenant Anderson taught, think places, not spaces. Five toons of eight instead of four of ten. Incompetent opponents. Excellent toon leaders, good soldiers."

Graff looked at Ender without expression. Waiting for what, Ender thought. Lieutenant Anderson spoke.

"Ender, what's the condition of your army."

"A little tired, in peak condition, morale high, learning fast. Anxious for the next battle."

Anderson looked at Graff, and Graff shrugged slightly. Then he nodded, and Anderson smiled. Graff turned to Ender.

"Is there anything you want to know?"

Ender held his hands loosely in his lap. "When are you going to put us up against a good army?"

Anderson was surprised, and Graff laughed out loud. The laughter rang in the room, and when it stopped, Graff handed a piece of paper to Ender. "Now," the Captain said, and Ender read the paper.

"Dragon Army against Leopard Army, Ender Wiggins and Pol Slattery, 2000."

Ender looked up at Captain Graff. "That's ten minutes from now, sir."

Graff smiled. "Better hurry, then, boy."

As Ender left he realized Pol Slattery was the boy who had been handed his orders as Ender left the mess hall.

He got to his army five minutes later. Three toon leaders were already undressed and lying naked on their beds. He sent them all flying down the corridors to rouse their toons, and gathered up their suits himself. As all his boys were assembled in the corridor, most of them still getting dressed, Ender spoke to them.

"This one's hot and there's no time. We'll be late to the door, and the enemy'll be deployed right outside our gate. Ambush, and I've never heard of it happening before. So we'll take our time at the door. E toon, keep your belts loose, and give your flashers to the leaders and seconds of the other toons."

Puzzled, E toon complied. By then all were dressed, and Ender led them at a trot

     Orson Scott Card

to the gate. When they reached it the forcefield was already on one-way, and some of his soldiers were panting. They had had one battle that day and a full workout. They were tired.

Ender stopped at the entrance and looked at the placement of the enemy soldiers. Most of them were grouped not more than twenty feet out from the gate. There was no grid, there were no stars. A big empty space. Where were the other enemy soldiers? There should have been ten more.

"They're flat against this wall," Ender said, "where we can't see them."

He thought for a moment, then took two of the toons and made them kneel, their hands on their hips. Then he flashed them, so that their bodies were frozen rigid.

"You're shields," Ender said, and then had boys from two other toons kneel on their legs, and hook both arms under the frozen boys' shoulders. Each boy was holding two flashers. Then Ender and the members of the last toon picked up the duos, three at a time, and threw them out the door.

Of course, the enemy opened fire immediately. But they only hit the boys who were already flashed, and in a few moments pandemonium broke out in the battleroom. All the soldiers of Leopard Army were easy targets as they lay pressed flat against the wall, and Ender's soldiers, armed with two flashers each, carved them up easily. Pol Slattery reacted quickly, ordering his men away from the wall, but not quickly enough—only a few were able to move, and they were flashed before they could get a quarter of the way across the battleroom.

When the battle was over Dragon Army had only twelve boys whole, the lowest score they had ever had. But Ender was satisfied. And during the ritual of surrender Pol Slattery broke form by shaking hands and asking, "Why did you wait so long getting out of the gate?"

Ender glanced at Anderson, who was floating nearby. "I was informed late," he said. "It was an ambush."

Slattery grinned, and gripped Ender's hand again. "Good game."

Ender didn't smile at Anderson this time. He knew that now the games would be arranged against him, to even up the odds. He didn't like it.

It was 2150, nearly time for lights out, when Ender knocked at the door of the room shared by Bean and three other soldiers. One of the others opened the door, then stepped back and held it wide. Ender stood for a moment, then asked if he could come in. They answered, of course, of course, come in, and he walked to the upper bunk, where Bean had set down his book and was leaning on one elbow to look at Ender.

"Bean, can you give me twenty minutes?"

"Near lights out," Bean answered.

"My room," Ender answered. "I'll cover for you." Bean sat up and slid off his bed. Together he and Ender padded silently down the corridor to Ender's room. Bean entered first, and Ender closed the door behind them.

"Sit down," Ender said, and they both sat on the edge of the bed, looking at each other.

"Remember four weeks ago, Bean? When you told me to make you a toon leader?"

"Yeah."

"I've made five toon leaders since then, haven't I? And none of them was you." Bean looked at him calmly.

"Was I right?" Ender asked.

"Yes, sir," Bean answered.

Ender nodded. "How have you done in these battles?"

Bean cocked his head to one side. "I've never been immobilized, sir, and I've immobilized forty-three of the enemy. I've obeyed orders quickly, and I've commanded a squad in mop-up and never lost a soldier."

"Then you'll understand this." Ender paused, then decided to back up and say something else first.

"You know you're early, Bean, by a good half year. I was, too, and I've been made a commander six months early. Now they've put me into battles after only three weeks of training with my army. They've given me eight battles in seven days. I've already had more battles than boys who were made commander four months ago. I've won more battles than many who've been commanders for a year. And then tonight. You know what happened tonight."

Bean nodded. "They told you late."

"I don't know what the teachers are doing. But my army is getting tired, and I'm getting tired, and now they're changing the rules of the game. You see, Bean, I've looked in the old charts. No one has ever destroyed so many enemies and kept so many of his own soldiers whole in the history of the game. I'm unique—and I'm getting unique treatment."

Bean smiled. "You're the best, Ender."

Ender shook his head. "Maybe. But it was no accident that I got the soldiers I got. My worst soldier could be a toon leader in another army. I've got the best. They've loaded things my way—but now they're loading it against me. I don't know why. But I know I have to be ready for it. I need your help."

"Why mine?"

"Because even though there are some better soldiers than you in Dragon Army—not many, but some—there's nobody who can think better and faster than you." Bean said nothing. They both knew it was true.

Ender continued, "I need to be ready, but I can't retrain the whole army. So I'm going to cut every toon down by one, including you—and you and four others will be a special squad under me. And you'll learn to do some new things. Most of the time you'll be in the regular toons just like you are now. But when I need you. See?"

Orson Scott Card

Bean smiled and nodded. "That's right, that's good, can I pick them myself?"

"One from each toon except your own, and you can't take any toon leaders."

"What do you want us to do?"

"Bean, I don't know. I don't know what they'll throw at us. What would you do if suddenly our flashers didn't work, and the enemy's did? What would you do if we had to face two armies at once? The only thing I know is—we're not going for score anymore. We're going for the enemy's gate. That's when the battle is technically won—four helmets at the corners of the gate. I'm going for quick kills, battles ended even when we're outnumbered. Got it? You take them for two hours during regular workout. Then you and I and your soldiers, we'll work at night after dinner."

"We'll get tired."

"I have a feeling we don't know what tired is."

Ender reached out and took Bean's hand, and gripped it. "Even when it's rigged against us, Bean. We'll win."

Bean left in silence and padded down the corridor.

Dragon Army wasn't the only army working out after hours now. The other commanders finally realized they had some catching up to do. From early morning to lights out soldiers all over Training and Command Center, none of them over fourteen years old, were learning to jackknife off walls and use each other as living shields.

But while other commanders mastered the techniques that Ender had used to defeat them, Ender and Bean worked on solutions to problems that had never come up.

There were still battles every day, but for a while they were normal, with grids and stars and sudden plunges through the gate. And after the battles, Ender and Bean and four other soldiers would leave the main group and practice strange maneuvers. Attacks without flashers, using feet to physically disarm or disorient an enemy. Using four frozen soldiers to reverse the enemy's gate in less than two seconds. And one day Bean came to workout with a 300-meter cord.

"What's that for?"

"I don't know yet." Absently Bean spun one end of the cord. It wasn't more than an eighth of an inch thick, but it could have lifted ten adults without breaking.

"Where did you get it?"

"Commissary. They asked what for. I said to practice tying knots."

Bean tied a loop in the end of the rope and slid it over his shoulders.

"Here, you two, hang onto the wall here. Now don't let go of the rope. Give me about fifty yards of slack." They complied, and Bean moved about ten feet from them along the wall. As soon as he was sure they were ready, he jackknifed off the wall and flew straight out, fifty meters. Then the rope snapped taut. It was so fine that it was virtually invisible, but it was strong enough to force Bean to veer off at almost a right angle. It happened so suddenly that he had inscribed a perfect arc and hit the wall before most of the other soldiers knew what had happened. Bean did a perfect rebound and drifted quickly back where Ender and the others waited for him.

Many of the soldiers in the five regular squads hadn't noticed the rope, and were demanding to know how it was done. It was impossible to change direction that abruptly in nullo. Bean just laughed.

"Wait till the next game without a grid! They'll never know what hit them."

They never did. The next game was only two hours later, but Bean and two others had become pretty good at aiming and shooting while they flew at ridiculous speeds at the end of the rope. The slip of paper was delivered, and Dragon Army trotted off to the gate, to battle with Griffin Army. Bean coiled the rope all the way.

When the gate opened, all they could see was a large brown star only fifteen feet away, completely blocking their view of the enemy's gate.

Ender didn't pause. "Bean, give yourself fifty feet of rope and go around the star." Bean and his four soldiers dropped through the gate and in a moment Bean was launched sideways away from the star. The rope snapped taut, and Bean flew forward. As the rope was stopped by each edge of the star in turn, his arc became tighter and his speed greater, until when he hit the wall only a few feet away from the gate he was barely able to control his rebound to end up behind the star. But he immediately moved all his arms and legs so that those waiting inside the gate would know that the enemy hadn't flashed him anywhere.

Ender dropped through the gate, and Bean quickly told him how Griffin Army was situated. "They've got two squares of stars, all the way around the gate. All their soldiers are under cover, and there's no way to hit any of them until we're clear to the bottom wall. Even with shields, we'd get there at half strength and we wouldn't have a chance."

"They moving?" Ender asked.

"Do they need to?"

Ender thought for a moment. "This one's tough. We'll go for the gate, Bean."

Griffin Army began to call out to them.

"Hey, is anybody there!"

"Wake up, there's a war on!"

"We wanna join the picnic!"

They were still calling when Ender's army came out from behind their star with a shield of fourteen frozen soldiers. William Bee, Griffin Army's commander, waited patiently as the screen approached, his men waiting at the fringes of their stars for the moment when whatever was behind the screen became visible. About ten meters away the screen exploded as the soldiers behind it shoved the screen north. The momentum carried them south twice as fast, and at the same moment the rest of Dragon Army burst from behind their star at the opposite end of the room, firing rapidly.

William Bee's boys joined battle immediately, of course, but William Bee was far more interested in what had been left behind when the shield disappeared. A formation of four frozen Dragon Army soldiers were moving headfirst toward the Griffin Army gate, held together by another frozen soldier whose feet and hands were hooked through their belts. A sixth soldier hung to his wrist and trailed like the tail of a kite. Griffin Army was winning the battle easily, and William Bee concentrated on the formation as it approached the gate. Suddenly the soldier trailing in back moved—he wasn't frozen at all! And even though William Bee flashed him immediately, the damage was done. The formation drifted to the Griffin Army gate, and their helmets touched all four corners simultaneously. A buzzer sounded, the gate reversed, and the frozen soldier in the middle was carried by momentum right through the gate. All the flashers stopped working, and the game was over.

The teacher door opened and Lieutenant Anderson came in. Anderson stopped himself with a slight movement of his hands when he reached the center of the battleroom. "Ender," he called, breaking protocol. One of the frozen Dragon soldiers near the south wall tried to call through jaws that were clamped shut by the suit. Anderson drifted to him and unfroze him.

Ender was smiling.

"I beat you again, sir," Ender said. Anderson didn't smile.

"That's nonsense, Ender," Anderson said softly. "Your battle was with William Bee of Griffin Army."

Ender raised an eyebrow.

"After that maneuver," Anderson said, "the rules are being revised to require that all of the enemy's soldiers must be immobilized before the gate can be reversed."

"That's all right," Ender said. "It could only work once, anyway." Anderson nodded, and was turning away when Ender added, "Is there going to be a new rule that armies be given equal positions to fight from?"

Anderson turned back around. "If you're in one of the positions, Ender, you can hardly call them equal, whatever they are."

William Bee counted carefully and wondered how in the world he had lost when not one of his soldiers had been flashed, and only four of Ender's soldiers were even mobile.

And that night as Ender came into the commanders' mess hall, he was greeted with applause and cheers, and his table was crowded with respectful commanders, many of them two or three years older than he was. He was friendly, but while he ate he wondered what the teachers would do to him in his next battle. He didn't need to worry. His next two battles were easy victories, and after that he never saw the battleroom again.

It was 2100 and Ender was a little irritated to hear someone knock at his door. His army was exhausted, and he had ordered them all to be in bed after 2030. The last two days had been regular battles, and Ender was expecting the worst in the morning.

It was Bean. He came in sheepishly, and saluted.

Ender returned his salute and snapped, "Bean, I wanted everybody in bed."

Bean nodded but didn't leave. Ender considered ordering him out. But as he looked at Bean it occurred to him for the first time in weeks just how young Bean was. He had turned eight a week before, and he was still small and—no, Ender thought, he wasn't young. Nobody was young. Bean had been in battle, and with a whole army depending on him he had come through and won. And even though he was small, Ender could never think of him as young again.

Ender shrugged and Bean came over and sat on the edge of the bed. The younger boy looked at his hands for a while, and finally Ender grew impatient and asked, "Well, what is it?"

"I'm transferred. Got orders just a few minutes ago."

Ender closed his eyes for a moment. "I knew they'd pull something new. Now they're taking—where are you going?"

"Rabbit Army."

"How can they put you under an idiot like Carn Carby!"

"Carn was graduated. Support squads."

Ender looked up. "Well, who's commanding Rabbit then?"

Bean held his hands out helplessly.

"Me," he said.

Ender nodded, and then smiled. "Of course. After all, you're only four years younger than the regular age."

"It isn't funny," Bean said. "I don't know what's going on here. First all the changes in the game. And now this. I wasn't the only one transferred, either, Ender. Ren, Peder, Wins, Younger, Paul. All commanders now."

Ender stood up angrily and strode to the wall. "Every damn toon leader I've got!" he said, and whirled to face Bean. "If they're going to break up my army, Bean, why did they bother making me a commander at all?"

Bean shook his head. "I don't know. You're the best, Ender. Nobody's ever done what you've done. Nineteen battles in fifteen days, sir, and you won every one of them, no matter what they did to you."

"And now you and the others are commanders. You know every trick I've got, I trained you, and who am I supposed to replace you with? Are they going to stick me with six greenohs?"

"It stinks, Ender, but you know that if they gave you five crippled midgets and armed you with a roll of toilet paper you'd win."

They both laughed, and then they noticed that the door was open.

Lieutenant Anderson stepped in. He was followed by Captain Graff.

"Ender Wiggins," Graff said, holding his hands across his stomach.

"Yes sir," Ender answered.

"Orders."

Anderson extended a slip of paper. Ender read it quickly, then crumpled it, still looking at the air where the paper had been. After a few moments he asked, "Can I tell my army?"

"They'll find out," Graff answered. "It's better not to talk to them after orders. It makes it easier."

"For you or for me?" Ender asked. He didn't wait for an answer. He turned to Bean, took his hand for a moment, and headed for the door.

"Wait," Bean said. "Where are you going? Tactical or Support School?"

"Command School," Ender answered, and then he was gone and Anderson closed the door.

Command School, Bean thought. Nobody went to Command School until they had gone through three years of Tactical. But then, nobody went to Tactical until they had been through at least five years of Battle School. Ender had only had three.

The system was breaking up. No doubt about it, Bean thought. Either somebody at the top was going crazy, or something was going wrong with the war—the real war, the one they were training to fight in. Why else would they break down the training system, advance somebody—even somebody as good as Ender—straight to Command School? Why else would they have an eight-year-old greenoh like Bean command an army?

Bean wondered about it for a long time, and then he finally lay down on Ender's bed and realized that he'd never see Ender again, probably. For some reason that made him want to cry. But he didn't cry, of course. Training in the preschools had taught him how to force down emotions like that. He remembered how his first teacher, when he was three, would have been upset to see his lip quivering and his eyes full of tears.

Bean went through the relaxing routine until he didn't feel like crying anymore. Then he drifted off to sleep. His hand was near his mouth. It lay on his pillow hesitantly, as if Bean couldn't decide whether to bite his nails or suck on his fingertips. His forehead was creased and furrowed. His breathing was quick and light. He was a soldier, and if anyone had asked him what he wanted to be when he grew up, he wouldn't have known what they meant.

There's a war on, they said, and that was excuse enough for all the hurry in the world. They said it like a password and flashed a little card at every ticket counter and customs check and guard station. It got them to the head of every line.

Ender Wiggin was rushed from place to place so quickly he had no time to examine anything. But he did see trees for the first time. He saw men who were not in uniform. He saw women. He saw strange animals that didn't speak, but that followed docilely behind women and small children. He saw suitcases and conveyor belts and signs that said words he had never heard of. He would have asked someone what the words meant, except that purpose and authority surrounded him in the persons of four very high officers who never spoke to each other and never spoke to him.

Ender Wiggin was a stranger to the world he was being trained to save. He did not remember ever leaving Battle School before. His earliest memories were of childish war games under the direction of a teacher, of meals with other boys in the gray and green uniforms of the armed forces of his world. He did not know that the gray represented the sky and the green represented the great forests of his planet. All he knew of the world was from vague references to "outside."

And before he could make any sense of the strange world he was seeing for the first time, they enclosed him again within the shell of the military, where nobody had to say there's a war on anymore because nobody in the shell of the military forgot it for a single instant in a single day.

They put him in a space ship and launched him to a large artificial satellite that circled the world.

This space station was called Command School. It held the ansible.

On his first day Ender Wiggin was taught about the ansible and what it meant to warfare. It meant that even though the starships of today's battles were launched a hundred years ago, the commanders of the starships were men of today, who used the ansible to send messages to the computers and the few men on each ship. The ansible sent words as they were spoken, orders as they were made. Battleplans as they were fought. Light was a pedestrian.

For two months Ender Wiggin didn't meet a single person. They came to him namelessly, taught him what they knew, and left him to other teachers. He had no time to miss his friends at Battle School. He only had time to learn how to operate the simulator, which flashed battle patterns around him as if he were in a starship at the center of the battle. How to command mock ships in mock battles by manipulating the keys on the simulator and speaking words into the ansible. How to recognize instantly every enemy ship and the weapons it carried by the pattern that the simulator showed. How to transfer all that he learned in the nullo battles at Battle School to the starship battles at Command School.

He had thought the game was taken seriously before. Here they hurried him through every step, were angry and worried beyond reason every time he forgot something or made a mistake. But he worked as he had always worked, and learned as he had always learned. After a while he didn't make any more mistakes. He used the simulator as if it were a part of himself. Then they stopped being worried and they gave him a teacher. The teacher was a person at last, and his name was Maezr Rackham.

Maezr Rackham was sitting cross-legged on the floor when Ender awoke. He said nothing as Ender got up and showered and dressed, and Ender did not bother to ask him anything. He had long since learned that when something unusual was going on, he would find out more information faster by waiting than by asking.

Maezr still hadn't spoken when Ender was ready and went to the door to leave the room. The door didn't open. Ender turned to face the man sitting on the floor. Maezr was at least forty, which made him the oldest man Ender had ever seen close up. He had a day's growth of black and white whiskers that grizzled his face only slightly less than his close-cut hair. His face sagged a little and his eyes were surrounded by creases and lines. He looked at Ender without interest.

Ender turned back to the door and tried again to open it.

"All right," he said, giving up. "Why's the door locked?"

Maezr continued to look at him blankly.

Ender became impatient. "I'm going to be late. If I'm not supposed to be there until later, then tell me so I can go back to bed." No answer. "Is it a guessing game?" Ender asked. No answer. Ender decided that maybe the man was trying to make him angry, so he went through a relaxing exercise as he leaned on the door, and soon he was calm again. Maezr didn't take his eyes off Ender.

For the next two hours the silence endured, Maezr watching Ender constantly, Ender trying to pretend he didn't notice the old man. The boy became more and more nervous, and finally ended up walking from one end of the room to the other in a sporadic pattern.

He walked by Maezr as he had several times before, and Maezr's hand shot out and pushed Ender's left leg into his right in the middle of a step. Ender fell flat on the floor.

He leaped to his feet immediately, furious. He found Maezr sitting calmly, cross-legged, as if he had never moved. Ender stood poised to fight. But the other's immobility made it impossible for Ender to attack, and he found himself wondering if he had only imagined the old man's hand tripping him up.

The pacing continued for another hour, with Ender Wiggin trying the door every now and then. At last he gave up and took off his uniform and walked to his bed.

As he leaned over to pull the covers back, he felt a hand jab roughly between his thighs and another hand grab his hair. In a moment he had been turned upside down. His face and shoulders were being pressed into the floor by the old man's knee, while his back was excruciatingly bent and his legs were pinioned by Maezr's arm. Ender was helpless to use his arms, and he couldn't bend his back to gain slack so he could use his legs. In less than two seconds the old man had completely defeated Ender Wiggin.

"All right," Ender gasped. "You win."

Maezr's knee thrust painfully downward.

"Since when," Maezr asked in a soft, rasping voice, "do you have to tell the enemy when he has won?"

Ender remained silent.

"I surprised you once, Ender Wiggin. Why didn't you destroy me immediately afterward? Just because I looked peaceful? You turned your back on me. Stupid. You have learned nothing. You have never had a teacher.''

Ender was angry now. "I've had too many damned teachers, how was I supposed to know you'd turn out to be a—'' Ender hunted for a word. Maezr supplied one.

"An enemy, Ender Wiggin,'' Maezr whispered. "I am your enemy, the first one you've ever had who was smarter than you. There is no teacher but the enemy, Ender Wiggin. No one but the enemy will ever tell you what the enemy is going to do. No one but the enemy will ever teach you how to destroy and conquer. I am your enemy, from now on. From now on I am your teacher.''

Then Maezr let Ender's legs fall to the floor. Because the old man still held Ender's head to the floor, the boy couldn't use his arms to compensate, and his legs hit the plastic surface with a loud crack and a sickening pain that made Ender wince. Then Maezr stood and let Ender rise.

Slowly the boy pulled his legs under him, with a faint groan of pain, and he knelt on all fours for a moment, recovering. Then his right arm flashed out. Maezr quickly danced back and Ender's hand closed on air as his teacher's foot shot forward to catch Ender on the chin.

Ender's chin wasn't there. He was lying flat on his back, spinning on the floor, and during the moment that Maezr was off balance from his kick Ender's feet smashed into Maezr's other leg. The old man fell on the ground in a heap.

What seemed to be a heap was really a hornet's next. Ender couldn't find an arm or a leg that held still long enough to be grabbed, and in the meantime blows were landing on his back and arms. Ender was smaller—he couldn't reach past the old man's flailing limbs.

So he leaped back out of the way and stood poised near the door.

The old man stopped thrashing about and sat up, cross-legged again, laughing. "Better, this time, boy. But slow. You will have to be better with a fleet than you are with your body or no one will be safe with you in command. Lesson learned?''

Ender nodded slowly.

Maezr smiled. "Good. Then we'll never have such a battle again. All the rest with the simulator. I will program your battles, I will devise the strategy of your enemy, and you will learn to be quick and discover what tricks the enemy has for you. Remember, boy. From now on the enemy is more clever than you. From now on the enemy is stronger than you. From now on you are always about to lose.''

Then Maezr's face became serious again. "You will be about to lose, Ender, but you will win. You will learn to defeat the enemy. He will teach you how.''

Maezr got up and walked toward the door. Ender stepped back out of the way. As the old man touched the handle of the door, Ender leaped into the air and kicked Maezr in the small of the back with both feet. He hit hard enough that he rebounded onto his feet, as Maezr cried out and collapsed on the floor.

Maezr got up slowly, holding onto the door handle, his face contorted with pain.

Orson Scott Card

He seemed disabled, but Ender didn't trust him. He waited warily. And yet in spite of his suspicion he was caught off guard by Maezr's speed. In a moment he found himself on the floor near the opposite wall, his nose and lip bleeding where his face had hit the bed. He was able to turn enough to see Maezr open the door and leave. The old man was limping and walking slowly.

Ender smiled in spite of the pain, then rolled over onto his back and laughed until his mouth filled with blood and he started to gag. Then he got up and painfully made his way to the bed. He lay down and in a few minutes a medic came and took care of his injuries.

As the drug had its effect and Ender drifted off to sleep he remembered the way Maezr limped out of his room and laughed again. He was still laughing softly as his mind went blank and the medic pulled the blanket over him and snapped off the light. He slept until pain woke him in the morning. He dreamed of defeating Maezr.

The next day Ender went to the simulator room with his nose bandaged and his lip still puffy. Maezr was not there. Instead a captain who had worked with him before showed him an addition that had been made. The captain pointed to a tube with a loop at one end. "Radio. Primitive, I know, but it loops over your ear and we tuck the other end into your mouth with this piece here . . ."

"Watch it," Ender said as the captain pushed the end of the tube into his swollen lip.

"Sorry. Now you just talk."

"Good. Who to?"

The captain smiled. "Ask and see."

Ender shrugged and turned to the simulator. As he did a voice reverberated through his skull. It was too loud for him to understand, and he ripped the radio off his ear. "What are you trying to do, make me deaf?"

The captain shook his head and turned a dial on a small box on a nearby table. Ender put the radio back on.

"Commander," the radio said in a familiar voice. Ender answered, "Yes."

"Instructions, sir?"

The voice was definitely familiar. "Bean?" Ender asked.

"Yes sir."

"Bean, this is Ender."

Silence. And then a burst of laughter from the other side. Then six or seven more voices laughing, and Ender waited for silence to return. When it did, he asked, "Who else?" A few voices spoke at once, but Bean drowned them out. "Me, I'm Bean, and Peder, Wins, Younger, Lee, and Vlad."

Ender thought for a moment. Then asked what the hell was going on. They laughed again.

"They can't break up the group," Bean said. "We were commanders for maybe two weeks, and here we are at Command School, training with the simulator, and all of a sudden they told us they were going to form a fleet with a new commander. And that's you."

Ender smiled. "Are you boys any good?"

"If we aren't, you'll let us know."

Ender chuckled a little. "Might work out. A fleet."

For the next ten days Ender trained his toon leaders until they could maneuver their ships like precision dancers. It was like being back in the battleroom again, except that Ender could always see everything, and could speak to his toon leaders and change their orders at any time.

One day as Ender sat down at the control board and switched on the simulator, harsh green lights appeared in the space—the enemy.

"This is it," Ender said. "X, Y, bullet, C, D, reserve screen, E, south loop, Bean, angle north."

The enemy was grouped in a globe, and outnumbered Ender two to one. Half of Ender's force was grouped in a tight, bulletlike formation, with the rest in a flat circular screen—except for a tiny force under Bean that moved off the simulator, heading behind the enemy's formation. Ender quickly learned the enemy's strategy: whenever Ender's bullet formation came close, the enemy would give way, hoping to draw Ender inside the globe where he would be surrounded. So Ender obligingly fell into the trap, bringing his bullet to the center of the globe.

The enemy began to contract slowly, not wanting to come within range until all their weapons could be brought to bear at once. Then Ender began to work in earnest. His reserve screen approached the outside of the globe, and the enemy began to concentrate his forces there. Then Bean's force appeared on the opposite side, and the enemy again deployed ships on that side.

Which left most of the globe only thinly defended. Ender's bullet attacked, and since at the point of attack it outnumbered the enemy overwhelmingly, he tore a hole in the formation. The enemy reacted to try to plug the gap, but in the confusion the reserve force and Bean's small force attacked simultaneously, while the bullet moved to another part of the globe. In a few more minutes the formation was shattered, most of the enemy ships destroyed, and the few survivors rushing away as fast as they could go.

Ender switched the simulator off. All the lights faded. Maezr was standing beside Ender, his hands in his pockets, his body tense. Ender looked up at him.

"I thought you said the enemy would be smart," Ender said.

Maezr's face remained expressionless. "What did you learn?"

"I learned that a sphere only works if your enemy's a fool. He had his forces so spread out that I outnumbered him whenever I engaged him."

"And?"

"And," Ender said, "You can't stay committed to one pattern. It makes you too easy to predict."

Orson Scott Card

"Is that all?" Maezr asked quietly.

Ender took off his radio. "The enemy could have defeated me by breaking the sphere earlier."

Maezr nodded. "You had an unfair advantage."

Ender looked up at him coldly. "I was outnumbered two to one."

Maezr shook his head. "You have the ansible. The enemy doesn't. We include that in the mock battles. Their messages travel at the speed of light."

Ender glanced toward the simulator. "Is there enough space to make a difference?"

"Don't you know?" Maezr asked. "None of the ships was ever closer than thirty thousand kilometers to another."

Ender tried to figure the size of the enemy's sphere. Astronomy was beyond him. But now his curiosity was stirred.

"What kind of weapons are on those ships? To be able to strike so fast and so far apart?"

Maezr shook his head. "The science is too much for you. You'd have to study many more years than you've lived to understand even the basics. All you need to know is that the weapons work."

"Why do we have to come so close to be in range?"

"The ships are all protected by force fields. A certain distance away the weapons are weaker, and can't get through. Closer in the weapons are stronger than the shields. But the computers take care of all that. They're constantly firing in any direction that won't hurt one of our ships. The computers pick targets, aim, they do all the detail work. You just tell them when and get them in a position to win. All right?"

"No." Ender twisted the tube of the radio around his fingers. "I have to know how the weapons work."

"I told you, it would take—"

"I can't command a fleet—not even on the simulator—unless I know." Ender waited a moment, then added, "Just the rough idea."

Maezr stood up and walked a few steps away. "All right, Ender. It won't make any sense, but I'll try. As simply as I can." He shoved his hands into his pockets. "It's this way, Ender. Everything is made up of atoms, little particles so small you can't see them with your eyes. These atoms, there are only a few different types, and they're all made up of even smaller particles that are pretty much the same. These atoms can be broken, so that they stop being atoms. So that this metal doesn't hold together anymore. Or the plastic floor. Or your body. Or even the air. They just seem to disappear, if you break the atoms. All that's left is the pieces. And they fly around and break more atoms. The weapons on the ships set up an area where it's impossible for atoms of anything to stay together. They all break down. So things in that area—they disappear."

Ender nodded. "You're right, I don't understand it. Can it be blocked?"

"No. But it gets wider and weaker the farther it goes from the ship, so that after a while a force field will block it. Okay? And to make it strong at all, it has to be focused, so that a ship can only fire effectively in maybe three or four directions at once.''

Ender nodded again. Maezr wondered if the boy really understood it at all.

''If the pieces of the broken atoms go breaking more atoms, why doesn't it just make everything disappear?''

''Space. Those thousands of kilometers between the ships, they're empty. Almost no atoms. The pieces don't hit anything, and when they finally do hit something, they're so spread out they can't do any harm.'' Maezr cocked his head quizzically. ''Anything else . . . ?''

Ender nodded. ''Do the weapons on the ships—do they work against anything besides ships?''

Maezr moved in close to Ender and said firmly, ''We only use them against ships. Never anything else. If we used them against anything else, the enemy would use them against us. Got it?''

Maezr walked away, and was nearly out the door when Ender called to him.

''I don't know your name yet,'' Ender said blandly.

''Maezr Rackham.''

''Maezr Rackham,'' Ender said, ''I defeated you.''

Maezr laughed.

''Ender, you weren't fighting me today,'' he said. ''You were fighting the stupidest computer in the Command School, set on a ten-year-old program. You don't think I'd use a sphere, do you?'' He shook his head. ''Ender, my dear little fellow, when you fight me you'll know it. Because you'll lose.'' And Maezr left the room.

Ender still practiced ten hours a day with his toon leaders. He never saw them, though, only heard their voices on the radio. Battles came every two or three days. The enemy had something new every time, something harder—but Ender coped with it. And won every time. And after every battle Maezr would point out mistakes and show Ender had really lost. Maezr only let Ender finish so that he would learn to handle the end of the game.

Until finally Maezr came in and solemnly shook Ender's hand and said, ''That, boy, was a good battle.''

Because the praise was so long in coming, it pleased Ender more than praise had ever pleased him before. And because it was so condescending, he resented it.

''So from now on,'' Maezr said, ''we can give you hard ones.''

From then on Ender's life was a slow nervous breakdown.

He began fighting two battles a day, with problems that steadily grew more difficult. He had been trained in nothing but the game all his life—but now the game began to consume him. He woke in the morning with new strategies for the simulator, and went fitfully to sleep at night with the mistakes of the day preying on him. Sometimes

Orson Scott Card

he would wake up in the middle of the night crying for a reason he didn't remember. Sometimes he woke with his knuckles bloody from biting them. But every day he went impassively to the simulator and drilled his toon leaders until the battles, and drilled his toon leaders after the battles, and endured and studied the harsh criticism that Maezr Rackham piled on him. He noted that Rackham perversely criticized him more after his hardest battles. He noted that every time he thought of a new strategy the enemy was using it within a few days. And he noted that while his fleet always stayed the same size, the enemy increased in numbers every day.

He asked his teacher.

"We are showing you what it will be like when you really command. The ratios of enemy to us."

"Why does the enemy always outnumber us in these battles?"

Maezr bowed his gray head for a moment, as if deciding whether to answer. Finally he looked up and reached out his hand and touched Ender on the shoulder. "I will tell you, even though the information is secret. You see, the enemy attacked us first. He had good reason to attack us, but that is a matter for politicians, and whether the fault was ours or his, we could not let him win. So when the enemy came to our worlds, we fought back, hard, and spent the finest of our young men in the fleets. But we won, and the enemy retreated."

Maezr smiled ruefully. "But the enemy was not through, boy. The enemy would never be through. They came again, with more numbers, and it was harder to beat them. And another generation of young men was spent. Only a few survived. So we came up with a plan—the big men came up with the plan. We knew that we had to destroy the enemy once and for all, totally, eliminate his ability to make war against us. To do that we had to go to his home worlds—his home world, really, since the enemy's empire is all tied to his capital world."

"And so?" Ender asked.

"And so we made a fleet. We made more ships than the enemy ever had. We made a hundred ships for every ship he had sent against us. And we launched them against his twenty-eight worlds. They left a hundred years ago. And they carried on them the ansible, and only a few men. So that someday a commander could sit on a planet somewhere far from the battle and command the fleet. So that our best minds would not be destroyed by the enemy."

Ender's question had still not been answered.

"Why do they outnumber us?"

Maezr laughed. "Because it took a hundred years for our ships to get there. They've had a hundred years to prepare for us. They'd be fools, don't you think, boy, if they waited in old tugboats to defend their harbors. They have new ships, great ships, hundreds of ships. All we have is the ansible, that and the fact that they have to put a commander with every fleet, and when they lose—and they will lose—they lose one of their best minds every time."

Ender started to ask another question.

"No more, Ender Wiggin. I've told you more than you ought to know as it is."

Ender stood angrily and turned away. "I have a right to know. Do you think this can go on forever, pushing me through one school and another and never telling me what my life is for? You use me and the others as a tool, someday we'll command your ships, someday maybe we'll save your lives, but I'm not a computer, and I have to *know!*"

"Ask me a question, then, boy," Maezr said, "and if I can answer, I will."

"If you use your best minds to command the fleets, and you never lose any, then what do you need me for? Who am I replacing, if they're all still there?"

Maezr shook his head. "I can't tell you the answer to that, Ender. Be content that we will need you, soon. It's late. Go to bed. You have a battle in the morning."

Ender walked out of the simulator room. But when Maezr left by the same door a few moments later, the boy was waiting in the hall.

"All right, boy," Maezr said impatiently, "what is it? I don't have all night and you need to sleep."

Ender stayed silent, but Maezr waited. Finally the boy asked softly, "Do they live?"

"Does who live?"

"The other commanders. The ones now. And before me."

Maezr snorted. "Live. Of course they live. He wonders if they live." Still chuckling the old man walked off down the hall. Ender stood in the corridor for a while, but at last he was tired and he went off to bed. They live, he thought. They live, but he can't tell me what happens to them.

That night Ender didn't wake up crying. But he did wake up with blood on his hands.

Months wore on with battles every day, until at last Ender settled into the routine of the destruction of himself. He slept less every night, dreamed more, and he began to have terrible pains in his stomach. They put him on a very bland diet, but soon he didn't even have an appetite for that. "Eat," Maezr said, and Ender would mechanically put food in his mouth. But if nobody told him to eat he didn't eat.

One day as he was drilling his toon leaders the room went black and he woke up on the floor with his face bloody where he had hit the controls.

They put him to bed then, and for three days he was very ill. He remembered seeing faces in his dreams, but they weren't real faces, and he knew it even while he thought he saw them. He thought he saw Bean, sometimes, and sometimes he thought he saw Lieutenant Anderson and Captain Graff. And then he woke up and it was only his enemy, Maezr Rackham.

"I'm awake," he said to Maezr.

"So I see," Maezr answered. "Took you long enough. You have a battle today."

So Ender got up and fought the battle and he won it. But there was no second battle that day, and they let him go to bed earlier. His hands were shaking as he undressed.

During the night he thought he felt hands touching him gently, and he dreamed he heard voices, saying, "How long can he go on?"

"Long enough."

"So soon?"

"In a few days, then he's through."

"How will he do?"

"Fine. Even today, he was better than ever."

Ender recognized the last voice as Maezr Rackham's. He resented Rackham's intruding even in his sleep.

He woke up and fought another battle and won.

Then he went to bed.

He woke up and won again.

And the next day was his last day in Command School, though he didn't know it. He got up and went to the simulator for the battle.

Maezr was waiting for him. Ender walked slowly into the simulator room. His step was slightly shuffling, and he seemed tired and dull. Maezr frowned.

"Are you awake, boy?" If Ender had been alert, he would have noticed the concern in his teacher's voice. Instead, he simply went to the controls and sat down. Maezr spoke to him.

"Today's game needs a little explanation, Ender Wiggin. Please turn around and pay strict attention."

Ender turned around, and for the first time he noticed that there were people at the back of the room. He recognized Graff and Anderson from Battle School, and vaguely remembered a few of the men from Command School—teachers for a few hours at some time or another. But most of the people he didn't know at all.

"Who are they?"

Maezr shook his head and answered, "Observers. Every now and then we let observers come in to watch the battle. If you don't want them, we'll send them out."

Ender shrugged. Maezr began his explanation. "Today's game, boy, has a new element. We're staging this battle around a planet. This will complicate things in two ways. The planet isn't large, on the scale we're using, but the ansible can't detect anything on the other side of it—so there's a blind spot. Also, it's against the rules to use weapons against the planet itself. All right?"

"Why, don't the weapons work against planets?"

Maezr answered coldly, "There are rules of war, Ender, that apply even in training games."

Ender shook his head slowly. "Can the planet attack?"

Maezr looked nonplussed for a moment, then smiled. "I guess you'll have to find that one out, boy. And one more thing. Today, Ender, your opponent isn't the computer. I am your enemy today, and today I won't be letting you off so easily. Today is a battle to the end. And I'll use any means I can to defeat you.''

Then Maezr was gone, and Ender expressionlessly led his toon leaders through maneuvers. Ender was doing well, of course, but several of the observers shook their heads, and Graff kept clasping and unclasping his hands, crossing and uncrossing his legs. Ender would be slow today, and today Ender couldn't afford to be slow.

A warning buzzer sounded, and Ender cleared the simulator board, waiting for today's game to appear. He felt muddled today, and wondered why people were there watching. Were they going to judge him today? Decide if he was good enough for something else? For another two years of grueling training, another two years of struggling to exceed his best? Ender was twelve. He felt very old. And as he waited for the game to appear, he wished he could simply lose it, lose the battle badly and completely so that they would remove him from the program, punish him however they wanted, he didn't care, just so he could sleep.

Then the enemy formation appeared, and Ender's weariness turned to desperation.

The enemy outnumbered him a thousand to one, the simulator glowed green with them, and Ender knew that he couldn't win.

And the enemy was not stupid. There was no formation that Ender could study and attack. Instead the vast swarms of ships were constantly moving, constantly shifting from one momentary formation to another, so that a space that for one moment was empty was immediately filled with a formidable enemy force. And even though Ender's fleet was the largest he had ever had, there was no place he could deploy it where he would outnumber the enemy long enough to accomplish anything.

And behind the enemy was the planet. The planet, which Maezr had warned him about. What difference did a planet make, when Ender couldn't hope to get near it? Ender waited, waited for the flash of insight that would tell him what to do, how to destroy the enemy. And as he waited, he heard the observers behind him begin to shift in their seats, wondering what Ender was doing, what plan he would follow. And finally it was obvious to everybody that Ender didn't know what to do, that there was nothing to do, and a few of the men at the back of the room made quiet little sounds in their throats.

Then Ender heard Bean's voice in his ear. Bean chuckled and said, "Remember, the enemy's gate is *down*." A few of the other leaders laughed, and Ender thought back to the simple games he had played and won in Battle School. They had put him against hopeless odds there, too. And he had beaten them. And he'd be damned if he'd let Maezr Rackham beat him with a cheap trick like outnumbering him a thousand to one. He had won a game in Battle School by going for something the enemy didn't expect, something against the rules—he had won by going against the enemy's gate.

And the enemy's gate was down.

Orson Scott Card

Ender smiled, and realized that if he broke this rule they'd probably kick him out of school, and that way he'd win for sure; he would never have to play a game again.

He whispered into the microphone. His six commanders each took part of the fleet and launched themselves against the enemy. They pursued erratic courses, darting off in one direction and then another. The enemy immediately stopped his aimless maneuvering and began to group around Ender's six fleets.

Ender took off his microphone, leaned back in his chair, and watched. The observers murmured out loud, now. Ender was doing nothing—he had thrown the game away.

But a pattern began to emerge from the quick confrontations with the enemy. Ender's six groups lost ships constantly as they brushed with each enemy force—but they never stopped for a fight, even when for a moment they could have won a small tactical victory. Instead they continued on their erratic course that led, eventually, down. Toward the enemy planet.

And because of their seemingly random course the enemy didn't realize it until the same time that the observers did. By then it was too late, just as it had been too late for William Bee to stop Ender's soldiers from activating the gate. More of Ender's ships could be hit and destroyed, so that of the six fleets only two were able to get to the planet, and those were decimated. But those tiny groups *did* get through, and they opened fire on the planet.

Ender leaned forward now, anxious to see if his guess would pay off. He half expected a buzzer to sound and the game to be stopped, because he had broken the rule. But he was betting on the accuracy of the simulator. If it could simulate a planet, it could simulate what would happen to a planet under attack.

It did.

The weapons that blew up little ships didn't blow up the entire planet at first. But they did cause terrible explosions. And on the planet there was no space to dissipate the chain reaction. On the planet the chain reaction found more and more fuel to feed it.

The planet's surface seemed to be moving back and forth, but soon the surface gave way in an immense explosion that sent light flashing in all directions. It swallowed up Ender's entire fleet. And then it reached the enemy ships.

The first simply vanished in the explosion. Then, as the explosion spread and became less bright, it was clear what happened to each ship. As the light reached them they flashed brightly for a moment and disappeared. They were all fuel for the fire of the planet.

It took more than three minutes for the explosion to reach the limits of the simulator, and by then it was much fainter. All the ships were gone, and if any had escaped before the explosion reached them, they were few and not worth worrying about. Where the planet had been there was nothing. The simulator was empty.

Ender had destroyed the enemy by sacrificing his entire fleet and breaking the rule against destroying the planet. He wasn't sure whether to feel triumphant at his victory or defiant at the rebuke he was certain would come. So instead he felt nothing. He was tired. He wanted to go to bed and sleep.

He switched off the simulator, and finally heard the noise behind him.

There were no longer two rows of dignified military observers. Instead there was chaos. Some of them were slapping each other on the back, some of them were bowed with their head in their hands, others were openly weeping. Captain Graff detached himself from the group and came to Ender. Tears streamed down his face, but he was smiling. He reached out his arms, and to Ender's surprise he embraced the boy, held him tightly, and whispered, "Thank you, thank you, thank you, Ender."

Soon all the observers were gathered around the bewildered child, thanking him and cheering him and patting him on the shoulder and shaking his hand. Ender tried to make sense of what they were saying. He had passed the test after all? Why did it matter so much to them?

Then the crowd parted and Maezr Rackham walked through. He came straight up to Ender Wiggin and held out his hand.

"You made the hard choice, boy. But heaven knows there was no other way you could have done it. Congratulations. You beat them, and it's all over."

All over. Beat them. "I beat *you,* Maezr Rackham."

Maezr laughed, a loud laugh that filled the room. "Ender Wiggin, you never played me. You never played a *game* since I was your teacher."

Ender didn't get the joke. He had played a great many games, at a terrible cost to himself. He began to get angry.

Maezr reached out and touched his shoulder. Ender shrugged him off. Maezr then grew serious and said, "Ender Wiggin, for the last months you have been the commander of our fleets. There were no games. The battles were real. Your only enemy was *the* enemy. You won every battle. And finally today you fought them at their home world, and you destroyed their world, their fleet, you destroyed them completely, and they'll never come against us again. You did it. You."

Real. Not a game. Ender's mind was too tired to cope with it all. He walked away from Maezr, walked silently through the crowd that still whispered thanks and congratulations to the boy, walked out of the simulator room and finally arrived in his bedroom and closed the door.

He was asleep when Graff and Maezr Rackham found him. They came in quietly and roused him. He woke slowly, and when he recognized them he turned away to go back to sleep.

"Ender," Graff said. "We need to talk to you."

Ender rolled back to face them. He said nothing.

Graff smiled. "It was a shock to you yesterday, I know. But it must make you feel good to know you won the war."

Ender nodded slowly.

Orson Scott Card

"Maezr Rackham here, he never played against you. He only analyzed your battles to find out your weak spots, to help you improve. It worked, didn't it?"

Ender closed his eyes tightly. They waited. He said, "Why didn't you tell me?"

Maezr smiled. "A hundred years ago, Ender, we found out some things. That when a commander's life is in danger he becomes afraid, and fear slows down his thinking. When a commander knows that he's killing people, he becomes cautious or insane, and neither of those help him do well. And when he is mature, when he has responsibilities and an understanding of the world, he becomes cautious and sluggish and can't do his job. So we trained children, who didn't know anything but the game, and never knew when it would become real. That was the theory, and you proved that the theory worked."

Graff reached out and touched Ender's shoulder. "We launched the ships so that they would all arrive at their destination during these few months. We knew that we'd probably only have one good commander, if we were lucky. In history it's been very rare to have more than one genius in a war. So we planned on having a genius. We were gambling. And you came along and we won."

Ender opened his eyes again and they realized he was angry. "Yes, you won."

Graff and Maezr Rackham looked at each other. "He doesn't understand," Graff whispered.

"I understand," Ender said. "You needed a weapon, and you got it, and it was me."

"That's right," Maezr answered.

"So tell me," Ender went on, "How many people lived on that planet that I destroyed."

They didn't answer him. They waited a while in silence, and then Graff spoke. "Weapons don't need to understand what they're pointed at, Ender. We did the pointing, and so we're responsible. You just did your job."

Maezr smiled. "Of course, Ender, you'll be taken care of. The government will never forget you. You served us all very well."

Ender rolled over and faced the wall, and even though they tried to talk to him, he didn't answer them. Finally they left.

Ender lay in his bed for a long time before anyone disturbed him again. The door opened softly. Ender didn't turn to see who it was. Then a hand touched him softly

"Ender, it's me, Bean."

Ender turned over and looked at the little boy who was standing by his bed.

"Sit down," Ender said.

Bean sat. "That last battle, Ender. I didn't know how you'd get us out of it."

Ender smiled. "I didn't. I cheated. I thought they'd kick me out."

"Can you believe it! We won the war. The whole war's over, and we thought we'd have to wait till we grew up to fight in it, and it was us fighting it all the time. I mean, Ender, we re little kids. I'm a little kid, anyway." Bean laughed and Ender smiled. Then they were silent for a little while, Bean sitting on the edge of the bed, and Ender watching him out of half-closed eyes.

Finally Bean thought of something else to say.

"What will we do now that the war's over?" he said.

Ender closed his eyes and said, "I need some sleep, Bean."

Bean got up and left and Ender slept.

Graff and Anderson walked through the gates into the park. There was a breeze, but the sun was hot on their shoulders.

"Abba Technics? In the capital?" Graff asked.

"No, in Biggock County. Training division," Anderson replied. "They think my work with children is good preparation. And you?"

Graff smiled and shook his head. "No plans. I'll be here for a few more months. Reports, winding down. I've had offers. Personnel development for DCIA, executive vice-president for U and P, but I said no. Publisher wants me to do memoirs of the war. I don't know."

They sat on a bench and watched leaves shivering in the breeze. Children on the monkey bars were laughing and yelling, but the wind and the distance swallowed their words. "Look," Graff said, pointing. A little boy jumped from the bars and ran near the bench where the two men sat. Another boy followed him, and holding his hands like a gun he made an explosive sound. The child he was shooting at didn't stop. He fired again.

"I got you! Come back here!"

The other little boy ran on out of sight.

"Don't you know when you're dead?" The boy shoved his hands in his pockets and kicked a rock back to the monkey bars. Anderson smiled and shook his head. "Kids," he said. Then he and Graff stood up and walked on out of the park. ∎